RED-HOT RAVES FOR *LAGUNA HEAT*!

"Slick and elegant...It's a swell book to read."
—*Los Angeles Times*

"A remarkable debut. Parker writes with a confident professionalism...and his book has a rich texture and a strong cast of characters."
—Lawrence Block

"A dandy detective yarn...It's an impressive and satisfying debut...The author has a flair for intricate plotting, swift pacing, and well-drawn characters that jump off the page. A fine mystery by an exciting new writer."
—*Dallas News*

"*Laguna Heat* is an exciting first. Here is an author who knows America's voice, and more than a little of its truth."
—Whitley Strieber

"This mystery has all the right elements."
—*Los Angeles Herald Examiner*

"An awesome evil festers in this Eden on the Pacific...An intriguing story of mystery and suspense."
—E.M. Nathanson, author of *The Dirty Dozen*

LAGUNA HEAT

T. JEFFERSON PARKER

St. Martin's Paperbacks

This is a work of fiction. Any resemblance between the characters and people who have lived, stayed in, or passed through the fine city of Laguna Beach is entirely coincidental.

LAGUNA HEAT

Copyright © 1985 by T. Jefferson Parker.

Cover photograph © J. Patton/Robertstock.com

All rights reserved.

For information address St. Martin's Press, 175 Fifth Avenue, New York, NY 10010.

Library of Congress Catalog Card Number: 85-10055

ISBN: 0-312-35707-9
EAN: 978-0-312-35707-8

Printed in the United States of America

St. Martin's Paperbacks edition / July 1986

St. Martin's Paperbacks are published by St. Martin's Press, 175 Fifth Avenue, New York, NY 10010.

20 19 18 17 16 15 14 13 12

To Robert and Caroline, for their faith
To Lori, for her patience

LAGUNA HEAT

PART ONE

ONE

A perfect morning in a city of perfect mornings, an artist would have worked, a god would have rested.

The convertible slowed as it approached the stables, then bounced from the road onto a gravel driveway. Its headlights swung left-to-right, acute angles filling with dust, while gravel popped under the tires like grease in a skillet.

The driver, by nature an early riser, had not been fully awake until moments before when a fawn wandered onto the road ahead of him. He had jerked the wheel and watched in panic as the animal froze, stiffened on bony legs, and turned its wide black eyes to the headlights. The hood of the car flashed by and blotted the fawn from sight, but no impact. In the rearview mirror the driver watched it flicker into the scrub oak near the road, legs, ears, a tail. A thirsty search in a parched summer, he thought. If adrenaline were coffee, he just got a potful. His name was Tom Shephard, his rank was detective, and he was the new and sole member of the Laguna Beach Police Homicide Division.

Shephard followed the wide driveway past a corral, turning off the headlights and engine when three figures coalesced before him in the grainy, salt-and-pepper light of morning. To the east an orange glow preceded the sun, to the west the black sky was already softening to gray. It would be a while before the sun mounted the highest hill and announced itself to the city, nestled and still sleeping against the Pacific.

He pulled the Mustang under a stand of eucalyptus. The scrubbed, high-pitched aroma of the trees engulfed him as he stepped out and shut the door, his legs still shaky from the near crash with the fawn. A comet-shaped leaf spiraled into his trunk as he searched for his flashlight, which he located in a box of rags and car wax. He tested it, pleased that the batteries were still strong. When he closed the trunk a mockingbird began its morning chatter, which followed him up the driveway to the three figures that stood, heads bowed, flashlights aimed in front of them.

On the ground was a hump, and over the hump was a blanket. Shephard recognized his fellow police by their outlines: to the right protruded the telltale belly of Sergeant Grimes; to the left slouched the almost shoulderless frame of Carl Pavlik, the crime scene investigator; between them, her stocky curves undaunted by patrol garb, stood Lydia Worth, farthest from the blanket and first to speak.

"I found him here in the driveway when I turned out to head back to town," she said. "The door of the house was open." She raised her flashlight beam, which crossed weakly to the house and shivered around the open door. "I don't know if it's Tim or not. But this is his house and stable."

Shephard knelt down and turned back the blanket. He had seen the mask of death in so many expressions, so many forms. A hundred faces, a hundred deaths, a hundred

3

chances to ready one's self for the next. But even a thousand wouldn't have prepared him for this. His knees weakened as he dropped the blanket and stood up.

"What d'ya think of that, Wonderboy? Your first murder in Laguna. Style, drama, the creeps. We didn't want you coming down from L.A. and thinking this was just a quiet little town." Grimes flashed his light onto Shephard's face. Shephard took it, turned it off, and handed it back.

"Lydia, is this where you usually make your turnaround?" Shephard's voice sounded foreign and disembodied, even to himself.

"Not until last week. I saw Tim downtown and he asked me to make a pass once a night. Before that I was using the road half a mile back." Even with the burnishing tones of sunrise playing against one side of her face, Shephard could see that Lydia Worth looked pale, stricken.

"Why the pass?" he asked. The headlights would strafe the house and the car could spook the horses. Horses, he thought. He hadn't seen any. For a moment he gazed at the skeleton of the empty corral.

"He was worried about prowlers."

"Rope off the driveway where it meets the road, please. Both places. Grimes, help her." Shephard's voice took a decided pleasure in the order to Grimes, who didn't budge.

"Think your big-city smarts can cut this one, Shephard?"

"With people like you helping, we can't lose, Jerry."

Grimes disgorged a grunt, which was immediately drowned by a phlegmy smoker's cough. Shephard offered him a cigarette but Grimes aimed his stomach toward the road and spit.

"People like me don't shoot kids," he said.

Shephard absorbed the insult without comment. He looked down to the blanket and lit the cigarette, believing that smoke might keep away the germs of death, just as it keeps away plague or mosquitoes. At any rate it was a con-

4

science-easer, and better than no breakfast at all. The smoke rushed to his head and mixed with the smell of eucalyptus, which made it almost pleasurable. Beside him, the crime scene investigator unwrapped a piece of purple aromatic gum and placed it in his mouth. Grape, a Pavlik staple. He pocketed the paper neatly.

"Carl, buddy. Happy August twenty-fifth," Shephard said.

"Morning, Tom. Yesterday my horoscope said question marks are on the horizon. Look at all of them." Pavlik pushed back his glasses with a thin finger. He was a slight man with straight black hair and the perpetual look of someone who has just got out of bed. Only his eyes were free of the general sense of dilapidation; they studied Shephard's face, then returned to the ground in front of them.

"Let's see what we can answer." Shephard pulled back the blanket and looked again at the black and blistered face, scorched hairless and still oozing fluid, cheeks and throat distended like a bullfrog in mid-croak. Protruding from the forehead was a blackened rock. Then he noticed the odor, localized but distinct. Burned flesh, he thought, sweet and repellent. He pulled away the blanket. The body was an obscene extension of the face: chest a swollen quilt of blisters, stomach and genitals overrun with blebs, legs and arms an edematous outbreak. The only evidence of clothing lay in the burnt fray of material around the body perimeter and the twisted leather belt still fastened at the waist. The buckle, large and ovaloid, had sunk into the flesh. Only the bottoms of his bare feet had been spared.

Shephard realized that he was scarcely breathing. He stood up, exhaled, took another drag on the cigarette. Slanting vertigo, a queasy slosh in the stomach. He watched Lydia Worth drag a pylon from the trunk of her patrol car while Grimes waited. "Shoot it, Carlos," he said.

Pavlik already had the camera out. He fastened the

5

strobe, set the meters, and began. The strobe blinked efficiently, the body seeming to shift positions between each shot. Shephard turned away and looked up at the sun, now bisected by the hill in front of it. He noted that the mockingbird was still singing happily, immune to what was revealed below. Pavlik ran through the roll of thirty-six almost without stopping. Shephard waved the camera away and bent back down.

He worked carefully but quickly, tilting back the head, prying open the mouth and easing two fingers inside. Out came a wad of dry paper, green and white. Then another, and another. Six in all, with more beyond reach in the throat. Pavlik held out a plastic bag and Shephard dropped them in, saving the last. The wad was the size of a golf ball but much lighter. He stood up and unraveled it beneath the intent, bespectacled stare of Pavlik.

Bills. Two hundreds, two fifties, two twenties.

"Three hundred and forty dollars," said Pavlik, a detail man. Shephard worked his fingers across the bills, locating in his flashlight beam the red and blue hairs, then dropped them into the bag. The crime scene investigator snapped it closed, as if the money might attempt an escape. Shephard looked down again.

Mouth agape, rock protruding from the forehead like a rapacious tumor, the face defied long observation. Shephard looked instead at his watch. A mile to the west he heard waves breaking on Main Beach, or perhaps the swooshing of cars on Coast Highway. The early morning air tasted good. The man was sprawled, legs and arms out, as if he had been dropped from above. Shephard followed an imaginary line from the sky to the body, his eyes at first refreshed by the slate gray clouds, then accosted again by the ugliness on the earth in front of him. The left hand lay open and relaxed, the right was clenched tightly, even in death. Shephard coaxed open the fist as Pavlik slid a sheet of clean white paper underneath. From the still-white palm tumbled a meager handful of hair, which Pavlik immediately bagged.

"Nice," he said.

"Stupendous," Shephard agreed, unfolding the blanket to cover the body. Pavlik reached out and claimed a burnt match from the ground not far from the dead man's head.

For a brief moment, the two men lost themselves in the search for more matches, a welcome relief from the close-up study of the dead. Finding none, they rose without speaking and followed the footprints toward the house. The prints were deeper and more clearly marked in the soft clay near the porch. Bending down with his flashlight, Shephard saw that one set had been made by bare feet and began not far from the porch steps—the distance of a running jump, he guessed—and continued in a staggering, disordered pattern. They ended at the body. Another set bore the signs of cowboy boots, deep heel, wide ball, and scant toe. The right heel was cloven sharply by a V-shaped divot in the back. These followed the bare feet halfway to the body, then veered into the gravel and reappeared in the soil, facing—not pursuing—the dead man's. Shephard noted other tracks, older and trampled over by the boots and naked feet.

"Shoot the fresh prints, Carl. Then rope them off. Get a good close-up of the right boot."

"Why did he run all the way around to get Tim from the front?" Pavlik asked gloomily.

He was right, Shephard thought. Tim, if it was Tim, had apparently run into, rather than away from, the person who had killed him. Unless the poor wretch had run all the way from the porch with a rock dividing his head. "It must have been easy," he said, pointing to the chaotic pattern of the dead man's prints. "He wasn't breaking any speed records."

Shephard went through the open front door and into a

well-ordered, cowboyish living room. The lights were on. A pair of Winchester lever-action rifles were crisscrossed over a brick fireplace, a Navajo rug lay centered on the wooden floor, the window curtains were plaid, the coffee table solid oak. One wood-paneled wall was generously graced with photographs and paintings of horses. The other was covered in shelves for books, plants, a small television set. A tall but neat stack of *Racing Form* newspapers rose not far from the fireplace. More lay scattered on the coffee table in front of the leather couch. Shephard checked the dates: July 21 and 28, August 4 and 11. Horse man, horse race fan, he thought. Why the empty corral?

Also on the table were two shot glasses and a half-full bottle of Jack Daniels whiskey. Leaning forward, he noted that both glasses smelled of alcohol. Lights on and drinks poured. An early morning drink with a friend?

Open and face down on the floor near the coffee table lay a Bible. Shephard lifted it with his fingertips and set it down on the couch. The book was worn but serviceable, the gold letters of *Holy Bible* worn away from the leather cover, the binding battered but the pages intact. The first page offered a fancy filligreed frame and the words "Presented To," followed by three blank lines. The smeared black ink of a sloppily imprinted stamp read:

> THI   BIB   PRO   OF
>   FO   TAT   I   N

The title page that came next had a colorplate called "Jesus and the Children." Printed in bright red ink under the words *Holy Bible* was a concise and neatly lettered message:

> *Liars Burn and Little Liars*
> *Burn First*

Shephard felt a faint, sideways flutter in his chest as he read the note again. Then the room darkened.

Pavlik stood in the doorway, his rumpled form outlined in fresh sunlight, the ever-present forensic case dangling from one hand. He set it down with a thud on the hardwood floor. "Robbins's people will be here in twenty minutes to get the body. Want to help me dust?"

"Do what you do best, Carl. I'm going to have a look at the house. Dust the book on the couch first. If there aren't any prints, I'll take it with me."

"Grimes get to you? He hates new-hires. It's a way of being colorful."

"You got it, Carl, buddy. A colorful individual."

"He'll loosen up. He doesn't have any idea what it's like in the City of Angels. I do, and I never want to go back." Pavlik blew a purple bubble and sucked it back in.

Neither will I, Shephard thought as he walked down a short hallway that led out of the living room. A full-length mirror at the far end threw back his reflection. He stopped a moment to look at himself, a habit that was less vanity than curiosity: Who am I? Every mirror seemed to offer a different story. Only the fundamentals remained the same, a tall and meatless body, straight shoulders, brown hair that a TV commercial would have dismissed as unmanageable, a face of harsh angles softened only by the drowsy mustache that was so well integrated with the rest of his face he might have been born with it. Beyond that, the mirrors disagreed. Some emphasized the bags under the eyes, an image of weariness. Others suggested a stark, almost monotonous intensity. Still others shaded, altered, colored, rearranged him as if by whim.

The first room off the hallway was a den. It was arranged with a passion for symmetry: the bed centered and flanked by identical nightstands with identical lamps, a poster of a galloping horse framed in the middle of one wall, smaller pictures facing each other from opposite ends of the bed, same horse, same picture. Nothing in the room, he noted, suggested a woman's presence. It was fanatically clean, fanatically unlived in. Shephard recognized the bachelor's dependence on order.

The large bedroom at the end of the hall was similar in spirit. On the nightstand stood two pictures, one of a man and a woman, one of the same man and woman with a small girl between them. The room was distinctly cool. The bed was made. An early morning drink with a friend he was expecting? Or was he used to rising long before sunrise and making the bed?

In the living room, Pavlik was on hands and knees, his face point-blank to a shot glass. One hand dusted the glass gently with a small brush, working white powder concentrically outward in short strokes. The other held a black sheet of construction paper behind the glass. Both were gloved in translucent white rubber, which Shephard noticed was approximately the pallor of Carl's face. Pavlik pulled back and exhaled, chewing the gum with vigor. "Fair," he said. "Nothing on the book. Leather's too old and porous. Interesting note on the title page, though."

Shephard slipped the book into his coat pocket and stepped outside. The morning was already growing warm, and the northbound work traffic on Laguna Canyon Road had thickened. He watched the coroner's van lumber to a stop behind Lydia Worth's patrol car, against which Grimes leaned, smoking a cigar. Grimes blew a blue haze as Shephard approached. Before it cleared, two more patrol cars crunched onto the driveway, followed by the white Chevy four-door of the department's publicity officer. The Chevy skidded to a stop and Pincus of Public Relations got out, late but officious. Shephard confronted Grimes's puffy, bulldoggish face.

"Grimes, take the houses to the west. Lydia, you take the ones east. Wake up the neighbors and find out if they saw or heard anything."

Grimes grunted and pushed off the car. Lydia accepted a cigarette from Shephard and lit it with a still-shaking hand. "I'm not used to this." She smiled weakly. "I talked to Tim Algernon five days ago, and now I can't be sure that's even him. If it is Tim, I can tell you he lived alone and has a daughter in town. Jane. He's owned the stables for a long time. He'd rent the horses for rides in the hills. Last week he told me he'd finally retired and sold off all the horses except one. A favorite mare."

At the far end of the driveway, the exit end for cars leaving the stables, Shephard looked for fresh tire tracks. But the gravel was well-worn, and the faint signs of travel could have been a week old or an hour new.

Outside the barn, the nicked boot again. One set of prints going into the open barn door, the same set coming back out. Shephard stepped inside. A light bulb burned overhead, halfway down the double row of stalls. The musty smell of hay and dung lingered, ingrained by now, he thought, into the wood itself. The silence inside was broken only by the muted hiss of cars heading out Laguna Canyon Road. He noted that the nameplates on the stall doors had been recently removed. Fresher paint was underneath, and screw holes were torn in the wood. Severing his sentimental attachments, Shephard thought. Like when he had taken down the pictures of Louise after their divorce. Only the nameplate on the first stall remained: BECKY. The favorite mare, no doubt.

Shephard discovered that the tack wall was empty. A complete sale, he thought. But wouldn't he have saved a saddle, bit, and harness for Becky? He found no riding gear anywhere in the barn.

Back outside, the fresh morning sun made his eyes ache. Paralleling more bootprints toward the corral, Shephard stopped at a patch of moist clay under a pepper tree and found what he was looking for. The right bootprint bore the nicked heel.

He returned to the body and stood over it, sensing the almost tangible aura that separates the dead from the living. He felt clumsy and out of place, like a tourist in a country where his customs and language don't apply.

From where he stood, Shephard could see the bootprints from the barn leading toward the corral. They ended at the now-open gate, obliterated by the deeper prints of hooves. Becky, he thought, a retired cowboy's pension. The animal had taken a wide circle around the dead man—spooked by the flames, Shephard assumed—then angled off toward an embankment behind the house. Her hooves had cut deep into the bank, then down to a wide stream bottom where the dry weeks of summer had reduced the water to a brackish slick. With the sun working steadily on his neck and mosquitoes whining in his ears, Shephard followed the tracks until they climbed up the opposite bank, continued west, and disappeared into a stand of scrub oak.

Not twenty yards away stood the saddled horse, idly eyeing the detective.

Beyond the oak lay a dense grove of eucalyptus. And beyond the eucalyptus, a ten-minute ride across the dry hills, lay the city.

TWO

The Orange County Coroner's facility is housed in a drab square building in Santa Ana, the only pretense at cheer being an orange band of paint that winds around it like a gift-box ribbon. The deputy medical examiner introduced himself as Glen Yee, then led Shephard down a clinical hallway toward a set of recessed double doors.

"Shephard, from Los Angeles?" he asked casually. Yee was short, primly dressed, and vaguely oriental.

"Right," Shephard answered, bracing himself for the inevitable condescension.

"Very unfair the way the press treats you in law enforcement. But welcome to Orange County. I grew up here, not far from Disneyland. When I was ten, this was a quiet little county filled with orange trees and political conservatives. But it isn't so quiet any more. Interesting, I think, that three of the first six men executed since the reinstatement of the death penalty grew up in Orange County. A modern place with modern problems," he said, shooting Shephard a concerned glance. "And we now have a modern forensic facility to help solve them." Shephard noted the pride in Yee's voice, the tone of a future administrator. "We built the facility one year ago. Before that, we shopped the bodies out to local mortuaries, and our examiners made house calls, so to speak. At a hundred dollars each, we ran up quite a bill."

"How much was all this?"

"About twelve million, but a money-saver in the long run.

Frankly, I think the success of 'Quincy' helped us pass the bond. This, for instance, is a fine feature."

Yee stopped about six feet from the doors and tapped his toe on a narrow black line. The doors slid open and waited. "The electric eye is positioned exactly one gurney-length away. The only doors in the county designed to be opened by the dead." Yee chuckled politely. Shephard lit a cigarette and stepped in.

White tile and formaldehyde, draped sheets, gray feet. The bodies were neatly lined along the wall in front of him while technicians worked busily at a counter opposite. Four high-intensity lamps hung at intervals from the ceiling, under which four tables offered bodies to the light of forensic science. Yee led Shephard past the first three. Drained of blood to a pale gray, chests open, staggered with factory-line precision across the room, the bodies struck Shephard as more automotive than human. Yee stopped at the last one, which was covered, and produced a clipboard.

"Tim Algernon, age sixty-four, male Caucasian. The dental check was easy because we had a name and not many dentists in Laguna Beach. Anyway, he was in good health until about five hours ago. At around six A.M. he died of a massive brain hemorrhage caused by the introduction of a foreign body through the frontal lobe. The foreign body appears to be a piece of common basaltic formation, but Robbins can tell you better than I can. In my opinion a fall, even a complete unconscious fall, could not have caused the kind of penetration we have here. I don't even think a rock that size could have been thrown through the frontal lobe. In short, it appears to me that someone literally bashed his brains out. Would you like to see?"

"No, but I will."

The head's features were indecipherable. Yee replaced the sheet.

"The body is seventy percent covered with third-degree

burns," he continued, stopping to run a thin hand through his black hair. "Basically every part of him not touching the ground, except for the bottoms of his feet. Ask Robbins again, he knows burns. I can tell you that Algernon hosted the fire, which implies an accelerant was used. Human skin of course is both porous and fire resistant, a trait shared by most green plants, incidentally. By resistant I mean that flame will not spread naturally." Yee interrupted his monologue to wink at someone across the room. Shephard turned in time to see a pretty blond woman re-bury her arms in a corpse.

"Now, we found something truly interesting here, detective. Lodged in the esophagus below the epiglottis were four collections of American currency. Twenty-two bills, totaling nine hundred and ninety dollars. Given the mint condition of the bills, I'd say he ate or was forced to eat them shortly before he died. Strange." Yee set down the clipboard and crossed his arms. His black eyebrows contracted thoughtfully.

"How much alcohol had he drunk?"

A trace of worry flitted across Yee's smooth face. "We didn't test blood alcohol. Generally—"

"Please do. You may find some in the stomach, too."

"Stop by after you see Robbins. I'll have your levels." The deputy medical examiner offered his hand and smiled.

"Thanks, doc. The new shop's a real dazzler."

"Welcome to Orange County, detective. I hope you receive better treatment here than you did in Los Angeles."

Better treatment, Shephard thought as he climbed the stairs to the research lab. Like he was being transferred from one hospital to the next. The face of Morris Mumford flashed inside his brain, then vanished.

Forensic specialist Ken Robbins was a dramatic counterpoint to the oriental preciseness of Yee. He stared at Shephard with puffy, red-rimmed eyes and wiped his glasses on a dirty lab coat. His head was large and block-shaped, covered with a mass of gray hair. Robbins dismissed formalities with western flair.

"Weird shit, Shephard," he said. "You're the reverend's son?"

"Right."

"Well, whoever engineered this little killing doesn't have much interest in our sweet Lord Jesus." The Bible in Shephard's pocket suggested the contrary, but the point didn't seem worth making yet. Robbins pumped Shephard's hand with easy power.

"What was the accelerant?" Shephard asked.

"You know burns?"

"A little."

"The accelerant was turpentine. Liberal doses. You probably saw that he was burned head to toe, front side. Flesh won't conduct flame on its own, so our man used turpentine. A good choice because it's cheap, easy to get around here, and it burns like hell."

"Nice comparison," Shephard said. "Turpentine is used to thin paints and lacquers. What else?"

"Got me, Shephard. All I know is dead people and what makes 'em that way. In this case, what actually made this Algernon fellow dead was a twenty-ounce hunk of basalt punched through his head. There she is." Robbins nodded to the triangular slab of rock that rested on a table beside an imposing microscope. The rock was fist-sized, sharp-edged, unremarkable.

"Common around here?"

"That's what the books say. Coughed up by ancient volcanoes and spread around by quakes and drifts. A rock is a rock. But those hair specimens you brought in might be a gold mine." Robbins pointed to the microscope and switched it on. Shephard bent down and peered through the eyepiece, adjusting the focus. Magnified, the hairs looked like the trunks of redwoods, complete with bark. Two such redwoods angled through the left side of the image area, while to the right rested a fat ring the apparent size and shape of a Cheerio. "On the left are two hairs from the collection you sent me. On the right is a cross-section from a third. The round center indicates straight hair. Oval center would indicate curly. You can't tell because of the lighting down there, but the hairs, all of them, follow a black-to-gray color pattern. Keep your eye on the hairs while I up the power and tell me what you see."

Shephard watched as the specimens tripled in size, their dull red tone fading still more with the higher magnification. "They got bigger."

"No shit. What else?"

"Mounds. Little mounds on them."

"Know what they are? Tocopherol acetate. More commonly known as vitamin E. If you use good conditioner on your hair, you probably have those blobs, too. That's the point, not everybody does. Did you get these specimens from a suspect?"

"Unless Algernon pulled out his own hair."

"Then you're looking for a man old enough to have gray hair, and I don't mean a streak or two. The original color was black, not brown. Jet black. Not a Viet Cong, either. The protein analysis says Caucasian all the way. His blood type is O. And he conditions his hair with something containing tocopherol acetate."

"That would make it an expensive product," Shephard noted, recalling that the contents of his own cheapish conditioner made a long paragraph on the label. And no vitamin E.

"And cheap people don't buy conditioner at all. Next."

Robbins slid out the specimen glass and inserted another, then turned down the power. Shephard regarded the single

17

tree trunk-like object, which was thicker, darker, and much smoother than the first. One end tapered to a nearly perfect point, the other was truncated cleanly. Midway, it was dented.

"What you're looking at is a camel's hair, believe it or not." Shephard entertained a brief and irrelevant vision of the killer arriving on the back of a camel. "It was in with the human hair. My first thought was a hairbrush. But it's much too thin."

"And why the tapered end?"

"Exactly my question. I was thinking it got pulled out of a sports jacket or a sweater."

Shephard turned up the power and watched the hair grow. More mounds. "But who would condition a jacket?"

"What?"

Shephard backed away and let Robbins study the camel hair.

"No shit. Didn't think to crank it up that high." Robbins stood and shook his head slowly. "You got me. And you got me on this, too." He replaced the specimen slide with still another.

Shephard gazed through the eyepiece at a stunningly beautiful sliver of blue. It was dark and rich as lapis lazuli. "Looks like a gem," he said.

"It's a cobalt compound," Robbins corrected.

Shephard looked again at the bright slash of blue. "Is it radioactive?"

"Give me another hour, I'll tell you."

"What's it doing in a man's hair?"

"That's your job, dick. Maybe he takes nuclear shampoos. I just dig the treasures, you spend 'em how you see fit. I'm still working on the fabric from his shirt, the dirt under his nails, some other angles. Fire doesn't leave us much to go on."

"It's a start. The killer rides a conditioned camel and

washes his own hair with cobalt. See it all the time."

Robbins shrugged, and guided Shephard to the door. "Say hello to your father for me. We ran around a bit together in his cop days down in Laguna. I haven't seen him since he started saving souls, but what the hell, it must be just as good as staring at stiffs all day. Good luck, Shephard. Weird shit."

Yee was hefting a handful of something into the scale above Tim Algernon's body when Shephard walked back into the morgue. The cargo dropped; the scale swung gently.

"Blood alcohol is point two," Yee said decisively. "That's legally quite drunk in this state. We found another two ounces of undigested whiskey in the stomach. I'd estimate he had his last drink no longer than fifteen minutes before death."

Shephard watched the scale reading settle at one pound, four ounces. "The money you found in his throat. Was it enough to choke him?"

"Oh yes. In fact that is exactly what he was doing before he died."

"Can a man make sounds when he's choking? Anything loud enough to wake neighbors?"

"You mean a scream. No, and I'm afraid this money will complicate your search for motive. Why would anyone put a thousand dollars in a man's throat when he could have put them in his own pockets?"

Shephard regarded Yee briefly, then turned toward the double doors. A good question, he thought, so good he'd been trying to answer it himself for the last six hours. Still without a workable solution, his mind resorted to the obvious. "Maybe they were full."

Yee shook his head and emptied the contents of the scale tray with the nonchalance of a janitor.

THREE

Back at the station, Shephard removed the Bible from his coat pocket and set it on the desk. The handwriting suggested order and calm: *Liars Burn and Little Liars Burn First.* Again he studied the incomplete, smeared stamp.

Thi   Bib   Pro   of
   Fo   tat   i   n

This Bible Property of whom? Shephard instructed the desk receptionist to handle all calls from the press, then replaced the Bible with a telephone book.

He decided to start with the best, on the theory that anyone who can afford to leave over a thousand dollars behind can afford the best hotel in the city, and that a person on foot might be in need of a room. Predictably, the Surf and Sand had been booked for the last month. So had the Martinique and the Hotel California. The Laguna Hotel reported a single check-in at eight that morning, a "young man with a nice suntan." The Whaler's Inn had accepted a family of five at nine o'clock, "full-on touristas," according to the clerk. Monday business was slow.

Shephard worked his way down the list of Laguna Beach hotels and motels, descending without luck to the city's worst, the Hotel Sebastian. He remembered it from his boyhood in Laguna as a hangout for third-echelon Brotherhood converts, the money- and high-seeking opportunists who took over Timothy Leary's organization in its last days. The owner, a James Hylkama, said that a man of "about sixty" had checked in, bagless, at seven that morning. He had given his name as William Hodges of Fresno and paid for three days in advance. Seven would be about the right time, Shephard calculated, for a man on horseback to go from Laguna Canyon Road to the edge of the city, then on foot to the Sebastian.

His phone buzzed and Chief Darrel "Pete" Hannover's smooth voice summoned Shephard to his office. The chief was sitting squarely behind his oak desk, elbows out and hands folded, when Shephard walked in. He was dressed as usual in a three-piece suit that suggested commerce rather than law enforcement, action rather than the polite sloth that was Hannover's trademark. He was known as a good administrator in a department with little to administer, and a good talker who rarely had anything to say. He motioned Shephard to sit down and offered him a cigarette, which Shephard accepted.

"As I indicated when you were hired, Shephard, my method is to stay out of the investigations and workings of my men and women. Laguna Beach has an average yearly homicide rate of point five, which translates to one murder every two years. This is the first one all year, and the most singularly hideous that I've encountered in thirty years with the city." He leveled a grave expression on Shephard. "I don't want to know who your suspects are, what your leads are, or what your hunches might be. Professionals work best sans encumbrance. I simply want quotidian assurance—for the mayor and myself—that you are doing everything possible to make an arrest. Do I have that?"

"Everything possible, absolutely." Shephard dragged deeply on the cigarette and regretted missing breakfast and lunch. The smoke dazed him.

"You know how I like to think of Laguna Beach, Shephard? And I'm sure the city council and Chamber of Commerce agree. I like to think of our city as a nice quiet little town where people come and spend their money in peace. A tourist town is only as good as its image. The only thing worse than murder would be a giant shark eating bodysurfers off Main Beach. You remember *Jaws*, don't you?"

"A fine film."

"My favorite part was the storytelling scene in the boat. The lost art of verbal painting. But I'm getting sidetracked, Shephard. My brain is on a right-side tack today. I just want you to know that I'm counting on you and depending on you. And I want you to depend and count on me, too. Say what people might about your father's former connections to this department, I can assure you that I hired you for your talent, not out of sentiment. Youngest detective on the L.A. force, weren't you?"

"That's right."

"And you got a handful of awards and commendations before the, uh, trouble, right?"

"Yes, sir, before the trouble."

"That's the kind of work I expect, Shephard. That's all; you can go now. By the way, how is Wade Shephard these days? I saw his television sermon last week."

"He's fine, chief."

"Pass along my regards, Tom. Au revoir."

Shephard drove the Mustang through the stop-and-go traffic on Coast Highway, heading south toward the Hotel Sebastian. In the crosswalk in front of him a band of saffron-robed Hare Krishnas chanted and banged drums, their robes fluttering in the afternoon breeze, their shaved heads shiny in the merciless summer sun. He recognized one of them as a boy from his high school chemistry class and offered a wave. The thin young man returned a mute stare to Shephard, then aimed his droning song back heavenward. Karma, he thought. Just what the hell is it? To the west, the Pacific sparkled and heaved against the dark rocks. While he waited for the light to change, Shephard regarded the water and sky, the covey of lovely legged women who walked along the shops facing the highway. The hometown hasn't really changed, he thought. But seeing his own reflection in the rearview mirror, he realized that something had changed, and that something was himself. The hair was thinner, the face no longer boyish, the eyes calmer and less eager. Ten years ago he had driven the same car down the same street, perhaps seen the same shops and tourists, but it didn't feel the same now. He had left Laguna at the age of twenty for the Los Angeles Police Academy, and had worked twelve years in L.A. Now he was back, without the wife he had taken with him, without the illusions of a simple life. Full circle, he thought, to the city of my birth. He did not consider himself disillusioned, simply non-illusioned. He had come to Laguna to start over. In the shower that morning he had told himself again that today he would start to start over. Was it the hundredth time?

The Hotel Sebastian hadn't changed, that much was obvious. He saw its dull yellow walls rising from the hill of iceplant on the inland side of the highway, a rickety structure that seemed always on the verge of collapse. The feeble stairway still zigzagged up from the sidewalk, the faded sign still proclaimed the Hotel Sebastian to be the "Jewel of the Pacific."

Shephard turned left on Serra Street, climbed sharply, and swung the car into the hotel courtyard. The first cottage on his right had a sign outside that read: MANAGER: JAMES HYLKAMA. He found a space beside the manager's slot and pulled in. The courtyard was gravel, bleached white by the sun and stained by lost oil and exhaust. A grove of eucalyptus trees loomed over the small cottages, which were arranged

23

in a horseshoe pattern. Shephard noted the rusted patio furniture outside the manager's office as he knocked. The man who answered looked like Mickey Rooney.

"Help ya?" the man asked, his voice deep and clear. Shepard produced his badge, and the door swung open. Inside, the room was sunny and neat and smelled of bacon. A large woman bent over an ironing board, bearing down on the wrinkles of a white shirt. She looked up and smiled, but said nothing. "I'm Jimmy Hylkama. This is Dorothy. What can I do you for?"

"I called an hour ago about William Hodges. I'd like to see him." The bacon made Shephard think of the breakfast he'd missed.

"Popular guy, that Hodges," Hylkama decided. He scratched his balding head, like an acting student doing perplexity. "He checked in at seven, and an old friend stopped by at nine. Now you. Trouble is, Hodges is gone."

"An old friend came by?" Shephard asked.

Hylkama augmented the story with histrionics. His pudgy hands seemed to take on a separate life, rising, dipping, returning like tethered birds to his body. Shephard listened intently, making notes in his small notebook. It took him only a moment to realize that Hylkama's gestures were not the cover of a liar but the accompaniment of a man who loved to talk. The lost art of verbal painting, he thought; Hannover should see this.

Unlike the man's active hands, his narrative was straightforward and orderly. At just after seven that morning, Hylkama was eating his breakfast of bacon and eggs. Dot had cooked it. There was a knock at the door, and Hylkama had opened it to find an "elderly type of man." He noted that the man was approximately his and Dot's own age, been married forty years by the way. He was short, average build, and dressed like many of his frankly down-and-out, alcoholic tenants. Gray-black hair, straight, a little on the long side.

24

Beard and mustache, neat. Hylkama's hands became circles, which he pressed to his eyes as he made his next point.

"His eyes," he said. "I remember his eyes. Big as golf balls and blue, beautiful blue. Right, Dot?"

"Very nice blue, Jimmy, but not that big. Regular-sized eyes, honey." She smiled again and descended on the next shirt. Hylkama ignored the correction and pressed on.

The man had taken a room for three days and paid cash in advance, which Hylkama said was a Hotel Sebastian rule.

"What kind of bills?" Shephard asked. "Denomination."

Two twenties, Hylkama said, old ones. He brought Shephard an old clipboard with one broken corner and a pad of yellow paper attached. The new guest had registered as William Hodges. Shephard noted that the signature was assured and precise. With prompting from Shephard, Hylkama revealed that, come to think of it, Hodges must have come on foot—he could remember no car, no bags. And cars at the Sebastian tend to stand out, he said, because so few of his tenants had them. Hylkama's hands loved this revelation; they fluttered, then clenched into tight, oh-the-pain-of-poverty fists. At any rate, he went on, two hours later, Hodges's old friend Michael Stett arrived, but when he took the extra key and went to cottage five, Hodges was gone. Hylkama took a moment to describe the general solitude of his guests, "lost to bottles for the most part," and how Stett's arrival had gladdened him. For Hodges's sake, of course. Because Stett was a snappily dressed fellow who arrived in a shiny dark blue Porsche that "sparkled like a jewel" beside Hylkama's own battered station wagon. With friends like this, maybe old Hodges has a prayer, Hylkama had figured.

"Why did Stett want the key? If he was a friend, wouldn't he just knock?"

"Because he wanted it to be a surprise. He didn't want to knock; he said he wanted to let himself in and give the old guy a real happy welcome home. In fact, he told me to call him quick if Billy came back, but not to let him know he'd been here. And he gave me this to help me remember." Hylkama's chubby fingers went into the pocket of his well-pressed shirt and with a flourish brought out a folded hundred-dollar bill and a business card.

The card, standard in all respects, said only *Michael Stett*, and gave a Newport Beach phone number.

"May I keep this?"

"Yes, you may. Mr. Stett asked that I keep his gift in strict confidence, but I do make it policy to help the police whenever possible. The Hotel Sebastian desires a respected place in the community. But I *would* like to copy that number."

The last person on earth I'd want to leave a secret with, Shephard thought. He pocketed the card after dictating the number to Hylkama, who wrote it down on the registry. With regard to the arrival and generous gift of "old friend" Michael Stett, Shephard turned over various possibilities in his mind, none of which seemed worth turning over.

"I'd like to take a look at cottage five," he said.

"Do you have a warrant, Mr. Shephard?" Hylkama suddenly looked grave.

"No. But if I did, I'd take that hundred of yours as evidence." Shephard watched Jimmy Hylkama's face relax, his exercise in sternness over.

"Sure, but don't forget to bring this back. It's my extra, because Stett walked off with the other one. Cottage five is opposite side, last one." Hylkama fetched a key from a desk drawer and handed it to Shephard. "Don't suppose you want to tell me what's going on, do you?"

"Routine stuff, Jimmy."

"I figured you'd say that. And it's okay with me. One thing you learn around here is don't ask questions. Most of the answers aren't very happy."

Shephard crunched across the gravel courtyard to the

opposite row of cottages and knocked firmly on the door of number five. After a moment's wait, he slipped the key into the lock and pushed open a door so thin and hollow it echoed when he closed it behind him.

His eyes got the facts but his nose caught the mood: old wood, old bedding, old lives. Disinfectant, mildew, dust, a feeble bouquet of detergent hovering just above the heavy smell of rot. The green carpet was worn heavily. The walls were paneled in pine halfway to the ceiling, and above that covered by green and yellow paper, most of which was still on. A gas heater stood in one corner, its vent shaft bent like a dislocated finger. The bed was pressed against the wall, neatly made but with a depression down the middle, body-sized. The pillow was dented likewise.

The other room served as a kitchen. The linoleum floor had cracked with age; the sink had yellowed and chipped. A set of plastic curtains lilted inward, then slapped against the window frame. Shephard spread them and found the window open; no screen.

There were no clothes in the closet, no personal items in the bathroom. A small medicine chest above the sink contained nothing but three rusted shelves and a cockroach that quickly disappeared into a crack. The shower was dry. Only the sink showed signs of recent use: the bowl was spotted with water, and the soap was still damp. Shephard pulled out the drain plug and ran his finger under the head. The bead of water that slid onto his finger was pale pink.

He returned to the main room and sat down. Hodges was neat, he thought. Stett, too. And they've likely got nothing to do with Tim Algernon. He rose tiredly from the chair, pulled open the top drawer of a nightstand beside the bed, and felt his heart accelerate.

A wallet sat neatly in the corner, well-worn brown leather, arched from use. And beside it was a can of turpentine.

27

Score one for law and order, he thought, his insides still jumping.

He carefully removed the wallet and placed it on top of the stand, prying it open with his fingertips and shaking out the contents. There were three one-dollar bills, a driver's license, and a ticket stub. Shephard read the license: Edward Steinhelper, born 1921, gray hair, blue eyes, 5 feet 9 inches tall, 165 pounds. The address was 8798 Fallbrook Street, Sacramento. So our man bullshitted Hylkama, he thought. Who wouldn't? The man in the picture was square-faced and grim, his hair swept back from a prominent forehead, his beard long and wide. As Shephard stared at the picture, he felt his mind dividing into its two professional paths, one leading him to study the face for what it was and what it might suggest, the other wandering deeper and less logically, trying to connect it to the thousands of faces in his past. They converged emptily. He turned his attention to the stub, dated August 24, Sacramento to Laguna Beach, Greyhound bus line 52, $16. Departing 6:30 A.M.

The bottom drawer of the nightstand was empty. Shephard took the driver's license, then put the wallet back in place. He shook the drawer, listening to the slosh of turpentine in the can.

Hylkama was at the ironing board this time, while Dorothy reclined on the sofa and smoked. Shephard knocked on the screen door, and Dorothy rose to let him in.

"Any luck?" she asked.

"Maybe. This Hodges?"

Mr. and Mrs. Hylkama studied the driver's license, Dot looming over little Jimmy's shoulder. Hylkama hesitated anxiously.

"Not him," Dorothy said.

"Definitely not," James agreed.

"How about Stett? Describe him to me, please."

"Big guy. Sporty type, muscles and all." Hylkama, of

course, made a muscle. "A real good dresser. Dark hair and dark eyes, about forty-five, I'd guess. Like I said, a funny friend for a guy like Hodges, being kind of a lowlifer himself."

"I'm going to have another policeman take a look at the room," Shephard said. "He'll bring back the key after that. Thank you very much for your help, Mr. Hylkama."

"Oh, sure." Jimmy seemed disappointed. "Anything else I can answer? You can see I like to help when I can."

"Not now. But you did a job, Jimbo, a real good job."

"Yeah, sure." Hylkama turned to his wife. "I'll take over, Dot. Here, let me . . . " He was moving toward the ironing board as Shephard left.

In the middle of the courtyard he stopped and considered Jimmy Hylkama's unfettered view of cottage five. Hylkama seemed like the sort to notice anyone leaving a cottage from a front door, he thought. The image of the screenless window fluttered into his mind, and he walked around the cottages to the back.

The back windows of the first four units were screened and curtained. A grizzled face stared at him through one as he worked his way past trashcans, litter, decrepit furniture, spare tires, and old newspapers of the kind that fill the backlots of the poor. At the last cottage he found the window screen flat against the earth.

Wonderfully preserved in the damp ground, a set of bootprints began just below the window and continued around the cottage. The triangular divot in the right heel was unmistakable. Shephard followed them until they disappeared at the stairway that led down through the iceplant to Coast Highway. Must have snuck out the back when he saw Stett coming, he thought. Good friends.

He took the stairs to the sidewalk and headed north to the pay phone at the Standard Station, where he dialed Michael Stett's number.

"Zero-five-five-zero," a woman's voice snapped.

"Tidy Didy Diapers?" Shephard asked nasally.

"You have the wrong number." She hung up.

Shephard waited a minute and dialed again. Same woman. "Tidy Didy Diaper Service?"

"You have the wrong number, sir, this is the number for South Coast Investigators."

He apologized, then called the station, where he requested a check on Edward Steinhelper of Fallbrook Street in Sacramento, and asked Carl Pavlik to get to the Hotel Sebastian as soon as he could. Pavlik was delighted. A few minutes later Shephard dialed South Coast Investigators.

"Zero-five-five-zero," she said again.

"Michael Stett, please."

"What is this regarding?"

"Estate work."

"Mr. Stett is not in. This is just the service. By whom were you referred?"

"I was led to believe this would be a confidential—"

"We are paid to screen the calls. We need a name and number where you can be reached."

"Randy Cox," Shephard said, and gave the number off the pay phone.

"I'll have Mr. Stett return your call when he arrives."

"You've been very kind," Shephard answered, but she had already hung up.

Pavlik arrived ten minutes later, standing in the doorway of cottage five, weighted down with his forensic suitcase. In his wrinkled and ill-tailored suit, he looked to Shephard like a forlorn salesman making his last call of the day.

"Carlos, buddy, partner, chum." Shephard felt a nervous voltage roaming his body. "There's a wallet and a can of turpentine in the nightstand. You may have some luck with the kitchen window. Get a sample of the water under the drain plug; it looks like blood. Try the pillow for hairs. Try

30

the foot of the bed for soil trace. Whoever checked in here washed his hands and laid down a while. When you're done, give the manager his key back. Arrange a stakeout for the next twenty-four hours. Get it done fast, leave no trace, and put everything back the way you found it. After that, book Hylkama and his wife for an hour session with the artist, Slobin. I want to know what this guy looks like." Shephard paused, running down his mental checklist. He carefully slipped the license back in the wallet. "And call the San Onofre nuclear power plant. See if they've got an Ed Steinhelper on the payroll."

"Sounds like you're in a hurry, Shephard. Anything exciting?"

"Just something I'd rather was over with."

"Yeah, what?"

"Getting my sanity back. Officially. If Steinhelper checks in, arrest him for murder. And shoot the bootprints; I think they'll match the ones at the stables." He tossed Pavlik the key on his way out.

"This stuff won't help us without a warrant, Tom."

"Carl, buddy. It already has."

FOUR

Shephard arrived at the Los Angeles County Medical Center to find that his psychiatrist had resigned shortly after lunch. He stood awkwardly over the receptionist's desk and tried to explain his predicament.

"This was my last session," he said quietly. He was particularly sensitive about mental health. "I'd like to get it out of the way."

"Last session? Name?"

"Shephard, Tom. I'm in the police program, for—"

"Oh, officer-involved shootings," she said cheerfully and much too loudly. Shephard imagined the other people in the waiting room staring at him. "Of course. Maybe Dr. Zahara can check you out. I mean, take over the check-out session." She giggled and dialed.

Dr. Zahara was a conspicuously pretty woman in her early forties, Shephard guessed, who was behind a large desk when he walked in. The room was comfortable and lit by a lamp that rested on the desk. Dr. Zahara smiled and slipped a pair of glasses over her green eyes.

"Sit down, Tom. Be comfortable."

Shephard sat and searched for a cigarette.

"Of all the damn things, our Dr. Abrams quitting like that," she said, shaking a shock of black hair and lighting a cigarette of her own. "I apologize. I'll be glad to administer this last session if you don't mind."

"I'm eager to be finished, doc." He felt slightly ungrateful.

"Counseling not to your liking?"

"Not really. Not this in particular, I mean. Just any." He finally found the cigarette.

She opened a manila folder and scanned the contents. "You've been with us for nearly a year. Thirty-two years old, born in Laguna Beach, graduated near the top of the Academy. Youngest officer to work detectives here, very impressive. Mayor's Plaque, Outstanding Rookie, Officer of the Year, City Council Commendation. Married at nineteen to Louise Childress, divorced at thirty-one." She lifted the cigarette to her lips and continued to read. "June of last year, Tom, you shot a man in the line of duty. A boy, to be precise, Morris Mumford, age sixteen. Resigned LAPD November, headed back to the hometown, and took work just about two months ago. Well, how do you like it?"

Shephard's mind flitted back to that drizzly summer night in Los Angeles, and to the face of the young man he'd killed.

"Oh. It was too quiet for a while. Today we had a homicide. I look forward to working it." Looking forward was excessive, he knew. Having to do it, the forced activity of a job was all it was. Still, he needed it.

"Why is that?"

"It's what I do best. 'Bathe oneself in the healing waters of action,' someone once said."

"That's true. You find your work rewarding?"

"It keeps me busy."

"Then what you find isn't necessarily more important than what it keeps you from looking at?"

Shephard searched her face as she searched his. "Keep reading," he said. "Abrams told me more than once that obsession with work is nothing more than 'an elaborate network of action to divert oneself from the pain of self-awareness.'"

"You've got a good memory. And what is it that you think needs healing?"

Here it goes again, he thought. Probing with their well-trained shovels. She put out her cigarette and folded her hands under her chin. Shephard took a final drag and crunched his out, chasing the last of the embers around the ashtray.

"I think the healing is more metaphorical than literal, doc," he said. Play the game, he thought, you're almost done with it.

Dr. Zahara smiled. "Why immerse yourself in work merely to 'keep busy'? A nice-looking young man like you must require a little more from his life than business. Metaphorical or not, it was your phrase."

Shephard began to feel claustrophobic, as if his shirt were

made of steel, shrinking in around him. His back was sweating. Hold on, he thought. Exude confidence.

"You've got the goods in front of you, doctor. I killed a boy. But some of the guys I worked with thought I did it too late, so they named me 'Too-long Tom.' My wife left me for a movie guy. My boss suggested I quit when the press and the ACLU came down. Last summer that was quite in vogue. These things all tend to make a man feel a tad lousy. When he works, he forgets them and pays the rent. When he comes to a doctor once a week to stroke the bureaucracy's guilt, he wonders why he has to sit still and talk about it. He starts to wish that his life was a secret, you know, doc? He believes he deserves a little privacy, just like anybody else. I know what needs healing. And I think the best way to do it is to forget myself. Not to dwell. You can drink things under, or screw them under. I work them under. Work is a vacation, doctor." Shut up, he told himself. Be healed.

"I hear anger in you. I probably shouldn't be sharing this with you, but . . . a note here from Dr. Abrams. May fifteenth: 'Getting response from patient nearly impossible. Cannot be provoked to talk, let alone to anger.' You just told me more in ten minutes than you did Dr. Abrams in a year. Why?"

"You're prettier."

Dr. Zahara fastened her calm green eyes on Shephard and nodded matter-of-factly. "Yes, I am." She flipped back the pages of his file. "You realize that this program was set up to help police officers cope with the trauma of a killing. I've seen lives ruined over shootings, no matter how clear it was to everybody that the shooting was necessary and unavoidable. I've seen the drinking you talk about, and the 'screwing,' as you call it. And I've seen a few men who keep things inside and deal with them on their own. Those types usually go one of two ways."

"Oh?"

"They either come through the episode strong and healthy, or they kill themselves. It's hard to tell which is going to happen. I lost a patient once whom I felt was making progress. This counseling might not mean much to you, Mr. Shephard, but it does to me. I don't want you to become my Morris Mumford."

"Sorry, doc. I won't kill myself. I don't have time."

She smiled and closed the file, letting her glasses dangle by a chain around her neck. "I see here that your mother died when you were very young."

"She was murdered. A man broke into the house when she was alone. I was a few months old." Shephard felt anger rising inside, the flippancy draining from his voice. "So I never knew her, and I don't see what that has to do with this counseling, if it's for a shooting trauma. The ACLU seemed to think that made me shoot the boy." He felt heated, clumsy, violated. Colleen Shephard was not to be disturbed. He watched the doctor shake her head slowly, wave a hand, and for the first time, blush.

"This counseling is to help make you a healthy person," she said quietly. She lit another cigarette. "Do you feel healthy?"

"I smoke too much, like you. I don't sleep enough, but besides that, I feel fine."

There was a long silence while Dr. Zahara studied Shephard and Shephard stared back.

"Have you seen other women since the divorce?"

"A few." He felt a shameful slide in his stomach as he reviewed his lack of contact over the last year. His one "date" had ended in the humiliation of trying to disprove what he had known anyway, that his desire had vanished. Since then it had been easier to be alone—a common reaction, according to Dr. Abrams. The silence of Dr. Zahara demanded that he go on. "Nothing steady," he said.

"Is that to your liking?"

"Sure. Play the field. I've never felt the need to be connected," he lied.

"But you enjoyed ten years of marriage?"

Enjoyed most of the time, he thought. Louise said he suffocated her, that she couldn't grow, couldn't breathe. And something about the difference between love and need. Don't need me, don't need me so much. And the harder he held on, the faster it fell apart.

"Since that, I mean," he said, a partial retreat.

"It's healthy to acclimate oneself to the opposite sex after the end of a long relationship. I would encourage anyone in your position to enjoy himself. Sometimes, the simple enjoying of oneself and another person can be tarnished by the end of a marriage. We have to learn to enjoy, if you will. That sounds contrary to nature, but it really isn't. It is one of the purest delights of being human, I think."

Shephard imagined Dr. Zahara pushing back her chair, standing and stretching languorously, coming toward him from around the desk, kneeling beside him to kiss his hand. Her skirt fell away as she stood up and his hand slipped into warmth and dampness. But when he stood to kiss her, her face cracked and blistered into Tim Algernon's and she erupted, laughing, into flames.

"I suppose that's true," he said. Had Pavlik gotten good latents from the turpentine can? Was the stakeout man awake, or napping behind his sunglasses? This Bible Property of whom? Why had the killer left nearly fifteen hundred dollars behind, then checked into a cheap hotel? Could the bills have been his to begin with? If little liars burn first, who second?

"Is there anything you would like to talk about?"

"No, thank you."

"Then you're released from our care as scheduled," she said. "I think you are dealing with your life in a, well, a quietly positive way. Please feel free to call me any time you wish; we can set up another session if you feel the need. You have a new life ahead of you, Tom, and I wish you all the good luck in the world." She stood and offered her hand. "Don't be afraid to look at yourself. It can only do good. Those secrets you feel the need of having, they're common to us all. Go ahead, work. Sometimes when we lose ourselves, we find ourselves, too."

Shephard's dog, Cal, welcomed him home with minimal interest and a guilty slink. Flipping on the kitchen light, Shephard discovered one of his shoes had been thoroughly chewed and slobbered upon, its leather lace masticated to pulp. Cal offered an unrepentant glance, then waddled off to the patio to be fed. Shephard avenged himself by carrying a box of doggie treats to the patio, commanding Cal to sit, then dropping a banana peel from the trash into his eager jaws. The mutt spit up the peel with distaste but attacked his dinner gratefully, Shephard making it extra large out of a sense of guilt.

After dinner they were friends again, Shephard pouring himself a large Scotch, Cal yawning, then falling asleep in the middle of the kitchen floor.

His evening project was to unpack the dozen boxes still stacked in the living room, but it had been his evening project for nearly two months. So much for the healing waters of action, he thought. He pulled open the top of one, confronted a framed photograph of himself and Louise dressed up Roaring Twenties style for a Halloween party, and lost heart again. Would Dr. Zahara be a good fuck? He pondered the question, but the exercise was cerebral rather than hormonal, and he got no answer. He replaced the picture face down and poured another drink.

Suddenly, the dazzling fleck of cobalt under Ken Robbins's microscope positioned itself square in his mind's eye, as if to blot out introspection. Shephard closed his eyes. The cobalt rotated of its own will, offering him rich blue facets and begging the question: What was I doing in the killer's hair? Then the blue gave way to the camel's hair. It displayed itself similarly and begged the same question. Had it come from the collar of a coat perhaps, or a hat? No one washes coats or hats in hair conditioner, he thought. The image dispersed and he opened his eyes.

Shephard recognized the process as what his father called a "Dick Probe." He was fourteen when he had asked Wade what made a good detective. Wade was sitting at the kitchen table, halfway through a quart of bourbon. A good detective works behind his eyes, he had said. When you look at something, don't think about it. See it. Think it later. Close your eyes and let it come back. Then you can hold it as long as you want and give your brain a chance to catch up. Especially with people; first impressions are usually wrong. Your mind knows more about what you see than it lets on, so you have to be able to bring things back. Some people call it imagination; the quacks at the Academy called it meditation on evidence. Me? He had smiled drunkenly. I call it a Dick Probe.

Shephard, old enough to get the joke, blushed, then laughed heartily to cover his embarrassment. Wade had retired to his room a short time later, bottle in hand, and when the door to the bedroom closed, Shephard did his first Dick Probe—on his father. When he closed his eyes, he saw not Wade but a bourbon-colored stallion galloping through the desert, dragging a lifeless body behind it.

Shephard lit a cigarette, stepped over Cal, and went into the living room, where he dug out a dictionary from a box of books.

cobalt, *n* [G *kobalt*, goblin, demon of the mines; term applied to cobalt by miners from ignorance of its value or because it was troublesome], a hard, lustrous, ductile, metallic chemical element, found in various ores: it is used in the production of alloys; its compounds are used in the production of inks, paints, and varnishes: symbol, Co.

cobalt blue, *n:* 1. a dark-blue pigment made from cobalt. 2. a dark blue.

Cal lifted a sleepy head when the phone rang. Shephard reread the cobalt entry as he lifted the receiver.

"Tom, it's Carl here." Pavlik sounded breathless. "The prints on the turpentine can match the ones on the glass at Algernon's. Whoever drank with him last night left that can in the Sebastian. I picked up some soil trace from the bedspread and got ferrous earth, the same as around the stables. The water under the drain had blood in it, type O, same as Algernon's. I called Yee. Robbins is working two hairs I got from the pillow and told me that the material fragments from the body haven't told us anything we didn't know at noon. The cobalt isn't radioactive to any degree that would matter, but it's the kind of thing someone *might* pick up if he worked with metal alloys. Some kind of light industry, maybe. Or, of course, if he mined the stuff. Robbins kept saying it was real weird shit here in Laguna."

Pavlik stopped, breathed rapidly, then continued. "Now get this. Sacramento says that Edward Steinhelper is an ex-con. He's done time for burglary, assault, embezzlement. He's been clean for three years but his wife told me he disappeared two nights ago with the car. *Still* gone. He worked for a shop in Sacramento until last month. His job was finishing furniture. Mr. and Mrs. Hylkama say the guy who checked in isn't the guy on the license, but maybe they're wrong. Steinhelper stinks."

Shephard considered the cobalt, its use in varnishes. "You lift any prints from the kitchen, near the window?"

"Nothing to lift, but I shot the boot marks. They eyeball

like the tracks we found this morning. Right down to the broken heel. You found the sonofabitch, Shephard."

"Who's working the stakeout?" he asked.

"Grimes. Said he needed the overtime."

"The whole night?"

"He said no problem. Slobin is meeting with the Hyl-kamas at nine tomorrow to do the Identikit."

"Good work, Carl, chum."

"Same back. I'm dead. See you tomorrow."

The idea of Grimes working the stakeout irritated him. He poured another Scotch and stared again at the unpacked boxes that constituted his new life. He smoked and paced the apartment, went to the patio to view the lights of the city below, and paced some more. Finally, just after midnight, he went downstairs to the garage.

He eased the Mustang onto Thalia Street and followed Thalia down the hillside to Glenneyre. The night breeze cooled his face, and he noted that the moon was nearly full. The tree-lined streets of Laguna seemed strange to him after years of working in the bright lights of L.A. Was there anywhere in L.A. as dark as this at night, he wondered? As he approached Serra Street, the smell of the eucalyptus engulfed the car and Shephard realized for the thousandth time just what it was that had brought the painters to Laguna at the turn of the century. Peace and quiet and a place to work. Even now, he thought, with the millions of tourists who swarm the town in summer, it was still the best place in the world to retreat, regroup, start again. He thought of the boxes stacked in his living room as he pulled into the courtyard of the Hotel Sebastian.

He cut the headlights and U-turned in front of a white sedan parked diagonally across from cottage five. Slowly he completed the turn and dipped back out of the courtyard to park on the street. Retracing his way on foot, he approached the sedan and had his worst fears confirmed. Even through the closed windows he could hear Grimes snoring. The rearview mirror had been angled for a clean line of sight to the cottage door, but Grimes's big head was wedged comfortably between the window and the headrest. Shephard stooped to the glass and studied the bulldog face, babylike now, at rest. He noted that the windows were filthy and wondered what Grimes could hope to see, anyway. What a way to earn your overtime, he thought. There were no lights on in the cottage, and no sounds except the occasional hiss of cars down on Coast Highway. Steinhelper could have come back any time, he thought. Be asleep inside right now. Might have been for hours.

He trod lightly across the gravel to the back side of the cottages. And as he rounded the corner of the first, he stopped short at the figure of a man, outlined in moonlight, standing behind the back window of cottage five. A beam of light appeared in front of the figure, then climbed to the window. Whoever it was took a step closer and pressed his head to the lilting curtains. The beam vanished.

Shephard marched toward the cottage, eucalyptus leaves crunching underfoot, and shouted, "Hey, bud. Out for a midnight stroll? Stay put a second, will ya?"

In the clear moonlight he saw the man pull away from the window and freeze. Shephard could make out a head of curly hair, rounded in outline. He looked big. Then he turned and lumbered across the backlot toward the sloping hillside that rose behind the cottages.

"Hey, don't go away! Laguna cops here! Hold it, sonofabitch." Shephard pursued, reaching cottage five and angling up the hillside. Eucalyptus loomed around him, and as he peered into the dark, he could see the big man's body zigzagging through the trees, his arms pushing off the cream-white trunks.

The hillside was covered with iceplant. Shephard

41

sprinted, slipped to one knee, rose, and slipped again. Down the second time, he saw that the man ahead of him had gone down, too. A muffled curse trailed back to him in the darkness. Up again, Shephard hugged the tree trunks for balance, launching himself from one to the next. Ahead he could see the man on all fours now, clawing up a steep embankment. Shephard dashed toward him and found himself on his face. He righted himself, churning his legs deep into the iceplant for footing. Somehow the man was widening the distance. Shephard was twenty yards behind him, down on all fours himself, pulling with his hands as his feet slipped and skidded. Everything seemed slick, as if drenched in oil. He saw the man disappear over the rise. Shephard reached the top a moment later and stopped to get his bearings.

The hillside rose steadily before him, and as he listened he could hear no movement in the dense cluster of trees. His breathing was deep and frantic, his vision poor in the murky shadows of the eucalyptus. He could feel his heart thumping in his ribs, his head, his ears. A quirk in the shadows ahead, then the snapping of a branch. "Hey! You! Stop right there. . . . " His attempted shout trailed off feebly into breathlessness and he started running again. As the man ahead darted into a clearing, Shephard saw him turn his head and look back. Then he lunged forward and disappeared into the trees again.

In the clearing, Shephard stopped and listened. His legs were heavy and he couldn't seem to breathe fast enough to keep his lungs full. Silence. He waited, studying the pale trunks of the eucalyptus trees, every one of them large enough to hide a body. Then, scanning the scene in front of him, he walked slowly forward, waiting for his game to break cover. This is the place to hide, he thought. The closely bunched trees blotted out the light from the moon. Still no other sound than of his own rapid breathing.

Doesn't the sonofabitch breathe too, he wondered? Too many cigarettes. Ahead of him the trunks sprouted like a regiment of towering soldiers, each a slash of bone in the blackness. Then a quick wisp behind him, head-high; no, he thought, and began to duck, but he was just beginning when the steel slammed into the back of his head and dropped him abruptly to his knees. Take a vacation, fucker—later Shephard was sure he'd heard the man say it—take a vacation because you're going to need it. Then the swift and wind-robbing jolt of a shoe in his stomach and his face pressing into iceplant.

The last thing he remembered was thinking how much iceplant tasted like blood.

FIVE

He awoke to a well-lit acoustic ceiling. The holes shifted and swirled, the squares stretched into rectangles and back again; a Beatles tune dripped from a speaker, watered down to almost nothing. He lifted his arm and read his name off the plastic bracelet. Spelled wrong. When he tried to raise his head, it erupted with a pain so severe it overwhelmed his mind like a tsunami and sent him floating back into unconsciousness.

Sedated dreams: gray forms looming with terrible size, slow-motion horses snorting from widened nostrils, mute women with perfect bodies, fires, voices, clouds. And later, when the sedatives began to wear off, he found himself in the dreams, an onlooker in a shadowed world of murmurs

43

and mood, like an ego-less baby seeing events around himself, trying to understand them, understanding nothing.

When he finally regained consciousness, his father and a man he didn't recognize stood over him. Wade looked stricken. Shephard groaned, testing his pain, then propped himself up on his elbows. "Hiya, pop," he slurred.

His father was dressed tennis, little white shorts and little white shirt. So was the man who was with him. "Take it easy, son. You'll rip your stitches."

"My serve. Love-fifty. Little white shoes, pop; Nikes?" His words were escaping without thought. "Get me a Scotch," he heard himself say.

"That's the spirit," said Wade's friend.

"Tommy, you remember Joe Datilla? The Surfside?"

Datilla stepped forward and smiled. He looked gray, handsome, fit. A sailboat tan and a health-spa body, Shephard thought. "Haven't seen you in years, Tom. I was with your dad when he got the news, so I thought I'd come along. I'll forgive you for interrupting our tennis." Shephard tried his best to focus. Joe. Of course.

"I 'member old Joe. And the health spa—the Surfside."

"Well . . . " Datilla smiled pitiably.

"It's the ritziest sun club north of La Costa," Shephard blurted. Wish the room would quit swimming. "I ain't no dummy. How are ya, pop?"

"You know how I am, Tom. How are *you?* And what happened?"

"Someone had a party on my head, but it's okay, I feel great. Know how hangovers make you feel profound? That's me. One big hangover. I'm going to become a poet. . . . "

Wade and Datilla laughed heartily, but his father stepped forward and ran his fingers across Shephard's face. He laid back down and touched his head, getting only bandage.

"Again, Tommy. What happened?"

Shephard offered a concussive narrative. It ended

abruptly when he felt exhaustion coming over him like a warm blanket. " . . . So that was my night. You do anything fun?" He settled back into the pillow.

"Did you get a look at him, Tom?" Datilla asked.

"How old a man?" asked Wade.

"One at a time, boys." He closed his eyes at a sudden crack of pain. "Yes, and forty. Give or take five years. Pretty damned dark out. Bring me the phone, will ya?"

Wade put his hand on the telephone and moved it away from his son. "A boy found you in the hills," he said. "When they brought you here, they called the department. The chief knows you're here, so don't worry about business right now. Just give my prayers a chance to work. Please."

Wade the Reverend, still thinking like Wade the Cop, Shephard thought. "Welcome back to the hometown," he said finally. "It's changed." He could hear Wade and Datilla chuckle, which mingled with the piped-in music and throbbed through his head.

"Won't be so bad," Datilla was saying now. "As soon as you're up and around, I expect to see you out at the Surfside. Come by any time. We'll have a drink, maybe go for a sail. You play tennis?"

"No. Could never figure out how to keep score."

"I'll teach you. I can think of a few ladies out there who might be intrigued by a detective."

"Yes. I'm an intriguing man."

"You're just a tired, beat-up man right now," said Wade. He stepped forward again, pressing his hand against Tom's shoulder. "We'll let you rest, son. Let's have lunch just as soon as you feel up to it. I haven't improved any as a cook, but you grew up on it, so it shouldn't kill you now."

"Leave that to the pros," Shephard said.

"What'd the sonofabitch look like, anyway?" Datilla said.

"Just a big guy with curly hair and no respect for the law."

"Well, I hope to heaven you find him."

"Amen," said Wade.

He was pronounced mildly concussed, but was released that afternoon to Pavlik. The crime scene investigator took Shephard to the Hotel Sebastian to get his car, driving carefully while Shephard slumped in the seat and watched Laguna Beach slide by the windows. Pavlik's voice seemed to slip past his brain without contact, Shephard hearing only snippets. Grimes picked a good time for a nap . . . got Hardy there now . . . watched the hotel for an hour myself . . . got the key . . . when I went in, everything was the same, same crappy old place . . . get some rest . . . got the stakeout myself tonight. . . .

The climb up the stairs to his apartment was endless, the steps somehow multiplying in front of him. He stopped halfway when he heard his neighbor's voice booming from the doorway below.

"Hey, Shephard, wanna grind?" He turned to focus on Sal.

"Just ate, Sal."

"What's that shit on the back of your head, man?"

"Just a little ding."

"You mean she closed her legs too fast." Sal bellowed, enjoying his joke immensely.

Shephard grinned, but a jolt of pain shot through his head. "Fishing the rocks tonight?" he managed.

"Up too late, bro, I'm in the coffin after the grind."

Sal roared a friendly insult to a woman passing on the sidewalk, and Shephard confronted his stairs for the second half of the journey.

Before he reached the porch he could hear Cal's quiet whining coming from inside. Shephard stopped by the door and listened . . . a long whimper followed by another, the dog catching his breath, then starting in again. The muffled thumps of struggle, then nothing. Shephard slid his key into the lock with one hand, brought the Colt Python from his holster with the other, and stumbled through the door.

Cal was flopping in the middle of the living room floor, hog-tied and gagged with masking tape. Shephard stepped past the dog, the pistol held in front of him, and moved slowly into the bedroom, where he saw that the covers had been slashed lengthwise with something very sharp. He went into the bathroom, then back out to the living room and the struggling mutt. He beheld his apartment.

The stereo speakers were smashed, the turntable arm twisted obscenely upward, the plants dumped from their pots onto the carpet, the lampshades crushed, his art collection—a single print of Hopper's *Nighthawks*—pulled from its frame then torn to small bits that were scattered across the floor. The boxes had been toppled and gutted, the sofa overturned, a photo album mangled and thrown atop the heap of what had once been a growing diffenbachia. He was trembling.

He untied Cal, who fled to the bedroom as soon as his legs were free. The dog was still whining when Shephard found him on the far side of the bed, scooped him into his arms, and brought him to the kitchen. Cal shivered as Shephard set him on the drainboard and tried to cut the tape from around his mouth with scissors. Back on the floor, Cal lay down and worked his paws over his nose, fly-style, trying to pull off the sticky bands. Shephard finally rubbed some vegetable oil into the dog's hair, lifting the tape gently and pouring a slender stream of oil as he went. Cal's right eye, puffed and bloodshot, regarded Shephard with unabashed terror. The other was swollen shut. Shephard's head throbbed as he worked bent over his dog.

The telephone rang. Shephard worked his way through the littered living room and picked up the receiver, saying nothing. A wonder it still works, he thought.

"Shephard?" The voice was muffled and low. He waited, realizing now why the phone hadn't been pulled from the socket. "Yeah, it's you, Shephard. I left the phone alive so I could call and ask you if you got the picture. Get it?" Shephard said nothing. "You get it. Do yourself a favor and beat it for a while. You'll make me very happy. How's the dog? Worthless in a pinch, you know." The man hung up.

Shephard went back out to the kitchen, poured a Scotch, and went back downstairs. He found Sal reclined on a sofa, balancing an ashtray on his stomach while he fiddled with a joint.

"Don't bust me, Shephard. I'm a good guy."

"You were up late?"

"Like you. Have a lady up there last night?"

"No, why?"

" 'Cause the fuckin' stereo was blasting for an hour. I figured you didn't feel like filling up the neighborhood with moans and groans." Sal's conversational voice was concert-pitch. It seemed to ricochet from one wall of Shephard's skull to the other.

"What time?" Shephard asked. The moans and groans were Cal getting kicked and his apartment being ransacked, he thought. That's why the bastard turned up the music.

"Little after one. You ought to . . ." Sal understood. He got up from the sofa, set down the ashtray, turned off the television, and shut the door. "What happened?"

"I had a visitor last night. Did you see him?"

Sal seemed to diminish in size and become more alert, edgy. "Yeah, I saw him," he said quietly. "I told you I was up. The door was open, I see everything that comes and goes around this ghetto. Tall and thick, good build, so I figured he was a cop. He came by the door about one, then the stereo. Back down a half hour later. The son-ofabitch was driving a Carerra and I wondered how a cop got the dough for one of those. Midnight blue, right un-

48

der the streetlamp in front. Everything okay up there?"

Dark blue, and Michael Stett shiny, Shephard thought. "No."

Sal eyed him warily. "Shit, Shephard. I'd have come right out with it but I wondered if you two were . . . well, shit, you know Laguna." Sal's hand fluttered on a limp wrist.

"He was alone?"

"Alone and not in a hurry from the way he walked. I had him pegged cop all the way. Sorry, bro."

Shephard helped the vet hold Cal's head still while the X-rays were taken. The doctor, a thick and docile man named Gillson, shot Cal with a long needle and told Shephard his dog would be all right. By the time the X-rays were processed, Cal was asleep and slobbering contentedly on Shephard's leg. His skull was fine, Gillson said, and the swelling would go down in a day or two. After that he wanted a look at the eye.

The doctor closed the door of the examination room and asked how it happened. Shephard told him it was an accident. Gillson sighed and lit a cigarette. "Plenty of good shelters in town if you're tired of your pet," he said.

Back at his apartment, Shephard carried Cal upstairs and set him down on the couch. Standing amidst his degraded home, he knew that there would be no fingerprints or significant evidence, none of the careless calling cards left by youngsters, junkies, amateurs. Nothing was missing. He was in professional hands. And the act of violation was complete: his knees were still shaking, his tongue felt thick and dry. He noted the roll of masking tape tossed into the corner.

The quiet of the evening heightened his sense of aloneness as he stared down at the literal ruins of his life. Outside he heard a car moving down Thalia Street toward the highway, the far-off dialogue of a television, a peaceful breeze in the trees outside the house. The disgust he felt as he kicked the ruined *Nighthawks* frame wasn't so much for the possessions in the house as for himself. Keeper of the peace, he thought. The keeper who can't keep his wife, the keeper who can't protect his home, can't prevent his own dog from having the shit kicked out of him. And with the disgust came anger. The healing waters of action, he thought. He poured down a Scotch and made another. He smoked three straight cigarettes, lighting the last with the embers of the one before it. He paced the kitchen, and stood looking out from the balcony.

Then it all became clear.

By eleven he had piled everything from his past—letters from Louise, pictures of Louise, pictures of himself and his wife together, the books she'd given him, anything that tugged from the past rather than called him toward the future—into the middle of the floor. To this he added the boxes wholesale, and the ruined possessions that lay scattered about. His head was killing him. By twelve he had tied it all up in the slashed bedding and dragged the heavy bundles across the street, where he hefted them into the dumpster of St. Michael's Church. It took several trips. There, he thought. In emptiness will be abundance.

He called Louise. A man answered politely and asked if he could say who was calling.

"Her ex, fuckhead. Put her on."

"Gladly."

Then she was there, Louise, he thought: lovely, bored, drifting Louise. "Hello, Tom," she said. He could hear the new life in her voice, its sweet assurance. "Robert here is giving me a funny look. Did you say something bad to him?"

"Absolutely not. Scout's honor. I'm just calling to tell you I've got a new life, a grand one. I know you felt a lot of guilt about me, but I want to let you off the hook now."

"You're drinking again, aren't you?"

"Sober every night for the last month. Got any movie parts yet?"

She paused. He could hear her breathing. "I'm not really at that level yet, Tom. Shampoo commercial, maybe."

"Get Robbie on the ball. He's big time."

She let the comment go. Don't be an ass, Shephard, he thought. That's not the point.

"How 'bout you?" she asked. "Are you seeing anybody?"

Shephard felt the Scotch hitting him, a stupid confidence. "In fact I am, Lou. Karen's her name. Does some acting up your way. Karen Smythe . . . was in the last Reynolds pic, you know, *Burt* Reynolds, forget the name of it, though."

"Well, that's fine, Tom. I'm really happy for you."

"Don't be. It's all a lie."

"I know."

"I moved back to Laguna."

"You should be happy there."

"Like to see you sometime, Lou. I think about you."

"Maybe, Tom."

By two he was asleep, and not long after accosted again by the imminent nightmare in which Morris Mumford pitched over dead on the grass while a cop tried to keep his own insides from spilling on the sidewalk. In the dream, as it had happened in reality, Shephard stood and peed his pants while his ears rang and the pistol in his hand grew too heavy to hold up any longer.

SIX

Early the next morning Shephard called on Jane Algernon. Her house was on Laguna Canyon Road a half mile west of her father's stables, tucked under a massive willow tree that cast shade over the entire front yard. He smelled the strong odor of fish and heard croaking sounds as he approached. There was a chain-link pen in front of the house containing a cement pool, a slippery animal of some kind, and a young woman wearing thigh-high rubber boots over her pants. She was bending toward the animal, offering a tidbit. Shephard guessed fish. The animal slipped into the water and the woman turned. She was large and pretty, and her dark hair was pulled away from her face.

"Seal?" he asked.

She looked at him like he didn't particularly matter. "Sea lion. You must be police."

"Detective Shephard." The sea lion surfaced and croaked. She tossed a fish into the air and the sea lion surged to meet it. "Can we talk?"

"Go ahead."

Shephard felt a chill, and it wasn't just the shade of the willow. "I'm very sorry. You have my condolences. Did your father live alone?"

"My mother died twenty-six years ago of cancer. He lived alone."

"What kind of man was he?"

She flipped another fish toward the animal and smiled

when it was caught again mid-air. The smile froze when she turned back to him. "I don't know. He ignored me, I ignored him. I'll tell you I loved him as much as any daughter can love a father. It was just better done at a distance, that's all."

Shephard lit a cigarette. "Frozen fish?"

"Fresh frozen."

"Of course. So, you can't tell me what kind of man he was?"

Jane Algernon sighed and put her hands on her hips. "A gambler and a drinker," she said. "That's how much I can tell you. Those are the kinds of things you need to know, aren't they?"

"Oh, yes, definitely," he said, pulling the notepad and pen from his pocket and scribbling nothing on the page. In matters of friendly questioning, Shephard had learned that preconceptions were something to be used. Played up. Street talk for street people, tough talk for people who watched too much TV, confidential talk for those who fancied themselves in the know, condolences to the needy few who turned to the police for sympathy and a shoulder to cry on. But people like Jane Algernon were the hardest: their superiority demanded submission. "Since he had the stables, I wonder if horses were what he gambled on."

She studied him briefly, then threw another fish, fresh frozen. The sea lion backpeddled with a croak, knocking his head on the cement siding. Shephard winced.

"Horses, football, fights. It was always that way. If you know Laguna, you won't have to ask me where he booked."

"Oh, you must mean Marty's Sportsplace."

"Tell Marty hello from me. It's about time he got some pressure."

"It sounds like you don't care much for Marty."

"I don't care for people who run others down, or those who snoop around after and try to clean it up," she said.

Shephard scribbled. "That's me, isn't it?" Her back was to him and she didn't turn around. He noted that her hair was held up by two chopsticks that caught the faint light streaming through the willow. Her legs were long and looked trim where they disappeared into the boots. When she bent down to get another fish, her arms were dark brown on top and lighter underneath. She had tucked her blouse into the khaki pants and the material stretched against her back as she stooped. She is beautiful, he thought.

"That's anybody, detective."

"Did he have any enemies? Anyone who might want to take his life?"

"If I thought there were, I'd have come to you first, wouldn't I?"

Shephard realized that he was getting nowhere, and that even in the mind of a mourning daughter who was bitter about things there would be a wealth of information, any crumb of which might prove useful. It was often the crumbs he needed most. Jane Algernon was miles away from offering any. He scribbled dramatically, flipping over a page, referring to it, then scribbled some more.

"What are you writing when I haven't told you anything?"

Shephard looked up and found her blue, angry eyes boring into him. "Just what I see," he said, finishing the entry with a flourish.

"And just what do you see, detective? Besides a hungry sea lion who would like the rest of his lunch."

"I'll tell you, Miss Algernon. First I see your father. Since you say you ignored him, you might want to know what he looked like before yesterday morning." Shephard called to mind the picture in Tim Algernon's bedroom. "He was a big man with a healthy head of gray hair and a love for horses. Loved to ride them, feed them, talk to them. Maybe they were something he loved even more after your mother died.

54

People focus a tremendous amount of love on animals sometimes, especially lonely people. It's a safe, easy love because animals don't demand much. But still it's love. I see him betting horses and drinking Jack Daniels, probably too much of it. I see him tired of running the business and selling off a dozen animals he loved and hated to see go. I see him saddling up that last mare, what was her name . . . ?"

"Rebecca," she said, her voice bordering on fury.

"Rebecca, but he liked to call her Becky. Anyway, they would wander off through the canyon. That's this canyon right here. Then, of course, I see what happened to him. I see him sprawled in the gravel outside the house he'd owned for forty years, a rock the size of a grapefruit planted in his brain, a thousand plus dollars in bills stuffed down his throat, and his entire body ruined by fire." From where he stood, Shephard could see that Jane's face had colored to an angry shade of red.

"Then I see you, his daughter, who lives walking distance from the stables. I see him drunk and saying things to you that you don't like. I see you watching him lose his money at the track. Feeding sea lions is a good profession, but it's like mine in that you don't make much money at it. You wondered why the dollars went to the track instead of down the road a bit. Bear in mind this is just speculation, Miss Algernon. I see you thinking he drank your mother into an early grave. I see you not quite forgiving him for it all the way. The last part of what I see I shouldn't bore you with, but you did ask. I see a daughter too full of guilt to admit she loved her father, and too angry at him to admit she feels betrayed. Too ashamed of herself for not doing anything to help him—and how could she?—to really try now that she has the chance to. I see a woman whose left chopstick is about to fall out."

Her hand shot to her head and poked the dangling stick back into place.

55

"And, of course, I have to see me, too, since I'm here. I see a cop with a patch on the back of his head who has to walk up to this woman and ask a bunch of questions she doesn't want to hear. He wants to hear them even less, but he believes in certain fundamental things, and one of those is that killers shouldn't go free. So he asks the questions. He gets no answers, and quite frankly he feels a bit foolish. When a beautiful woman makes a man feel small, he feels real small. But he *is* a professional. He wants answers, he needs help. He scribbles a bunch of shit in a notepad hoping she'll think he's as dumb as he acts, and she'll finally have to ask him what he's writing. And you did, Miss Algernon."

Shephard looked at the notepad and slid it back into his coat pocket. She was still staring at him, her eyes a cobalt blue, he thought. Demon of the mines.

"And just what is it you would like to know?" she asked quietly. It sounded like a hiss.

"I'd like a recent photo of your father. I need a sample of his handwriting. I need the names of his friends, regular business clients, gambling buddies, drinking partners. I'd like to see his business books. I need one hour with you in his house, with you talking about him however you want. What I need might be between the lines, so anything goes. You tell me what you want to tell me. Whoever killed him planned to kill him. It wasn't for money. Somewhere in that house, somewhere in that mind of yours is a reason."

"Is that all?"

Her voice has thawed, he thought. "Yes."

"Fine. Then get off my property and out of my sight. Good-bye. And, detective, it's got nothing to do with your patch. That's the most interesting thing about you." She turned and brought another fish from the bucket, tossing it by the tail to the sea lion. "What was your name?"

"Shephard."

"I might want to remember it the next time I talk to the chief. He's a neighbor, you know."

"Oh, right. Here's my card." He worked a business card into a diamond of chain link. "I'm sorry, Miss Algernon. My mother was killed when I was young, so I can understand what you're feeling. You don't really get over it, you just learn to turn it off. You can keep him okay, inside yourself." And not to be disturbed, he thought. Like Colleen. "Do you know Ed Steinhelper?"

"Get out." She stared at him as he turned away from the fence and headed back to the car.

Shephard found Marty Odette's black 280Z parked outside the Sportsplace on Coast Highway. The plates said MARTYZ and the car shone like obsidian under the nine o'clock sun. The tourist traffic had already begun to thicken; the smell of brine and suntan oil was wafting in from the beach. Shephard remembered the Sportsplace as a boy: a dark, loud bar where men went to watch sports on a large screen and where betting was rumored to take place. He had learned some years later that Marty Odette had done a short stretch for bookmaking, but he kept his profile low in Laguna. The cops didn't bother Marty because they liked his bar. Marty Odette had been good friends with Wade Shephard, before Wade had found God. Shephard hadn't heard his father mention Marty in years. Stepping into the bar, Shephard couldn't shake the image of Jane Algernon from his mind.

The morning drinkers in the Sportsplace were like morning drinkers anyplace: quiet, friendly, determined. An eight-foot-long airplane propeller still hung behind the bar. Beer seemed to dominate the counter. Shephard ordered coffee. The woman next to him looked about seventy and she smiled at Shephard. He nodded and took a stool.

"Don't I know you?" the man behind the counter asked.

"Tom Shephard."

"Tommy Shephard, goddamned." He reached over and pumped Shephard's hand.

"How are you, Marty?"

"Look around you," Odette said, spreading his arms like a pastor raising his congregation. "I'm great. Business is up. And you? How's Wade? I saw him on the TV Sunday night, a real good sermon. It made me feel like a sinner so I turned it off, but what a delivery he's got. Building some big hospital down in Mexico, isn't he?"

"The Yucatan, near Cozumel."

"After all he's been through, what a guy. What a miracle worker he's turned into." Odette was a stocky, gray-haired man with a wide face and a smile that was quick and didn't quite line up right. He poured Shephard a coffee and then poured one for himself.

"Got any help this morning, Marty?"

"Sure."

"Why don't you see how it tends bar?"

Odette's manner quieted a notch as he untied his apron. "Sure, Tommy." He disappeared to a back room and returned with a young man following him. "Come on back."

The office was a large room with no windows, one desk, two chairs, and three telephones. They sat and Odette poured two short Scotches, a medium-priced brand.

"You heard about Tim," Shephard began. "I'd like to know if he was bringing you much business."

Odette sipped his drink. The phone rang and he said to call back. "Beer drinker," he said. "And a helluva good guy. He'd come in Friday nights for beers, Mondays during football. A heavy beer drinker, Tim." The phone rang again and Marty said to call back. Then he punched the com line and told someone at the other end to answer the goddamned phone. He hung up and smiled. "Keeping the distributors off my back is a full-time job."

"I'm not talking beer business, I'm talking book," Shephard said.

Marty shook his head with finality. "No more, Tommy. I'm out of that for good. That's why we're drinking this"— he held up his glass—"instead of Glenlivet."

Shephard could hear the phone ringing outside in the bar area. "When did you see him last?"

"Friday night."

"Anything unusual?"

"Yeah. He had a friggin' Bible on the counter with him. I asked him if he was getting born again and he told me to shut my mouth. Funny place to see a Bible in a bar, but this place is like home to a lot of the guys." Odette checked his watch too casually.

"I'm in a hurry, too, Marty. I want to find out who killed Tim Algernon. The people making those calls want to know your odds on the thoroughbreds at Hollywood Park tonight. And don't try to tell me they want to know what kind of gin you're pouring because that insults my intelligence and tends to piss me off. I just need three answers and I'll be out of here and you'll be back in business. One, did Algernon win big last week?"

"Two thousand on a horse called Blue Moon. Fifth race at the park last Thursday."

"How did you pay off? What kinds of bills?"

"Hundreds, fifties, twenties. I don't know how much of which. It wasn't old, wasn't new, just bills." Marty slugged down his Scotch and poured another. Shephard's was still untouched.

"Who handles your rough stuff?"

Odette stood up and leaned over the desk toward Shephard. "No, Tom. That I don't touch, and never have. The guys who play here are buddies, that's it. No roughing up, no nothing. Shit, everybody in Laguna's got two things, money and a suntan. I don't have no trouble with that.

Nickel an' dime." He sat down and leaned back. "But speaking of muscle, I just thought of something that might help you. Tim asked me for Little Theodore's number when he was in. I gave it to him. You know Little Theodore?"

"Sure."

"Maybe he can help you, Tommy." Shephard stood up and drained the Scotch. Odette remained sitting, and a worried look crossed his face. "Not gonna close me up, are ya?"

"I'm homicide, Marty. Haven't killed anybody, have you?"

Odette grinned. "Anytime. Stop in anytime, Shephard. I owe you one. I just got my jet license. We'll go up for a ride sometime, okay?"

"One more thing. What did Tim drink if it wasn't beer?"

"Jack Daniels, always."

"Anybody here know Tim hit it big on Thursday?"

"Everybody did. He saw to that. But like I said, all the guys here are buddies. Anybody shady, I throw 'em out. Swear."

"Jane Algernon sends her regards."

Marty shook his head sadly. "A knockout," he said, as if another one had gotten away. "And a class bitch, too. Feel sorry for her though, under the circumstances. Send her mine back, Shephard. By the way, what happened to your head?"

He stopped at a pay phone and called South Coast Investigators. This time his call rang straight through to the offices. The woman who answered the phone was polite, young, and British, and she set up an appointment for Randy Cox to see Michael Stett about some estate work. Shephard fabricated a story about a rich dead Uncle Larry and a vindictive sister who wanted it all. She was sure Mr.

Stett could be of help. "One o'clock this afternoon," she concluded. "Cheerio."

A collection of notes from Pavlik awaited him on the desk. The handwriting, like the man, was not much to look at but thorough and to the point.

> Robbins matched the hairs; same man at stables and hotel. Nothing new on first samples.
> No one came to cottage five last night. Chief implied stakeout to end midnight tonight. Flair for the dramatic as always. How's the head?

And the last, written at 8 A.M., when Pavlik was on his way home after twenty-four hours of work:

> Called Steinhelper's wife again. He showed up late last night. Said he was mugged and spent a few days with friends. She said he looked it. Was drinking with a guy up in a Sacramento bar called O'Malley's on the twenty-third, he says. Offered him a lift home and got conked. Beat him to the punch, probably. Cops on the follow, but story tracks. It looks like Hylkama was right. Steinhelper isn't our man.
> Slobin did the Identikit sketch, attached.

Shephard cleared the notes away from the Identikit sketch and positioned it squarely in front of him. The face looking up at him was taut and slender, eyes wideset and intense, nose thin, mouth full and upturned at the corners into an inadvertent, wry look of superiority. The beard was trimmed back, framing the hard face. The hair was straight and fell onto the forehead from a center part. Overall, a haughty expression, a handsome face.

It had the quality of all Identikit sketches, Shephard thought, as his mind wandered and searched backward for connections: it could be anybody and it could be nobody. No one looks like a killer, or does everyone?

SEVEN

outh Coast Investigators was located in Newport Center, a sprawling commercial complex marked by buildings that looked distinguished and trees that looked planted. The English receptionist was fair-haired and freckled, welcoming Shephard, a.k.a. Cox, with a warmly professional smile. Her name was Marla Collins, and she told him she was only temporary until fall, when she would be back in school. Shephard took a seat on a black leather sofa and awaited Michael Stett.

Half an hour later he was shown into a roomy office. The man who looked up from the desk, then stood to offer his hand, was tall and muscular as Hylkama had described, an athletic-looking man with dark curly hair and brown eyes. His face was deeply tanned, deeply lined. The nameplate on his desk said BRUCE HARMON. He grabbed Shephard's fingers rather than hand and pumped a punishing hello.

"Sit down, Mr. Cox," he said curtly. "Estate work?"

"I requested Mr. Stett," he protested meekly.

"Not available, but I own this joint and I'll be of help if I can."

"I was told Mr. Stett was very good."

"He's no longer with us, I'm afraid. Now, I understand you had an Uncle Lawrence of some means who left you a settlement that your sister believes should go to her. Let me get the ground rules straight, Mr. Cox. South Coast Investigators is a licensed and certified company working on a straight thirty percent commission of all settlements made to its clients. We don't involve ourselves in estates under ten thousand dollars, although we are engageable to determine the size of an estate. That can be quite a costly and time-consuming venture. People aren't always completely, well, up-front. Are those terms agreeable to you?"

"They sound all right."

Harmon was the right size, Shephard thought, and he had the right attitude for breaking heads and dogs. Even money he's got a Michael Stett card collection somewhere.

"How much, roughly, do you think you have coming to you?" Harmon set his elbows on the desk and leaned forward onto his knuckles. His forearms were thick and his neck massive, exaggerated by the tight polo shirt he was packed into.

"Oh, about nothing," Shephard said.

Harmon's eyes narrowed angrily before he had the chance to reinstate his professional manner. He smiled. "Nothing?"

"I don't have a rich Uncle Larry, and if I had a sister, she could have anything she wanted. What I do have is an interest in the murder of Tim Algernon."

Harmon leaned back and pulled a cigarette from the pack on the desk. "And I suppose you're not Randy Cox either," he said.

"Shephard, Laguna Beach Police." He produced his badge. Harmon didn't look at it.

"Well, shit, Shepard, why didn't you just say so? I'm a private eye, not Jesse James. I help you guys any chance I get. Why all the drama?" Harmon smiled.

"Cops are usually bottom of the list on a businessman's calendar, especially a man in your business. I figured a little bait might get me in here sooner."

Harmon laughed heartily, but his eyes said I'd like to break your neck. "Somebody conk you?"

"Somebody conked me outside the Hotel Sebastian."

"Well, what can I help you with? I'll tell you right now I don't know a damn thing about this Algernon guy except what I read in the papers."

"Algernon was killed about six o'clock Wednesday morning. The man who did it left the scene on foot and made it to the Hotel Sebastian by seven. He left less than two hours later. He got two visitors, one was me and the other was you. I want to know why you were looking for him."

Harmon shifted heavily in the chair. "How do you know all that?"

"Hylkama told me a friend of his new tenant showed up a half hour before I did. He had Michael Stett's card and your face."

Harmon reached into a desk drawer and brought out a tape recorder. He turned it on, tested the microphone, and set it at the end of the desk closest to Shephard.

"Don't mind, do you?"

"Not at all."

"Now, you say I was at the Hotel Sebastian on Monday morning, looking for your suspect, I take it. Can you substantiate that?"

"I could by bringing Hylkama down here, but that's not what I'm after. You'd be making a lot of dumb trouble by trying to tell me this isn't your card." He placed Michael Stett's business card on the desk. Harmon glanced at it and nodded.

"I cover when I can. Yeah, it's my card and there isn't any Michael Stett."

"Then what's up, Bruce, buddy?" Shephard put the card back in his pocket and lit a cigarette.

Harmon leaned forward again on his massive arms. "What's up isn't for me to know, Tom, buddy. I've been retained by an attorney to locate Ed Steinhelper. Since he's my client, we enjoy a legally confidential relationship, which means I don't have to tell you shit about him and he doesn't have to tell you shit about me. And as employees of *his* client we all three share the same confidential relationship. What it all boils down to, Shephard, and I give you all that legal crap for the record only, is that I don't know why I was hired and I don't care. As far as you're concerned, I'd like to help, but I can't give you much. I didn't find him, if that helps."

"What did you find?"

"Same thing you did. Nothing."

"I'd hate to think you found what you needed and locked it up in that safe in the corner," Shephard said.

Harmon looked at the safe, then back to the detective. "And I know you can get a warrant and have it opened. But I'll save you the trouble by telling you there isn't anything in it."

"And if there was you'd move it by the time I got back here."

Harmon smiled and nodded. "Hell, wouldn't you?"

Shephard knew that getting such a warrant would be impossible. He also saw that the man sitting across from him knew the law as well as he did. Probably an ex-cop, he thought. He would get nothing from Harmon. But the next best thing was to try for a glimpse of what it was he wouldn't get.

"How did you know he was Steinhelper when he checked in as Hodges?" Shephard asked. He watched Harmon closely.

Sometimes, while the brain takes its milliseconds to form a response, the eyes in front of it will hesitate and go blank: the mind concentrating only on the task at hand. Harmon's eyes dulled fleetingly, then came back to Shephard with redoubled confidence.

"Hodges is a common alias," he said slowly. "For Steinhelper, I mean." Good, Shephard thought, smiling. Harmon turned off the tape recorder casually.

"You want him?" Shephard leaned forward in his chair.

"'Course I want him, that's what I was hired to—"

"I got him." Shephard offered a blank stare.

Harmon's face flushed slightly, its wrinkles seeming to deepen. If he were a TV show, Shephard thought, it would be time for a word from his sponsors. Harmon offered a stranded smile. "You do?"

"I do." Shephard waited. "I got him the same place you did. Out of that wallet in cottage five."

"Get out of here, Shephard. Your games bore the shit out of me."

"No charge, Bruce. I'll tell you where he is because I think you're such a swell guy. Come on, turn your machine back on and get it down. He lives on Fallbrook Street in Sacramento with his wife, and that's where he is right now. He got mugged and lost his wallet."

Harmon stood up, and for the first time since Morris Mumford faced him with a hunting knife on a drizzly night in L.A., Shephard felt afraid. Harmon's face was a heavy yellow, his eyes almost too sunken to see. For a moment, the room seemed to diminish around his bulk.

"Get out, Shephard. Or I'll break your bones."

Shephard stood up with an exaggerated sigh. "Sorry I couldn't make your job easy, Bruce. Buddy. Chum. You must be getting a thousand or so to find this Steinhelper fellow. But I understand how it is. You don't want me to tell you where he is because you weren't hired to find out where he is. You're a lousy liar and a lousy dick, too. You're not a bad back-seat lawyer though. You like dogs?"

Shephard opened the door. Harmon was still standing behind the desk, his huge hands open at his side.

"One more thing, Harmon. This man you're looking for is a killer. If you find him first and I don't hear about it, you go to jail for obstruction. Promise."

He slammed the door and walked slowly toward Marla

Collins's desk. He heard no footsteps from the office, no opening of the door behind him. Standing in front of her desk, he smiled and shook his head.

"Did you get everything you needed?" she asked cheerily.

"I don't understand," he said.

"Don't understand what, Mr. Cox?"

"How a girl like you can work for a guy like him, Marla. Maybe you'd explain it to me sometime if I were to call you."

"Well, I don't think—"

"Please give your number to me, Marla."

"Collins, Corona del Mar," she said worriedly.

"Keep it quiet," he said, nodding toward the office.

"I will."

He stepped outside to a raw sunlight, the manicured emerald lawns of Newport Center, and the deafening roar of a power mower being ridden across the grass by a Mexican in a big hat.

He had stepped down a short flight of stairs to the underground parking structure before he was fully aware that he had done it. At first the shadows offered relief from the bright morning, but as he moved past the cars in their stalls, he was aware he was looking for something. Nameplates were bolted to the wall over the appropriate stalls: ADAMSON & LIFSCHULTZ ATTORNEYS AT LAW, THE FAIRCHILD GROUP, GOOD LIFE MAGAZINE, LYTTLE PUBLIC RELATIONS, MAGNON ASSOCIATES, ORLANDO FOR HAIR, STANLEY PEAVEY, D.D.S. South Coast Investigators had two stalls reserved, one for clients and one for Mr. Harmon. The client space was empty, but glinting tastefully under the neon light in front of Mr. Harmon's sign was a midnight blue Porsche Carerra.

Shephard brought his face up close to the tinted window. A CB radio, telephone, and radar detector graced the dash and console, while the back seat contained nothing but tennis gear. Just looking at it made his head hurt, all ten stitches. He noted the license plate, overcame a strong urge to kick the door, then turned and walked back out to the sunlight.

Back at the station he gathered what he could on Bruce Harmon, most of which came from Chief Hannover, an acquaintance. Former Newport Beach police sergeant, distinguished service, retired ten years ago to go private, active socially in Newport Beach, a "respected if not altogether well-liked" man, according to the chief. "Bit of a brute," he added confidentially.

The afternoon consumed Shephard in routine, giving him a relentless headache. He called the hotels and boarding houses again, but no one close to answering Hodges's description had checked in anywhere. Neither Robbins nor Yee had found anything new. Marty Odette had called and left a number for Little Theodore, which Shephard tried throughout the afternoon. Wade had called twice. Eight newspapers had called, ranging from UPI to Laguna's *Tides and Times;* Shephard scooped up all the numbers and dumped them into the trash. Joe Datilla had sent him a bottle of premium Scotch and a get-well card.

It was nearly four o'clock before he got through to Little Theodore. His voice was guttural, harsh, and rude as always, and strangely welcomed by Shephard. When he hung up, he entertained the image of Little Theodore—all six feet four, three hundred and fifty pounds of him—sitting in the first pew of Wade's newly opened Church of New Life one sweltering Sunday, sweating conspicuously but still concentrating on Wade's sermon. Little Theodore was something of a friend. They arranged to meet at eight o'clock at the Norton Hotel in downtown Santa Ana. Shephard left the station at six to give himself time to prepare the Jota.

He uncovered the machine and wheeled it to the center of his garage. Chrome and black, it sparkled under the single bulb in the ceiling with the splendor of a warhorse preened for battle. The handlebars were short and well forward, the seat narrow and built for one. The seamless gas tank was swept low beneath the seat, a small but flattish tank that would offer his knees a hold through the racking jolts of low-gear speed. The bars, the seat, and two tiny footpegs just above the back axle were the only connections between rider and the hundred and fifty horsepower engine that at high rev could render him deaf and half-blind with velocity and sound. Shephard had owned several motorcycles and driven many more before settling on the LaVerda Jota. He was not the kind of man who often owned the best of anything, but to him, having the Jota was a necessity that transcended its price. He had found the German machines too sluggish and domesticated, the Japanese bikes lacking in character, the American models more nostalgic than functional. But the Jota—which meant a kind of frantic dance in Italian—was perfection. More than perfection, he thought as he opened the fuel lines and checked the gas level; even more than perfection it was release. Aboard the Jota, there was always release.

A minute later Laguna Canyon Road was disappearing under his headlight, his skin tightening against his skull. He took the curves in long bites, leaning into them and accelerating out, straightening the bike and laying himself almost flat in a fifth-gear crouch when he hit the passing lane and shot past cars that seemed to be backing up. He wore goggles to keep bugs from hitting him and tears from spreading across his face, keenly aware that at the Jota's speeds a helmet was vanity. The deep, hollow rasp of the engine droned under him. Telephone poles bunched closer and closer together. Hilltops slipped by against the pale night as if on fast film. Halfway down the road he found his rhythm, bounding back and forth between the lanes for high-apex turns that ended in straights of purest speed.

Downshifting into fourth, Shephard leaned into the long arc that connects Laguna Canyon Road to Interstate 5 and climbed onto the freeway at a modest ninety. From behind a lumbering truck, he crossed three lanes with a faint tilt of bodyweight and braced himself against the footpegs for the blast into Santa Ana. The airport lights flickered before him and were gone; the stars blurred as Irvine became Tustin became Santa Ana, and just when the entire continent seemed to be spreading itself out for him, slowly, like a lover across a bed, the First Street sign flashed by and he had only a mile to cut his speed. In a moment of lucidity before he turned off the freeway, Shephard likened the trip to making love, or what he remembered of it.

He found Little Theodore's chopped Harley Davidson parked across two spaces outside the Norton Hotel. The night was warm and there were mariachis playing in the café next door. He looked through the window at them: short, wide men dressed in black, their music happy and imprecise, the guitar lagging the rhythm by a fraction of a count.

The hotel lounge was dark and smelled of beer. Little Theodore took up most of a corner booth, dressed as always in a black T-shirt from which his huge arms emerged, mirrored sunglasses, and a broad black hat. Shephard noted an addition to the hat: a band of silver dollars wrapped around the crown. Little Theodore's beard was still red, tangled, gigantic. Before him on the table were two glasses and a full bottle of tequila. A grin cracked across his face when he saw Shephard. "Hey, little jackass," he called. "Come over here."

Shephard sat down and Theodore filled the glasses. The Cuervo Gold made Shephard shudder when it went down. Sitting with Little Theodore is like sitting with the past, he thought as Theodore refilled the glasses. He hasn't changed in ten years, not since Wade first hired him as a temporary bodyguard.

"Someone bash your brain pan?" the big man growled.

"It's too hard for serious damage. Just a little dent."

"I've been looking forward to this all night, little jackass. Man shouldn't drink alone." Theodore hooked down the tequila and set the glass on the table with a slap. The shot glass looked like a thimble in his hand. He pushed Shephard's face to the side. "Who did it?"

"Someone who doesn't want me working the Algernon case. You heard about it?" Shephard drank his second glass.

"Heard about it? It's all over the goddamn papers. I figured you'd be callin' me soon."

"The guy who hit me is a private dick named Harmon. He's an ex-Newport cop, a sergeant. He took me out at the Hotel Sebastian and wrecked my apartment when I was sleeping it off."

Theodore filled the glasses again and leaned forward. "You mentioned business on the phone. Want me to break his arms?"

"No. I need him functional so I can get to his boss. But I do have some business. Tim Algernon got your number from Marty the Friday before he was killed. Did he call you?"

Little Theodore shook a cigarette from a pack on the table. "Yeah. Friday night about eleven."

"And?"

"Hey, slow down, pissant. We got to drink, we got to ride, we got to talk. We got time to get to everything."

"I'd like to get to this first. I've got a dozen scraps of evidence and not one good reason why someone would kill Tim Algernon. But I think he knew it was coming." Theodore sighed and downed his tequila. Shephard did likewise.

"He was scared," said Theodore. "Not whinin' scared, but casual, take-your-time, beat-around-the-bush scared."

"What did he want?"

"First he wanted to know if I was working much these

71

days. Then he wanted to know how my book was selling. Tell the truth, I barely remembered the sonofabitch. Played some horses with him once is all. Half an hour later, the story comes out. Says he's worried some punks know he's got money stashed on the grounds. He wants me to move in as discouragement. Room, board, five hundred a week. Which totals about a thousand a week the way I eat and drink."

Shephard pondered the story. "Why was he worried, anything specific?"

"Just worried is what he said. He's a big mouth when he wins big and drinks, so I figured he'd talked and was gettin' spooked. Anyhow, I said no. I got a new old lady and she's a real treat to drag this old sack of fat into bed with at night. Got my own place, the book is sellin' good, me and Ray is going to write up another one. Shit, what I want to go live in some manure heap for?" Theodore shrugged. "Now this," he said quietly, returning his attention to the tequila. "Now he's a dead man. Didn't mean to hold out on ya. Was gonna call, case you didn't first. Drink up, Shephard. We're all dead too soon."

Shephard drank and felt the tequila eroding his sense of control. Just as well, he thought. He lit a cigarette, which returned him to calm.

"Whoever killed him didn't want any money. We found him in the morning, with over a thousand dollars worth of currency stuffed down his mouth. You say he beat around the bush. What about?"

"Told you. Everything and nothing. The book, the work, the bullshit." Theodore leaned back; the booth shook.

"When did he want you to start?"

"Next morning."

"Did he go up in price, or offer the five hundred right off?" Just how desperate had Algernon been?

According to Little Theodore, Algernon had started with an offer of three hundred, then gone up to five. Then, sounding drunk, he "got weepy" when Theodore said no. Then he hung up, and that was the last that Little Theodore heard of him until his wife read him the story in yesterday's paper. Shephard had forgotten that Theodore could neither read nor write. I only know how to spell ten words, he liked to brag, and all of 'em's dirty.

"Whoever killed him smashed his head with a rock, then set him on fire. Whoever killed him sent him a Bible with a little hate mail attached. Whoever killed him has someone else in mind, too, if I'm reading it right. I missed him by two hours at the Sebastian. He's in town. I know it."

Little Theodore poured them two more shots and downed his instantly. Shephard obliged, put down the glass, and found himself looking at another full one. Again they drank. The music wavered in his brain, the smell of the cactus steamed up into his nostrils. Theodore capped the bottle and grinned.

"Let's ride to your poppa's church and finish this bottle," he said. "I'm feelin' too big for this little shithole, and sittin' with a scrawny cop don't do much for my reputation. Besides, a little motion might be good for the memory." He pushed away the table and righted his tonnage, wobbling slightly as he made his way for the door. Shephard glanced at the bartender, who shook his head.

They rode deeper into Santa Ana, through the barrio and its quiet low houses and graffiti-covered walls, past the snug suburban tracts with their houselights dying out even at ten o'clock, across the tracks and the switching yard to the Church of New Life grounds. The night was warm and fragrant. They rumbled into the parking area of what had once been a drive-in theater. The Church of New Life wasn't the only one in Southern California to start in an old drive-in. The first of Wade's sermons had been delivered to worshippers in cars who listened through speakers hung on their windows. The old movie screen was still standing but had been converted into a billboard that displayed biblical scenes, changed seasonally. In the midsummer darkness Shephard could make out the figure of Christ in white on the screen before them, a halo around His head, children at His feet. Shephard's vertical hold was slipping. Jesus rose and fell like a television picture on the blink. Theodore cut the engine of his motorcycle and handed him the bottle. Around them, the speakers of the Church of New Life spread out like rows of well-pruned grapevines.

"This cactus makes my brain loose," Theodore began. "I'm rememberin' some more of what Algernon told me. He said punks knew he had money at first, then it got changed to sound more like one punk—kept sayin' him this and he that. I think he was drunker'n hell too. Said this guy had it in for him a long time. Got reasons to believe he's comin' back to get me, he said. Come to think of it, it sounded less like money than hurt he was after. He said havin' a hog like me around might keep him safe. He said he'd pay for his sinnin' when he was dead and he wasn't in a hurry to get that way. Yeah, that's what he talked like." Theodore reclaimed the bottle and gulped. "And he told me he wasn't worried just for himself, but some other people, too."

"Any by name?"

"He said, I think there's more than me in danger. A fine old woman who lives in town might be, too. Hope it's Greeley, he said. What the fuck, I said, call the cops, Tim. He said it wasn't the kind of matter cops could handle. Guess he was right on that one, eh, Shephard?"

Theodore growled and wheezed: a laugh. Shephard, feeling the lugubrious effects of tequila, took the statement broadside and felt shamed. It was a feeling he'd had often as a rookie, often too in his first few years as a cop. But over time he had built up that protective coating that any cop who stays a cop needs. Wade had lost his stomach for it. No surprise. Somewhere it must all be stored up, he thought, as Theodore passed back the bottle. Somewhere inside everything that you deflect collects. He knew it was true. When he drank he could feel those deflected items stirring, some thick and sad, like those he had felt just now, others jagged and painful, like a river of broken glass trying to get out. His father had told him once that cops are the true garbage collectors of society, that cops see, consume, and store the million instances of ugliness that everyone else wants to put out of their lives. The suicides, the murders, the slow poisonings, the "accidents" where a sober young man plows a new car into a lightpole at a modest and accurate forty miles an hour. We see it, Wade had said; the rest just get it from the papers.

"How's the old man?" Theodore asked.

"Strong. Happy. Not the same man I grew up with."

Theodore seemed to ponder this. He rubbed his beard and spit. "What do you think it was got him into the God business instead of bein' a cop?"

Shephard had thought about it often himself. "He said once that the pains of loss are the bricks of miracles. I think that might explain it." Shephard was aware that his mind, now tequila-drenched, was not altogether clear. He thought of Jane Algernon and wondered what she was doing.

"That's good. I'd use it in one o' my books 'cept there ain't no miracles in the story of a fat bodyguard like me. Pass that bottle, jackass."

"Wonder if it's worth it?" Shephard asked.

"What worth what?"

"The pain, just for a miracle."

Theodore responded only after a long, silent pause. "Everybody's got the hurt. Takes a special sort like your old man to turn it into somethin' decent. Miracles go around to lots of folks, they don't just go into somebody's wallet. Most of us can't make no miracle even if we tried. We just rot and die. 'Course, anybody knows the hurt, your old man does. Tequila, young Shephard?"

Shephard took the bottle, which seemed suddenly heavy, and drank. His thoughts rioted. "When I was a kid, he used to leave at night with a bucket and a fishing pole. Told me he was going fishing. But he never came back with anything. This was once a month or so, every few weeks. So one night I followed him. I had a little motorcycle then, so I cut the lights and he didn't know I was behind him. All the way to the pier south of town. He left his bucket in the car and walked onto the pier. I followed but stayed so he couldn't see me in the shadows. He walked right down the center of it, never looked to one side or the other, walked with his head down faster and faster. Had to hustle to keep up. And when he got to the end he just kept on walking, right over the edge and into the water. He'd told me a hundred times not to jump the pier because once a month the tides are low enough to kill you. He never even looked over the side. He didn't want to know. He just walked off the edge and swam back to shore. I watched him and stood there an hour trying to figure out why he did it. I couldn't figure it out. Still haven't. Nothing but rocks under that pier at low tide. Dried his clothes at a laundromat so I wouldn't know."

"What with your momma bein' shot dead, maybe it was understandable. I ain't no genius, but I figure having your old lady dying in front of you must make for a whole heap of miracle bricks." Theodore held up the bottle and the moon perched on top of it. "Maybe they was gettin' too heavy for him."

"I'm basically uncompromising when it comes to loss," Shephard announced, his words now running well ahead of his ability to think. "I mean there's too much of it to even be an issue. You go to sleep, you get up. Morris Mumford is a helluva loss to me. But I'll be damned, Theodore, if I was standing there again if I wouldn't shoot him again, too. Maybe that's the cactus talking. Maybe those are just words. Maybe that's just a miracle brick Morris paid for and nobody's ever gonna pick up."

"You ain't no reverend, Shephard. You're just a scrawny cop with too much tequila in him. Pass that tequila, faggot."

Shephard felt an overwhelming desire to do something, but the feeling passed.

"What happened to that sonofabitch shot your momma? Dead, ain't he?"

"Yeah. Died in prison a while ago."

"Well, don't go gettin' hard on yourself," Theodore growled. "The world ain't set up for doin' decent. Look at it. Some dumbass kid takes a knife to a cop because the cop's the closest thing he can hate. You shoot the kid so he don't do the same to you. The newspapers make a buck sellin' it, the lawyers get rich talking about it. And some pecker in office makes a committee to study the problem. Nobody gives a shit about Morris in the end, except maybe you. You're probably the only one who'll remember him twenty years from now."

Shephard weighed this argument against another jolt of tequila, and found it wanting.

"He had a girl," he said. "I saw her."

"She'll do better. So don't worry it to death. The only people who do any good in the world are whores and bartenders. Don't worry it. It don't look good on you."

"I guess we got off the topic."

"We didn't have no fuckin' topic. Hang tight, little runt. You want me to break that feller's arms, just gimme a call."

Suddenly the roar of Little Theodore's Harley burst across the night, pounding Shephard from a hundred inebriated angles, rattling his teeth. He pushed the starter and the LaVerda joined the outrage, a hoarse, low growl that spun higher and faster as he twisted the throttle. Theodore hurled the empty bottle into the darkness and his bike jerked ahead. They rode slowly through the lot, side by side past the billboard of Jesus and the children until they hit the boulevard and bellowed away in different directions.

Shephard returned to his denuded apartment early in the morning. Stripped to bare essentials, the place suggested beginnings or endings, but no present. And what is the present but an exit from the past and a waiting for the future, he wondered gloomily as he leaned over the toilet and gave up his tequila. Crossing the bathroom he caught his reflection, spectral and hollow, studying him from the mirror. "I'm starting over," he mumbled.

He called his father. "Was it worth it, pop?"

"Tommy? It's—"

"Quarter 'til three. Was it?"

"Was what? Have you been drinking?"

"A tad. Gotta tell me. Was the miracle worth the pain?" Shephard's voice sounded as if it came from underwater.

A pause. "Tommy, go to sleep. I'll talk to you when you're sober."

"And one more thing . . . " Shephard tried to gather his thoughts, but they seemed to be fraying like cut rope inside his head. "The pier. How come walking off the pier with nothing but rocks once a month? I'm talking clarification."

"Tommy? Let me tell you something. Don't look for the bad. Don't play the dark notes, son, until they're all you've got left to play. Forgive what you can't change. Can you understand that? Now go to sleep. I'll see you for lunch on Friday, all right?"

"Clarification."

Wade hung up.

A few minutes later Shephard was asleep, relinquishing his dreams once again to the boy with the knife.

EIGHT

He pulled the Mustang off Laguna Canyon Road and parked under the willow tree. The coffee from his Thermos was hot, and the morning news was filled with money market advertisements and city council trivia. Across the yard he could see that his card had been removed from the chain-link fence, and that the sea lion was slouched like a giant slug against the side of its pen. Shephard's head ached vengefully, hangover on top of concussion, but his mind was clear and uncluttered. He chewed four aspirins and waited for Jane Algernon.

Half an hour later he heard a door slam and she appeared on the porch. She shot a disdainful glance his way, then walked across the yard in front of him, stopping to pull the waders from the clothesline. She was dressed in a sweatshirt and shorts, and Shephard felt like he shouldn't watch her step into the boots, but he did anyway. He took a hot gulp of coffee and stepped out of the car.

"Miss Algernon, delightful we meet again," he said with cheer. She glared at him as she turned to a freezer beside the house and pulled out a bag. Her face looked haggard and sleepless. Shephard watched the fish slide like melted silver from the bag into a bucket at her feet. She took the bucket to a garden hose and rinsed off the sea lion's breakfast. When she stepped into the pen the animal rushed to her side with a croak, raising its slick head to be stroked. She patted it and dropped a fish into its mouth. Like Cal without ears, he noted. "Fresh frozen?"

"Oh," she said with a smile. He had never known a smile could be so damaging and beautiful at the same time. He felt impaled on it. "It's the detective again. I used to enjoy these few moments alone, every morning, but not since he started coming here. What can I do for you, little man?"

"I wondered if you changed your mind about helping me. The handwriting samples I asked you for. The picture of your father, the business books. I want you to tell me about him. I thought that you might—"

"But I haven't. And I won't. And strange as it may seem, if you park in my driveway or come onto my property again, I'm going to call the police." She dropped another fish, which was caught mid-air and mid-croak. The animal spun in self-satisfaction, slid into the pool, sped around it without visible effort, then slapped back out and stopped at her feet again. Head-first everywhere, he thought, like Pete Rose.

"Miss Algernon, I have reason to believe that—"

"He has reason to believe," she told the beast. "He had no reason to believe before, but now he does. Did the detective find God last night?" She dangled a fish, and Shephard studied the length of her body, the rounded, lovely thighs above the rubber.

"Reason to believe that other people may be in danger from the man who killed your father," he blurted quickly.

She shook her head and aimed the smile at him again. Looking at it, he felt loathsome, freakish. She studied him for what seemed an hour, then reached some kind of conclusion. She turned back to the animal, still dangling the fish.

"Now the detective is bluffing the witness," she said. "But that's okay, because really, he isn't here." She tossed the fish into the pool and the sea lion heaved after it. Shephard waited a long time for her attention to return to him, then began to wonder if indeed he were not really there.

With each throb in his head, patience waned. Screw it, he thought.

"Not here? Yeah, I'm not here." He was less aware of stepping across the yard to the garden hose than he was of simply watching himself do it. He watched as he picked up the nozzle, carried it to the pen fence, and hosed down the young woman inside. The water burst into shiny spray as it hit her, dazzling in the morning sun. "She lives in town somewhere. I don't know her name, her age, or why she's in danger. She might even be you," he heard himself saying. She faced him throughout the soaking, arms at her sides, hair clinging to her face in wet strands, her face clenched in hatred, the sea lion croaking gleefully as he put his stream-lined face into the bucket of fish she had just dropped.

He hooked the nozzle into the chain link when he was finished. "Your father lived the last days of his life in terror, I just found out. He knew what was going to happen, and it did. If he never told you about it, I guess I can understand why. Have a wonderful life, Miss Algernon."

Back in the Mustang, he was pleased to find his coffee still warm.

Then, a sudden beating on the window beside his face. Through the glass her voice was muted but clear, as if on a telephone.

"Bastard! Open that door, you bastard!" A black wader thumped against the glass. Then her fists, small and pink, flattening not inches from his head. Her eyes were wide, her hair soaked and sticking to her face, her voice shrill and desperate. "Open that door, you bastard!" Her fists hit the window in thuds, like big drops of rain. Shephard stared through the glass at her, then pointed at the door lock, which was all the way up. She threw open the door and pounced, nails, teeth, fists pounding wildly—he heard them hitting the dash, the leather seats, even the horn once, which honked quickly and sent the sea lion into a frenzied croak—then a moment's pause before a black wader blotted out the sunlight to his left and thwacked against his head with the sound of a mop hitting a floor. He was aware of his shirt tearing, a hot gouging in his ribs, and the repeated curse, "I hate you, I hate you, you little bastard!"

They spilled onto the lawn, where Jane, wader still flailing, found distinct advantage. Shephard covered up under elbows and hands, trying to keep the stitches intact. The wader slammed methodically into his ribs and head, punctuated by gasps and broken phrases. "You . . . bastard . . . get you . . . sonofa . . . " Shephard heard the sea lion clapping and croaking at the chance finally to be the spectator.

The blows began to slow and the words started to lose their fury. Her voice dissipated into tired panting, then a final grunt as she slammed the wader once more into his ribs, then let it fall to the ground. Still covering himself, he could hear her a few steps away, sobbing fast and shallow as if she were choking. He lowered an elbow for a look.

Her back was to him; she had her face in her hands. Her shoulders shook. The noisy sea lion looped his pen again, fired with excitement.

"Shut up, Buster," she said. "Just shut up."

Shephard plopped back into the car and poured some coffee into the plastic cup. The back of his head was sticky and his shirt blood-stained at the elbow. From a safe distance he offered Jane Algernon the coffee. She looked at him through a shock of matted brown hair, an expression not of victory or surrender, but relief. Brushing the hair away from her face, she shook her head. Shephard backed off and lit a cigarette.

"Okay," she said evenly, though her voice trembled. "Let's get some ground rules straight. I'll help you if I can. I'm too tired right now to care who killed my father, but if someone else is in danger I feel . . . obligated to help. I can get you the handwriting, his business ledger, some photographs. And I'll tell you what I can about him on the promise that you'll leave your cheap, goddamned budget psychologizing out of it. I don't need your analysis, I don't need your guilt, I don't need you."

The inside of Jane Algernon's cottage was small but neat. In contrast to the disheveled exterior, the living room gleamed with modern, high-tech appointments: a glass coffee table sat in the middle, surrounded by chrome and green velvet chairs, a low couch that matched them, a square glass end table. From one side of the room a long-necked chrome lamp swung outward to hang above the table; in the other stood a mirrored shelf containing stereo components and a small television, surrounded by plants. A breakfast nook built off the living room had more chrome and glass and a palm tree in a high chrome pot. The walls were pale salmon, the carpet a blue-gray. Shephard sat down in front of the coffee table. She crossed in front of him and disappeared into the bedroom. A moment later she was back with a damp washcloth, which she tossed to him, and a photo album that she opened over her legs when she sat down on the couch.

"Nice place," he said, dabbing at his bandage. Not so nice a lady, he thought. She glanced at him and handed him a snapshot.

"My father and Rebecca, taken last year. He was in good shape for a man his age. Tall and strong." Shephard examined the picture in the ample light of the living room. Tim Algernon sat atop the corral, Rebecca standing at his side, her face pressed into his open hand. Jane reclaimed the picture and put it back in its place. Then another, this time of her father and herself inside what looked like a barn. "That was taken five years ago. It's the most recent one of

83

us together. Like I said, we hadn't been close the last few years."

"How often did you see him, recently?" She put back the picture. Shephard brought out his notebook, which was sadly bent from the fray.

"See him? Once a month maybe. Hi, how are you, that was all. People grow apart."

"Yes. May I?" Jane handed Shephard the photo album, then crossed her long legs over the velvet and leaned back. "When was the last time you saw him?" He leafed through the book. Tim Algernon riding Rebecca, Jane atop another mare, Jane with Buster the sea lion in his pen, Jane and a young man with their arms around each other, a close-up of Buster, a quiet shot of sunlight on a vase of flowers. He looked up.

"Two weeks ago," she said. "About." She looked down, brushed something from her leg, then stared at Shephard.

"What did he say? Did he come here or did you go to see him?"

"He came here," she said quietly. "He sat where you're sitting now, and we talked for a few minutes. Nothing in particular." She turned to face the sunlight that slanted through a window. Shephard studied her profile: her nose straight and thin, her lips full, the eyelashes golden in the rush of sun.

"Was he worried, preoccupied?" He continued his study of sunlight and woman, a combination he decided was insurmountable.

"My father was very calm," she said, still facing the light. "That comes from breaking horses as a young man." She looked at Shephard. He ducked into the photo album.

"Uh, finances. In order?"

"He made enough money to gamble away and drink on," she said sharply. "He was bad at gambling, good at drinking."

84

Shephard heard the bitterness in her voice. "Do you own this house, Miss Algernon?"

"What do you care? I thought you'd decided I was bitter because he didn't help with money." She brushed her hair from her face and looked back out the window.

"That was just to piss you off." He stared at her legs, for the moment supremely happy.

"Well then, one for you, detective. I rent. Father was never interested in helping out that way. Booze and horses had first priority."

"It's hard for people our age—how old are you, Miss Algernon . . . ?"

"Twenty-nine."

"To finance homes themselves. I've wished my father had been in more of a position to help me when I was looking to buy. Resented it a little, too."

She turned to him, a dull gaze. "I'm not interested in your resentments, detective."

"Then I figured that love and common courtesy must count for something too. That's more than a lot of people ever get."

"I'm happy for enlightment," she said. "But I always thought that poverty makes us all look a bit ridiculous."

Shephard heard the rage working its way back into Jane Algernon's voice. His head began to ache again, as if in warning. "I'd like to see his house now."

"No." The reply was curt and final. She stood, went to the window of the breakfast corner, then turned to look at him. "I'm sorry, but I don't think I could . . . look at his things right now. I don't feel I can do that kind of thing just yet. Do you understand?"

"Yes, and that's why we have to go now. I need you in a mood to talk. Filters off, feelings raw. Do you understand?" He stood and set the photo album on the coffee table. His heart was beating with inexplicable speed. He wondered if it was the coffee. He watched her round the kitchen table, look out the window again, then disappear into a back room.

A moment later she was back, with a purse slung over her shoulder and a pair of pumps on her feet. "You first, detective." She motioned to the door. "You stare at my legs any longer, they're going to fall off."

They stood on opposite sides of Tim Algernon's den, the small bed between them, the identical pictures of the same horses peering over each of their shoulders. Jane had picked up a small trophy from the dresser.

"What I remember most about growing up were the good times we had here at the stables," she said, handing him the trophy. "But dad used to talk about this club all the time. How grand it was." She handed him the trophy, which read: TIM AND MARGARET ALGERNON—THIRD PLACE DOUBLES —SURFSIDE MEMBERS TOURNAMENT—1947. "That's the Newport Beach club. Mom and dad were members until the early fifties, until she got sick, I guess. He was always talking about the great days at the Surfside, the two of them playing tennis and sailing. Kind of idealized it, maybe."

She took the trophy back from Shephard and set it on the dresser. The house had made her pensive, as he had hoped it would. He followed her as she rambled, remembered. In the living room, Jane stood in front of the big fireplace and looked into the ashes. "When I was a girl, we were close. Even when I started getting to be a woman, he was kind of a father and a mother. I guess I was eighteen maybe, before I saw the drinking doing its work on him. He'd go up and down—manic. High as a kite, then too depressed to get out of bed. Get violent too, but not with me. I watched him punch one of his horses in the face once, because she bit him. He was a strong man." She laughed quietly, tears welling in her eyes. "Yeah, I might have blamed him for mom dying, even though I never knew her. I blamed him for blowing his money at the track, drinking, passing out in the stable feed trough, things like that."

Jane turned her weakening face to him. She ran her hand against her eyes, then returned to the ashes. A strand of dark hair fell across her face, hiding it from him.

"He was an easy man to be hard on," she said finally. "And I took advantage of it. By the time I started college I was truly ashamed of him—the way he'd carry on in town. People always telling me stories about him, where he ended up some night, how he fought, got sick. A village idiot, a clown. And gambling away the money. I could have used a little help. We all could, I guess. Anyway, there was something cold inside of me, and I knew he felt it."

Shephard could hear her voice wavering, and Jane trying to force it under control.

"So I'd just slam him against that coldness, give him what I thought he deserved. It hurt him—I know it hurt him. Somehow, that only made me feel more right in doing it."

When she turned again to Shephard she was red-faced, beginning to sob. He sat down on the couch, put a *Racing Form* across his knees and studied it. "Everybody blames himself when a parent dies," he said. "My mother was killed when I was four months old, and when I got big enough to realize I didn't have a mother I blamed myself for it. You grow into it, like a shirt. But go ahead and feel sorry for yourself if it makes you better." From the corner of his eye he saw her head cock sharply in his direction.

"Up yours, Shephard. I can cry if I want to."

"Long as you understand you're crying for yourself."

She was in front of him, thighs positioned straight before his face, her hand beginning its arc from outside his vision but descending with a swoosh through the air, gaining speed as he dropped the newspaper, caught her wrist, and forced her down, all in one motion. He stood and shoved the

Racing Form into her hand. It dropped to her lap when she brought her hands to her face.

"There's two kinds of crying, Miss Algernon. You cry for someone else and you choke the sounds right out, and it sounds like a dog gagging on a bone. You cry until your tears are gone and there's nothing left to come out except maybe your guts. But when you cry for yourself, it sounds long and sad, like music. Like you sound right now. You haven't cried for him yet, you're still working on yourself. How come?"

It was easier than he had thought it would be. When she looked up at him, he saw it was over. Her eyes were big and blank, and she spoke quickly, as if disgorging something poisonous, long-held.

"It wasn't two weeks ago when I saw him last," she blurted. "It was Friday afternoon. He came to my house and stunk like whiskey, and I was revolted. I screamed at him. And he told me he was scared and wanted to know if . . . if . . . " Her head was shaking.

"If he could stay with you?"

"For a few days, he said. Someone was going to hurt him and he was afraid. But he always said such crazy things when he was drinking. I said he was just *imagining.* Jesus Christ, I told him he was just drunk and stupid. I finally gave him a little peck, a little ugly peck on the forehead, and then, I sent him out. God, I sent him out."

"Who was going to hurt him, Jane?"

"*Someone.* He said someone was coming to get him. But he didn't say who, or why, or for what, and I'd heard him say things before that were wild. I thought he was maybe just lonely, tired of living alone."

Her last words were little more than a whisper, blown tearlessly in at the end of her storm. She had dropped her face into her arms, dark hair cascading over her knees and dangling in mid-air as she shook her head in disbelief.

"What else, Jane?"

"He said, there might be others in trouble too. That it wasn't just him."

"Who?" Shephard watched the tears dropping onto Jane's feet, the liquid shiny on her skin. He could scarcely hear her.

"He didn't say. The whole world, maybe. He just didn't say."

Jane pitched over onto the cushions, drawing up her knees, burying her face in a pillow. Shephard saw her shoulders beginning the first shudders of what would be another storm. Worse this time, he thought. For her father. He spread an afghan over her quaking body, and went into the kitchen.

In a drawer near the telephone Shephard found a small address book, which he quickly leafed through, then pocketed. No Greeley was listed. He remembered Theodore's words. Why would Algernon hope it was Greeley in trouble? Tim Algernon was a consistently sloppy secretary. One look at the address book told him that it wasn't Algernon who had written in the Bible. Then who had? Had the killer written it himself, after the act, a triumphant good-bye? Or, perhaps, had the Bible come to Algernon earlier, the threat that had made Tim come to Jane and call Little Theodore for protection? If so, how had it arrived? Personal delivery, or by mail?

Shephard walked outside. With fumes of garbage wafting up into his face, he systematically pulled the contents from a trash can on the side of the house. Halfway down through the mess, smeared with the sticky pitch of orange juice concentrate, he found a plain brown wrapper, Bible-sized and torn open. He retrieved it with some sense of accomplishment, then set it on the ground, where he brought the fragments back to their original form.

Tim Algernon's name and address were written across the paper in the same ink and same neat hand as in the Bible that contained the threat. The postmark was Wednesday, August 20, Sacramento. Three days before Ed Steinhelper was rolled. Four days before whoever took his wallet came into Laguna on Greyhound line 52. Eight days ago, he noted: five days before Algernon died.

He found Jane on her father's couch, breathing deeply, covered by the afghan. Looking down at her, he felt a fluttering inside, of wings perhaps, as if a covey of quail were about to take flight. Then, the same frantic impulse to act that he had felt the night before, the urgent but undirected desire to do something. The conflux of feelings was rapid and contradictory. Paternal: he could adjust the pillow under her head, pull the afghan more comfortably to her waist. Carnal: he could simply stare. Professional: he could wake her. He felt paralyzed, or was it, he wondered, dumbfounded? He smiled stupidly. His path of action became clear. He walked quietly across the floor and shut the door behind him, sure he had done the right thing. As he moved through the bright noon heat he realized how long it had been since so little had mattered so much.

He felt altered, as if his system had just received a transfusion of something new.

NINE

A telephone company printout listed all calls made from Tim Algernon's phone the week before he died. Shephard was handed the information by a reluctant company manager, who reminded him that the release of such data was illegal, then hustled him into a small room that contained a desk and chair. The manager's patience seemed fatigued to its breaking point when Shephard requested a number-indexed directory. The manager delivered it after a punishing wait, sighed, and shut the door.

Using the directory and Algernon's address book, Shephard translated the called numbers into names, and listed in his notebook parties called, times, duration of calls. After an hour's work, it appeared that Algernon's "fine old woman who lives in town" was one Hope Creeley. So Theodore got it a little mixed up, Shephard thought. To "hope it was Greeley." Not bad for a man who can't read or write. Her address was listed as 9487 Waveside, Laguna Beach, and Tim Algernon had called her a total of twenty-four times between 5 P.M. Saturday, August 23, and Sunday, August 24. Twenty-four calls of a minute each. The last was made at 11:54 Sunday night, six hours before Algernon had had his last whiskey with the man who killed him. What can a terrified man say in twenty-four one-minute calls that he couldn't say in one twenty-four-minute call, Shephard wondered. He dialed Hope Creeley's number from the booth outside, got no answer, and dialed again.

Back in the Mustang, he headed for Waveside Drive in the north end of town.

The house was a tidy, three-story Spanish-style manse with a clay tile roof and a spacious portico whose shade smelled of citrus to Shephard. He pushed the doorbell, which after a momentary silence prompted a muted chime from deep inside the house. Just to the right of the wooden door, a mailbox contained three envelopes. He removed them, glanced at the first and saw that it had been delivered that day. He rang again. No answer.

A wrought-iron gate opened onto a walkway that led around the right side of the house. Shephard pushed it open, the hair on his neck rising when it squeaked like fingernails on a chalkboard. The walkway was narrow and shaded from the house next door by a tall fence of redwood. It opened to a generous backyard that in spite of its size was still cloistered from the neighbors by three large avocado trees, growing in a semicircle against the back fence. Between the dark green avocados stood lemon trees, their round, symmetrical bodies sprinkled with fruit. The cement patio spread out before him like an island in a sea of grass, covered with chairs, tables, lounges, a barbecue. He judged it a peaceful backyard.

To his left he saw that the sliding glass door was open nearly halfway, the edge of a white drape lapping outward in the breeze. The family dog, a smallish breed by the look of it, had fallen asleep inside the house and its head was dangling over the tracks of the door and onto the patio. Not much of a watchdog, Shephard thought, considering the whining gate. He whistled quietly, but the dog still didn't budge. The breeze stirred a windchime, scattering random music.

Shephard whistled again and went across the patio to the dog. Standing over it now, it was clear to him that the animal was dead. It was a basenji, eyes half open, its tongue dangling out, the tiny chin stained with blood.

Pushing back the drapes, he stepped inside. He stood and listened for a moment, hearing nothing. The living room was hushed in shadow and emitted none of the lingering friction of recent activity. The upholstered chairs were humped quietly around a low coffee table, a piano with covered keys blended into the darkness of the far corner, a meager portion of light forced its way through the drapes and washed almost unnoticeably into the pale green carpet. Shephard drew the Colt Python from his shoulder holster, but it felt wrong in his hand. Moving into the dining room, he put the pistol back.

Why is it so difficult to see a dining table and five chairs and not imagine people sitting there, he wondered. But the dark walnut chairs, polished exuberantly and waiting just so, were vacant. The armoire towering behind them twinkled with crystal even in the dreary light. The kitchen showed no signs of recent, or any other kind of use.

"Mrs. Creeley?" Shephard's voice echoed quickly. He backtracked to the basenji and found that his powers as an investigator of human affairs meant little in the world of dogs. The throat seemed large, the neck swollen, but didn't basenjis have a thickened, Egyptian head? The blood on the chin suggested strangulation, or did it? The expression on the dog's face told him nothing. Standing once again on the pale green carpet, he regarded the staircase that began at the far side of the living room.

He climbed to the second story, aware for the first time that the house, despite the opened patio door, was stuffy and ill-ventilated. Each of three bedrooms on the floor was decorated with a zeal for American Colonial: hardwood floors covered with red throw-rugs, white and blue bedspreads across which huge eagles cocked their heads, massive maple headboards cut with Colonial heft and grace. The effect was museumlike, he thought, more to be looked at than lived in. Nowhere were there signs of a family's energy, that wake of activity that leaves at the very least a chair out of kilter with its table, a coat tossed across a bed or sofa, a dish in the sink.

The stairway carpet changed from green to white where it began its rise to the third story. Shephard felt a quick flicker of vertigo when he reached the final floor: the relentless white skewed his sense of balance. He called again.

The third floor was as vast as it was colorless. The white carpet opened before him to a capacious anteroom whose walls, furniture, even fireplace, were crisp white. Unlike the downstairs rooms, the anteroom stood bleached in sunlight, which entered two west-facing windows unobstructed by shades or curtains and parceled itself into bright rhomboids on the carpet. Shephard noted again, as he had as a child, that in shafts of sunlight dust settles upward rather than the more logical down. He crossed the pristine carpet to a set of double doors, white, at the far end. Swinging them open he found still more of the pale carpet, expanding before him into the master bedroom.

Shephard thought it was the brightest room he'd ever seen. A cream-colored settee was backed against the wall to his left, over which hung a mirror framed in white that reflected more white from across the room. In the center stood a king-sized bed that seemed magnified by its lack of color. Shephard suffered the momentary illusion that everything was made of plaster. When he pressed his hand against the bed, the soft texture felt incongruous.

He stood in the bathroom doorway, faced with a full-length reflection of himself. The mirrored partition gave way on the right to a large vanity area consisting of two sinks fitted with white porcelain fixtures, a mirror that ran the length of the wall in front of the sinks, a white wooden chest fastened to the far wall beside a toilet, and a sparkling bidet. He turned back to the bathroom entrance, moved past the entryway mirror again, and found himself in a similar room: white walls, white tile.

But rather than a toilet and bidet, along the far wall was a bathtub, and Shephard's first reaction when he looked at it was, Well, my sweet God Jesus, there is something that isn't white.

Lying in the tub is something definitely not white.

He backed against the wall as a flood of sweat erupted along his back, and stepped back out to the bedroom. He stood watching the dust settle upward, breathing rapidly.

Then a series of mental detours, in the form of questions. When did Jane Algernon awaken? Did Cal like last night's dinner? How long could a dog survive on a strict vegetarian diet? Why does dust settle up? Who cares? Then there was the problem of his pistol. He drew it, put it back, drew it again: somehow he felt better with it dangling from his hand as he walked back into the bathroom and approached the tub.

The vortex of all the whiteness that spread around him was a naked woman. She was blackened so badly by fire that she seemed to have been reduced to some birdlike creature, a pterodactyl perhaps, with claws at the end of feeble wing-arms, a puffy underbelly, foreshortened legs that spread open obscenely and looked as if they could do little more than grasp a branch or fold flush to the body in flight. He saw a narrow face on which only the eye sockets and mouth were recognizable. One of the tiny hand-claws clutched the end of a shower curtain rod, which was blackened to its midway point. The shower curtain itself lay jammed into a white wicker wastebasket.

The discoverer of such secrets is always first aware of his own uselessness. And Shephard, much as he had done when he looked down at the sleeping mystery of Jane Algernon, looked down at this changed woman and wondered what to do. He wanted to cover her. He felt as if he should pray. He knew he should call other policemen to divvy up the problem: Pavlik to the minutiae, Pincus to the press, Grimes to the crowd that would form outside and inquire shyly about the nature of the tragedy; Chief Hannover to the mayor, Lydia Worth and other officers to search the neighborhood fruitlessly, Robbins to remove the body, and Yee's dispassionate hands to interpret it. And he, the detective, to gather the essential from what the others found, fit the pieces together, discard the falsehoods, and approach the killer on his own.

Good Jesus Christ, he thought. What he really wanted to do was sleep. His legs weakened as he backed to the wall and eased himself down it, the Python clanging and spilling from his hand when it hit the tile.

PART TWO

TEN

I t wasn't until late that night that Shephard found what he was looking for in the three-story mansion of Hope Creeley. And having found it, some time passed before he knew that he had.

After the strength returned to his legs, he had risen to call Pavlik, then stood waiting in the kitchen, locked in a waking dream. Even when the crime scene investigator arrived, Shephard was unable to fully break from the penumbral trance that enveloped him. The entrance of Pavlik played itself out with the familiarity of déjà vu. Shephard watched through the front window as he lugged his forensic case up the driveway, stopping not once but twice to check the address against a slip of paper in his free hand. He greeted Shephard with a haggard, 2 A.M. smile even though it was two in the afternoon, and followed the detective upstairs to the white acreage of the Creeley bedroom.

Staring down at the twisted body in the bathtub, Shephard offered some flattened words about "another stiff" and "getting to work," hoping to ease Pavlik away from the numbing reality of it. But the words were wasted. Pavlik slunk back out of the bathroom as Shephard had and stood in the brazen sunlight of the bedroom, his mind, Shephard guessed, filling itself with the same kinds of deflecting questions that had filled his own. They returned to the tub side by side, like teammates breaking huddle, silently buttressing each other by their mutual presence, concentrating with an intensity geared to leave no room for fear or revulsion. They worked quickly, and the pace accelerated. Pavlik's Baggies and petri dishes suddenly seemed to blossom upon the bathroom floor. They sorted scrapings of flesh and ash from the body and tub, hair samples from the floor and beside the body, more from the wastebasket after they had removed the wadded shower curtain using a pair of cooking tongs that Pavlik claimed, in his increasingly animated chatter, were far superior to the wooden ones extolled at the Academy. The gathering of the evidence progressed smoothly, until the question of the woman's eyes arose.

"Looks like she's watching us, Tom," Pavlik said. Shephard ignored him until he noticed that Pavlik had quit working and sat silently looking at the woman's face. "Can you close her eyes for me, Tom?" His face had soured to gray and there was a nervous urgency in his voice. Shephard tried to smooth the woman's eyelids down but couldn't quite manage it, neither left nor right. Pavlik leaned forward and tried it, too, but had no better luck, then mumbled something about the glow in her eyes and no damned eyelids anyway. Then he was running his hand along the body, his voice running high as he tilted her head both ways, then leaned over and promised to find her eyelids. Shephard remained silent, watching his shock-bound partner.

With a trembling hand, Pavlik finally retrieved two fleshy sections from the far side of the body. Each was decisively cut along one side and sprouted hairs along the other. He carefully handed them to Shephard, as delicately as if they had been artifacts, chattering all along about why he became a cop and fishing with his brother on the Bend in Oregon and something about sex, before he collapsed cross-legged on the floor and turned his frantic, crushed gaze to Shepard. After a long and wordless rest, Pavlik carefully put away his dishes and bags, replacing them on the floor with his fingerprinting utensils.

"Sorry," he said.

The investigation in Hope Creeley's house dragged on with unbroken monotony for the entire afternoon. By the time they had packed up the forensic gear and called Ken Robbins's bodysnatchers, Shephard was exhausted. As he stood and looked out the window of Hope Creeley's bedroom, he realized it was not just from the physical tedium of bending, scraping, dusting, spraying, lifting, and photographing for three straight hours. More than the physical frustration of the work was the mental fatigue that comes from knowing that all the work will amount to nothing. The fatigue from realizing—as Shephard had realized even as Pavlik was walking up the driveway and checking the address—that he wasn't doing the job wrong, he was simply doing the wrong job.

The idea had hit him quickly.

That night he sat up under the single lamp remaining in his razed apartment and made out a list of predictions on what Robbins and Yee would find. He anticipated that the accelerant would be turpentine again, that at least one of the scores of human hairs collected would match the ones found in Tim Algernon's tightly clenched fist, that the killer had entered sometime during the early morning or evening through the unlocked sliding patio door, that the dog's neck would be broken or his throat crushed. In short, a repetition of the sundry, fragmented, peripheral, and presently barren intelligence that he already possessed. He drank a Scotch and smoked. Later, with the wretched image of Hope Creeley in his head, he wandered with Cal through the city, a tall figure in a wrinkled jacket, his gaze rarely leaving the dark sidewalks, his lanky body bent forward at the waist as his long legs carried him with effortless and deceptive speed.

For the first time since he had looked down on the disfigurement that was once Hope Creeley, Shephard felt the protective numbness lifting from his mind. He realized as he passed the quaint and long-closed shops of Forest Avenue that the murder of Hope Creeley had taken the case from routine homicide—if there was such a thing—into a darker, more menacing realm. A realm governed by logic and purpose, still well hidden. So well hidden, in fact, that not even three days of exhausting work had allowed him to guess an answer to the most fundamental question: Why? Wade had often told him that solving a premeditated murder was nothing more than the reading of a story. To understand the murder was to understand the plot, he had said. Crimes of passion and crimes of profit offered their scenarios to even the least competent detectives, who had only to read stories that a child could understand. According to his father, every motive was a beginning. The motive became flesh through action.

But a murder without a motive seemed to him like a story without words, or one written in a strange language. Shephard, his angular face beveled into shadow and light by the streetlamp, grappled with the comparison. Somehow, it seemed apt. A book composed by a mind not easily grasped, he thought, like that of a madman or a genius. As he crossed Coast Highway and made his way into the cool onshore breezes of Main Beach, he had a premonitory fear that fingerprints, Identikit sketches, hair specimens, blood samples, and flecks of cobalt could pile up from his desk at the station to the roof of the universe and still amount to nothing but an indecipherable language. A book without under-standable words, he decided.

When he came to the shoreline, Shephard turned south and paralleled the effervescent violet of whitewater that swirled and broke about his feet. He thought of Jane. A party was taking place around a campfire on the sand, the people lit to copper by the flames, their laughter reaching him in snippets interrupted by the waves. A boy and a girl, still wearing bathing suits, broke away from the group and ran after each other into the water, the girl shrieking before she jumped. Another couple stopped to offer him a puff of sweet marijuana, which Shephard politely declined. But the lovely aroma that trailed them as they left, so ripe with forgetfulness and the promise of dreams, tempted him as he hadn't been tempted in years. Since he was a boy, in fact, and walking along this same beach with Louise. He smoked a cigarette instead, recalling that he had in fact accepted the joint from Louise, eagerly and with feelings of great sin. They had finished it and laughed until they found a dark parting in the cliffs, then snuggled in to kiss and grope and decide once again, with a profound swelling in his heart and ache in his groin, to wait until they were married. They had tried, and almost made it too, though it hadn't been all that long to wait. Just like Louise to say, let's try, but not be able to quite do it, he thought. But that was another matter, his defense perhaps.

Louise, he thought. Was the reality love, or the end of love?

Just before midnight he stood in front of Hope Creeley's Spanish-style home, fingering in his pocket the key he had found in her kitchen drawer. After admonishing Cal gently, he brought it out and let them in.

Cal immediately followed his nose, cruising the hallway for smells, veering unexpectedly and for no apparent reason, stopping suddenly as if something in the air had commanded him to. Shephard took to the house also, wandering, meandering, looking but not knowing for what. Certain fragments found their way into the pockets of his coat: Hope Creeley's address book, which contained Tim Algernon's number as well as his father's; an unopened telephone bill; a handful of matchbooks that had been decoratively placed in a brandy snifter; a shopping list written in a cramped, nervous hand.

Dimly, Shephard remembered a bedroom wall covered with framed mementos and photographs. On the second floor he found it, in the last of the three bedrooms.

While Cal sat attentively at his feet, Shephard regarded the framed history. Hope Creeley at high school graduation; in a newspaper photograph that showed her as a Red Cross worker; in a portrait taken as a young woman, standing in her wedding gown with the groom, pushing cake into each other's mouths. She was a handsome, slight woman, with a plain but friendly face rimmed with light curls. There was something self-contained about her, Shephard thought. Even in the picture of her wedding day, he detected something remote and controlled in her smile. A smile of agreement, conformity, not mirth or abandon. The same smile Hope Creeley wore aboard a motor yacht where she stood on deck with two other couples.

The photograph was blurred by age. He recognized the couple to Creeley's left: Mr. and Mrs. Wade Shephard. And the third man was familiar. Shephard closed his eyes and tried to dredge the man's name from his memory. A handsome, outdoor-looking man, someone to whom life had been good. The face taunted, but remained anonymous.

Below the yacht picture was a shot of Hope Creeley and her husband standing in front of a tennis net, their racquets in their hands, a trophy at their feet. Embossed into the matte border in fine gold letters was the legend:

The same tournament Tim and Margaret Algernon had played in, he thought. Shephard removed the picture from the wall, examined it under the direct light in the center of the room, and replaced it. Cal yawned and wandered away. The photographs seemed to end around 1950, he noted, as if everything memorable in the woman's life had been completed by then. He turned off the light and headed for the third story, wondering why it was such a bad year for Surfside tennis players.

He crossed the white expanse of the anteroom and stood beside the nightstand in the bedroom and noticed something for the first time. No wonder we missed it, he thought. White, like everything else in the room, it blended chameleonlike into the wall behind it. But one look at it explained why Tim Algernon had called twenty-four times instead of once.

Like a million other frustrated callers around the world, he had gotten the answering machine rather than his intended party.

Shephard sat down on the bed, turned the rewind switch, and waited for the tape to stop. It didn't have far to go. Then he pushed the play button, lay back on the hard bed, and stared at the ceiling.

A man's voice, calm and peaceful: "This is Reggie, Hope. Just called to say hello. Did you see the yellow rose by the hedge this morning?"

A woman's voice, older, enthused, concerned: "It's Dorothea again, Hope. Thank you so much for your contributions to the Society. I can't wait to read it and I know the pictures will be a delight. Please come see us again soon. Bye now."

Then, a deep voice that spoke slowly and deliberately:

"Hope, this is Tim. Sorry I missed you. We have to get together and talk, please. My number is 494-1318. Goodbye."

The same voice: "Tim Algernon again. I hope you're on vacation. Please call me as soon as you get in, it's very important."

The next caller listened to the message, waited, and said nothing. It took him five seconds to hang up. Shephard stopped the tape, rewound it, and listened to the empty five seconds again. The sound of cars on a fast street, and one horn honk.

Tim Algernon called again: "Tim Algernon, Hope. Call me as soon as you get this message. Promise?"

The first caller, still calm and peaceful: "I hope everything is okay there, dearest Hope. Perhaps we'll have breakfast again? Toodles." He hung up.

Then a long wait, traffic moving in the background again, and the distant peal of bells. The voice came fast and hurried: "Did you get my little package, Hope? I'll bet it made your skin crawl, didn't it? You don't have to call me because I'll be calling on you. No matter what you do."

There was a pause while the traffic and bells continued in the garbled background. Then the voice continued: "Look to God, look to heaven, and look to hell, Hope. It's so nice to be back in Laguna Beach. Hello, hello . . ." The caller hung up.

Shephard lurched up from the bed, rewound the last message, and played it back. Again the long pause, the cars and bells. The hurried, severe voice, speaking as if he had to get the call over with so he could get on to business.

Followed by Tim Algernon again: "Sorry for all the calls, Hope, but I've got something urgent to see you about. Please call me. If I could explain it in thirty seconds, I would. Again, it's Tim Algernon, 494-1318."

And Algernon again: "Hope, call me immediately. I think you may be in danger and I know that I am, too. Please call Tim. Hurry."

Then a new voice, or rather, two of them. First a pert "Oh," as if in mild surprise, then a pause, followed by a voice that Shepard recognized immediately: "Hello, Mrs. Creeley. We're returning your confidential call of yesterday. Please call us anytime."

Marla Collins and Bruce Harmon, he thought: confidential as hell.

Then the hurried voice again, this time sending a nervous chill up Shephard's spine: "Poor Timmy, poor Tim. Haven't you heard?" There was more traffic in the background before he hung up. It was the last call on the tape.

Shephard rewound again to the threatening message. He listened to it twice for the words, which he scribbled into his notebook as they were spoken, and once to count the bells ringing the time in the background.

There were seven.

"Good old Saint Cecilia's," he mumbled to Cal as he stood up from the bed. "She always tells us the time, doesn't she, Cal? Even with all the traffic on Coast Highway."

Shephard removed the tape in case some other interested party—Bruce Harmon, for instance—should want to hear it. With the first inklings of luck stirring inside him, he stood up. Cal was already asleep on the floor.

Little package, he thought. Little package. He wondered if it might be book-sized.

The inklings of luck were true. Not that any great amount of it was needed to pull out the nightstand drawer. But there was the Bible, nestled in the corner beside a bottle of nail polish and an unopened packet of cotton balls. The inside of the back cover bore a stamp more decorative and informative than the stamp on Algernon's book, a fancy, cheerful filigree that read: *Forest Avenue Books, Happy Reading.*

The book was not new. But he reasoned that the handwriting on the first page was. The ink was red and the familiar penmanship was ordered and skilled:

For the Lord your God is a devouring Fire,
A jealous God,
He is coming to make His misery yours.

To the collection of matchbooks, address books, and notes in one pocket, Shephard added the Bible in the other, forming a ballast for the long walk home. Outside the door, approaching the darkness of a hedge, he found the small yellow rose that Reggie had asked about. He wondered if she had seen it or not.

He covered the miles back to his apartment quickly and easily, well ahead of purposeless Cal.

ELEVEN

The proprietress of Forest Avenue Books welcomed Shephard with one of the overly grateful smiles worn by the owners of floundering businesses. She was old, pert, and leather-faced, and studied Shephard with the intensity of a hawk over a good field. He introduced himself and brought Hope Creeley's Bible from his pocket.

"I'd like to know if you sold this book recently," he said.

The woman introduced herself as Sally Megroz. When she took the book, her bony hands dipped from the weight.

She flipped to the first page and brought her face close to the paper, nodding.

"That's me," she said. "Sold it early in the week. Let's see just when it was."

She worked her way to the register desk and pulled a dusty, flimsy cardboard box from under the counter. With a lick of her finger she parted the stuffing of pink receipts. She brought three close to her face before she nodded again and looked up.

"Monday the twenty-fifth. Three dollars because it was used. Only book I'll sell used." She handed Shephard the slip and stepped back. "You know about Hope Creeley, I suppose." Her voice was suddenly accusing.

"Yes," he answered. "Did you know her?"

"Did I know her? Of course I knew her. She was a regular customer. I don't understand why there are always enough police to write parking tickets on my customers but not enough to keep something like that from happening." She met Shephard's stare with a defiant raise of the chin.

"We do what we can, Mrs. Megroz. What did the person who bought this Bible look like?"

"A very nice older man. Came in about two. I had him pegged for religion or self-help when he walked in. I try to guess which section they'll head for. I was right." Self-help or religion, he thought, Jesus. She returned the receipt to her derelict box.

"What did he look like?"

"Shorter than you but taller than me. Medium kind of build. Older gentleman, graying and very sweet. He wore a beard. He was dressed in old clothes, so at first I thought he was one of the new winos in town. They come in for the summer from the harsher climes, you know." Come south from Sacramento for the summer, Shephard noted.

"Did you talk with him?"

"Yes, in fact he admired the painting there." She turned

and pointed to a violent seascape hanging on the wall behind her. A ship was being dashed on the rocks of some unforgiving coast, its crew flinging themselves into the sea. He thought of his ruined print of Hopper's *Nighthawks*.

"Admired it?"

"Very much," Mrs. Megroz said defensively, as if Shephard's judgment in art was suspect, or perhaps retarded. "He said the strokes were very confident and the colors well orchestrated. I added that the emotion was what I liked. Not that all paintings should be so extreme. But I admired the gumption,. you might say. He said that the painting was obviously done from the heart, not the brain."

"What else? Anything?"

"That is all I remember."

"And he paid cash?"

"He did."

"Tell me," Shephard said as he brought the Identikit sketch from his coat pocket. "Have you ever seen this man?"

Sally Megroz brought the drawing to her nose and for a long time it didn't come down. When it did, her face had gone pale. "Monday. That's him," she said quietly. "Why is such a nice man as that wanted?"

"He killed Hope Creeley, Mrs. Megroz." Shephard let the statement take effect before he continued. "And anything you can tell me may help us find him. Unless you'd rather have me writing parking tickets." He looked through the glass door to the cars jammed into the parking slots on Forest Avenue.

"He got one," she said.

"One what?"

"A parking ticket!" Sally Megroz's voice climbed an octave as she spoke. Her eyes narrowed, as if she were getting some kind of revenge, long overdue. She recalled how he had paid the money, gone to the door, then turned around and come back in. He said the police were giving him a ticket so he may as well browse a minute longer. "Damn the cops again, scaring away my customers," she added. "But I eat my words, sir. I'm damned happy about this." Her chin trembled and tears welled in her eyes.

Shephard steadied her frailty with a consoling hand. "You've done well, Mrs. Megroz," he said, inwardly grinning at his good fortune and the high bureaucratic irony of a killer being issued a parking ticket. "Can you tell me what kind of a woman Hope Creeley was?"

Sally Megroz's face hardened into a mask of loyalty, compliance, eagerness to help. She described Hope Creeley as a very private and very kind woman. She was a great reader of biography and history. She had recently brought a collection of pictures and a diary to the Historical Society, a donation that had thrilled both Mrs. Megroz and the society director.

On the inside track of his memory, Shephard heard again the second caller on Creeley's answering machine.

"Dorothea?"

"Dorothea Schilling. We were so happy to get them. Hope was very aware of the sweep of history in our little town." Shephard put the Bible back in his pocket. Sally Megroz took a step forward and spoke confidentially. "If you want to know about her, you should get Dorothea to show you the photographs and diary. Really, she was more an acquaintance than a true friend. A very private woman."

Like Tim Algernon, the very private man, Shephard thought. And like Algernon, a former member of the prestigious Surfside Sail and Tennis Club of Newport Beach.

"Did you see his car?" Shephard asked hopefully.

She turned her pale gray eyes to him and shook her head slowly. "At my age, these old eyes miss a little. I could see Tammy the meter maid writing a ticket out the window and the car was red. I'm sorry, but that's all I can tell you."

"You've been very helpful." Shephard gave her a card and

shook a cool, unresisting hand. "If you think of anything that might help us, give me a call. Immediately, if you see that man again."

He stopped at a pay phone to relay the parking ticket search to Pavlik. The crime scene investigator had rebounded since his grim encounter with Hope Creeley; his voice was excited again, his words coming quickly. Robbins and Yee had started early on the body, he said. Robbins had called to report that again turpentine had been splashed in liberal amounts over the body. Yee's lab had already issued a preliminary cause of death, unremarkable considering the evidence: death by burning. Pavlik took to the parking ticket search like a bird to the sky, ringing off in a hurry and telling Shephard to call in an hour. "Let's nail this sonofabitch," he said.

Dorothea Schilling of the Laguna Beach Historical Society looked historical, Shephard thought as he introduced himself. She was bundled in a pink sweater, even though the day was already eighty and the musty Society rooms were unventilated and stifling.

After Shephard asked to see Hope Creeley's recent donations to the Society, Dorothea led him to the back of a second room and pointed to a lumpy couch. "Right here is where you sit," she said. With his back to the doorway, sinking into the couch so far he wondered if he'd ever get back out, Shephard waited for her to return. Some time later she was back, pushing a dull gray cart with a loose wheel that squeaked and wobbled. Finally she was before him, smiling, offering a low, wide box that bulged at the sides. "I thought you might like some peace and quiet," she said.

He studied the box. "How about the diary, Dorothea? May I see that too?"

She shook her head gravely. "I'm sorry, but Hope's desire

is that the diary remain sealed until five years after her death. It's a matter of—"

Shephard brought out his badge. "I forgot to mention, Dorothea, that this is police business."

She nodded, brows furrowing. A moment later she was back with a heavy, leather-bound book.

He felt like the prisoner of an overly kind aunt, but the feeling was not altogether unpleasant. She brought him a cup of instant coffee so strong that it was undrinkable, so hot that the plastic spoon had wilted into uselessness. He thanked her profusely, smiling as she hobbled off to the front room cinching the bright sweater around her neck.

The box contained newspaper clippings taped to notebook paper. The articles were yellowed and weakened by time, and the tape had collected a dark residue of dust around its edges. But each sheet was dated in the upper right corner, and they were arranged chronologically. Shephard set the stack on the couch beside him, glanced at the vile coffee, and started at the beginning.

Hope Augustine had first surfaced in the press in 1943, when she was pictured in the *Laguna Week News* as one of several local women honored for her work with the Red Cross. She was third from the left in the group shot, a dreamy smile on her face, her hair held severely back with a clip. The article said that she had recently returned from service overseas. Later that year she was again pictured in the *Laguna Week News*, this time for organizing a volunteer support group for the South Laguna Hospital. The group called themselves the Angelitos—Little Angels—and the other women were like Hope Augustine: young, pretty, happy. They had dedicated themselves to outpatient care and fund raising. Hope was president. She was quoted succinctly in the short article: "I think work like this is the least we can do in wartime."

A year later she was pictured in the engagements column

of the same paper. Her betrothed was Burton Creeley, an accountant and partner in the newly formed Surfside Sail and Tennis Club in Newport Beach.

No wonder she was a member, Shephard thought. Had she known Tim Algernon then?

Apparently, Hope Augustine had become Hope Creeley and moved to Newport Beach, five miles north of Laguna on the same unspoiled coast. The *Newport Ensign* picked up her story again in late 1944, when she was pictured as the new bride of businessman Creeley. He was beside her in the wedding shot, a frail, dapper man who was five years her senior. The couple appeared regularly through 1944 and 1945, favorite targets of party-going photographers. They were pictured aboard yachts, at ground-breaking ceremonies for additions to the Surfside Club, in tennis garb at post-tournament parties. One photograph was similar to the one he'd seen in Creeley's house: Hope and Burton standing on the Surfside court, a trophy at their feet. The happy couple continued their public lives through the forties, always surrounded by the postwar gaiety and newfound opulence of the Surfside Club.

Then Burton Creeley was dead. An article dated September 26, 1951, said that fishermen had discovered his body dashed against the rocks of the Newport jetty. The next day's *Santa Ana Register* said that Creeley was known to swim every evening in the ocean, sometimes in the channel at Newport, sometimes south in Laguna Beach where the currents were known to be treacherous. Burton Creeley was officially classified as the victim of a swimming accident by the Newport Beach Police on September 29.

But on the next day, the *Register* ran a short article with a large headline, claiming that Creeley had been seen by two friends in Laguna shortly before the accident had taken place. A follow-up story stated that the friends turned out to be two gas station attendants who "believed" they recognized Creeley from newspaper photos. A Newport Beach police captain wryly questioned how a body could wash six miles north, around a jetty, and end up in the Newport Channel in less than a night.

The press lost interest, and Hope Creeley disappeared from the public eye for twenty-four years.

Shephard felt a keen sadness as he looked at the next picture. It was dated November 28, 1975, and showed Hope Creeley, thin and undeniably without happiness, staring back at the photographer. She had organized a support group for the South Laguna Hospital again, and again they called themselves the Angelitos.

Hope Creeley had never looked so far away from heaven, Shephard thought. The women around her were young and vibrant, as she had once been, but Hope Creeley looked pained. Her eyes were still large, but her face had shrunk around them, sagging heavily at the mouth. A year later she was pictured again, this time receiving an award from the hospital's board chairman, whose beefy grin dominated the one-column shot.

Hope Creeley's forced and very minor smile was the last one of her public life.

Shephard turned the last clipping onto the pile beside him and lit a cigarette. A sad life and a sadder death, he thought. But why would an avenging God come to make His misery hers? Hadn't she had enough?

The cigarette tasted raw and bad. He dropped it into an ashtray and watched the smoke lift upward through the stale air. Behind him, from the Historical Society lobby, he heard Dorothea Schilling sneeze, open a drawer, dryly blow her nose. She doesn't even know yet, he thought.

He hefted the leather-bound diary onto his lap. As he scanned through the book, he saw that the handwriting evolved from a graceful, purposeful flow to a more pragmatic

114

curtness, and finally into wild scribbles that made up the last several entries.

The opening passage was dated January 1952. Four months after her husband's death, Shephard thought. He felt the pain in her words as he read:

> *I have fulfilled one half of my New Year's resolution by beginning this diary, and I'll fill the other half when I join the Angelitos again. The truth is I'm awfully tired of the support group, even though momma and everyone else tells me to get out of the house and participate. But every time I feel any energy, it takes me back to a time when such things meant something to me. Now, being part of a group is just like taking dead flowers and putting them in the vase I used to put Burt's roses in. And speaking of that vase, I put it on the kitchen table today and watched the sunlight break through it into a small rainbow. It was lovely but I cried. I feel him everywhere. Mother says I should slowly remove such things from my life and only hold onto the good memories. This seems like good advice, to hold onto only good things. But I'm not sure what to do with the vase. Can good things hurt, too?*

Shephard pondered the question respectfully as he turned to the next entry. It was two months later, March 21, 1952:

> *I'm still having the cramps and jitters inside me. When I think of loving Burt, they get worse and it's like my mind is trying to forget but my body wants to remember. Sometimes I wake up so hungry for him that my face is wet from tears, and other things are wet too. It isn't easy for a woman to be alone after being loved by her husband so much. I know that I was not the only woman he made love to, but I know that he never loved her the way he loved me. She is a slut, but I'm not bitter. There is simply no room for bitterness. My heart actually feels like there is something around it, squeezing sometimes. I shopped for two again today, but I felt bad by the time I got to the*

cereal and had to put my sunglasses on. I still haven't joined the girls at the hospital yet. But so sweet, some of the letters the patients have written. Maybe when I put some weight back on. Ten pounds down from only a hundred to start with and all the clothes look funny. Still never hungry. It feels so strange when men look at me now.

The next entry, made on March 26, 1952, unnerved him:

Poor Wade Shephard and poor Colleen. Just because bad things happen to us is no reason to forget the bad things that befall others. Wade and I had dinner once last week but we didn't find much to talk about and it was a very dark event. He got drunk and I did, too, but it was not a cheerful drunk but a gloomy one and over early. People like us should be good for each other. But I would rather be with someone whose life has been easier on them. I'm sure he thought the same of me. Joe was still very nice to arrange it. He has been so good, getting his pharmacist to fill the prescriptions for me, and no charge, even. The pills, they make me feel dumb and warm and forgetful. I guess sadness gets bigger when you share it. Wade has lost weight, too. Must have looked funny to the others at the club, two weight-losers and mate losers. At least Burton was an accident. I have no doubt that Azul killed Colleen, he was such a violent and uncaring man. I'll never understand what so many of the women saw in him. Joe was most helpful in helping me prepare my testimony. Good God, my problems are small compared to Colleen's. Or Wade's. Wish I could sleep regular hours. Sleep, now there's a powerful drug.

Shephard finished the entry and tried to picture his father and Hope Creeley dining in some dark corner of the Surfside Restaurant, forcing conversation and drinking for relief. But Hope Creeley's cramps and jitters seemed to transfer themselves to his own stomach. The passage about Wade and Colleen was violation. He felt awkward, angry—the same feelings that he had had as a child, a fist-clenching, biting, wildly violent passion to destroy the mention of his mother's death, yet to preserve her memory inviolate. Shephard lit another cigarette and let the calming nicotine swarm his brain. The memory of his mother was not memory at all, he thought, but the creation of it. He had never known her. Yet he had labored to imagine what he might have known. And the Zaharas and Creeleys of the world were intruders, the memory-wreckers. Safe and warm, he thought. What better judge than me to edit my own past?

A trickle of sweat dropped down his back as he wiped his forehead with a sleeve. Drop it, he thought. Healing waters. Unprofessional, intrusive, destructive. He pressed ahead. The next entry was made one year after Burton's death, September 26, 1952:

> Exactly a year now since Burt drowned. It was a lovely day today but it made me remember because seasons will make us do that. Even without the lights and decorations, if December came around you would still think of Christmas. It's in the blood, I guess. A very busy month, moving to Laguna. The Surfside was simply too haunted for me—having to see the things that made me happy and even the things that didn't, like Helene. And all the people talking behind my back about her and Burt. Nobody says anything to me. I feel sorry for her. But Laguna is small and beautiful and not so many people know me, so they don't look at me with those damned pitying eyes. Everything is growing so fast, so many new people. Something inside of me is changing. I don't have the pains and cramps so often and my bones don't feel like they're made of iron anymore. I got out of bed early today. I no longer like my bed so much. Not that I want another man. Think about Burton so much still. Had my first period in a year last week. Think I was bleeding when he died. My new neighbors here are quite nice. The

Ottens on the left and Laras on the right. The little Lara girl is so cute, all cheeks and freckles. Of all the things Burt left me, I wish that one of them could have been a child.

He skipped ahead nearly ten years, to May 5, 1962:

Big race to Ensenada today from the Surfside. I'm writing this from aboard Joe Datilla's boat, the Priceless, which is why the handwriting is so nutty. Maybe the gin too. It's been a great race and I think we're somewhere in front. Joe hates to lose and takes everything so serious. This is supposed to be my turn to sleep, but too much coffee and excitement, I think. Reggie Otten said he'd leave his wife for me yesterday, and I told him not to be so silly. Such a sweet little man, and a good neighbor.

December 7, 1963:

Whenever I hear this date my blood seems to go metallic and something rings in my ears. I can still remember what I was doing when we were attacked. I was playing with Skeeter in the front yard and dad had just heard on the news about Pearl Harbor. He was screaming and bellowing at mom, then she was crying and quick on the telephone with her friends. I kept looking up in the sky and wondering if I might see a Zero, and dumb Skeeter just barked. What a horrid winter this has been. I can still hear the drums and see that dark processional at John Kennedy's funeral, and those pictures of Jackie with the blood on her legs and everyone saying what a coward she was for trying to climb out. Poor, poor woman. The wind blew all day here when they buried him and it was a bad day. I feel so low now, I'll write another time.

Shephard moved ahead twenty years, to the last entries in the book. Hope Creeley's handwriting had decayed into a heavy and erratic scrawl, sometimes angling up the page, sometimes down. He could almost feel the pressure of her

118

hand as she tried to keep the pen steady. August 25, the day that Tim Algernon had been killed:

    I've never had such a feeling of foreboding in all my life. Today I got out of bed and went to the garden. Someone had pulled off two of my best roses in the night. Reggie kept following me up and down the hedge yesterday and tried to kiss me by the perennials. He wants an answer about the movies, I know. So lonely since his wife passed away. Then the afternoon paper came and Tim Algernon dead. I went to the bathroom and was sick but nothing came up. Even Skeeter seemed slowed up today. The first Skeeter was a better dog until the trash truck hit him. The new Skeeter is a good dog and I like the way his tail curls and his ears point. I like the barklessness of him. A silent dog is almost a perfect dog. Tim kept calling but I never returned them, and now I wonder if the police should know. I want to be left alone, no Tim and no one but Skeeter and me and he can't even bark. Poor Tim now. One of the old Surfside gang and such a nice big man. So much bad has happened to so many of us from back then. Bad luck hangs in the air like the pyramids at El Giza. The world is so big, but so empty. The wind especially, like the day they buried the president and it just kept blowing like breeze off the ankles of God. I wonder if part of Burton is flying around in it sometimes. I know now, as I look back, that I held onto him too long after he was gone, just as I held onto him too hard when he was with me. It seems impossible that a person might do something so simple as loving wrong. I'm sure Burton is somewhere out there in that wind. He always wanted flying lessons.

Then, the last entry, made two days before Shephard had found her body, August 26:

    Been inside for two full days now. Won't answer the phone and don't want any more mail. What is happening? Got this very nice Bible in the mail Tuesday with a very bad note inside the cover. I've called the police twice but hung up. Joe Datilla said not to worry because it was

*probably a bad joke or the wrong address but my name was
right on the package. Been rubbing my eyes all day for
some reason. Called Reverend Shephard today but he was
out. I don't know who would send me such a thing. Joe
says just stay home and take care of myself and work on
my writing or something even though I told him I was
tired of it. He's always been so respectful since Burton.
They were always at odds but such good partners, Datilla
and Creeley had such a good ring to it. I'm sure he felt
responsible for Burton because he was weaker and they
argued and gossip had them enemies but not true at all.
There just seems no end to the bad luck. The Shephard
boy is now a policeman and working on Tim. I almost
called him but I hung up. I am just a foolish old woman
and really not that old at all. I remember him when he was
little, always baseball and bicycles for little Tom Shephard.
Born into all the messes that happened before. We should
all move a million miles away from where we start off.*

*The old pictures make me sad. Going to pack all this up
today and take to Dorothea at the Historical. I'm sick of
writing, and who cares about the old times anyway? Time
for me to be rid of it all and start on something else.
Perhaps knit more. Who would send me such a bad thing
as that Bible? I feel safe in the house here like Joe said.
Saw Wade Shephard's sermon on the TV last week and
really very good. He's grown into such a strong, good man
after all the hell he was in after Colleen died. Skeeter
misses his walks. Just thought of it now, but it's been three
years since I've been to the beach, although I can see a
little bit of it from the third floor here, and with the white
all around me and the quiet, the ocean doesn't seem as
terrifying as it used to. Tried to get my life as white as
could be. That sounds like laundry. Always think of parts
of him being in the ocean. But that is over now.
Everything seems over now for some reason. I'm tired.
Good night Burton.*

As if approving an official statement, Hope Creeley had
signed the last page. Shephard saw that the signature, unlike

the scribbled entry, was clear, confident, and graceful. A final testimony to spirit over gloom, hope over despair. In some small way, he thought, she had won.

And so, in a way, had he. A path was opening before him now, and it pointed straight to the Surfside.

Behind him, Shephard heard the door open, the jingling of a tiny bell, and Dorothea Schilling's frail voice welcoming a new browser to the Society. The voice of the man who answered her was deep, clear, and unmistakable.

"I'm Toby Benson with the *Times,* doing a story on Hope Creeley. I understand she made a donation to the Society recently. May I see it?"

Mrs. Schilling explained that the contributions available to the public were already being enjoyed by one history buff, and that Mr. Benson could join him in the back room. A moment later, Mr. Benson's large and well-dressed form was standing over Shephard, his face hardening as he looked down. Shephard stood up and left the diary and clippings on the couch.

"Bruce Hard-on, buddy, chum. How the hell are ya?"

Bruce Harmon reddened, and Shephard was aware of the rage percolating through the big man's body. In the cramped room, he looked even larger than before, and less predictable.

"It's public record now," he said slowly. "Public record now that the Historical Society has it." Dorothea Schilling's wide-eyed face peeped from around a wall.

"They don't have it, Bruce. I do. If you want a look, tell me who sent you to take it."

Harmon's eyes found the diary and box of photos laying on the couch beside Shephard. His instincts told him to smash what was in his way, Shephard guessed; his brains told him to wait. And Shephard's own instincts told him to arrest Harmon for obstruction and hold him forty-eight hours before not bringing charges, which would be thrown out by the district attorney anyway. But something beyond instinct told him that Bruce Harmon was worth more left alone, that the free are at liberty to make mistakes. Cop and ex-cop read each other's thoughts with identical speed and accuracy. At the same time, they offered each other the slow, premeditated smiles used by police officers throughout the world, smiles as dry and mirthless as sand, meant to lull, confuse, disarm.

On his way out, Harmon nearly capsized Dorothea Schilling, who had just come around the corner bearing another cup of scalding coffee. He grunted past her, slamming through the door. She watched him in cowed embarrassment.

"So many of them lose interest," she said confidentially. And she reluctantly consented to let Detective Shephard keep the Creeley diary for "a day or two at the most."

From a pay phone on the highway, Shephard called Pavlik and found that a red 1964 Coupe de Ville had been ticketed outside Forest Avenue Books at 2:12 P.M. on Monday, August 25. The car was a convertible and the plates read 156 DSN, California. And due to Sacramento's usual computer logjam, Pavlik lamented, he still didn't have the name of the registered owner. It had not been reported stolen.

A busy killer, Shephard thought as he hung up. He walked to the Mustang and leaned against the black body, hot in the late morning sun. Looking across Coast Highway to the ocean that twinkled silver-blue on the horizon, Shephard took out his notebook and charted the killer's movements. Nine days ago, the man had mailed a Bible to Algernon from Sacramento. On Saturday, three days later, he had rolled Steinhelper and taken his wallet. Sunday, he arrived from Sacramento in Laguna on Greyhound line 52. By six Monday morning he had removed Algernon from the realm of the living. By seven he had checked into the Hotel Sebastian, washed up, paid in advance for three days, and left his can of turpentine and his stolen identification in the night-stand drawer. A very busy man.

Shephard realized with modest but welcome clarity that the stolen identification had been left behind on purpose. Good, he thought, our man is thinking of us.

By nine, Shephard figured, the suspect had left—just after Bruce Harmon, and just before Shephard himself, had arrived. At two o'clock he went to Forest Avenue Books, purchased the used Bible, possibly sat under the shade of one of the city's venerable eucalyptus trees as he penned the brief but terrifying note to Hope Creeley, then walked across the street to the post office and mailed the book. It had arrived at Creeley's mansion a day later.

One day after that, he had gone to Creeley and done what he said he would do, and the misery he made hers was considerable. Had he cut off her eyelids so she would have to watch? Shephard shivered.

Sometime before Monday at 2 P.M. he had found a car.

And sometime before Tuesday he had found a safe place to sleep.

He was working methodically, accurately, quickly. Working like he knew the city.

Shephard pulled the now-wrinkled Identikit sketch from his pocket and studied it under the glare of the sun. The wry, confident face studied him back.

TWELVE

His father had insisted on an early lunch. The table of his Arch Bay Heights home was set for two, and the Reverend Wade Shephard, tanned and serene, was quick to offer his son a glass of white wine. Wade, by personal decree an alcoholic, no longer drank, but the wine was present at every meal as an invitation to guests and as a test for himself. The liquid splashed tunefully into the goblet; his father smiled. It was the reverend's smile, not the policeman's, Shephard thought as he sat down. As a boy he had been intrigued by his father's smile, its wariness and suspicion, its taunting secrecy. But the smile of Wade the Reverend was forgiving, warm, public.

"I apologize for the early hour, but I've got a wedding this afternoon," he said. "Two young people from the congregation, charming couple. How's the head, son?"

"Healing rapidly."

"Good, good. Wouldn't hurt to lay off the booze," Wade said with encouragement. "You sounded pretty hammered the other night. It's so good to see you again, Tommy. What do you hear from Louise, anything?"

"A little. She moved into a friend's home in time for the peak tanning season. Malibu."

Her friend was Robert Steckman, the movie producer, and his smooth voice returned to Shephard's ears as he sipped the wine. She's too beautiful to be unseen by this town, he had told Shephard at a party one night. Steckman had "found" Louise at Bullock's Wilshire, where she worked, and they had developed a quick and cheerful friendship that Shephard mistrusted and felt excluded from. Too beautiful to be unseen, he thought. And now, a year later, Steckman had taken her into his Malibu home, undoubtedly to be seen.

"You sound bitter, son. A door is closed and a window opens. When you find a young woman whose soul is your soul, take her as a wife and love her with all your heart." Wade's voice was the same mellifluous, optimistic one that he used for his televised sermons.

Shephard nodded. "I did that," he said.

"Only a fool would close the window," his father said quietly.

"You haven't raised a fool."

"No. I haven't." Wade sipped his coffee, and as his father lowered his face, Shephard saw a change of expression so subtle only a son might register it. For an instant, the face of Wade the Cop passed across the face of Wade the Reverend, like the shadow of a bird across water. Then it was gone and Wade looked up. "You know, I think that everything I've done in my life—from the time I married your mother and every day after she left us—I did in some way for her. Even before I met her. Somehow I was acting for her, anticipating her. And judged by some standards, I have done wonderful things. The power of the Lord has given me a large congregation that grew from almost nothing. Do you remember the first sermon in that makeshift chapel that still smelled like popcorn? With Little Theodore sitting there in a sweat?" He paused, as he did on television, for effect. "Then a huge chapel in which to worship. And the beginnings of a hospital in Yucatan, where we can carry the mercy of God to those who need it most. And I have been given some beautiful things, too. A lovely house in a beautiful city, good friends, health. But you know something? I would trade it all to have her back with me."

Wade brought a napkin to his mouth, patted, set it down on the table in front of him. Shephard poured himself another glass of wine. His father smiled.

"I think, of all the joys on earth, that the love shared by a man and a woman is most sacred, Tommy. And human, too. When I loved Colleen I told myself that it was the best of what I would ever do. I was your age when I thought that. And now, it's thirty years later and I feel the same thing. I would trade it all to have her back in this house with me. You'll never hear that in a Sunday sermon, or maybe you will, but it's true. The times we had, the laughter. Even the sorrow we shared . . ." Wade smiled again and it wasn't the public version, but a private reminiscence, a reverie about something fine.

Shephard felt like a man listening to an advertisement for something he couldn't buy. The image of Louise reclining on a Malibu sun deck flitted into his mind, followed by one of Jane Algernon standing in waders, aiming her lovely and hurtful smile across the yard at him.

"The hospital in Yucatan," he said, "will it be big?"

"Two hundred beds, Tommy. And the donations keep rolling in. We're about to break ground, and she's going to be beautiful. I decided to call it the Sisters of Mercy Hospital. Come back to the den, I'll show you the blueprints."

Wade led him from the dining room into the living room, then down the familiar hallway to the den. The presence of his old house, the home of his boyhood, brought back to Shephard a horde of memories that fought for attention all at once: walking down this same hallway in his baseball cleats and getting a wild bawling out by Wade; the same hallway where Pudgy, Shephard's beloved mutt, had scampered a million times and slammed into the wall, unable to negotiate the sharp turn to Shephard's bedroom; that bedroom, first on the right, where he had retreated to play with Christmas presents, cried at the first heartbreak of romantic love in the fourth grade, slept long and feverishly through the chicken pox, constructed out of cardboard his first motorcycle, stared through the window when the rain fell so hard in 1960 that three houses in the Heights had slipped into the street, and sat benumbed before the small television set the day of John Kennedy's funeral watching the motorcade labor through the streets—Hope Creeley had been right, the wind was foreign and merciless that day.

Even the smells seemed haunted: his father's invariable Sunday morning menu of pancakes, bacon, and eggs; the dank and muted smell of sulfur brought up in the water system; the undercurrent of saltwater that was always stronger in summer; the smell of dried eucalyptus leaves, Wade's favorite, which were always placed around the Shephard house in vases; even—and Shephard believed as they stepped into the den that he could smell it still—the high-pitched stink of his father's bourbon.

As they went into the den, he realized that what was so strangely timeless about the old house was simply the obvious. Wade hadn't changed it in thirty years. No new paint, no new carpets, no drapes, no new furniture. Why hadn't he noticed it before, he asked himself. Because there was nothing to notice?

The Sisters of Mercy blueprint hung from the den wall by thumbtacks. Wade trained the beam from a track light —one new addition, Shephard noted—onto the smeared design and put on his glasses.

"Two stories and two hundred beds," he said proudly. "One hundred private, the rest in groups of four, six, and eight. A full maternity ward and pediatrics section because the birth rate in Mexico is phenomenal. The hospital itself will be on Isla Arenillas, south of Cozumel. Ten years ago, the villages around were nothing but a few huts and a Pemex

127

station. Now they're towns. Five years from now they'll be wonderful little cities full of tourists who are going to pay good money and bring good business to places you've never even heard of yet. The Yucatan is going to be the new Mexican Riviera, and the Sisters of Mercy will be there to help." Wade turned to his son with a contented but oddly skewed grin. "I don't really know where I got the idea to do this. I just woke up one morning and that's what I wanted to do. I believe I was guided by the spirit in my decision. Strange, but I'd never even been to Mexico."

"You've been guided a long way from home, pops."

"A few years from now, I'll be gone and I'll have left four miracles behind me. A church and a hospital, a wife and a son. I'm proud of that. I think it's an honor to add something before you go."

Wade glanced at his watch and flicked off the track light.

They returned to the dining room, where Shephard helped his father clear the table.

Through the sliding glass door that led to the backyard, Shephard watched the sea heave steadily into Arch Bay. The surging blue was broken only by the bright dabs of color that were his father's roses, a Wade passion for as long as he could remember. The rose bushes ran the entire length of the wide backyard. They had supplied Shephard with scores of gifts over the years. He remembered particularly a small bunch he had picked for Louise on the occasion of their first date, a mixed bouquet of reds and whites, which he augmented with bright yellow blossoms of sourgrass weed that grew unfettered in a far corner. She had been nearly ecstatic, and Shephard was moved by her reaction in a way that only a boy of sixteen can be. He thought back to that night as he set his wineglass in the sink. After going to bed he had mentally composed love poems to Louise, which he imagined turned into deep blue birds that flitted out of his room and winged through the night to her bedroom. And, too moved by emotion to sleep, he had left his room and gone into the backyard, where he faced in the direction of his beloved's home and spread his arms to draw in the telepathic poem-birds that she was assuredly sending back to him. He had maintained this dramatic pose for a few long minutes, convinced that the world had never known a love so pure and powerful. Pudgy had sat idiotically in front of him, head cocked, waiting for something to happen.

As he thought of Louise, he felt bad.

Those early years had seemed endless, he thought, setting the plates and a coffee saucer into the familiar sink. They had seemed endless, and then they vanished.

Wade filled the sink and began washing the dishes, and in automatic response to the years of teamwork that had made the Shephard house spotless, Tom took his time-honored position to his father's left. He dried. The view through the kitchen window was pristine. A bank of clouds wandered across the sun, casting a momentary darkness over the day and turning the shiny water to a dark blue. Cobalt blue, Shephard noted, like the flecks in Larry Robbins's microscope. He worked the Identikit sketch from his pocket and flattened it on the counter beside his father. Wade studied it, shook his head, looked again. "No."

"Did you know Tim Algernon?" Shephard asked.

Wade handed him a plate and nodded. "Hard to live in this town for thirty years and not know Tim. We played a little tennis together at the Surfside back after the war. Never friends, just acquaintances." His father's voice suddenly found an edge. "I heard it was pretty bad." He looked again at the sketch, then moved it aside.

"He didn't have a face. We had to run a dental on him just to make the identification."

Shephard purposefully offered his father little information; Wade's line of questioning would reveal his own instincts on how to handle the case. There was a long silence as Wade rinsed the sink and doused it with cleanser. Then, as he had done a hundred times before, he wiped the counter once before swinging himself up onto the tiles, where he sat with his back to the ocean. Shephard dried the last of the silverware and hoisted himself likewise onto the opposite counter. His father's face had lost its warmth.

"Money?"

"That was my first thought. Until I found over a thousand dollars in bills stuffed down his throat. There was more in the house, and plenty of hardware someone might want." Shephard waited again.

"Then what does that leave?"

Shephard looked into the face of Wade the Cop. "An old detective friend of mine told me once that men get killed for four reasons. Money, a woman, silence, and revenge. Algernon didn't have a woman."

Wade seemed to ponder the statement. Then: "Now do you understand why that old detective left that world for a better one?"

"I think so. But there must be silence and revenge in your world, too."

His father grinned broadly. "We try to keep it to a minimum."

"Algernon was killed early Monday morning. On Wednesday, Hope Creeley had a visit from the same man. He held her down in the bathtub and cut off her eyelids before torching her, and everything—"

"Cut off her eyelids?"

"The only way I can figure it is that he wanted her to watch," Shephard said.

His father shook his head. "I guess that's how I'd read it too," he said quietly.

"And the same guy did it. He sent Algernon a Bible with a threat written in it. The same for Creeley. The woman at Forest Avenue Books said the Identikit sketch matched her customer. She had him pegged for religion or self-help."

"An astute observation, I'd say."

"The connection between Algernon and Creeley is the Surfside Club. They were members at the same time, but it was a long time ago—"

"One connection, maybe," Wade interrupted. "I hope for your sake there's more than just that."

"It's all I've got. Maybe Joe Datilla can open some doors."

Wade's face seemed torn between professions: the suspicion of the detective and the gentle disappointment of the reverend both registered. "Joe will do everything he can for you," he said, and for a moment was lost in thought. "I can't think of two more opposite types. Algernon, as I remember, was a quiet man, big and strong, an athlete. Hope Creeley was married to Burton Creeley, who was part-owner of the club. She was a vivacious, very social woman before he died. Of course after that, she just seemed to fade away. I'm sure that living there at the Surfside was more than she could handle."

"You knew about Helene?"

"Everyone knew about Helene Lang."

"What happened to her?"

Wade looked down at his feet as they dangled by the cupboard. "Like Hope Creeley," he answered finally. "She just seemed to fade away. Left the club after a while, I think."

"Where did she go?"

"I don't know, Tom. I quit going there after your mother passed away and it was quite a while before I had the desire to play tennis with the old gang again. So I lost touch. Just as well, I think. I'll tell you, after the war I came back from the Pacific, glad to be alive with a little peace in the world. A year or two later I met Colleen and I don't have to tell you that that was the happiest time of my life. The whole world seemed to breathe a big sigh of relief. People moved west to Southern California; the factories that were building planes went back to building station wagons, and it was wonderful. A whole country full of teenagers is what it felt like. Then a long run of, well, call it bad luck if you want. A strange feeling it was, sitting in the Surfside Lounge after Colleen and Burton. I guess the dream had to end. It felt like . . . growing up, maybe. It sobered us. It aged us. It woke us up from a good sleep." Wade reached down and wiped the counter once with the towel. "It's still a hard time to talk about," he added as he slid off the counter and checked his watch.

"Thanks, pops," Shephard said.

"Hey." When he looked up, his face was full and flushed, a dose of the Reverend Wade Shephard. "I've got a couple of young lovers to marry. And when you're ready, I'll do it for you, too." He smiled broadly. "No charge."

THIRTEEN

Shephard sped north on Coast Highway toward the Surfside Club, helping himself to the vacant fast lane and holding the Mustang to a mild eighty. An afternoon breeze had eased onto the coast, the first stirrings of a shift from low to high pressure. By evening the wind would hit seven knots, he guessed, frosting the sea with whitecaps and clearing the smog westward for a high-gloss sunset. He pictured himself sitting on the patio of the Hotel Laguna, working on a double Scotch in the company of Jane Algernon while the sun went down behind Catalina Island. Unlikely daydreams, he thought. But as Jane Algernon's sleeping figure passed across his mind he again felt that fluttering inside, the covey of quail gathering before flight. He savored the brief sensation, but forced his mind onto other things, telling himself not to surround molehills of emotion with mountains of meaning.

The all-news station featured an interview with a university psychologist, an expert in law enforcement, who posited that "not all police are the cold-blooded killing machines that many people think them to be." On the contrary, he told the interviewer, some undergo horrible traumas during and after fatal shootings. The nightmares, divorce, and eventual suicide of one such case were noted, and the summation was that people should have more compassion for the cop on the beat.

The report yanked Shephard back to that freakishly drizzly night last August. He had responded to a call from an officer in distress and arrived at the residential street off Pico Boulevard to find a cop being held at bay by a man with a knife. The scene played itself out again: Shephard cutting the lights of the unmarked car, cautiously approaching the two men framed in the headlights of a black and white, moving closer to see that the officer's hands were held out with the palms up. He could still hear the calm argument, something about whatever was wrong with the cockroaches didn't require a knife and maybe jail. Then the cop dropping his hands and the man with the knife dropping his for a moment before he swung upward in a quick arc and the officer went for his gun: Shephard could never clearly remember who moved first. He saw the short trajectory of the blade outlined in the headlights. Then the jerking of his right shoulder and the muzzle flash of the Python .357. And the roaring in his ears as the cop went down and the man pitched over backward onto the wet grass, all in a warm drizzle that cast a spectral sheen over the scene. Then that endless moment of indecision while he felt the urine spreading down his pants, and moved closer to see the officer on his knees, bent over, cradling a handful of his own insides, and the young man with only his foot moving and his chest turning dark in the rain. Looking down on him, Shephard saw that he was just a boy.

Shephard lit a cigarette to break the reverie, then pushed to a music station. The song was dreadful but helped to erase the vision of Morris Mumford from his mind. At night it was different. At night, Morris lived inside him and did as he pleased.

The traffic thickened as he approached Corona del Mar. By the time he reached the first traffic light, the cars had coalesced into an unmoving mass of colors, shining chrome, puffs of exhaust. Children bustled up and down the sidewalks, across the crosswalks, through the stationary traffic. They carried the accoutrements of beach kids: boogie boards, swim fins, portable radios, skateboards, blankets. Shephard watched a thin, tan boy with a sunbleached mop of hair bob down the sidewalk in front of him, the Tom Shephard of another lifetime. He was carrying a pair of swim fins and a beach towel over his shoulder. Shephard called out over the door of the convertible: "Hey, how are the waves?"

The boy turned without breaking stride, shot Shephard the thumbs-up signal, then turned back to the bright sidewalk before him. Walk it all the way to Alaska, Shephard thought. His own pale reflection in the rearview mirror, cigarette dangling from under the drooped mustache, was the face of someone who no longer bore relation to the waves at Corona or to the boy on the sidewalk, he thought. Closer to the corpse in the bathtub, or the one in the dirt of Tim Algernon's driveway. Closer to cigarettes. Closer to death. Closer to the middle, closer to the end. Maybe it was he who should walk to Alaska.

The light changed to green and the cars lurched forward to wait at the next one.

Ten minutes later he had emerged from the Corona del Mar snarl, opened up his speed past Newport Center and the office of South Coast Investigators, and eased down the long slope of highway to the bay bridge. The Balboa Bay Club slipped by to his left.

The first yellow apartments of the Surfside Club appeared to the west, dwarfed by high palm trees that tilted in the breeze. As he swung into the Surfside entrance and stopped at the guard house, Hope Creeley's words found their way to his mind. Bad luck in the air at the Surfside. The guard was a trim man of about sixty, Shephard guessed. He stepped from the house with a humorless expression, a clipboard in his hand. Shephard smiled and noted that the guard's holster was on his left hip but he held a pen in his right hand.

"Thinking about a suite," he said. "Like to have a look around." The guard perched himself over the car, bent down to have a look inside, then made a brief study of Shephard. "Tom Johnston is the name."

"Appointment, Mr. Johnston?"

"Lease lines were busy all morning. Drove in from L.A. anyway. The city is driving me crazy."

"Like that this time of year. Sign in, please." He passed Shephard the clipboard, who registered with a bogus Beverly Hills address and phone number. The guard—Shephard saw that his name was Arthur Mink—read the information and pointed behind the guard house. "Guest lot around and to your right. Have a nice visit, Mr. Johnston. The leasing office is next to the lounge on A Dock."

Shephard followed the two-lane road around the guard house and along the flank of the Surfside convention room, where it opened onto a wide expanse of mostly empty parking spaces. The few cars there were clustered around the tennis courts. He put the Mustang between a Rolls-Royce Corniche and a black Seville, and as he swung open the door saw that all of the court marked 7 was taken up by Joe Datilla. The other courts around him were full and several patient players were waiting for their turn, but Datilla was on his alone, driving serves from a bucket of yellow balls at his feet. Shephard admired his precision: stoop for a ball, a breath and an arching of the back as he tossed up the target, a quick rotation of torso and arms as his legs straightened and the racquet rose to full extension, then snapped down. Follow through, return stance, a pleased nod as the ball screamed over the net and smacked into the far quadrant.

Shephard stood at the chain-link fence and witnessed two more serves before Datilla looked over his shoulder. His scowl turned to a smile.

"Tommy Shephard! I'll be damned." Racquet in hand, he came to the fence and swung open the gate. Datilla's handshake was firm and warm, the kind of handshake that says you're part of the team. "How's that head doing? You were a little drugged when I saw you last."

"Just fine. That Scotch made it a little more palatable."

"The least I could do." Datilla's eyes searched Shephard's face for a brief moment. Shephard noticed that he wasn't sweating. "What brings you to the Surfside? Everything okay?"

"I'm fine, but my city's a little on the nervous side. Two murders in one week. Broke all records."

Datilla sighed. "All I can say is I'm glad I'm not in your business. Any good leads?"

"Let's talk a minute, Joe."

Datilla moved his racquet to the other hand and pointed to the bench by the fence. "You got it, Tom. Anything I can do."

They sat down, Datilla pulling a maroon windbreaker

136

over his suntanned body, Shephard lighting a cigarette. Datilla looked like a man who could afford to be good to himself, Shephard thought, and was.

"The victims are Tim Algernon and Hope Creeley," Shephard began. "They used to play tennis here. Did you know them?"

"Very well. Hope was married to my partner, Burton. Tim and his wife Margie were charter members. We opened just before the end of the war."

"Did they know each other?"

"Oh sure. Small group then. Your father and mother were with us. Good times."

"Were they involved?"

Datilla brushed a hand through his silver hair. His eyes were blue and perplexed when it came away.

"In what?" he asked.

"Each other."

The perplexity turned to relief. "No." He smiled. "Not those two. Tim was dedicated to his wife. Straight shooter all the way. Hope was very much in love with Burton, too. They had their differences, but I don't think Tim Algernon was one of them."

"Enemies, jealousies, rivals? Anyone who didn't like them?"

Datilla propped the racquet against the bench and slowly shook his head. "You know, Tom, after the war we got together here whenever we could. Hard play, hard drink, nothing but fun. Believe me, we'd earned it. Any rivalries we had were settled right on these courts. Skin-deep rivalries, nothing more than that. And forgotten in the lounge when the beer started flowing. Sorry, no."

Shephard was suddenly aware of the threadbare line of investigation that had led him to this point. Two dead people, each members of the same tennis club nearly thirty years ago. Datilla seemed to read his thoughts. He took up the racquet again, twirled it in his hand, waited for Shephard's next question.

"Whoever killed Algernon and Creeley didn't do it for money. He's left plenty of property behind in both houses. The killer threatened them both. He's doing what he says he'll do. Algernon was an older man who ran a stable and bet a little on the horses. Creeley was a civic-minded gal who stayed inside with a dog that couldn't bark. Algernon tried to warn her. Called twenty-four times and got a machine. I don't get it. Why would someone want to do that to an old woman like Hope Creeley?"

Datilla stared at the cement. He zipped up the windbreaker, then slowly unzipped it, his hand performing the action disconsolately, automatically. "I've been asking myself those same questions since I first heard about Tim." Datilla's eyes were moist. "Tommy, I can't imagine a reason. The harder I try, the less I believe it's happened. Maybe the killer picked out the two people who deserve it least. Is that a lead?" He smiled weakly and shook his head.

Shephard stubbed out his cigarette in an ashtray beside the bench and inquired casually if Datilla had any doubt that Burton Creeley had drowned.

"Not after I saw him in the morgue," he answered.

"By accident, I mean," Shephard corrected. "There was speculation in the papers, Joe, that it was more than an accident."

Joe Datilla's face darkened, but his blue eyes stayed cool, controlled. "Third-rate theories from fourth-rate newspapers, Tom. You've got to know how that works, after all the press you got last summer." His voice had heated. "Those bastards will print anything that takes up space. I resent what they implied when Burton died, and I'll never forgive our wonderful free press for that. It taught me a lot, though. Like keep your mouth shut. The week after Nixon resigned there were rumors in the papers that he was staying here on my boat, *Priceless*. Not true. But I wouldn't let the press in here to see for themselves, and they took me for part of a cover-up. Personal grudge, sorry."

Shephard nodded. Then: "Burton was cheating on his wife."

Datilla met Shephard's gaze with a deadpan expression, his eyes steady and calm. "Burt Creeley was a man of endless energy and enthusiasm," he said. "And some of those energies found regrettable outlets. Tom, I always thought he was foolish to risk what he had with Hope, but another man's business is just that. The woman he was seeing was sick. A slut. Nymph."

Datilla explained how Miss Helene Lang's application for membership had slipped by him. He usually screened the applicants, especially those applying to live at the Surfside, personally. Somehow, the beautiful and rapacious Helene had slipped in under the door. It was only after a time that she began to show her "true colors." Datilla said that after seeing what they were, he'd tried his best to stay away from Helene Lang.

"A man who can't control himself is a fool and a danger to himself," Datilla said. "I've seen a few get swallowed up by their own accidents. No one's perfect, Tom, but I could never see Burton and her . . . besides the fact she was built nice and knew how to show it off. Hope was lovely, too. There's a line you have to draw when what you risk is worth more than what you're getting. A sense of proportion. You don't bet a hundred to win fifty. Burton didn't make little mistakes like most of us. Too sharp. He must have saved them all up for a big one. Helene Lang was it."

"And did it cost him?"

"It must have. It cost his wife more, which was sad. And she handled it like the class act she was. Tremendous woman." Joe sighed again and twisted the racquet in his hands.

139

"She thought highly of you, too. Called you several times before she died, didn't she?"

Datilla glanced up, his face in a look of stiff amusement. "Oh? Well, of course, but how . . ."

Shephard explained the diary, while Datilla's face softened.

"Yes, naturally. Must be very interesting to read."

"Where did Helene go, when it was all over?"

"She was hospitalized for a nervous breakdown. Then she went back home. New England, I think it was." Datilla gazed pensively at the strings of his racquet, as if Helene Lang might materialize from the empty squares.

The silence became awkward, and Shephard let it stand. But again he felt his line of questioning double back on itself, forming a circle, a zero. Datilla was as cooperative as he could want. Why wouldn't something give? He watched a woman walk onto the balcony of a third-story penthouse, shake a beach towel, then disappear back through a sliding glass door.

"It's out of proportion, Joe," Shephard said listlessly, more to himself than to Datilla. "Like you say."

"What's that, the club?" Datilla followed Shephard's gaze to the penthouse.

"No, the killing. There's no sense of balance. It isn't formed correctly. It's like that bet in poker you talked about. Too much for too little. Unless we're talking about stakes that aren't on the table yet."

"It looks that way, doesn't it?"

"What do you get for the penthouse, Joe, ocean view?"

"Two thousand a month, plus membership and dues. That's the basic. You can write your own ticket from there but it only goes one way."

"A sweet few acres here, Joe."

"Seventy-five in all. Where else in Newport Beach can you find a parking lot with room in it?"

"A smart buy, the club."

"Tommy, I'll tell you something about this club. But while I do it, I want you to see something that I think you're going to appreciate. Come with me, let's take a little walk."

Datilla led them past the other courts, which were alive with players, shouts, the hollow pop of racquets hitting balls. He waved and nodded, and Shephard noticed that many of the players watched them walk by, their expressions locked into those reverential near smiles reserved for the rich.

"You say the club was a smart buy," Datilla began. "But what it really was was a lucky buy. I was just a shade over twenty when I came back from France and the war. I had two loves—tennis and cars—and my dream was to make enough money to give me both. A year later, I had a club and it was called the Surfside." Datilla paused to smile at a lovely brunette in a tennis skirt. She smiled back at him, then at Shephard. Maybe it *is* who you know, he thought abstractedly.

"Real estate was cheap then, so cheap you'd laugh if I told you what my first ten acres here cost. I didn't have a leg to stand on financially, but some friends arranged a loan through the bank. Collateral was my tennis racquet, I guess. Started with a clubhouse and a few courts, and when the membership began to pick up, I sunk what money I could into more land."

Datilla pointed ahead as they walked. Shephard followed his hand to the sprawl of apartments that loomed in the near distance. "All that was just bayfront sand," he said proudly. "And finally I bought it all up. By 1948 I had so many people joining this club I was turning them away, and still building as fast as I could to accommodate them. So I got my tennis, Tommy. Smart buy? Maybe. But I think that luck was a big part. Keeping this place going is harder than getting it built. When you accumulate things, you accumulate worry. I've lived by one philosophy since the club was built. I don't take chances. I cover my bets and play conservative. It's more important to protect what you have than to reach out for more, don't you think?"

"Right on, Joe," Shephard answered, wondering if there were enough common ground in their two ways of life to merit any understanding of Joe Datilla's philosophies. He thought of his ransacked apartment, comparing it to Datilla's Surfside.

The tennis area ended at a tall wing of apartments on the left and a large open patio to the right. Centered in the patio was an Olympic-sized swimming pool, in which a solitary swimmer—an older woman by the looks of her—churned methodically down the middle lane. They followed a walkway past the pool and its bright yellow deckside furniture, a tennis pro shop, an open-air lounge. The bar was already littered with afternoon drinkers, dressed in tennis clothes and chatting energetically. Shephard thought it looked like a commercial for something—beer, or the good life, maybe.

Then came the men's and women's spas, a low building surrounded by the unmistakable odor of sweat, steam, disinfectant. They turned hard right at the end of the men's locker rooms and descended a short flight of stairs that ended in a pair of blue doors. Datilla fumbled for his keys with one hand, but the other found the door open. He held it for Shephard and stepped inside.

The first thing that appeared out of the darkness was a tiny, poorly lit stand at the far end. Sitting under the single hanging lamp was a blue-uniformed guard, apparently reading. The door thudded shut behind him, then the entire underground cavern flashed alive with light. He felt Datilla's hand on his arm, guiding them toward glittering automobiles.

"My other love," Datilla's voice continued behind him. "My true loves, my wives, my concubines, my children.

These are my babies, Tom. Thirty-eight of them, counting the Sportster I use around town."

"Ah. The collection. I've heard about this."

They stopped. Shephard felt in need of a tour guide. Most of the cars were foreign, strange machines that he had rarely seen on the road, all polished to a frenzy of color and chrome. He recognized a Ferrari Boxer, a vintage Mustang convertible much like his own, an Alfa Romeo Veloce, but that was all. The rest evaded description.

"I could tell you about the Mondial over there in the far corner," Datilla said. "Or the Maserati here on the left, or the Silver Shadow in the middle there. But I'm not into cars for what they're worth, I love them for what they are. I've got a 'seventy Honda mini-car buried out there somewhere, a beautiful little machine that gets about sixty miles on a gallon of gas and corners like a go-kart. I've got a homely old Rambler here because at times I feel like a homely old man. There's a new RX-7 on the far side; it's a car that a million people own and a classic since it first came out of Japan. A car for every mood, Tom. They're here to impress nobody but me. I love them all the same, too."

Shephard gazed out over the cars.

"I've got a full-time guard to watch them, but not full-time enough," Datilla said. "Believe it or not, I lost one Monday morning. Somebody came right in and took it. Broke my heart. A red Coupe de Ville convertible, pristine and fun as hell to hit the town in on a summer night. Gone. Hope they find it soon."

"What year?" Shephard asked, warming to a possibility.

"Nineteen sixty-four."

"Monday morning you said? Late or early?"

"Must have been late. I tracked down the guard a day later and chewed his ass good. He said he left for an hour because he needed to go to the bank. Should have fired old

Mink, I suppose. Didn't even lock up. Shit, can you imagine?"

"Do you remember the plates, Joe?"

"Gave it to the Newport cops Wednesday. Hold on."

"I'll keep a special eye out."

Shephard watched as Datilla disappeared into the sea of cars, working his way to the tiny guard hut in the far corner. The timing was right, he thought. The car stolen Monday morning late, in time for a stop by Forest Avenue Books. But why hadn't it shown on the Stolen printout from Sacramento? Datilla came back with a grubby slip of paper, which he handed to Shephard, and the answer was clear: 1AEA 896. Different plates, different car. Just another finger pointing to the Surfside. Were they all coincidence? He pocketed the slip anyway, out of habit. Datilla thanked him profusely for the personal attention. Shephard showed the Identikit. Datilla looked for a long moment, shaking his head.

"Sorry, Tom. Kind of looks like anybody, you know? Anyway, I've bored you with my enthusiasms. Let's get up where the sun still shines." Datilla locked the doors behind them, and checked them twice.

The sunlight was dazzling.

"How about a tour of the club, Tom? Plenty you haven't seen."

Shephard offered his hand. "Joe, buddy, you've been a tremendous help. If you don't mind, I'll wander around a bit, then head back."

Datilla looked slightly disappointed, but rallied. "Fine, young man. Tell your father hello for me. And watch yourself around here, plenty of young ladies to get you in trouble. If any mention a taste for a distinguished gentleman of the older persuasion, give my number quick." Datilla pumped his hand, then turned and headed back toward the courts.

Shephard waited a moment, then backtracked to the walkway that led past the pool. The woman was still swimming; she stopped at the end of a lap and smiled at him, then pushed off.

The walkway ended at A Dock, where tinny Hawaiian music issued from the lounge. He stepped onto the wooden docking, feeling the gentle sway of the structure, watching the huge yachts dipping and rising slowly overhead. The sunlight blared off their white hulls. He squinted and read the names: *Priceless*, Datilla's vessel; *Interceptor*, *Marybeth*, *Comeback*. Above him, he watched a crewman dangle a broom over the hull of *Priceless* and scrub an invisible blemish. Keeping a ship like that clean isn't a job, he thought, it's a career.

Then, as surely as he was studying the yachts, Shephard knew that someone was studying him. The feeling came, passed, came again. When he turned to look over his shoulder, the woman from the swimming pool, dripping wet and balancing a highball in her hand, was looking at him from the A Dock lounge.

He turned back and meandered down to the lesser vessels of B Dock.

Footsteps on the wood, the clapping of sandals not in a hurry. Then a gruff woman's voice behind him. "Looking to buy?" it asked.

Shephard turned to face a pair of washed-out gray eyes, a deeply creased face, a head of dripping black and gray hair, two large bosoms. The highball tinkled in her hand and the scar on her wrist was obvious. "Not exactly," he said.

"I'm Dorothy Edmond. I used to own a Ditmar Donaldson ninety. John Wayne told me it was the only ship on the water he liked better than the *Goose.*"

"That's very nice."

"Don't bore me, young man. Phonies always bore me."

She cracked a shrewd but not unfriendly smile. "I've seen more of the world than you dream of and I'd go back for seconds if I had the time." He noticed that the eyes were red-rimmed and that her breath carried more alcohol than was missing from one highball. "Now, let me guess. You're a captain looking for a ship?"

"No."

"A mate looking for a captain?"

"No again."

"A tennis hustler looking for a match?"

"No."

"How about a dick named Tom Shephard wondering why two old-timers from the Surfside got burned up?"

He studied Dorothy Edmond's red-rimmed gray eyes, which said nothing back.

"Oh damn," she said suddenly, looking behind her down the dock. Joe Datilla was hustling toward them, tennis racquet in hand, cursing the crew of the *Priceless* as he went by. "Forget what I just said for a half hour. Then call me."

Datilla was dripping sweat. Must have been some bucket of balls, Shephard thought. He smiled quickly at Shephard, then turned his aggravated face to Dorothy. "Dot, trouble with Bank of Newport. Barnes and Kaufman are on their way here for bad news on the Carlsbad escrow. Meet them when they get here, keep them out of my hair for an hour while I run some figures. They're due at three. Hustle up, please, honey. I told you about this yesterday, dear."

"Oh, Joe, tell them to go home." She beamed, twirling the drink.

"That's ten minutes," he said quickly. "Go to, Dorothy. I need your persuasive skills."

She upped the glass and got only ice. "Just when I thought I had a young buck interested in my old bones. I'll get you for this, Joe Datilla."

146

Datilla grinned as Dorothy broke away and climbed the ramp back to the lounge. "Sorry, Tommy, these things come up. Anything I can show you?"

"Sorry to be in the way, Joe. I've got to head back. Just wanted a look at the fabled A Dock."

Datilla walked him toward the guard gate, most of the way in silence.

"I hope Dorothy didn't shake you up too bad. She's a great gal, but the liquor reaches the danger limit by about noon. Apt to say some pretty irresponsible things sometimes. Been social director here from way back."

"No problem, really." They shook hands again before Datilla veered hurriedly off toward the A Dock lounge.

Shephard was met by a red-vested valet at the guard house. He described his car and handed over the keys. Mink, he noticed, was still on duty, sitting alone on a stool. Shephard approached and offered a cigarette, which Mink accepted.

"Find a place?" the guard asked.

"Had a long talk with Joe. No openings, but I'll wait." Shephard lit a cigarette of his own, and decided to go fishing. "By the way, he asked me to tell you that Barnes and Kaufman canceled."

Mink responded wonderfully, reaching immediately for the clipboard. "Who?"

"Barnes and Kaufman, Bank of Newport. They were set for three."

"Not through this gate they weren't."

So Joe Datilla didn't like Tom Shephard and Dorothy Edmond together, Shephard thought. And why *hadn't* he fired Mink, anyway?

"Never mind, I must have gotten the message wrong. . . . Joe told me he got a Cadillac stolen Monday. Bad news when the thieves find their way into a club like this."

The guard shook his head and slammed down the clipboard. "Easy stealin' a car with no guard to watch it," he said flatly.

"Heard the guard had some banking," Shephard said optimistically, careful to attach no blame.

"Banking nothing," said Mink. "Joe told me to take the day off. It was my shift in the garage. Miss a day and lose a car. What luck. But the boss says jump, I ask how high. I needed a day off anyway. Who doesn't? Hell, he signs the paychecks."

The valet arrived with Shephard's car, screeching to a stop in the outbound lane beside the guard house.

Shephard tipped the boy heavily, lost in speculation. He turned south on Coast Highway, back toward Laguna, and stopped at the first pay phone he could find. At the end of half an hour, Dorothy Edmond time, he dialed her number. He was surprised to find her listed. The whiskey voice at the other end was unmistakable.

"Yes?"

"Dorothy Edmond, Tom Shephard."

"Who?"

"Tom Shephard. Just talked to you there at the club."

"I'm sorry but you didn't. I've been sitting in this apartment all day. Are you a crank?"

Shephard wanted a minute to consider the possibilities, but he didn't want to lose her.

"No, honey," he answered quickly. "Are you?"

She hung up.

He listened for a moment for any signal of intrusion on the line, but heard none.

When he called back, the line was busy, and when the operator broke in for him, she got only static. Off the hook, she said. Try later?

148

FOURTEEN

Chief Hannover was pissed. His voice over the office line was shrill, and when Shephard found him at his desk he was sitting upright, wide-eyed, and had managed to gnaw the end of a yellow pencil down to wood. He kicked out a chair to Shephard and slid backward in his own. Hannover was dressed as usual in an expensive suit that looked cheap on him, a three-piece gray silk outfit that seemed to shine, troutlike, at the wrong places. He leaned back to reveal dark crescents of sweat seeping onto the armholes of the vest. His hair, slightly too long, was held in place with spray. When Shephard sat, Hannover pounced on his desk intercom and ordered Cadette Annette to hold all calls for "one quarter of an hour." This done, he slid again on his chair, eyeing Shephard.

"I'll have to lapse into the colloquial in order to get my point here across with as much brevity as possible," he said, then fumbled in the box on his desk for a cigarette. Shephard lit it, and one for himself. Hannover squared himself in the chair. "We are fucked. Mayor Webb called me at home last night and we had a long talk. God, can that woman talk. To put it bluntly, Shephard, she's terrified, both personally and professionally. She herself received"— Hannover broke off the sentence to scoot forward, pick up a slip of paper, and wave it at Shephard—"thirty-six telephone calls between nine and noon today. All from horrified citizens wanting to know what is happening in their quaint little seaside town. And in turn, she asked me that same question. Shephard, you're familiar with the fate of Inca bearers of bad news?"

"They were beheaded."

"I felt quite like one of those unfortunates today when I tried to explain to her that we haven't even established a motive as yet. Luckily, we've progressed as a civilization since the times of beheadings. Instead, there has been a subtle improvement, which allows the offending messengers to erect a temple of truth or a cloud of smoke, as necessary, to trumpet or obscure their position. Of course you know what I'm talking about, don't you?"

"A press conference."

Hannover drew deeply on his cigarette, then looked at it. His voice was deep and smoke-choked. "You're going to handle it, Shephard. Two of the three networks are sending news crews, the *Times, Register, Pilot,* and all the local papers will be there. You don't look happy."

"I don't like reporters. And they don't like me."

"I can understand that. But as detective in charge, you are the best man for the job."

"What about Pincus in Community Relations? It *is* his job. . . ."

"No one believes Pincus," Hannover said glumly. The Community Relations Office had been his idea, a "liaison between the department and the community it serves." But the recently hired Pincus had turned out to be lazy, happy, and deeply indecisive, turning calls over to the chief rather than fending for himself. "The *Times* won't even talk to him anymore. So it's your show, Shephard. I know the press kicked you around a little up in L.A., but I'll tell you right now that the Orange County press is a different animal. Not so . . . carnivorous," he said, pleased with his word choice. He smiled at Shephard briefly. "I want to give you some basic parameters between which you should stay."

150

While Hannover talked about parameters, Shephard's mind wandered back to reporter Daniel Pedroza of the *Times*, who had hounded him so thoroughly after the shooting. He had become like a shadow, waiting for Shephard outside the station when he arrived at work, lingering in the parking lot at quitting time, tying up his phone line with innumerable calls, filing a mountain of stories. The stories called the integrity of Shephard and of the entire department into question. When Shephard quit returning the calls and refused further interviews, Pedroza had even showed up at his house one night. In fact, the night after Louise had said she was leaving him, and Pedroza had asked if they might talk about some "more personal aspects" of his post-shooting trauma. Shephard had hurled a near-empty wine bottle at the reporter, then read the next day of his "violently irrational" behavior. Pedroza hadn't mentioned the wine bottle.

Even Daniel Pedroza, however, was no match for the ACLU lawyer who had grilled Shephard at the inquest. The attorney had implied that the murder of Shephard's mother had stamped upon him a deep and malevolent hatred for "alleged criminal types." Deep in the bowels of L.A.'s City Hall, sweltering in the late September heat, Shephard's heart had pounded with such anger that he was sure it was being picked up by the reporters' tape recorders.

"Are we clear on those?" Hannover was asking. "Play them back, Shephard. It's important we present a united front at this point in time."

"Stress that the killings of Algernon and Creeley may be connected, or may not be. We don't want to arouse any more fears than we have to. Don't mention the threats, the eyelids, or the voice on the answering machine because we need something to use on a suspect. Stress again that the force has redoubled its efforts, and that a task force is working around the clock to bring a suspect under arrest. Remain calm, polite, and assured at all times. Pass out the Identikit sketches in case any of the local papers haven't seen them. And insist on makeup for my forehead because I'm sure to sweat under the lights."

Hannover nodded with approval throughout the litany, then smiled and leaned back again in his chair.

"You've got a mind like a steel trap, young man," he said finally. "And remember you're representing the city of Laguna Beach, home of the Festival of Arts. The conference is set for four, so you've got about five minutes to get handsome. Just like your father, Shephard, you're going to be a TV star."

The conference room was already steaming in the raw glare of the television lights when Shephard walked in. He sat down at the end of a long table, declined makeup, and broke into a sweat. Danny Pedroza sat down next to him.

"Thought I left you in L.A.," Shephard said.

"I thought I'd left you there, too." Pedroza looked at Shephard's head. "Somebody hit you with a wine bottle?"

"Just a hangover."

"I've been trying to get a job in Orange County for three years. You know, sun and waves and pretty girls on every corner. None of this kind of crap."

Shephard studied Pedroza's smooth, youthful face, the short black hair, the pearly grin. "Me, too. But people keep killing each other and reporters keep asking questions. No end to it, I guess."

One of the young cadettes walked into the conference room, drawing stares and a cumbersome silence as she came to Shephard and plopped a stack of Identikit sketches down on the table. When she left, Pedroza leaned closer. "What's this about the eyelids being snipped?" he asked in a whisper.

"News to me," Shephard said out loud, looking straight ahead. Where do they find out this stuff, he wondered.

"You denying it?"

"I never said it."

"Is it true?"

Shephard considered his response as Hannover's parameters dissolved in his mind. "What if it were?"

"Then I'd like us to print it."

"The chief wouldn't, Danny. We need something for the suspects to choke on."

"I can respect that."

"Would you?"

"I respected that wine bottle." Pedroza paused, then leaned closer again. "Both off?"

The NBC director was motioning for Shephard to stand, snapping his fingers and checking his light meter. Shephard nodded to Pedroza, returned the glare of the lights as best he could, then stood.

Looking out at the conference room, he saw only the blizzard of lights, hot and relentless, and heard the clicking of tape recorders, the shuffle of pens and pads. Shephard began his briefing, talking to the faceless crowd before him.

"Monday at six A.M. a routine Laguna police patrol discovered the body of Tim Algernon outside his home on Laguna Canyon Road," he heard himself drone. Good, he thought, maybe they'll all fall asleep. "The Orange County Coroner's office reported later that day that Mr. Algernon had expired from severe hemorrhaging in the skull caused by trauma. The trauma was caused by a rock." Shephard continued to stare into the camera, careful not to wipe his face with his hand, as he was tempted. "The body was then doused with common turpentine and set on fire. Three days later, on Thursday at approximately three P.M., the body of Mrs. Hope Creeley, age sixty-three, was discovered in her Laguna Beach home. Mrs. Creeley was pronounced dead by reason of severe burns early the next day by the coroner. Certain similarities that have occurred in the two cases open up the possibility that the murders may have been the act of one man." Hannover's absurd "parameter" rang somewhere in the back of Shephard's echoing brain. "But it is not our opinion at this time that the murders are definitely connected." He heard a low groan issue from the glare to his right, followed by a grumble from the other side of the table.

"Investigation has led us to believe that the suspect is a white male, age sixty, medium height and slight build. Eyes are blue and hair is gray, worn longish, and a beard. He may be driving a 1964 Cadillac Coupe de Ville, convertible, red. The plates are one-five-six DSN. At this point we have not established a motive. Questions?"

The voices blasted at him chaotically, like leaves blown by wind. They tangled all at once, repeated, dissipated to a few, then singled to one that issued from just behind the camera.

"Do you believe the same person is responsible for both murders?"

"We're not sure. There is a possibility."

The same voice: "How good is that possibility?"

"There are indications for and against. Speculation would be premature."

Then a woman's voice, harsh and hurried: "Then it's possible that there are two maniacs running around this town burning people to death?"

"We haven't ruled that out," Shephard said, nearly choking on the idea.

A new voice: "Was Mrs. Creeley sexually assaulted?"

"No."

"Was Mr. Algernon?" A grumble from the reporters.

"No."

The first voice: "You say no motive has been established. Can you tell us what motives have been ruled out?"

"Robbery. Substantial amounts of property were left at both scenes. No property that we know of has been taken."

The woman again: "Then in the absence of apparent motive, we may be talking about thrill killing?"

"That is a possibility."

A young man's voice: "Mr. Shephard, do you have a witness to either murder?"

"No."

"Where did you get the description of the suspect and his car?"

"I can't reveal that at this time." Shephard felt a fat bead of sweat travel down his forehead toward his nose. Should have taken the makeup, he thought. The lights in front of him burned into his eyes. No wonder they use bright lights for interrogation.

"Is the car stolen?" Good question, Shephard thought.

"We believe so." Then why no record in Sacramento?

"Was the rock that killed Algernon thrown or driven into his head manually?"

"Driven manually," Shephard answered.

Then the first voice: "Did Mr. Algernon and Mrs. Creeley know each other?"

"Yes." There was another rush of questions, which finally filtered down to one. His eyes burned.

"Do you believe they were involved in any illegal activity?"

"No, we do not."

The harsh woman's voice again: "Romantically? Were they involved with each other romantically?"

"No. They were friends at one time."

"What time was that?"

"Still friends, I mean. Friends for a long time."

"Do you think that this may be the work of more than one man?"

"We believe the suspect acted alone. It is possible that he had help."

The young voice: "What kind of help?"

"We have no evidence; it is simply not ruled out at this time."

"Do you think it is significant that both victims lived alone?"

"It is harder to kill two people than it is to kill one, if that's what you mean."

"Not exactly."

Then a woman's voice, harsh and fast, from the back of the room: "Detective Shephard, isn't it true that you resigned from the Los Angeles Police Department after the fatal shooting of Morris Mumford last year?"

Shephard stared lamely in the direction of her voice. "Yes, that is true."

Her voice again: "I'd like to know if the subsequent trauma of that shooting and resignation has in any way affected your handling of this case."

The room was so quiet Shephard could hear the whirring of tape inside the camera, or was it the whirring of blood inside his head? He silently cursed the woman, the light, himself. The silence was lasting too long.

"Of course not."

Her voice shot back quickly: "What about stress? I'm curious if stress has in any way impaired your search for what is obviously a single and very single-minded killer." Jesus, he thought, who is she?

"Stress? No, I don't think it has."

She was on him again. "We appreciate your avid concern for the facts, detective, but I'd like to know about your feelings. This is a small town whose murder rate has quadrupled in one week. The cases are being handled by a very young detective who was recently forced to resign from a larger and more potent force. What are your feelings now? What about your fears and doubts, Detective Shephard. Do you have any?"

The drop of sweat found its way to his nose. He wiped

it with what grace he could muster, then stared toward the voice as the lights bore into his eyes. He heard the door open and quietly close. His mind began to eddy: How was Cal's swollen eye? How much vacation time did he have after two months on the job? Was the table below him real wood or wood-look? He thought of Jane. Then he heard himself talking, slowly, conversationally, as if to a friend over the telephone.

"Fears and doubts? Sure, I've got the same fears and doubts you'd have if you walked into a bathroom and found a dead person in the bathtub. It scares you. It makes you feel cursed and unclean, like you want to take a long shower or swim way out in the ocean. And you doubt if the same man did the same thing the next night in the next house that you'd get there in time to prevent it. There's enough fear and doubt to choke on for a lifetime. As far as why I'm running this investigation, well, it's my job. I work here. That's all."

Shephard nodded once to the cameras, then sat back down, wiping his forehead with his sleeve. Pedroza whispered "Bitch" in his ear, then stood and disappeared. Shephard's eyes reeled from the lights. Blue dots spun and expanded, so clear and bright that they seemed real enough to reach out and touch. He clumsily removed a cigarette and someone lit it for him. A few of the reporters gathered in front of him, helping themselves to copies of the Identikit sketch, respectfully quiet. Then a stocky young blonde was standing in front of him, slipping a reporter's notebook into her purse and staring down.

"Tina Trautwein," she said, "*Daily Pilot*. I hope I didn't get too personal. Our paper believes in getting deeper than the headline." Then she turned with a swirl of light hair and muscled her way through the other reporters to the door. But Shephard never saw her go through it, buried as she was by an orb of bright blue light.

The technicians broke down the lighting tripods while the director ordered them to Algernon's Riding Stables for an "on-location background intro." The director lit a cigarette and leaned against the wall while his crew scrambled. "Tough job, eh, kid?"

"Beats washing cars," Shephard said without forethought.

He brought an Identikit sketch to the table in front of him and buried himself in it. The last of the reporters filed out. The face seemed pleased by the way the conference had gone: it looked up at him with a wry smile that seemed to say, "Well, Shephard, I'm so happy to hear about your fears and doubts. Wouldn't you like to know what's next?"

Next, he thought. Damn.

The door closed and the room was quiet. Finally. Peace and quiet. Then he was aware of someone sitting at the far end of the table, just on the fringe of his returning field of vision. He looked at her, then to the side, as he would at night to see a distant road sign. A young woman in a light blouse, tan arms, dark hair. Shephard rubbed his eyes and sighed, prepared for neither the wrath nor the icy beauty of Jane Algernon.

"I came to see you," she said. After the pressing voices of the reporters, her tone sounded subdued, reasonable, even pleasant.

"To sue me?"

"To thank you. For . . . helping me break through. I don't have a lot of people I talk to on a regular basis, so I'd kept a lot of things inside where they turned bad. You saw that, and I thank you for, well, for seeing it."

Across the table her eyes looked bright blue, and it wasn't the flash dot any more.

"You should have held a press conference," he said wearily. "They would have seen it."

Jane Algernon neither smiled nor spoke. She set a purse

on the table and brought out an envelope, then a small box, which she slid down the table to Shephard.

In the envelope he found Tim Algernon's bank statement, another snapshot of him, and a letter written to "Rita." The box contained a tooth of some kind, yellowed, small, not sharp.

"Buster dropped it," she said. "He's still a pup. The California Indians considered the teeth of the sea lion to be good luck. Good luck to you from Buster and me."

The change in Shephard's spirit was fundamental: he could feel something coming into him, other things going out.

"I let myself into your conference," she continued. "But when that woman started asking questions, I wished I hadn't. You handled it rather well. You said you wanted to go swimming in the ocean when you saw Hope Creeley. I knew what you meant because I do that every night. I swim in the ocean." She stood up and walked to the door. She shifted her purse from one shoulder to the other, then back again. "I guess I could stand here all day and move this silly thing around, couldn't I? What I mean is, I swim at Diver's Cove at nine every night, and if you'd like to swim tonight I'd . . . I wouldn't mind the company."

Shephard considered her loveliness, her rage, her strength, her pain, her invitation. As he looked at her, the list went on and on.

"I'd love to be the company," he said finally, and then she was gone.

The California DMV in Sacramento had unsnarled its computer jam sometime during Shephard's press conference. Pavlik had left a note on his desk in his inimitably cramped, precarious handwriting. The registered owner of the car bearing plates 156 DSN was Dick Moon of 4887 S. Coast Highway in Laguna Beach.

Shephard pocketed the note and slipped out the back entrance of the station, watching—out of habit it seemed by now—for Daniel Pedroza loitering near the Mustang. But his car was unattended, and he was relieved as he pushed it into gear and backed from the shade of an olive tree into the fierce Laguna sun.

Ten minutes later he drove into the parking lot of Moon Chevrolet and parked beside a new Camaro. The dealership owner was a portly man wearing a polka dot shirt with a collar so wide it looked like wings. He introduced himself as Dick Moon.

"Lot of people think we named this place after the moon," he said with a bright smile. "But Moon is me. Now, what can I get you into, young man?"

Moon's grin disappeared when Shephard expressed interest in an aging Cadillac with the plates 156 DSN. He waddled ahead of Shephard, leading them back to the sales office, where he consulted a logbook. Moon ran his fat finger down the column and shook his head.

"Got no such car on the lot. We got a sixty-nine Valiant with those plates, no Caddy."

"I'd like to see it," Shephard said.

Moon bit the end off a cigar and pointed it behind him. "She's round back," he said. "Real cute little thing."

Around back, Shephard found the cute little thing slouched alone beside the trash container for the parts department. The paint was peeling as if from a severe sunburn, the windows were clouded with dust, one tire was flat, and the car listed heavily to port. Moon arrived behind him, announced by the aroma of cigar.

"Not the car she used to be," he confessed.

But very interesting just the same, Shephard thought. Joe's Cadillac might be in service after all. "Where are the plates?" he asked, studying the naked plate holder dangling from the front.

160

"Stolen probably," Moon said. "Wouldn't be the first time."

Shephard rounded the car and found the back plate gone, too. Pinched Datilla's Caddy and swapped plates. Clean.

"How long has it been here?"

"Couple of months. Took it in trade, God knows why." Moon puffed thoughtfully. "Hey, GM's doing backflips to move these new Camaros. Car of the year. I'll get you into one for peanuts and give you top dollar for the Ford. What can you go each month?"

Shephard had knelt near the front of the Valiant, inspecting the license plate holder. "Oh, no thanks, Dick. Just looking today."

"Well, go ahead. And come back when I can get you into something you deserve."

Moon waddled away, trailing cigar smoke. Shephard tried the doors but found them locked. No wonder the Cadillac hadn't shown up on Sacramento's stolen list, he thought.

When he turned to head back to the Mustang, the bells of St. Cecilia's—whose towers rose just one block to the south—chimed a tuneful six o'clock. He stopped and listened, hearing the caller's voice imprinted over them, taunting Hope Creeley through her answering machine. Two points for the 4800 block of South Coast Highway, he thought, and for a moment experienced the cool anxiety of standing somewhere he didn't belong.

From the sidewalk in front of Moon Chevrolet, Shephard could see two pay telephones, one beside the gay bar called Valentine's, the other in front of a liquor store across the street.

First he called Pavlik, to report the stolen plates to Sacramento. Then he called Dorothy Edmond again. After a half dozen rings, her whiskey voice answered in a husky hello. She spoke quietly and sincerely, apologizing for evading him earlier, explaining that certain Surfside personnel were given to listening in at the club switchboard.

She insisted that they meet the next morning at eleven anywhere that served a decent Bloody Mary. They agreed on Kano's, a fashionable retreat in Newport Beach, that opened early on Saturdays for brunch and had a good bar.

FIFTEEN

Diver's Cove was dark by nine o'clock. Shephard picked his way down the concrete steps to the beach, which was foreshortened by high tide. He lit a cigarette and walked across the sand to the near side of the cove, where he sat on the hull of a beached catamaran. A light evening breeze tapped the halyard against the mast above him, ringing a pleasant tune that carried a short distance, then vanished. The rocks of the cove cut a silhouette against an indigo sky, while the ocean gathered and dispersed the lights of nearby houses. The moon had grown since he had last noticed it, perched above the tequila bottle held by Little Theodore, and now sat far offshore, spreading threads of wavering light into the water below.

He felt giddy, nervous. How long since he had known that expectant apprehension? His insides fluttered, settled. There was a sense of velocity, too, something like the first back-straightening jolt of the Jota in low gear, something one-way and irrevocable. He imagined Jane Algernon asleep on her father's couch, her legs tucked under the bright afghan. She said nothing about a swimsuit but he had stuffed one into the pocket of his jacket just in case. What

162

if she swam naked and expected the same of him? His stomach went queasy as his mind filled with scenes of his last woman: the glum apologies, the strained second efforts, the final capitulation followed by heavy doses of guilt and whiskey. And the worst part was that the desire was there, but fouled, short-circuited.

The hollow sound of wooden sandals on concrete echoed behind him. Shephard turned to see a figure in white descending the steps, then heard the thud of shoes hitting sand. He watched her stoop, pluck the shoes from the ground, and continue across the beach toward him, while her dress—he could see it was a dress now, white and loose —lifted in the onshore breeze. A large athletic bag hung from her shoulder. She stopped a few feet from him, backlit by the houses, one side of her face picking up the light from the moon. Shephard stood.

"There are only two rules I have out here," she said quietly. "One is no words, the other is no worries. Do those sound all right to you?" Behind her, a house light blinked off.

"They sound easy," he said.

"Here," she took his hand. "This way."

They paralleled the shore, moving north. Shephard stopped to take off his shoes and socks and roll up his cuffs. The water splashed warm against his ankles as they sloshed along the beach. Ahead of him he could see a tall outcropping of rocks in the near distance. When they got closer, a dark bird left the top with a heavy beating of wings. The waves, small and cylindrical, smacked sharply against the high-tide beach. Shephard thought about her rules. They seemed aptly chosen. Each time the brine swarmed around his feet and receded, he felt as if a measurable quantity of words and worries were being carried away by the sea. By the time they reached the rocks he seemed lighter, less bound to what was behind them. His heart pounded nervously.

The rocks formed an archway. Shephard's stomach fluttered again as they ducked into a darkened vault that was protected on three sides by rock and open at the top to the sky. Inside, it was quieter and warmer. He could hear the breeze whistling through the cracks, overtaken by the rhythm of waves.

A wide angle of light opened the darkness around him. He watched as Jane pressed the flashlight into the sand and set her bag beside it. Without looking at him, she turned away and began to unbutton her dress.

Shephard watched, dumbly rapt, as the dress slid from her back, revealing Jane Algernon's wide and slightly muscled shoulders. A swimmer's back, he thought, scalloped and lean, tapering to a narrow waist. Then, as the dress fell to her knees and she bent to step out of it, he studied her high, firm buttocks and strong thighs, which were sculpted flawlessly. Her legs were long and without waste. No bathing suits, he thought, as she wrapped a large towel around herself and turned to face him.

For a brief moment Shephard felt that rare emotion, the opposite of déjà vu: not that he had been there before but that he would never be there again.

Was it pleasure, invitation that crossed her face as she returned his stare in the dim light? Fear? He was aware of the moment as precious, inviolable, singular. It felt strange to be so sober, so acutely present. The ocean that rushed against the rocks was inconsequential and far away. She seemed to have gathered all his awareness into a single vector that, even without moving or speaking, she drew in toward herself.

Shephard turned and undressed, feeling her eyes on him as surely as she had felt his. The light went out and she found his hand again, leading him out to the darkness. They waded carefully through the tidepools until they hit the sand, and by the time she was waist-deep, Jane had slipped under a wave. Shephard followed, the warm water stinging the cut on his head, his belly touching the smooth sand bottom. He kicked and stretched his hands out in front, feeling another wave surging overhead, pounding his feet as he went under. How long since he had been in the water? He counted the years but lost interest. Up again, he could see that the water was faintly luminescent, tinged blue-white by the moon. Jane broke into a crawl stroke ahead of him. The flutter of her kick made a sparkling trail behind her, but she was a quiet swimmer and moved through the water with an effortless, languorous rhythm.

He kicked hard and pulled deeply to keep up with her, careful to leave a few meters between them. Past the waves he felt the bottom falling away and knew that even a few yards from shore the ocean was much the same as it was many miles out: strong, unfathomable, unforgiving of all that is not part of it. And just as the first lappings of the waves had seemed to draw little parts of him away with them, he could now feel larger portions leaving too. He recalled that he had been married once but wasn't sure to whom. He believed that he rented an apartment somewhere in the town behind them but couldn't quote an address. He knew that he was a cop on a murder case but couldn't remember the specifics. He wondered why he had ever quit surfing. But the regret soon vanished. He didn't know why and didn't want to know. Was it possible to continue this way to Hawaii, or perhaps to an uninhabited tropical island where he and Jane could live on fish and fruit, procreate wildly, found a race? It seemed a possibility.

Then, ahead of him, Jane Algernon's face collected in the darkness and it was smiling.

"Are you scared? The rocks are under us, not far," she said. Shephard could feel the churning of her legs as she kicked to stay afloat. Her hair was slicked back and the bones in her face caught the moonlight.

"No. Are you?"

"I do this every night." Her voice was a whisper, excited and conspiratorial. "This is as far away as you can get from yourself and still get back. Do you know what I mean?"

"I feel it. I couldn't have said it."

"It's reductive. I'm Jane Algernon and you're Tom Shephard. That's all I know right now because compared with this ocean, nothing else matters. I know when I get back that everything will make sense again. Different sense, but still sense." She lapped up a mouthful of water and sprayed it into the air. "Look. She's our mother. She's our great organizer."

"You broke your rules," he said, moving closer.

"They don't apply out here. Nothing applies but what you are right now. What are you?" Her breath smelled as if it came from somewhere rich and clean.

"Words or no words?"

"Whatever it takes, detective."

The months of inertia changed to months of hunger as Shephard reached out and placed his hands on Jane Algernon's face. He could feel her legs and arms straining as he eased her still closer, close enough to taste the warmth of her breath. His legs pumped the water. Inside him he felt a sweet riot breaking out, birds on the wing, electric, agitated, nerve-spun. Her mouth was warm and the water running around it was cool and salty. He kissed it, then across her cheek and down her neck—she said something but he didn't hear what—until he dropped his hands to her waist and lifted slightly, bringing her breasts high enough to take one nipple between his lips as gently as if it were a drop of water. She pressed against him, legs still lunging, arms falling to his buttocks then around, and Shephard realized his strength as she took him in her hands, tenderly, like a treasure consigned to her care. Their legs mingled, locked, released. He closed his eyes and found her mouth again; he was streaking

166

through space. His hand fell to her legs and she eased them apart, his fingers finding warmth and slick abundance, a woman's quiet affirmation that even the ocean could make no less of. Shephard could feel it around his fingers, his palm, as if it were draining, spilling in a rush. And while he pushed inside her she climbed him, arms around his neck, the bottoms of her thighs around his ribs, her warmth breaking away from his hand and colliding with his stomach, hot where the cool water had been. He churned harder to support them both, guiding her buttocks down, around him, then moving inside her, a flawless connection that began tentatively and went deeper while she kissed his mouth, nose, ears, eyes. She whimpered with each snap of his legs and he hoped that he would be strong enough. Moving forward, he found a rock and braced his feet against its rough edge. She leaned back and fanned her arms in the water. Her torso shone pale and slick in the moonlight and Shephard could see her hair floating around her head. He brought her harder against him.

She cried out as the first voltage erupted inside her. He could feel it, like electricity, quick and tense. Then another, and she groaned and drew herself back up to him, arms locked around his neck as another surge broke inside. Shephard slowed, resting as they sank down, then pushed off the rock for a heave upward. She clutched his flanks with her thighs. They strained together, until Jane's legs stiffened, rigid around him. He was aware of her shrieking, of his own rapid breathing, of the weakening of his legs. But the first stirrings of his own release brought their own energy, and while she clung to his body with ebbing strength he worked the last of his power, slowing, then feeling everything inside him moving to her. The frenzied birds took flight, and Shephard lifted his face skyward as if to watch them go, as a rich release shuddered out of him and seemed to last for hours while she tightened and drew it out, and out, and out still more, so that when it ended Shephard thought it was still going out of him and maybe always would be.

Floating. Face to the stars on a bed of ocean. Beside him a woman's hair, blending with his own. Her arms working the water slowly, her breath still rapid but descending. Shephard was aware of his own heartbeat, magnified by the water, a fast thudding, a precise mechanism. Funny how the stars multiply the longer you stare, he thought. A dozen, two dozen, then a thousand pinpoints in the fabric of night. Then Jane asking if he saw the Big Dipper—yes—and a thousand other scenes nobody has named. And while her breathing slowed still more she asked him to swim another hundred yards out or so, to the Inside Indicator, a rock, her goal on nights such as this.

They breaststroked slowly to the Indicator, whose side was cold and sharp under Shephard's fingers as he reached out to steady himself. "The real lovers go to the Outside Indicator," she said. "We may go there some night." Both resting on the rock, they kissed again, but long and slow this time, a kiss only for the enjoyment of kissing. Then she slipped down and away and disappeared under the water until she surfaced a few yards closer toward shore, stroking evenly for the cove.

Exhausted, he followed.

Back in the cave they dried—she had brought two towels—and faced each other as they dressed. From her bag she brought a small Thermos and two cups, which she filled with coffee that was still steaming. She packed the flashlight last and they walked unsteadily back down the beach, and up the concrete steps to the sidewalk.

"Back to the real world," he said. But it seemed intensified, hyper-real. He heard the faint patter of a moth in the lamplight above them, watched a spray of headlights from an oncoming car, turned back to Jane Algernon, whose face was beautiful and calm. "Let's go to the hotel. Have a drink. We missed the sunset but we can see the moon."

"No, Tom. But thank you. Be my friend. I need time. Please."

Shephard considered her words, her face, the beauty of her body. And it seemed that for what she had offered, she was asking little in return.

She came close to him and wrapped her arms around his neck, bringing his mouth close for a kiss. She rested her head on his chest for a long moment and when she turned her face to him he saw that she was crying.

Then she was moving down the sidewalk, the sound of wooden sandals on concrete, the moth above her head tracing halos of light in the beam of the streetlamp.

SIXTEEN

Shephard got Marla Collins's number from the operator, took his telephone to the center of the floor, and sat down. He was chilled and sandy, but the salt felt rough and good on his skin. Cal took an interest in the salt, licking his elbow until Shephard spilled him over for a belly scratch. Cal quivered a hind leg as if he were doing it himself. Marla Collins sounded less businesslike than she did at South Coast Investigators, her voice slurred and nearly obliterated by loud music.

"Marla, this is Randy Cox. I met you at work. . . ."

"Randy Cox, you're as phony as a flocked Christmas tree," she said without humor.

"I'm not much on flocked trees myself. I suppose Bruce blew my cover. I'm Tom Shephard, Laguna cops."

"Well, I'm still just plain old Marla, so what do you want?"

"You don't sound too happy."

"It's Friday night and I'm having a party. Except I didn't invite anybody. The wine is gone and the record skips. Other than that I'm happier than hell. Tommy, dear, excuse me while I pour a vodka." The line banged at the other end and Shephard heard the last of a Pretenders song before she picked up the receiver again. "Don't mean to pout. Now, what do you want from Marla Collins?"

"I want to know who Bruce Harmon works for. Any and all clients over the last two months." The record ended and Shephard heard ice clinking in a glass.

"Bruce wasn't too happy when you left that day."

"I wouldn't be happy if I was covering up a murder."

"Oh my. Don't you coppers lean toward melodrama."

"A man named Tim Algernon was burned to death Monday morning in Laguna. No melodrama. The guy who did it checked into a hotel an hour later. But he had a visitor before I got there. The visitor was your Mr. Harmon, but he didn't bother to use his real name. And since he says he's engaged by an attorney, that's all he'll tell me. Anybody with air in his lungs could tell there's more." The ice clinked again and Shephard heard Marla Collins gulp.

"I don't know how much air I've got left, but I *do* have a job. That's not all bad."

"I can pay you a little."

"You missed the point by half a mile. The point is that people have a right to do legal work, right? I mean, what if Bruce is on the up and up?"

"Then that's where it will end. I was hoping you could tell me that I'm wasting my time. Maybe he's got a legitimate concern. Tell me he does. Make me happy."

There was a long pause at the other end. Shephard heard the crackle of a match being struck close to the receiver.

"You know, Shephard, and bear in mind that this is a bottle of Zinfandel and a stiff vodka talking, I must say that I'm a little disappointed in your call. I thought that maybe this Randy Cox thought plain little Marla had her charms."

"Maybe he did."

Another long pause. "Sorry. I say things I shouldn't when I'm pissed. Do them, too."

"And regret them?"

"Sometimes I take the chance. I'd take it tonight. Busy?"

"Somebody just took the same chance and she looked a little bad when she walked away. That might make a difference to us both."

"If you mention it, it does. Look, Shephard. Call me back sometime. I'll think about it. I'm not in the business of biting the hand that feeds me. Tell the truth, I'm not sure if I like you or not."

"Neither am I. But I am sure that Bruce Harmon has been a few places he didn't belong. He seems to show up close on the heels of dead people. You can tell me who pays him to do it."

Shephard could hear her draw on a cigarette. When her voice came back, it was thin and smoke-filled.

"He's such an ass," she said flatly. "Nothing surprises me any more." He thought she was about to talk, but she offered only a quick cheerio and hung up.

At eleven o'clock he watched the rerun of his father's Sunday sermon on Wade's TV channel, KNEW. The service was unorthodox by denominational standards, a Church of New Life trademark. First, a gospel rock group called The Word took the stage and launched into a country-and-western ballad based on the life of Christ. The church cameramen moved in and out for close-ups, fades, montage shots

171

of the band, and intercut them with frequent moves to the audience. Shephard studied the faces. They were young and healthy, attentive to the music. The camera found a young mother and her infant, whom she was rocking gently to the beat of the song.

Three songs later the band left the stage and his father strode on, dressed as always in a light suit and white shirt, open at the collar. His hair shone silver in the bright lights, his face was flushed, rosy, alive. He took his place behind a modest pulpit and raised his hands for the applause to stop. When it did, he smiled into the camera and studied the faces before him.

"When I look out to your faces I see the power of the Lord at work," he intoned. "Praise Him!"

"Praise the Lord," his audience shouted back.

He smiled again, then leaned forward and looked at someone in the first row. "Very few of us here this morning really *know* each other," he began. "I see husbands and wives, brothers and sisters, good friends. But of the thousand people in this temple now, all worshipping Him, how many do you really know?" He searched the audience as if trying to answer the question for himself. "I would think that no one here today truly knows more than two or three of the people sitting in this House of God." Then quietly: "I know I don't."

He leaned back, looked down in front of him, then back up to the cameras. "I heard a joke the other day about a person from Poland. And one the day before that about a person from Mexico. And one about a Jewish man, one about a salesman, one about a black. You have heard the same jokes. These jokes get laughter, don't they? Do you think they are funny? I have to confess that I sometimes do, until I stop for just a moment to examine why. Do you know why we laugh? We laugh because jokes like these give us the chance to share one of our most common traits. A trait that many of us have in abundance, and all of us have in some small measure at least. *Ignorance.* We delight in sharing our own ignorance of other people.

"When we laugh at these jokes, we are not laughing at the Polish man, or the Jewish person, or the traveling salesman. We do not *know* them. We do not know the person in the joke. And to relieve ourselves of that duty, we accept the joke and believe that one race or type of person is lazier, dumber, more penurious than another. This, my friends, is what passes for funny. And this, my friends, is ignorance."

Wade leaned back, then turned and lifted his palm in the direction of the cross behind him. The camera lingered on it, then returned to him.

"Jesus knew these people. He told us to love them as we love ourselves. Jesus would not have laughed. Jesus saw the soul. And knowing that we could not do as He did, He offered us simple advice: 'Judge not, lest ye be judged.' "

Shephard watched his father lean forward and study the faces in front of him. The smile was gone, replaced by an expression of challenge.

"Many years ago, before I knew the Lord, I was walking down a street in Laguna Beach. I saw a man walking toward me. He was old and his clothes were tattered and his beard was long and stained. So when he veered in my direction, I told myself I *knew* this man. I had seen many like him, in many cities around the world, men with the same thirsty look in their eyes. Men who had given up on the world. Men who found their peace in a bottle. And because I was young and brash, and knew everything about the world, I told myself I would trick him. So when he stopped in my path and opened his mouth to speak, I spoke first. I said, 'Buddy, can you spare a quarter for a little wine?' "

Wade chuckled. His audience chuckled, too, uneasily. He pushed forward again on the podium. "He looked at me, surprised, I thought, that I had beaten him at his own game.

173

Then he rummaged through his pockets and brought out a quarter and a booklet. And he said to me, 'Take this, too, young man, and read it while you drink the wine.' It was a small, worn booklet containing the sayings of Jesus Christ, who in the beginning said, 'Judge not, lest ye be judged.'

"And I will tell you, I felt small. Small and ignorant and foolish. So, when I see someone I do not know, or hear a joke about someone I do not know, or hear rumors about someone I do not know, I think back to that day and see that old man's face as he offered me the quarter and the sayings of Jesus. Judge not, judge not and you will not have to worry about being judged yourself."

Shephard got a beer from the refrigerator, then flipped to the eleven o'clock news, where he saw himself standing in the harsh lights of the conference room, droning through his opening remarks. He looked nothing like the man on KNEW: his face was a sickly white and a glaze of sweat shone on his forehead. There was no life in his voice, it could have been the fabrication of a computer.

The anchorman's voice sounded over his own: "In an interesting sidelight to this story, it was the same Detective Tom Shephard in charge who recently resigned from the Los Angeles Police Department after the fatal shooting of a black youth last year. That killing was the twelfth last year by LAPD officers. . . ."

As he spoke, the conference footage gave way to a grainy, late night recording of the Mumford scene. Shephard watched as two officers carried the body toward a waiting van, its red lights pulsing. In the background was Morris's home, and somehow the news crew had rounded up his father and mother, who stood on the sidewalk where their son had fallen, staring at the camera while a reporter pressed a microphone toward them. The woman wept uncontrollably while the man, his eyes wide with sadness, tried to explain that Morris was just a kid.

174

"Detective Shephard, thirty-two, had this to say when questioned about living with the stress of a fatal, officer-involved shooting," the newsman continued, and the footage changed back to the Laguna police conference room, where Shephard stared stupidly into the camera and asked, "Fears and doubts? Sure, I've got the same—"

He flipped the channel back to his father's sermon and uncapped the beer. Wade was talking about the inner life and how the person who is beautiful on the outside can harbor a "heart of sickness," while the person with a diseased body can harbor "a heart of truth and beauty."

Shephard gulped down the beer and applied Wade's theory to Wade. Did he know his father? Maybe. Did he understand him? Maybe not. He thought back to the man whom he had grown up with, the cop who drank hard and came home at night to roam the house mournfully as if it were a city gutted by plague. Somehow, young as he was, Shephard had thought he understood. His father was simply looking for someone who was no longer there. Just as he was. Just as he had sometimes wondered what his mother's hair felt like, or the sound of her voice.

And he had understood the man who would disappear for long weekends fishing in the mountains and never come home with fish. Shephard understood that it was the mountains that drew him, not the fish. He had known the man who attacked everything he did with a terrible intensity, the Wade who had painted a strike zone on the garage door for his son to pitch against, then bludgeoned the door full of holes with a baseball bat when the zone came out crooked. He had known the man who walked purposefully down the center of the pier once a month and fell off into the darkness without so much as a look beneath. Somehow, he had even understood this: Wade was simply trying to lose himself. Shephard had even emulated this strange midnight ritual. He thought of those nights when his father left "for a walk,"

175

and he would start up his small motorcycle, crisscrossing his way out Laguna Canyon Road, forcing the oncoming traffic to career out of his way, to screech in panic stops.

It made sense. Lose oneself. Was it finally to find oneself, as Dr. Zahara said?

And he understood the Wade Shephard who had taken him out to dinner the night before he left for the Police Academy in Los Angeles. Wade had drunk profusely and encouraged Tom to follow. They obliterated their own good sense by ten, and by midnight, sitting in the corner of a noisy Laguna Beach saloon, his father had taken on that glazed look of a drinker who simply cannot put himself under. The elusive wave of darkness wouldn't find him. And at exactly 1 A.M.—Shephard had looked at his watch for some reason just before it happened—Wade's face had drained of color, his eyes had widened as if someone had just put a match to his foot, and he had slumped forward, knocking the small table and its drinks onto the floor.

He understood: it had been coming all night.

But the face on the screen belonged to a different animal, Shephard thought. It was fuller, and his smile had blossomed into a happy, generous gleam. His eyes were wider, and clear. The expression on the Reverend Wade Shephard's face said, "I'm here, take me, I will be of help to you." Even his voice had changed.

Shephard searched that face for answers. Were the dark eyes of Wade the Cop simply searching for what Wade the Reverend had found? Was the monthly jump from the pier only a preparation for the leap of faith? Was the anger a pathway to patience?

Shephard thought back to the first and only time that Wade had told him about the death of Colleen. It was early evening and he was in his room, thinking of the next day, his first day of school. He was counting dust specks in a shaft of sunlight that slanted through the window. Wade came in and sat quietly on the bed, his face grave and dark. He held a newspaper clipping, which he stared at for a long moment before he spoke. Then he told Tom that his mother was dead, as he knew, and that she had been killed by a man with a gun. The man's name was Azul Mercante and he had broken into their house when Colleen was alone. He had tried to take advantage of her in a way that men could do to women. But his father had come home and fought with Azul, who used the gun on Colleen before Wade could stop him. Azul had gone to prison, and would be there for many years. Fingering the news clipping with a trembling hand, Wade had showed it to his son. Too young to read, Shephard had merely looked at the pictures, one of his mother and one of his father. Wade explained that Colleen was safe and warm in heaven, where good people go. If other children in kindergarten talked of their mothers, then Tom would have to understand that he could not. This was nothing to be ashamed of. All he needed to know was that Colleen had loved him more than anything else in the world and she always would. Shephard had nodded and understood: after all, it was rather simple, wasn't it? His father hugged him, and hid his face as he walked out of the room and shut the door behind him.

He had happened across the news article and photos a year later, but shut the drawer quickly when he saw what was in it. His father's explanation was enough. She was safe and warm in heaven where good people go. Besides, he had thought of her from time to time, and built an image of her, a voice, a feeling. At times, he knew she was nearby, looking in through a window perhaps, or somewhere under the bed, making sure that he was all right. And as warm and substantial as Wade was, when Shephard cried with the pain or humiliation that only the young can feel so desperately, it was always Colleen's breast that took his tears. She was there, he knew it. She just was not the kind of mother you could see.

And twenty-five years later, as he sat in the living room of his naked apartment, he felt her presence still. A sensation from something no longer there, from a phantom limb, from the ghost who had given him life.

He had nearly dozed off when the phone rang. It was Jane Algernon.

"I didn't mean to be short," she said quietly. "I didn't mean it that way. You made me look at myself. You made me feel something again. Thank you, Tom Shephard. And I want you to know I'll do what I can to help you. I owe it to whoever else might be next. Maybe I even owe it to you."

"Don't try to do too much. You can get too close to things sometimes."

"I've spent most of my life trying to stay far away."

Shephard pondered her words. What a strange, fine thing it was, to be called on the telephone. He wondered what to say, and had just settled on *sleep well tonight, Jane,* when she put the phone back in its cradle.

SEVENTEEN

He had almost passed the darkened booth in Kano's when a cigarette lighter clicked and a long orange flame coaxed the face of Dorothy Edmond from the shadows. Shephard sat down and found himself surrounded by the smell of smoke and lilac perfume. Her face was made up cadaverously. The deep lines that had shown up so clearly in the sunlight were now buried in powder; the red-rimmed gray eyes were framed in a glittery makeup that caught the light of the table candle; her full lips had been painted an unnatural violet. And the gray-black hair that had dangled nearly to her shoulders on the Surfside dock was now hidden beneath a lavender scarf that was pinned on one side by a diamond cluster. Shephard settled into the overly luxuriant booth. The restaurant seemed barely living: a man in a dark suit hunched over a drink at the bar, while near the window a young couple sat with their backs to the lounge, silently watching the ships bobbing in the harbor.

A waitress appeared. Dorothy Edmond tapped her empty glass with a pale, jewel-heavy hand, and Shephard ordered a beer. As she turned to watch the waitress leave, Shephard noted the handsome profile of her lined face. Beautiful, he thought, and corrupted. Like obscenities in Spanish. Her black dress was cut low enough to reveal a withering, sun-dried cleavage. She brought her hand to her mouth and quelled a rattling, phlegmy cough.

"That cough is my best friend, detective. We go everywhere together." As she studied him, Shephard felt like a slave being inspected by a prospective buyer.

"Joe wasn't too happy to see us talking," he said finally.

"Joe isn't happy about anything he can't control," she answered, as if it were an aside to be dispensed with quickly. "You probably noticed that he plays tennis without a partner. Fewer surprises, and only one winner."

The drinks arrived and Shephard reached for his pocket, but Dorothy cut him off. "We're on a tab," she said. "I'd wear a hole in that pretty young hand of yours if we weren't." The waitress laughed with the forced enthusiasm reserved for good tippers. When she had gone again, Dorothy sipped her drink—Shephard noted that it was straight gin—then coughed into her hand. "Are you happy?" Her voice was raw and low and she asked the question as if everything that would follow depended on his answer.

"Reasonably. I got divorced last summer and pistol-whipped last Monday, but I'm a strong finisher."

"Trifles," she decided after a long pause. "It doesn't really matter because you'll be less happy when you leave here, and less happy than that later. Welcome to the club."

"Are my dues current?"

Dorothy Edmond set down her glass and shot him an inhospitable glance. "Don't be glib, young man. And understand two things before we go any farther. One is that I'll tell you nothing that isn't true. The other is I'll tell you nothing I don't want to. We can get along as two people helping each other, or you can heave your bureaucracy at me. But it won't work. I don't mind hell, I've been there."

Before Shephard could form a reply, the woman's face contorted and her hand shot up with a handkerchief in it. The cough exploded as she turned her head away.

"Bless you," he said.

"Yes, God bless Dorothy." She pulled a long cigarette from a silver box on the table and Shephard lit it. "I'm going to tell you a little story, detective. When it's over, I might entertain a question or two like you did on TV last night. Until then, you just listen.

"It begins with a young man named Joe, who was one handsome devil and a good tennis player. He served his country in the war, then settled on the coast along with a million hopefuls like him. His family was in Georgia, living on a rather large estate that wasn't theirs. His father was the groundskeeper, his mother a maid. Young Joe picked up his tennis on the estate courts, made love and proposed marriage to a bitterly ugly daughter, and was ejected from the scene with dispatch. Poor man, it must have been like sitting in a restaurant where you can't afford anything on the menu." She drew heavily on the gin.

"And young Joe was a dreamer. He dreamed of his own estate; of registering the name Datilla on the society pages; of money, class, power. A common enough dream. But Joe knew that to dream is to sleep, and he was no sleeper. He fell in with some rich friends in Newport Beach—Pasadena wealth summering in Orange County. Mostly the women. In Newport Beach you are society if you look society and act it. Joe did, and some friends pulled strings for a nice loan to start a club. A tennis club, ritzy and exclusive. His meager capital required a partner. Call him Burt. And together they bought a hunk of the California coast so cheap you'd laugh if I told you how much. The first courts went up a few months later, with a small clubhouse and a lounge.

"Everything worked. Burton was an accountant by training, and he knew how to maximize the money. Joe was a hustler and knew how to make rich people feel rich. His years as a servant's son paid off regally. After the war there was a hell of a rush into Orange County, and they'd bought in just before it started. A rush and a baby-boom, detective, which deposited on our shores a million happy infants like yourself. And for every new member who joined and paid the handsome dues, Joe and Burt took a little money aside and put it back into the Surfside Club. It grew like those babies did. It was strong, healthy, and happy. They incorporated and took thirty percent each for controlling interest."

Dorothy took a long drink from her gin and lit another cigarette. Shephard's beer had scarcely dwindled.

"But it didn't take a snake to point out the apple," she continued. "By 1950, the land value had gone up by half. Members and money seemed to fall from the clouds. Apartments, suites, two restaurants, a dock modestly named A Dock by pedestrian Burton. The sailing contingent was something they hadn't catered to or banked on, but Joe saw they were naturals for his Surfside. So Joe and Burt began to disagree. They were faced with a fortune that neither one even imagined when they started. Why two people can weather the hard times together and then fight when the sun shines is a question that I've never been able to answer. But, hell, it happens to marriages all the time.

"Joe saw the club as a big but exclusive plantation, like the one he grew up on. A money-maker plain and simple. But Burt began talking about incorporating as a municipality. He was talking about a sprawling little city on the coast, where people might buy in at a reasonable rate. He saw a planned community, with its own shopping centers, private beaches, a progressive school system. He was thinking democratic. He was talking to the papers and getting a bit of the spotlight that had always been Joe's. All Joe could do was smile and play along. Like any good businessman, he knew the value of sterling public relations.

"Not falling asleep, are you, detective? The story is just starting to get good." She drank again from the gin, and though she was nearly finished with her second double, Shephard saw no change in her pale gray eyes.

"Burt was a married man, but he was in love, too, and it wasn't with his wife. You might call the other woman Helene. They were not altogether discreet, Burton and his mistress. His wife, Hope, remained in a state of disrespectful shock and made no waves. Helene was a wonderful mistress, I suppose, and a clever woman. I might try to explain to you how she got Burt to will his thirty percent of stock to her, but I never really understood it myself. She was a detestable woman in my view, but she got what she wanted, almost all the time."

Dorothy had just pronounced her judgment on Helene when she was rocked by another spasm of coughing. Shephard wondered for a moment if she would get her breath again. Then, as the silence settled around the table, she brought out another cigarette and accepted the light from Shephard.

"You're pretty," she said, as disinterestedly as if she were commenting on the weather, or on a dress. "You looked like a real nervous young man on the tube last night. I flipped channels to compare you to Wade. Well, put it this way, if you're interested in a broadcasting career, don't be." She eyed him lasciviously, which Shephard found unnerving. The wrinkled breasts flattened under her dress as she leaned back for a deep drag on the cigarette.

"I'm just a cop for right now."

"So," she continued. "When Burton drowned in the bay one night, the Surfside suddenly had a new partner. Helene and Joe were now in control, and they were delighted."

Shephard weighed her words against what he knew of human behavior. "Joe and Helene drowned him?"

Dorothy set her drink on the table, fitting the round bottom into an imaginary circle on the wood. "It's so nice to talk to someone who understands," she said.

Shephard also weighed her smile against what he knew of human behavior, but nothing came out of it. It was a familiar, knowing smile, but beyond that there was something relieved, almost confessional about it. As he looked again into her eyes, he felt himself in the presence of someone whose life was nothing like his own. She seemed to have orbited elsewhere, seen different places, answered to different codes. He wondered if this was the difference experienced by the rich. But he wondered, too, whether Dorothy Edmond had enough money in her purse to pay for the drinks.

"Joe and Helene drowned him," she said, repeating his words. Coming from her, they seemed to mean something altogether different. "You see, Helene never really gave a damn about Burton. She and Joe saw the possibility and decided to give it a try. She would pretend love for Burt, and Joe would kill him when the stock was within reach. It wasn't very imaginative, but it was functional. Joe always had a way with things that worked. That was 1951, if you're keeping track," she said. "And it almost didn't work. You'll be especially interested in this part, Tom Shephard, both as a man and as a student of murder. That is what you are, right? Burton swam every night, sometimes in the channel in Newport, sometimes south at Diver's Cove in Laguna." Shephard imagined the Inside Indicator rough against his hand, the warmth of Jane's lips as she kissed him there.

"Yes, I've been to the cove," he said.

"Nice place to swim. The plan was to bring some of Joe's not very respectable friends down from L.A. to do the job. And to do it in the Newport waters where Joe's friends on the department would be slow to consider it as anything more than an accident. But Joe's L.A. friends didn't know the Newport Channel from Minneapolis, and they followed Burton to Laguna one evening and held him under at Diver's. By the time they got halfway back to L.A. and called in their results to Joe, Burt's body was floating in unfriendly waters. Of course, one phone call was all it took for Joe to get still another friend—isn't it interesting how many some people can acquire?—to rescue poor Burton from Diver's Cove and bring him north to the channel rocks. Those rocks did a nice job of ruining any evidence of struggle. And he was a tough little man, Burton. There must have been quite a struggle."

She coughed more quietly. Shephard sipped his beer and decided against a cigarette.

"That's just a little sidelight I thought you'd be interested in," she continued. "The papers even had hold of it. A couple of service station men recognized Burton as a customer the night he supposedly drowned in Newport. But the Newport cops closed the case, and the Laguna cops had no reason to open it back up in their own front yard. Would you have?"

For the first time, Shephard thought that she was playing with him.

"You might have to," she said.

"What happened to Helene? Back to New England?"

"Yes. New England. That's as good a place as any, don't you think?"

He weighed her words against his own circumstances, trying desperately to get a foothold on the way she thought. To see the world—if even just one corner of it—the same way Dorothy Edmond saw it. Certain images gathered in Shephard's imagination. The peaceful smile that Dorothy had offered Joe Datilla on the dock, her subservient role as emissary to the fictional bankers, her inviting attitude, the partially exposed breasts. Had she herself been hopeful of Joe's attentions? Had she perhaps been in love with Burt? Was everything she had said some massive, choreographed lie? The liquor was enough to twist her, he thought.

In times of confusion, Shephard resorted to the obvious: "Tim Algernon and Hope Creeley got burned to death in my city last week. What does all this have to do with them?"

"My, my," she answered quickly, as if he had just taken a swing at her, "how the young man bucks. I'll bet you're a tiger in bed, telling all those little beach girls just where you like it best."

He tried to think a way into the mind of the woman who sat next to him, but again he could not.

Shephard was never sure if he could have prevented what happened next, or if he had caused it, or if it was simply the last act in a script she'd written—one he couldn't understand. With one hand Dorothy Edmond snapped her fingers in the air, and the dark-suited man at the bar snaked off his stool and moved toward them. With the other she brought a large white envelope from her purse and handed it to Shephard. It was stiff and heavy.

"A little gift from the personal safe of Joe Datilla," she said. "Remember the old advice from Plato? 'Know thyself'?"

He nodded.

"Take it."

She rose from the booth in a swirl of smoke and lilac perfume, waving an irritated hand at the man who had dropped a fifty-dollar bill on the table and now stood waiting. "Bring the car, David," she said. "I'm perfectly capable of walking to it myself."

Then she disappeared unsteadily into the lobby.

In the dim candlelight Shephard examined the contents of the envelope. It contained two items, one a current California license plate—1AEA 896—the other a check for twenty thousand dollars from Joe Datilla to Wade Shephard. It was canceled and dated September 20, 1951.

EIGHTEEN

Ken Robbins sat amidst the clutter of his forensic lab and grunted off the stool when Shephard walked in. His white smock hung untied around his bulk and was stained with something that Shephard assumed was lunch. Stooped and massive, he looked like a man with scarcely enough energy to hold himself up, but behind his thick glasses Shephard saw the excitement in his eyes.

"Wouldn't have called you up here on a Saturday, but I got something that won't translate over the phone." He shook his big head dramatically. "Those reporters sure gave you a grilling the other night. Thought you handled it okay.

Take my advice, though, once you get on their bad side, just quit talking."

Robbins led Shephard across the lab to a long table that lay against a wall of windows overlooking the smoggy city. In one quick glance, he could see the heart of the county's government and the bowels of its poverty. To the east, the new Federal Building rose above them, and behind that the tall stiff towers of the jail. The Santa Ana Civic Center sprawled from behind the jail, and in the milky smog that seemed to hover everywhere, the County buildings etched their diminishing outlines against the suburbs. But to the west Shephard saw the gutted remnants at the end of what was once Fourth Street—century-old storefronts, hotels, and restaurants built out of brick that had lost its color. Their facades were festooned with construction company signs that announced the beginning of the end. The destruction had already begun at the north end of the street. Piles of rubble, cordoned off and alive with workers, lay where the old heart of the city had once beat. Farther down the street, Shephard could see the next set of businesses that were doomed, their fronts already so lifeless it looked as if they had given up long ago. Pawnshops, Zapaterias, Joyerias, the Palace Hotel, the Norton, where he had met Little Theodore, cafés, bars. End of a chapter, he thought as he turned to Robbins.

Three microscopes were set up on the table, each with the specimen slides already inserted. Robbins checked the first, then motioned Shephard to do the same. "Some you've seen, some you haven't," he said, stepping away.

Shephard gazed into the eyepiece at the rich blue slab under the glass. Robbins's voice came from behind him, patient but intense.

"Recognize it?"

"Cobalt."

"Right, or almost right. I got cobalt when I did the scan

the day you were here, and the reading was so high I let it slide. Shouldn't have. What you're looking at is a cluster of cobalt particles suspended in a base of oil. Try the next one, dick."

Shephard moved to his right. The color that hit him as he bent to the eyepiece was as rich as the blue, but brighter. He hadn't seen such a flagrant yellow since he stared at the sun once as a boy, then closed his eyelids and viewed it through his own skin.

"What we have here is the element cadmium. I found it connected to a hair on that dead dog's neck. Routine scan, you know, but that yellow burned my eyes like it's burning yours right now. You don't find cadmium very often, about as often as you find cobalt or a beautiful woman who doesn't know it. So I ran it through the scanner slow and got the same oil trace I found in with the cobalt. Not that it meant shit to me at the time."

In the last microscope Shephard found the same truncated branch—camel hair—that he had seen a week ago. It was magnified to show the mounds of tocopherol acetate.

"Here's the skinny," Robbins said as Shephard worked the focus and continued to study the hair. "Last week you bring me a handful of gray hair from the fist of a dead man. I named it killer's hair. And attached to that hair is a fleck of cobalt you don't find a helluva lot these days. And a piece of hair from an animal that doesn't even grow on this continent. A few days later more hair from the same guy. Both the camel hair and the human hair conditioned with the same stuff. This time there's a piece of cadmium in the hair of the dog this guy has choked."

Robbins threw off his lab smock and headed for the door. Shephard followed him to a small alcove filled with coffee and junk food machines. Robbins was silent while his coffee "brewed"; then he sipped and eyed Shephard over the cup.

"So I go home after the cadmium day and I'm halfway

through a martini—a big one—and my wife asks what I did. It isn't easy to explain what I do. But I was feeling good, so I told her about the cobalt and the cadmium and the camel's hair dented in the middle. All of it. And she smiles and says, Robbins, you're a dummy sometimes. All it took was a little art back in college to know that cobalt and cadmium are used in oil paints and camel hair brushes are what you put them on the canvas with."

Robbins treated Shephard to coffee, light, then slurped loudly from his own cup and continued.

"I said that's great, Carole, but you don't condition paintbrushes. She tells me sorry, but that's exactly what a serious painter does. They wash their brushes in shampoo and condition them with the best stuff they can afford. It keeps the filaments clean and supple. And when I pictured that camel's hair again, I saw that we were just looking at the wrong end when we said it wasn't from a hairbrush. The straight end goes into the metal that holds it in place with the others. That's why it's dented halfway—from the metal. That explains the oil base, too. Cobalt blue and cadmium yellow. I called a local art house this afternoon and they sell it all the time."

Robbins trailed slowly back toward the lab, his head bent to the coffee. Inside he shut the door and looked at Shephard with a smile. "You got a killer who paints. An artist. Only in Laguna, young dick. Weird shit."

An hour later Shephard entered the Laguna Art Mart with a stack of Identikit sketches in his hand. The clerk was a sweet young man who bore some resemblance to Elvis Costello, but with a pot belly. His name was Frank and he took the Identikit sketch, holding it close to his plastic-rimmed sunglasses.

"Oh God no," he said quickly. "I'm sure I didn't sell any Winsor and Newtons."

"Winsor and Newtons?"

"Paint," he said flatly. "If you want paint with real cobalt and real cadmium the only thing I sell is Winsor and Newtons. The best. Five ninety-five big tube three ninety-five small." Shephard wondered if Frank had dropped commas from his vocabulary. "Aisle one," Frank said in a blur, then threw back his head and went to help another young man struggling with a large picture frame.

Shephard found the paint tubes locked in a case on aisle one. He noted that Frank was correct in his prices. Leaning up to the glass, he spotted both Cobalt Blue and Cadmium Yellow among the uniform tubes. On the other side of the aisle were the paintbrushes. The camel hair brushes were moderate in price and came in a wide selection of shapes, sizes, and lengths.

As Shephard worked his way through the store, showing the Identikit to the clerks, he decided that the Art Mart must be the largest employer in the city. A toothy blond girl said he looked familiar but that she probably would have remembered because you have to unlock the case to sell Winsor and Newtons, and so far as she knew she hadn't. A wide and serious woman with a head of healthy brown curls told Shephard that she had sold so many Winsor and Newtons in the last week that she couldn't remember them all.

"Can you remember who bought them?" he asked earnestly.

"Come on, man," she said. "I'm an artist, not a clerk. A face is a face."

A red-headed boy with bright green eyes studied the Identikit sketch and pursed his lips grimly, as if wondering whether or not he should take a bet. He finally decided no and told Shephard to try Ella's Corner because the best artists in town didn't shop Laguna Art Mart anyway.

An hour later he merged onto Coast Highway and the slow knot of tourist traffic.

Ella's Corner was just that, a nook filled with art supplies, owned and maintained by a substantial woman named Ella. She examined the Identikit patiently, once with her glasses on and once with them off. A poodle wearing a knit vest poked from behind the counter, smelled Shephard's shoe, and clicked away.

"I didn't exactly sell him the paints," she said finally. "He said he didn't have any money, so I took one of his works in trade. I do it a lot. That's probably one of the reasons this is Ella's Corner and not Ella's place, house, or castle." She smiled beautifully and leaned over the counter, watching her poodle wander toward the easels. The dog turned a pair of gooey eyes to Ella when she called its name. "The painting is hanging over there." She pointed behind her and called the dog again.

Shephard picked his way through the crowded store to the far wall, which was covered with frames suspended on wooden pegs. Balanced above the top row was a large painting that grabbed his attention and sent a sparkle of nerves down his back.

It was done in reds and blacks, thickly applied, a dense canvas that was as visceral as any painting he had ever seen. In the upper left, a figure in black loomed from an angular bench of some kind, while below him a man with his back to the viewer gazed upward. Jutting from the center of the scene and disappearing off to the right was a thin stable of sorts, filled with beasts that had horses' heads and the bodies of men. As Shephard stared at the presiding figure, it seemed at first to be a hooded man, then a demon, then perhaps a woman with severe black hair, then a large reptilian bird. Slashed in black across its shadowy form was a dark protrusion. An arm? Wing? Cape? And deep in the dark recess of the head, two deep red sockets glowed dully.

He started when Ella appeared beside him.

"Unsigned," he said.

"Powerful," she said, cocking her head gallery-browser style, "but rather opaque. I kind of liked it after all the chintzy seascapes we see in this town. This painting has guts. So what the heck. I give up fifty dollars' worth of paint and fifty dollars' worth of canvas and brushes so he can do another one. It's a fair shake even if I can't sell it. You don't sell nightmares in Laguna. Of course we've got enough real-life nightmares to keep us busy for a while, don't we, detective?"

Shephard shrugged and continued to study the painting.

"No offense," she said pleasantly. "I recognized you from the television news."

Shephard accepted a cup of herb tea and sat with Ella for nearly half an hour, asking her every question he could think of about the man who had done the painting. But in the end her information was thin: he had come in one afternoon early last week, gone straight to the best paints and supplies, stacked them on the counter, and said that he was a great artist with no money but a painting he could give her in trade. He had then gone back downstairs —she had watched from the window—and brought back the canvas, framed, from the trunk of an early model red convertible Cadillac parked at the curb in front.

"How many blocks are we from St. Cecilia's Church?" Shephard asked.

"Just three," she said, then talked more about the strange painting, the humorless intensity of the man, his very near resemblance to the Identikit sketch that she now studied again. After a long pause she took the poodle up onto her ample lap and stroked its head. "Did he kill the old folks here in town?" Her eyes looked resigned.

Shephard nodded and touched the fluff of the dog's head. "How much would you like for the painting?"

* * * *

It fit nicely into the trunk of Shephard's own convertible, which was parked, as the Cadillac had been, at the curb in front of Ella's Corner.

With the evening traffic at its worst, Shephard took to the city on foot, moving north on the crowded sidewalk to the neighborhood overlooked by St. Cecilia's Church.

His pace was quick, despite the throngs of tourists and beach-goers. He angled through the crowd, a lanky figure in a loose jacket, tall enough to be almost conspicuous, but otherwise unremarkable except for the Band-Aid that graced the bald spot on the back of his head.

Through a break in the buildings he saw the ocean, a smooth plate of bronze in the windless evening. The same ocean that had cradled Jane and him, he thought, and the same one that had swallowed Burton Creeley. He paused for a moment, as the pedestrians eddied around him, and witnessed the ocean as an admirer, perhaps a friend. The sun had begun its slow descent over Catalina, and Shephard could see the profile of the island, as choked in smog as the city of Santa Ana had been a few hours before. Then, back to the street where the shadows were as long and solid as dashes of gray-green paint.

Two blocks short of St. Cecilia's he stopped again to survey the task before him. The west side of the highway was a solid front of shops, galleries, and apartments. To the east, the highway sprouted two hotels, a bed-and-breakfast house, and more galleries, the windows of which caught the sun and threw it back at him in bright rectangles of copper. With the stack of Identikit sketches in hand, he slipped through the crowd and into the first gallery, an incense-reeking little place called Outer Visions.

He was met by a huge canvas that hung on the far wall and easily dominated the dingy room with its electric blue hues. In the center of the painting was a life-sized depiction of Jimi Hendrix playing his guitar right-handed. The gallery manager sat at a desk, swamped in the smoke of incense rising from a brass burner in front of her. She eyed Shephard suspiciously through the blue smoke and finally rose to approach him.

He complimented her on the incense, which she said was homemade and named Hodgepodge. She showed a momentary interest in the Identikit but hadn't seen such a man and promised to call if she did. He left a card and stepped back out to the highway to cleanse his Hodgepodge-filled head with the sharp aroma of the ocean.

One door north was the Haitian Experience. The gallery windows were filled with small, bright, primitive works on canvas and wood. The owner introduced herself as Beverly Doan and spoke with a chipper British accent about the "primitive heathenism," "sensual innocence," and "magical visions" of the Haitian painters. She explained that her largest seller was S. W. Bottex, a Haitian known for his childlike enthusiasm and innocent energy.

"You can see it all in this one," she said, leading Shephard to one wall that was Bottex-covered. The scene was of an old man and a young girl sitting outside a wooden shed. Serene as the scene was, the canvas vibrated with hot pinks, bright yellows, and rich cinnamon reds.

Sensing his hesitation, Beverly Doan eased Shephard away from the Bottex to another wall featuring smaller paintings done on wood.

"You've probably never heard of some of these artists, and you probably never will," she said matter-of-factly. "They are desperately poor men and women who live in the city and work night and day on their art. I'm biased, of course, but it all has an enchanted quality for me. It speaks of voodoo, poverty, sensuality." She offered Shephard a quick smile. "But it's never forlorn or bleak. The Haitians are a happy people and a spiritual people."

Shephard brought Beverly Doan's attention to the drab sketches in his hand and felt bad for interrupting her charming enthusiasm. Something as unhappy and dispirited as the search for a killer didn't seem to fit with the Haitian Experience. She had seen the picture in the *Tides and Times*, and the face meant nothing to her.

"Think about one anyway," she finally said. "A little Haiti can brighten up any home in the world." She took his card with a polite smile and said she'd put him on the mailing list.

He continued, gallery after gallery, sketch after sketch, until the sun had gone down and the city hung in the brief penumbra of pre-darkness. Headlights flashed on, storefronts came alive for the night, traffic thinned, and the heartbeat of the city slowed for dinner, family, friends. The night was warm, and still no breeze had arrived. Shephard noted the last streak of orange over Catalina. He passed St. Cecilia's Church and glanced in at the burnished silence of the chapel and the dark wooden cross that hung behind the altar. There were flowers and a white-robed father, with his back to Shephard, arranging them. The pews were empty but polished. A short block from the church he found another row of galleries. One specialized in seascapes, one in the work of a prominent Laguna artist, one in budget-priced posters.

But none of the owners had ever seen the man in Shephard's Identikit.

Farther north he crossed the highway, jaywalking nimbly through the oncoming pairs of headlights. By then the stack of sketches in his hand was smaller, and the bottom ones were limp and ragged. He passed them out to the Gallery Andrea, the Coveside Gallery, and Gallery Laguna. Then the Jones/Churchill/Adams Gallery, the Gallery Panache, the Gallery Elite; Artiste's, the Seaside Gallery, the House of Art, Svendell's, Mason's. Some of the owners had seen the Identikit—none had seen the man it pictured. Finally, his legs beginning to fatigue and his stomach gurgling for dinner, he stopped at a dark, dusty store called Charles's, whose owner offered him a cup of coffee from a nineteenth-century cup and saucer.

Shephard declined the coffee and watched the man study the Identikit. His face reddened. He brought his hand across his hair—an involuntary urge to cover himself, Shephard thought—then shook his head slowly.

"No. No, I'm sorry," he said finally. He gave Shephard a diluted smile. Shephard saw that his business cards, arranged in a porcelain tray atop the counter, said *Charles Mitchell.* "What did he do?"

"He killed two people in town, Mr. Mitchell. They were about your age. Good people."

Charlie Mitchell's hand shot again to his thinning hair. "The Fire Killer?"

"He's still in town. He's a painter. Trying to sell some of his work to the galleries. Maybe he tried you." Shephard watched Charlie Mitchell lift his teacup with unsteady fingers. He sipped quickly, set down the cup, and sighed. "Have you seen him?"

"Dammit. I'm afraid . . . it might cost me."

"Cost you what?"

"That depends on you."

"Then I guess you'll have to depend on me, Mr. Mitchell."

The owner sighed again, then turned to a cabinet behind the counter. "Borderline, some of them," he said with his back to Shephard. "The ones that work require a state and local check, as you well know. And a fifteen-day wait. The ones that don't work are classified as antiques, and we sell them as-is, no forms, no wait." He brought a large wooden case to the counter and lifted the lid. Inside were five derringers, and space for one more. "When a customer looks dependable, I'll sell him a gun without the usual forms. I reason that anyone spending good money isn't going to use it on someone else."

Shephard pointed to the Identikit and Charlie Mitchell looked very disgusted with himself. His entire face lit with red; his ears seemed ready to bleed. "When?"

"Yesterday. Friday. An old Colt thirty-two. Jesus Christ. He was an old fellow and very polite. And he paid . . . oh hell, he paid cash."

By nine o'clock Shephard had worked his way into the gay sector of town, the hub of which was the intersection of Crest Street and the highway. Things were still quiet, although the streets were beginning to fill up with the men who nightly crowded the bars, hotels, beaches, and stores until the early hours of morning.

At Valentine's, the most popular gay bar/hotel in town, Shephard ran embarrassedly into an old schoolmate, who was about to show two men to their room when he looked at Shephard and smiled enthusiastically. He gave the key and instructions to an assistant—a boy who looked no older than fifteen—then shook Shephard's hand politely. "I remember you from high school, I think," he said. "I'm Ricky Hyams."

"I remember you. Tom Shephard." Shephard noted that Hyams had permed his hair and put on weight since he'd seen him last. He was dressed preppie—penny loafers, a pink golf shirt, and cotton trousers—and Shephard detected a hint of liner on the eyes.

"Are you looking for a room?" he asked happily.

"No, thank you," Shephard answered, aware of the stares from two gentlemen who loitered near the lobby cigarette machine. "But I am looking for—"

"You're a policeman, aren't you? That's right, you left for Los Angeles with Louise Childress right out of high school. Did you get married?"

"Yes, two years later."

"How is she? Louise was always so funny."

"Well, fine. It didn't work out all that well."

Hyams nodded understandingly and shot a quick glance to the men by the cigarettes. Then back to Shephard.

"It's hard to get along. Always will be."

When the assistant returned, Hyams left him in charge of the desk and led Shephard into Valentine's main bar. The place was dark and still quiet. The disco music, strangely subdued, issued from two large wall speakers. A network of tiny lights on the ceiling and walls blipped to the beat of the music, pulsing with each quiet thump of the drum.

"We've got two dozen rooms upstairs and behind," Hyams said proudly. "The dancing doesn't start really happening until about ten. Food is good and everybody gets along. First time you've been in?"

Something in Ricky Hyams's voice told Shephard that he was being looked on as a convert. He nodded abstractedly and handed Hyams the Identikit. In the beam of a small flashlight, Hyams studied the sketch momentarily, then looked up. It was apparent to Shephard that something in Hyams's mood had changed.

"Never seen him," he said with a tone of regret. "Sorry. He'd look better without the beard. Might try some of the other places. There's the Little Shrimp or the Boom-Boom Room, you know." Hyams gave Shephard the sketch and wiped his hands against his trousers. "If I see him I'll give you a call, okay? I see lots of faces around here."

"But not this one?"

"I already told you once." Hyams sounded hurt. "And I promise I'll call. Look, Tom, I'm getting ready for a big night. But come back earlier sometime. We can laugh about the old days at Laguna."

Even at ten o'clock, when Shephard was approaching the last row of galleries south of the gay quarter, the night was still warm and balmy. He had tried the Little Shrimp and the Boom-Boom Room and been met with the same regrets, received the same promises to call if the man was seen.

In a brightly lit gallery called Laguna Sunsets, he found a tired woman counting out the register. She smiled wanly when he walked in. She counted out a thin stack of money and slid the drawer halfway back into the register. Still shuffling the bills in her hand, she glanced at the sketch that Shephard had laid on the counter in front of her and nodded.

"He came in this week," she said. "Monday, maybe Tuesday. What's he wanted for?"

"Murder." She looked back down at the money in her hand and continued counting. Must have been a tough day, Shephard thought. Even murder doesn't get a reaction. "Did he buy? Sell? What did he want?"

"Seller," she said. "He had two canvases with him, and said he had more in the car." She dropped the money in a sack and put the sack in her purse.

"And?"

"Couldn't do it. Too bleak, too black. I sell art but I don't sell gloom. Why should someone look at something that makes them feel dark inside?"

The question struck Shephard as deceptively simple, and the answer he gave seemed deceptively complete. "The same reason someone would paint it," he said. "Because that's how they are."

"Then he was real dark, I'd say. He showed up a few days

later. Yesterday, I think. He stuck his head in the door and said he didn't need any cretin gallery owners anymore. Said he had a new car and lots of money. He pulled out a wad of bills and waved them at me. Robber, too?"

"Just a killer."

"Well, at least he knows what he wants," she said, turning the Yes We're Open sign to Sorry We Missed You.

The woman's exhaustion seemed to draw out his own. He walked her out of the shop and watched her disappear down the sidewalk, walking slowly and stiffly. His car was waiting up the highway, two very long blocks away.

He drove out Laguna Canyon Road until he saw the willow tree sagging its green shadow over Jane's house. A light was on inside, and when he parked he thought he saw her behind a window. He ran his hand through his hair and took a deep breath. Buster began yelping in his pen. He rang the doorbell twice, holding an Identikit sketch, his ostensible reason for coming there. Half wishing he hadn't come, he rang again. Why is this so hard? Ah, he thought, footsteps from inside . . . but it was only the thump of Buster's slick body on cement. From behind him the beast croaked with stupid verve. He felt a dribble of sweat making its way down his back, wondered if he smelled bad.

He rang once more, then turned away, started the Mustang and headed—for what reasons he wasn't sure—to Tim Algernon's stables up the road.

There was a light on at Tim's house too, a feeble glow from the living room.

As the car crunched across Algernon's driveway, the sound of the tires, the tall shadows of the eucalyptus, and the sight of Tim's ranch house brought all the grim events of last Monday back to Shephard. Six days, he thought: two murders, no suspect in custody, no motive. He could see Jane's father sprawled in the dust with a rock dividing his face, hear the mockingbird chattering away above him. And as he stepped from the car Shephard smelled smoke—the real thing, he thought—and with a sudden lurch of fear, searched the smell for something human.

The porch boards bent and creaked as he moved to a front window. Inside, the fireplace was alive with flames that cast an orange glow on the room. She sat on the floor facing the fire, her back to him, and a stack of cardboard filing cabinets beside her. She was wearing a blouse and jeans, and Shephard could see her hair held again by chopsticks, dark bangs curling across her forehead.

He knocked quietly on the door, and called out. A moment later she cracked it, studying him through the protective sliver, then pushed it open wide. He noted the puffiness of her eyes, the tissue in her hand. "You scared the hell out of me," she said, closing the door behind him.

"Sorry. I saw the light."

She tossed a sofa pillow in front of the fireplace, motioned to it, then sat back down. Shephard saw a stack of papers on the floor, documents of some kind, and bills.

"Little warm tonight for a fire, isn't it?" he asked.

"I've been freezing all day. Freezing in the middle of a hot Laguna August." She picked up a pile of papers, then plopped them back down. "One thing I can say for my father is he was organized. I think he kept *everything* in these files. I mean, he's got canceled checks to the phone company going back ten years. Billings from newspapers, all his feed and tack receipts, tickets from Christmas presents. Anyway, I guess I'll throw them away."

Shephard watched the flame shadows playing across Jane's face. There was a little pile of wadded tissue beside her. He unfolded the Identikit sketch and handed it to her. She stared at it, looked blankly at Shephard, then folded it back up and put it in a file folder. "You've got his organized blood," he said.

"Funny, you go back and look again at somebody who was

always there, and they're different. I never realized it, but dad must have spent everything he had when mom was dying. It was a long decay, you know. Cancer in the lips, then the tongue, then down to the throat. It must have been awful." Jane tapped a short stack of papers. "I added it up, from curiosity. Just under forty thousand dollars to try to beat that cancer."

"Sounds like a million might not have been enough to help," he said.

Jane shrugged. "Can't put a price on a life. You say dad had almost a thousand dollars forced into him before he died. I've been thinking about that. Seems to me, it was payment offered. Trying to save his own life with a little money. And whoever killed him wouldn't take it. Would rather have tortured him and humiliated him with it." A big tear rolled down Jane's cheek; Shephard watched her dab it away with a fresh Kleenex. "That seems an awfully cruel thing to do."

Shephard nodded, thinking of Hope Creeley as she watched her own eyelids coming off. "And unnecessary."

"Unnecessary? A policeman would say it like that, I suppose."

Jane tossed the tissue into the fire, raised up her knees and rested her chin on them. Shephard moved closer and put his arm around her, rubbing her back with his fingers. The fire popped, and he heard the cars heading out the canyon road, tourists from the art festivals returning inland. He was close enough to smell the shampoo in her hair; he dipped his nose to it, taking in the freshness. Tocopheral acetate? "I've been thinking of you," he said. "Wondering what you're doing, how you are. I'm real . . . taken. That sketch I brought is really just an excuse to see you, though you probably figured as much. Last night was really fine, Jane."

Then she was up, standing in front of the fireplace and looking down at him. "Yes, it was. But Tom, don't make too much of it, okay? We kind of short-circuited everything out there by the Indicator, and I blame myself. I'm not sorry for what we did, just for all the things that come with it. Maybe some of what you've been thinking, I've been thinking too. But sometimes I just want it all real slow, Tom." She smiled. "Though that may be hard to believe. You can't count on me. I've been around, and there's something real hard inside me I can use when I want it. I'll tell you about my men someday, maybe. Then things will make a little more sense, I hope."

Shephard nodded: to some statements there is nothing much to add, he thought. "Well, yeah. Take things as they come, I guess." He stood up and kissed her cheek.

"Good seeing you, Tommy."

He stopped at the door and said the same thing back.

Later that night he hung the painting from Ella's on his living room wall, where Hopper's *Nighthawks* had been. Compared to the red-black nightmare that now dominated his home, Hopper's ode to loneliness had seemed almost cheerful, he thought. Beside the painting he thumbtacked the Identikit sketch, the face that included all the darkness of the painting, and then some.

And still, Shephard noted, still the sonofabitch smiled.

NINETEEN

Early Sunday morning Shephard found Little Theodore slouched against the sissy bar of his motorcycle at the back of the Church of New Life drive-in lot. Sunday had broken bright and clear over the County, with a desert breeze washing away Saturday's stifling smog like a wiper on a windshield. The wind was warm, but promised even at seven o'clock to become hot before the morning was gone, a dry, scrubbed, high-pitched wind that stung Shephard's nostrils as he pulled the LaVerda up beside Theodore. The big man was working on a half gallon of Gatorade, which he offered to Shephard.

"Hotter'n a whore on payday," Theodore said, and cast Shephard a giant smile. Shephard noticed that Theodore had washed his hair and that the black T-shirt, stretched tight around his arms and almost to breaking around his belly, was conspicuously clean. He gulped the thirst-killer and found it unspiked. "You got me a tad drunk the other night, little fella. Felt like a stomped-on toad next day."

Theodore hooked the theater speaker to the handlebar of his bike and it crackled to life with the sounds of a steel guitar. He turned it down, his massive head bent in concentration as he fiddled with the knob. When he got the volume to his liking, he leaned back against the Harley's bar. Shephard noted the twisted, dried something that dangled from the arch of the bar top.

"Dried apricot?" he asked as a warm puff of wind sent it swaying.

Theodore tilted his head up for a look, then shook a slow no. "Bit off a woman's ear in Cheyenne. Imagine a little gal trying to stick me with a knife? And don't go asking why, little jackass, them days is long over." Theodore gave his bike a shake and watched the ear dance, a smile breaking through his beard. "Long over. Just a little reminder of what a woman can do to a man. Hey, pissant, you looked a little nervous on the TV the other night. Got to learn some polish, you want to be famous as me someday."

Shephard handed Theodore the Identikit sketch, then adjusted himself comfortably on the seat. The ride into Santa Ana had been fast: his heart still hadn't settled. But the thrill was nothing even close to the one he'd felt that night at Diver's Cove when Jane Algernon took him in and arched her back into the stars.

"I got a memory like an elephant, and this bastard ain't part of it. I'll hang onto it though, never know these days."

Wade's voice came through the speaker, and Theodore labored forward to turn it up. Shephard sat squat-legged on the seat, gazing out at the ocean of cars covering the drive-in lot. The battered rear ends of old Pontiacs, Chevys, and Fords. Still the poor people who come to the drive-in church, he thought, just like in the beginning. Wade always reminded him of that.

He closed his eyes as Wade began the sermon. A jetliner droned somewhere overhead, so high that the murmur of its engines seemed to come from one part of the sky, then from another. He breathed deeply and the warm wind struck his face. When he opened his eyes he saw only blue.

Wade began talking about the power of prayer and how it should not be taken lightly. The Lord is not a mail-order catalog, he said. Then he started comparing the power of prayer to a secret weapon, which must always be used wisely. But the sound of his voice, the droning of the plane overhead, and the warmth of the day soon transported Shephard into a reverie from which he caught only snippets of what was being said by his father.

He closed his eyes again and still saw the blue sky and it reminded him of the fishing trip he'd taken with Louise to Montana. He remembered turning her over the damp brown stump in the clearing and the comic dilemma of making love while a bear lumbered into their vision not fifty yards away.

"The Lord has dealt bountifully with you," his father was saying, and Shephard agreed. They had always liked it outdoors, and even in Silverlake he had rigged a mattress on the patio for summer nights. The air always seemed better outside, and they had to be quiet because of the neighbors, and one morning Shephard woke up to find a pink mosquito bite on her ass, but they laughed. Same patio where they had the party and he had seen that look pass between her and the producer, who ducked under a paper lantern to load a cracker with dip. Too beautiful not to be seen. And he and some others packing their noses in the bathroom. Shephard was curious, but some things a cop can't do even if his wife can.

Wade's voice came slowly over the speaker now: "The Lord has provided such wealth," he said. "But still when we find something we cannot buy, we always say we're too poor to buy it rather than we're not rich enough to buy it. And even then we forget the abundance that is heaven and the poverty of spirit that is hell."

Shephard brought his feet to the seat and rested his head on his knees. The wind gusted around him and tilted the motorcycle gently. Right, he thought, always richer than we think we are. He remembered holding so hard to her when she was slipping away, so that the harder he held, the faster she slipped away—like a watermelon seed between your fingers. Forget it, he thought, forget yourself like you told Dr. Zahara. But then there was the divorce, in his memory a hazy flurry of forms and negotiations, of obligatory cruelties inflicted from both sides to make the separation complete. One night still remained in his mind, a night when they had made the settlements and it must have been the mutual relief that brought them together once more to make love furiously and tenderly, both aware that it was finality, not promise, that had brought them to their last joining, and they did all that they had ever done as if in a summation before the good-bye. Louise had been too proud to demand much in the settlement, he thought; just sullen and guilty. Even the lawyers had remarked that theirs was a model divorce, but it was clear to Shephard that neither of them wanted much of what they had built together, though for different reasons.

"So no matter how little you may think you have and how little you think you will have, you can turn the water to wine and the loaves to plenty if you do as Christ and use faith." Wade's voice was powerful, even through the tiny speaker.

Shephard shifted his weight and glanced across at Theodore, whose hat was pulled down. The silver dollars shone brightly in the sun. The half gallon of Gatorade rested on his belly, cradled by his big hands. For a moment Shephard wished to be a simpler animal.

He gazed out again to the beaten cars around him. The lot was full except for the spaces at the back, and Shephard wondered why people liked being near the front even when there was nothing to be nearer to. But it was the County's poor who had been the foundation of the Church, and they didn't seem to mind that the Reverend Wade Shepard now delivered his sermons from the pulpit of a million-dollar dome made of blue glass. He could see the top of that chapel over the roof of a dusty Chevrolet. Its smooth panels glittered and shifted in the bright morning sun, a three-story sapphire. From inside the gem, Wade continued:

"Blessed are the poor in spirit, for they shall inherit the earth." There was a long pause, and when Wade began again the tone of his voice had changed. "Before we bring to an end our service for today, I would like to take a moment to bring you some good news. A good friend of the church, one of our supporters from the first days, has expanded his generosity to our new project, the Sisters of Mercy Hospital on Isla Arenillas, Mexico. Some of you may know him, his name is Joe Datilla, and he told me just yesterday that he is prepared to offer us a wonderful gift. You all have heard about the terrible events in Laguna Beach last week. Joe, just yesterday, established a reward fund for information leading to the arrest of the Fire Killer of Laguna. That reward will be one hundred thousand dollars to the individual who provides information on the case, matched by one hundred thousand dollars in donation for the Sisters of Mercy Hospital."

Shephard could hear the crowd come alive through the speaker. Then a raucous cry came up from the cars in front of him and they sprouted arms that waved from the windows. There were hoots, shrieking whistles, applause, and finally a chorus of honking horns that drowned out the next of Wade's words. Someone threw a beer can. Little Theodore let out a throaty rasp, broke into a cough, and pressed down the horn of the Harley, which responded with little more than a tweet. "Great deal," he growled. "Fuckin' A."

"Join me in praying that the Lord will deliver this tormented man to us," Wade said finally, "and that to him His mercy shall be given."

The Reverend Wade Shephard's office was hidden in a far corner of the massive new chapel. As Shephard walked through the door, a woman with her back to him turned and an embarrassed smile crossed her face. Wade was standing across from her, behind a desk, and Shephard's entrance seemed to take him by the same surprise. The woman excused herself and Wade sat down, still dressed in the cream-colored suit he wore for the televised sermons. His smile was pleased, expansive. "I wasn't expecting you so soon," he said pleasantly. "Surprised by Joe's offer?"

"Well, yes. Very powerful," Shephard said, not sure whether he was really surprised or not.

"Reward money works wonders sometimes, as I've told you."

"I can understand his helping the church. But why me?"

Wade leaned back in his large padded chair and crossed his hands over his stomach. Shephard saw something well pleased in the gesture. "I suppose only Joe could answer that. Of course, he bounced the idea off me before it was settled. Frankly, Tom, I think he's as appalled at what has happened in Laguna as you and I are. Don't forget, he's not just helping you," he said kindly.

"Two hundred thousand is a lot of appalled," Shephard said. He thought of Datilla serving on the tennis court alone, then of Dorothy Edmond's words. He isn't happy about anything he can't control. And it was Shephard's nature, or at least his training, to look for what was expected in return when a gift was offered.

"Of course, he's very interested in the hospital, too," Wade said. "I can see the questions swirling behind that glum young face of yours, Tom. I raised a good detective. But don't be afraid to accept a miracle. Expect them, accept them."

Wade's voice was confidential, his smile assuring. And his advice seemed to lift Shephard's concerns out of an arena he wasn't yet willing to leave. He nodded. "I met Dorothy Edmond on Friday," he said. "She didn't exactly portray Joe as a miracle worker."

"Oh?" Wade's smile had turned wry, as if he knew what might be coming next.

"Do you know her?"

"In a sense, yes. 'I knew her once' might be a better way to put it. She was and still is a very unhealthy woman."

"She coughs a lot."

"She does at that," Wade said gently.

"She told me some, uh, disturbing stories about Joe."

"Don't be disturbed. I told you a thousand times who the best liars are. Do you know?"

"Those who believe their own lies," Shephard answered quickly.

"She must be one of them," Wade said.

"I want to give them to you just the same. I saw Joe last Thursday. When I was leaving the Surfside, Dorothy took me aside and said she knew something about the murders. When I met with her the next day, she told me a long tale about Joe and a woman named Helene. Joe mentioned her, too. Helene Lang."

"I knew her, too," Wade said with a new smile. Again he leaned back and crossed his hands.

"She told me that Joe fought with his partner, Burt Creeley, and arranged to have him drowned in the bay at Newport. Helene had professed her love to Burt and had managed to alter his will so that his thirty percent of the Surfside stock came her way if he died. According to Edmond, Joe and Helene Lang were in it together. They planned it in advance so Joe could get the stock control. She said Burton's ideas were too . . . democratic."

As Shephard recounted Dorothy's story, he was aware of its gross unlikelihood. Coming from his own mouth it sounded impossible. But from Edmond, as she had sat in the cloud of smoke and lilac perfume, it was convincing enough to be real.

"I read parts of Hope Creeley's diary," he continued,

210

bringing fresh conviction to his voice, "and the affair checks out. She wrote about it, knew about it." Shephard stopped for a moment to ponder his collapsing narrative. Wade was listening patiently, calmly studying his son's face. "She said I'd have to 'reopen' the case if I wanted to get to the killer of Hope and Tim Algernon. Then she told me to know myself. Even if everything she said were true, I still don't see how it connects. But if she's pointing a finger, it's at Joe Datilla."

"Murder is a rather heavy finger," Wade answered. "Did you wonder why she was telling you this?"

"It's not the kind of story you'd want to keep inside, if it were true," Shephard answered after a pause. The truth was, he hadn't been able to figure out why she had come to him with it.

"Or even if it weren't." Wade sagged forward and poured himself a glass of water from a pitcher on the desk. "I don't know what she would gain by telling you something like that. I've known Dorothy Edmond for many years, and I've prayed for her many times. If Joe didn't have the heart to keep her on at the Surfside, she'd probably be back in one of the hospitals. She's been in quite a few, you know."

"No, I didn't know that."

Wade pushed himself up from the large desk, taking his glass of water. He looked through the blinds out to the Church of New Life drive-in lot. When he turned back to Shephard his face was drained of joy, like a fighter answering the bell for a round he can't win.

"I knew her quite well when she was engaged to Joe," he said finally. Shephard saw that his hunch had been right: she was a jilted lover, out of hope and ready for revenge. Fool, he thought. Ass. "The reason she's so intimate with the details of Helene Lang's life is because . . . she *is* Helene Lang. She's gone by a dozen names in the last thirty years. Dorothy Edmond is relatively new."

Shephard felt his ears warm with embarrassment, like a schoolboy who has multiplied the numbers he was asked simply to add. Wade sipped the water and set the glass back on the desk.

"The Creeleys, Joe and Helene, your mother and I were all pretty close for a while. Joe broke the engagement when he found Burton, his partner and closest friend, with Helene snuggled nice and tight below deck on Burt's boat one night. It broke his heart, Tom. True, she had convinced Burton to will his stocks to her, but it sure wasn't Joe who engineered that." Wade moved again to the window. When he drew up the blinds, Shephard could see the drive-in far below, the trees around it swaying in the growing wind. The last of the cars waited at the exit.

"Of course Helene was disgraced. She was a beautiful, powerful woman, but she started to crack when the entire club found out what she had been doing. When Joe found them that night on the boat, he roughed up Burton pretty good. Helene, too. Some of the people around the club probably knew already, but they had two black eyes and a broken engagement as evidence. Still, Helene Lang wouldn't let go. She stayed there at the Surfside, an outcast from Joe, an outcast from the life of the place. She drank. Made a spectacle of herself more than once. Then she cut her wrist one morning. The maid found her. It was Joe who took her downstairs and put her in his car for the hospital. The doctors didn't have any trouble putting her back together, but they weren't sure she was stable enough to let out. They kept her for observation. Which went into treatment. It never stopped. She still goes to a psychiatrist three times a week, or rather he goes to her. Joe Datilla pays for it. When she squandered all the money she had, she had to sell the stock and Joe bought it. That was years later. He didn't have to, but he threw in a suite as part of the deal. He never could turn her out, Tom."

212

Wade sat back down and poured more water. Shephard saw the pained look on his face, the row of tiny droplets above his lips. He had told his son—many years ago when he was a detective, too—that a cop's job wasn't to ponder human nature, just to understand it. Maybe those years of understanding the human animal had led him to God, Shephard thought.

"Tom, I'm sorry I didn't tell you before, about Helene. I'm not sure why she would tell you what she did or didn't do. Her doctors probably couldn't tell you. She probably couldn't either. Maybe she feels like it's time to confess. Maybe to hurt Joe. Maybe she doesn't feel anything I would even understand. But I'll tell you this. I'm deeply sorry that she did. I'm deeply sorry that you fell into it. I know how bad you hurt after the shooting, and Louise. I wanted Laguna to be a fresh start for you. I'm sorry she brought this onto your shoulders. I apologize for her." Wade's voice was shaking as he spoke his next words. "It's hard for me to talk about, son. It takes me back to a good time that turned out so bad for so many of us. I don't know how you're going to find out who killed Tim Algernon and Hope. You may never find out. But you're not going to find it at the Surfside. Handle it your way. Do what you think is best. But don't let the bitter heart of an old woman hurt you. She may be dangerous. And not only to herself."

"She showed me a check that Joe had written to you," Shephard said, staring down at the floor. "I don't know why. She wouldn't say why."

When he looked back up, there was a wry grin on his father's face again. Wade shook his head slowly. "I shouldn't make light of anything that has happened here today," he said. "And certainly not scoff at the strange imagination of a sick person. That was the down payment on the house I brought you up in, son. Joe had the cash, and his terms were easier than the banks could offer. Every interest point I could save was worth it, you know why?" Shephard honestly didn't. "Because I was twenty-eight years old and I had a son on the way. I figured the least I could do was put a good roof over his hard little head. I knew you'd come out hard-headed."

Wade moved behind him and began to rub his shoulders. Shephard marveled at his father's ability to make him feel like a boy again, a boy in good hands. An entire congregation must feel the same way, he thought: Little Theodore and a thousand more.

Outside, the sun was fierce and the wind had stiffened into a bone-dry Santa Ana. A family left the chapel for their car, and a little girl lifted her dress to catch the gusts. She giggled while her mother scolded and dad looked on, smiling. A good roof over her hard little head, he thought.

The LaVerda jerked to life under him like an animal with a mind of its own. It carried him across the city to the Newport Freeway, which would lead him nearly to the steps of the Surfside Club. Shephard, the hard-headed driver, believing that lies have reasons.

TWENTY

Arthur Mink stepped from the guard house and approached the LaVerda, holding onto his hat in the swirling wind. The palm trees of the Surfside leaned drunkenly, their fronds sweeping toward shore, their trunks seemingly ready to snap. Mink's bony vulture's face gave way to a smile. "Nice bike," he said.

"Thanks," Shephard answered. "It works. I'm here for a ten o'clock appointment with"—and he almost said Helene Lang—"Miss Edmond." Mink scanned the clipboard. "She sounded a little sauced when she called," Shephard said, "I'm not sure if she even remembered to . . ."

"Never mind. If I kept out all the people she was too drunk to call in, she'd never get any visitors. Wind's a strange one, eh?"

"Early in the year for a Santa Ana," Shephard said.

"She's in Suite Two-oh-seven, over B Dock on the water."

The motorcycle rumbled past the Surfside convention room as Shephard headed for the guest lot once again. He paused a long moment beside the near tennis court, where a young couple still volleyed despite the treacherous wind. The woman's scarf maintained a stiff starboard pitch, matched by her hair, which was as wavy and golden as Colleen's. Her partner, a big sturdy man, could have been Wade thirty years ago, Shephard thought. And the racquets could have been wood and the couple on the next court Tim and Margie Algernon, Burton and Hope Creeley, or Joe and Helene. The woman chased an errant ball to the fence, looked at Shephard briefly, then turned away in a flurry of windblown gold.

Shot in her own home by a man who tried to rape her, he thought. I hope it never happens to you.

The halyards of the B Dock yachts banged against their masts, a communal plea to be turned loose into the sea rather than remain chained to land. They rose and fell chaotically, while behind them the open bay churned and heaved. Shephard turned his back to the ships and squinted at the room numbers on the apartment doors. He could hear the Hawaiian music from A Dock. The curtains on Suite 207 were drawn tight.

The stairs to the second story were at the back. Halfway up he stopped and watched a maid push her cart along the walk below, a white towel peeling from the stack and a brown hand snatching it in flight. On the second-floor walkway he paused again to enjoy the Surfside view. To the west, a huge American flag stood stiffly over A Dock, while below it the palm trees bowed as if in supplication. Shephard realized that with no people on the courtyard below him and no cars in sight, the view he now saw could have been the same as it was in 1951, the year of bad luck at the Surfside. The same buildings, the same palm trees, the same ocean in the near distance, green, white-capped, violent. For a moment the feeling was unnerving, as if he had slipped back in time with the mere climbing of stairs. Other remnants from the early days of the Surfside came to mind. The same owner. The woman not thirty feet away in Suite 207. A cop named Wade Shephard, who had probably once stood on this same balcony thinking perhaps of his son just as his son now thought of him. Hell, he thought; should have stayed in L.A. At least the skeletons in the closet were my own.

He knocked on the door and waited while a cat moaned from the other side, miserable but patient. A door that nobody is going to open sounds different, he thought. He tried the knob and found it unlocked.

"Miss Edmond? Yoo-hoo, Dorothy?"

Inside, the suite smelled unmistakably of cat dung. In the vague light he watched a thin white animal cross the floor, stretch, then angle against his leg.

"Miss Edmond? Miss Lang? Whoever you are today, are you home?" He flicked on a light. The cat pointed its nose tentatively at a bowl near the door, where a can-shaped glob of food was slowly diminishing under a swarm of ants. Enough food for a week, he thought. "Eat up, cat. Protein." The cat, which Shephard noted was cross-eyed, moaned again.

He stepped over it and stood in the middle of the small living room. The suite was airless and nearly dark from the drawn curtains. He turned on a lamp and discovered that he was standing amidst thirty years of Surfside history, framed and dusty, hanging from the walls. Quite a social director, he thought; pictures of everything. Here was the cast that had become so familiar to him over the last week: Joe and Helene on the courts with Wade and Colleen; Burton and Hope Creeley at rest in the Surfside Lounge, martinis raised.

A home with nobody in it sounds like a door with nobody to open it, he thought. He raised his voice once more to confirm her absence, and it echoed briefly, unanswered. Gone for the weekend, and enough food for the cat. He noted that the litter box in the corner was well used. Outside, the wind buffeted the windows and the living room drapes lilted. When he opened the window, a gust of dry wind blew in. The cat moaned again.

Shephard leaned up close to a large photograph of Helene Lang and Joe Datilla sitting in a car. The car was a red convertible Cadillac. For a man who had "tried hard not to know her," his attentive smile, relaxed expression, and the comforting arm he'd wrapped around Helene looked like not much of a try at all. Why had he even bothered to lie, Shephard wondered. It must be common knowledge.

The same car that was stolen last week. The same car now at the disposal of the Fire Killer. In spite of the heat, Shephard felt a chill register down his back. To the left of the picture was a smaller one, vintage black and white, of Wade and Colleen Shephard standing on A Dock. Wade was on the left with his arm around her. Colleen was smiling at the camera, a broad and delighted smile. Wade was looking at her, or perhaps at the other man who stood to her right, also with his arm wrapped around Colleen. His face was lost in shadow, but somehow familiar to Shephard. He searched his memory for an earlier encounter with the man, but found none.

The hallway of Helene Lang's suite was covered with

more pictures, dozens of them. As Shephard stopped to study them he noticed that her collection began in the living room and continued chronologically down the hallway. The last photograph before the closed bedroom door was of a group of people he had never seen, the new wave of Surfside members. Their dress was extravagant and obvious. Mid-sixties bellbottoms and miniskirts, too much jewelry, long hair.

When he pushed open the bedroom door and saw Helene lying comfortably in her bed, he knew that something wasn't right.

"Helene, wake up," he commanded. Moving across the bedroom in the dank half-light, he saw her peaceful face; the empty bottle of gin on the nightstand; the prescription bottle beside it, empty too; and now the cat, which had silently entered behind him and leaped onto the bed, purring and rubbing its head against the woman's face. When Shephard reached down to shoo the cat away he looked into the half-open eyes of Helene Lang and knew that she had been dead for several hours.

The cat slunk to her face for another rub and Shephard slapped it away. He found her carotid and pressed it, uselessly. His ears were ringing, and he felt a bloated thumping in his chest.

Shephard saw that Helene had left an envelope resting on her chest. *To Joseph* was written on the outside in a calm and lovely script. He stood for a moment and tried to quiet his pounding heart, but the attempt was as futile as trying to find life in Helene Lang's quiet artery. With a silent nod to his own ungodliness, Shephard took the envelope, shut the door behind him, and returned to the stale kitchen. He sat down, and heard Helene Lang's whiskey voice as he read:

> *My Dear Joseph,*
> *It was only a few days ago that I realized how long I've*

*been waiting for this. Strangely, I am at peace now. I leave
with much bitterness and regret, but I bargained for them
both, as you well know. The real sadness about life is all
the time it gives us to do what we can never undo. If I
spent my time too close to the shadows I have no one to
blame except myself. And what is it about those shadows
that draws some of us, like moths to light? I suppose there
is a sunny world somewhere, but it never much interested
us, did it, Joe? For what we did to Burton I should burn
twice in hell, and would do it gladly if it could bring him
back and make things right. But that is childish, and we
have been anything but children. Regret is a luxury that
even I have outgrown. The one good thing I did on earth
was love you, but Jesus, why does He give us the hands to
do what we imagine? Finally, I will hurt you too, but the
confession I made was for myself, and believe me I needed
it badly. Even after all we have done I cannot be a part of
what you do now. I have made arrangements to bring the
proper people to the proper places, and should they fail
and you succeed, no one will be wronged more than they
have been wronged already.*

    I love you, Joe, but I wish I'd never been born to do it.
    Peace to you someday, too,
    Helene

The cat jumped onto Shephard's lap and rubbed its nose
against the corner of the letter. His nerves jolted and he
pushed the animal back to the floor. The wind outside
assaulted the windows and the glass shivered so vehemently
that Shephard wondered if it might break and bring the
whole storm into the suite. He smoked a cigarette and
flushed the butt down the kitchen sink, then smoked another. If Helene Lang was just a crazy liar, she had played
it right down to the end, he thought. A lot farther, it
seemed, than anyone would have asked her to.

For the next hour, Shephard went through her suite. He
again studied the photographs in the living room and hall.

He carefully rifled the kitchen drawers. In the second room off the hallway, guest quarters, he inspected the closet and found it nearly empty, but lingered over a collection of personal papers and snapshots that were pushed far into the recesses of a dresser. Letters from Joe, innocent lover's notes; a dried and ancient boutonniere with pin still intact; a baby picture unmistakably of Joe Datilla.

Back in the bedroom, which now seemed to smell of death, he worked his way through the large walk-in closet. Helene Lang's wardrobe befitted the social animal: cocktail dresses, dinner dresses, business suits, all bunched along one wall, gay colors and fine fabrics. The clothes were pressed together without regard for wrinkles or freshness, some of the slinkier gowns having slid to an end of their hangers, which now dipped helter-skelter from the weight. Another wall was dedicated to sport clothes and sweaters. The floor of the closet looked like a sale bin in a discount store: it was littered with dozens of shoes, which formed a small hill of mismatched colors and shapes. A group of bathing suits lay in one corner, the top one still damp from a recent swim. The suits below lay in a heap that smelled of chlorine and mildew.

The bathroom was roomy but dominated by crud. Black mold stained the bottom of the shower door, the linoleum cracked and peeled upward in one corner, and a furry orange rug was wadded around the toilet base, either to stop a leak or warm the feet.

Helene Lang must have done her entertaining at the lounge, Shephard thought, if she did any entertaining at all. The sink dripped, and the mirror above was so smudged that it offered only a translucent approximation when he looked into it. He wondered if an approximation was all Helene had wanted.

In the bedroom proper he flipped on the light and regarded it fully for the first time. The room was large but sparsely furnished, giving off the same air of carelessness as the closet. A simple director's chair sat by the far corner near the window, overhung by a lamp. To his left Shephard noted a potted palm, and above it on the wall hung an oversized rubbing of some Mayan deity, its mouth agape and filled with large round teeth, a rattle—or perhaps some weapon —clutched in its hand. A dresser stood beside the bed, drawers open and spilling underclothes of varying purpose. Beside the empty bottles on the nightstand stood a clock radio whose digital readout flipped to 10:14 A.M. as he watched.

Shephard found what he was looking for under the bed, that final catch-all of the bad housekeeper. At first the weight of it deceived him, seeming too heavy to contain the news clips that any social director would collect. But after he had worked the cumbersome blue trunk into the corner of the room and opened its solid lid, he saw that thirty years of Surfside history had been bound in leather volumes, one for each year. The covers were uniform navy blue, with gold lettering for the date and the words *Surfside Club.*

He sat down in the rickety director's chair and turned on the lamp above him. Gazing across the room, he thought back to his late night walk on the beach—it was just two days ago, he counted, but it seemed more like a thousand —when he had felt the murder of Hope Creeley transforming from homicide into something even darker, less negotiable. As he had described it to Datilla, it was proportionless, without balance. Had the killer bothered to take even five dollars, an earring, a television, then at least some idea of form and shape would have been suggested. But he saw the case as utterly without reason. I have come closer only to remain far away, he thought. True, he had given the killer a face and fingerprints, a car, a talent, a set of coinciding descriptions fit for the Academy textbooks. But he still couldn't answer the question, Why?

As he sat with the heavy trunk at his feet, Shephard remembered the strange feeling he'd had on the balcony only moments before, and it dawned on him that he was working a case in the present, when all indicators pointed toward the past. It was clear that the Surfside had been the stage for things beyond his understanding, and that all the players—Algernon and Creeley, Datilla and Helene, even Wade—were unfurling their bony fingers toward the trunk before him. He looked at the bed, wondering if she would have approved. And as he stared at her lifeless chest, hoping like a small boy that maybe she would come to life again, Shephard knew that Helene Lang had all but led him to this place, to her life and death.

He knew, too, that the trunk would include Wade and Colleen, Datilla and Helene, Tim and Margie, Burton and Hope. They seemed tangled, inextricable, one and the same. As he reached for the volume marked *1951*, his rational side urged him on while his instincts rebuked him, and for a moment he felt as if his hand were moving both toward and away from the book, like a cat feeling water with a hesitant paw.

But in the end it was more Helene Lang's advice to know thyself than his own sense of duty that led him to take the volume and bring it to his lap. Outside, the wind shuddered into the windows again and he felt chilled, though sweat was tickling down his head. Her words echoed as he began reading: Welcome to the club.

TWENTY-ONE

The year had started quietly. The first pages were neatly pasted with shots of New Year's Eve parties, and long lists of attendees. Shephard found that Joe and Helene were the featured players, although Burton and Hope Creeley were pictured three times. The gala mood quickly gave way to the more trivial goings-on in the Surfside: wedding announcements, births, deaths, and scholarships awarded. These smaller events were contained in a modest members' newsletter called *Surfsiders*. The editor was Helene Lang.

As spring arrived, so did the tennis season, and the scrapbook soon filled with tournament pictures, mostly clipped from the newsletter. The May edition announced the building of a new wing of suites on the club's north shore, and contained a brief message from co-owner Joe Datilla, who was pictured smiling at the ground-breaking ceremony. Burton Creeley stood beside him, spade in hand, but it was apparent that the photographer's interest was in robust Joe.

Shephard studied Burton Creeley's face and posture. It was easy to imagine him falling for the charms of a woman like Helene, whom Shephard found nearly out of the frame, casting a warm smile in Creeley's direction. He was small, almost hunched, and he looked uncomfortable in the dark suit. His smile was wan and forced. But as hungry as a man like him might have been for a sultry woman like Helene, Shephard thought, there was still something hesitant in his

223

look. It was hard to imagine him cheating on his wife
. . . and on his best friend.

The spring season gave way to a rash of summer parties:
women in light, sheer dresses, men in strangely outdated
casual wear. In one picture, apparently taken on the Surfside
beach, Wade and Colleen Shephard posed with their new-
born son, Tom. Well, Shephard thought, Helene's trunk
contains another surprise. Wade looked big-chested and
proud, and Colleen's lovely face was turned downward to his
own. The cutline read: "Mr. and Mrs. Wade Shephard show
off their new son, Thomas Wade. He was born four weeks
ago and tipped the scales at six pounds and four ounces.
Congratulations to members Wade and Colleen!"

On the next page he found a *Register* article on Burton
Creeley, the "silent owner" of the prestigious Surfside Club
of Newport Beach. It was Creeley's contention that the club
could soon blossom into a little city of its own, complete
with roads, schools, shopping areas, and, most importantly
of all, access for everyone to the golden bayfront property
of the club. He spoke of the Surfside as his "vision" and
"dream of tomorrow," and in the accompanying photograph Creeley seemed physically enlarged with his own
ideas. His smile was more relaxed, and there was a muscular
tension to his face. The reporter had apparently asked if
there was some disagreement in the upper levels of Surfside
management as to what the future of the club would entail.
"There is always a degree of give and take," Burton had
answered. "That's what makes great ideas even greater. I
can tell you that Joe and I see wonderful things ahead for
this club."

But the summer gaiety ended abruptly on September 9,
when Surfside member Colleen Shephard was shot and
killed by a man named Azul Mercante.

Shephard read the article again, the same one that Wade
had shown him that evening before his first day of school.

And just as it had done all those years ago, the picture of Colleen brought an overwhelming sense of violation to him, a sense of being intruded upon, penetrated, opened. He stared again, and felt again the loss of something he had never known, the itch in the phantom limb.

LAGUNA WOMAN SLAIN
Policeman Husband Watches in Horror

A Laguna Beach woman was fatally shot earlier today in her Arch Bay Heights home while her husband helplessly looked on.

Colleen Shephard, 22, wife of LBPD officer Wade Shephard, was shot once in the chest by a gunman who fled the scene. Police are now searching for the suspect.

According to Police Chief Donald Pantzar, Mrs. Shephard was apparently alone in her home when the gunman broke in and attempted to rape her. Her husband, returning home for lunch, found his wife being accosted in the living room. The suspect, whose name is being withheld on order of the chief, allegedly pulled a handgun and fired the fatal shot.

A fight for the gun ensued between Mr. Shephard and the man, who escaped on foot.

Mrs. Shephard was pronounced dead on arrival at Community Hospital in South Laguna Beach.

Police say that the murder weapon has been recovered and believe the motive for the break-in was rape.

The Shephards are four-year residents of the city. Earlier this year they had their first child, a son.

Shephard turned the page, relieved to find a full-page shot of fifty-four debutantes coming out at a Surfside-sponsored party. He studied their faces, trying to forget the story from the page before. Their cheery faces seemed to belong to a different world.

But two pages later he was plunged back into the murder of his mother, front page:

MURDER SUSPECT NABBED
Police Capture Laguna Beach Man

Laguna Beach Police yesterday arrested their prime suspect in Wednesday's murder of Colleen Shephard.

Azul Mercante, 25, also of Laguna, was arrested in his Temple Hills Terrace home after a brief struggle, police reported.

LBPD Captain Lonny Wilcox said that a loaded shotgun was found in the suspect's home.

Mercante was identified by the victim's husband, Wade Shephard, as the man he found accosting his wife in their Arch Bay Heights home Wednesday around noon.

In a press conference held yesterday, LBPD Chief Donald Pantzar stated that Shephard, a LBPD officer, had attempted to subdue the man when a struggle ensued. According to Pantzar, Shephard lost his gun to the intruder, who then turned it on Colleen.

Shephard attempted to revive his dying wife while Mercante allegedly fled on foot.

The suspect barricaded himself in his home and held police at bay for an hour with a shotgun, Pantzar said. He surrendered at 2:30 P.M. and no shots were fired.

The District Attorney says no charges will be filed until the preliminary investigation is completed.

There was a dim photograph of the family's Arch Bay Heights home beside the article, with the crude but informative caption: "Colleen Shephard, 22, was shot to death in this house Wednesday." Shephard's stomach had knotted, and sweat soaked his shirt. He stood up, set the volume on the director's chair, and stared through the blinds to the green bay surging below him.

The news of Mercante's arraignment was covered in a short article on the next page of the scrapbook. Assistant District Attorney Jim Peters was pictured beside the piece, as was the suspect, covering his face in his hands. Shephard knew that with formal charges brought a mere two days after the arrest, Peters must have considered his case a good one.

An eyewitness was enough to make any D.A. drool. Peters was a middle-aged man with a thick, combative face and a nose like a heavyweight's. Mercante retained a public defender by the name of Eugene Weingarten.

Another article on the same page told of Mercante's outlandish behavior at the jail. After refusing food for two days, he gashed his head on the bars of his cell in a "sudden fury, while screaming his innocence." The day after his arraignment, Mercante was removed to the criminal ward of the county hospital for "further examination and for his own protection."

With the coming of fall, the Surfside quieted. The big event of October was an annual yacht race that originated at the club and terminated in Ensenada, Mexico. The local press failed to recognize the serious side of the event and referred to the annual beer-drenched race as "The Booze Cruise." Surfside dockmaster Dick Evans was featured in a newsletter interview, trying to restore some sense of maritime drama to the race. "We like to think of it as a race for both the serious and the recreational yachtsman," he said. Another newsletter photograph showed the foundations of the new wing of suites, which were framed against a Surfside sunset and looked like ruins more than beginnings.

A trial date for Azul Mercante was set. The opening day would be Monday, October 14, and the presiding Superior Court Judge would be Francis Rubio. The article noted that Rubio, at the age of fifty, was the youngest judge on the Superior bench.

Then came the September 26 article Shephard had seen in Hope Creeley's collection, the brief account of Burton's tragic drowning in the Newport Channel. The whole *Surfsiders* newsletter was devoted to the memory of the co-owner. The title-page masthead, usually done in a lighthearted sea green, was a somber black. Creeley's portrait took up nearly a quarter of the first page, and beside it was a touching obituary written by none other than Helene Lang. She called him a "visionary" and a man "to whom the future was always a place of happiness and hope, a man whose loss dims the hopes and happiness of the futures of us all." Joe Datilla wrote a guest column on his personal friendship with Burton, the long days and worried months that constituted the birth of the club. "Somewhere inside myself," he wrote, "even during those times when it seemed our project might fail miserably, I always retained a solid foundation of optimism. Looking back on those times it is easy for me now to see that it was the endless faith of Burton that shored me up. He was a man who proceeded utterly without doubt and utterly without malice to anyone. He was the best of what a man, and a businessman, can be."

Shephard was struck by a third-page photograph, taken only a month earlier, of Burton and Hope Creeley side by side on the Surfside tennis courts. Her smile was reluctant and elusive as always, but her husband seemed to be brimming with vigor. They couldn't have been much over thirty years old.

A bad summer for the Surfside, he thought. As Creeley had written in her diary, bad luck seemed to hang over the club as over the pyramids at El Giza. He glanced up at the Mayan deity on the wall, which from his angle seemed to be doing a death dance on the silent chest of Helene.

He lit a cigarette and used a potted plant for an ashtray. He could hear the wind outside mounting for another attack, and when it hit, the glass behind him rattled with a vengeance. He shifted in his chair, the smell of his sweat rising around him, mixing with the dry aroma of smoke.

Helene had also clipped the *Register* article on the alleged sighting of Creeley in Laguna Beach the night he died. Shephard thought back to her account of the bungled murder, the hoods from Los Angeles unable to tell the Newport

Channel from Diver's Cove. And friends to bring the errant body back north to Newport Beach. But the cops had scoffed at the idea of the body drifting north, and when Shephard considered the logistics of such a drift, he couldn't help but scoff too. What if Helene had told the truth about the drowning? Even if she were as sick as Datilla and Wade had said, might she have still sprinkled her fantasies with bits of truth? Which bits, he wondered, and whose truth? But the newspaper's heated call to reopen the investigation dwindled into disinterest, and the next page of the scrapbook contained only a small article stating that Azul Mercante's trial for murder had been postponed three weeks and a large photograph of a Surfside Halloween gala in which the celebrants dressed up as ghosts.

On the next page of the Surfside scrapbook, the trial began. Weingarten immediately made headlines by requesting not a jury trial but a trial whose outcome would rest solely in the hands of the Honorable Francis Rubio. From his own experience in court, Shephard knew that the request was extremely rare and inevitably was made by defendants who believed that their chances with a jury were nil. Nevertheless, the Academy cliché that an innocent man will demand a trial by judge was sometimes true. Judges were less susceptible to pressure from the press, less impressed with the gyrations of prosecutors, and—perhaps from human reluctance to single-handedly pass judgment —often more attentive to the details of justice than a tired and underpaid jury might be. They were harder to fool. He also knew that judges tended to consider the evidence rather than the man, and could better differentiate between the act and the actor.

But the move to a trial by judge seemed futile as he read Jim Peters's opening remarks. His first statements portrayed Mercante as a dangerously aggressive "playboy," a man whose "very concept of women leads to serious questions about his state of mind at the time of the crime." He promised to produce adequate testimony to demonstrate Mercante's "everyday" behavior as potentially ripe for this kind of sexual crime. And the cornerstone of his prosecution, as he put it, was to produce a murder weapon clearly covered with the fingerprints of Mercante and reveal the results of paraffin tests, which would show that the defendant had in fact fired the fatal shot.

Weingarten's opening remarks were brief and to the point: Azul Mercante was a good friend of the Shephards, especially of Colleen, and had visited the house in goodwill, with honorable intentions. According to Weingarten—and the assertion made Shephard sneer with contempt for the man's stupidity—Wade Shephard had come home unexpectedly, and in a jealous rage fired at Mercante and instead hit his wife. He failed to address the fingerprints and the berium and antimony—the two telltale residues left by the explosion of gunpowder—that were found on Mercante's right wrist.

Shephard read the testimony with a slow anger shifting inside him. But it was apparent to him, as he began the article on the next page, that Mercante couldn't even hold up his end of Weingarten's thin charade.

MERCANTE GAGGED IN COURT

Murder defendant Azul Mercante, accused slayer of a young Laguna Beach mother this summer, was ordered gagged yesterday by Judge Francis Rubio.

Rubio's action took place after Mercante continually interrupted the proceedings with violent outbursts directed at prosecutor Jim Peters. The judge told Mercante that any further outbursts would land him outside the courtroom of his own trial.

Mercante's shouting came during the testimony of police researcher Dwayne Maxwell, who said that a paraffin test of Mercante's skin shortly after his arrest was positive.

Mercante screamed that the berium and antimony found in his skin were there because he is an artist and the paints he works with contain these substances.

The trial is now in its second week.

With a giddy feeling of pursuit, Shephard flipped quickly to the next page of the scrapbook. It was now Weingarten's turn to build a case, and he began by summoning several witnesses who testified that Mercante was in fact a frequent tennis partner of Wade Shephard and "apparently" a friend of both Wade and Colleen. Weingarten brought Wade to the stand on a Thursday morning. For nearly the entire day he questioned Wade's relationship with his wife, with the members of his department, and finally with Mercante, whom Wade described as "a volatile man but apparently a good man." He went on to state his shock in finding Mercante trying to accost his wife. Wade called their relationship one that was "building toward friendship," but that he only saw Mercante as a casual acquaintance at the Surfside Club.

Shephard was not surprised to read that Mercante was a member.

Weingarten finished the day's proceedings by bringing Dwayne Maxwell back to the stand to state that berium and antimony were common components in the paints used by fine artists and that such residues might stay lodged in human skin for "several days." Mercante was carried screaming from the courtroom after breaking his gag, and was banished by Rubio for the next two days.

The two names that jumped off the next page brought Shephard a swirling sense of exhilaration.

The next day's witnesses were Tim Algernon and Hope Creeley.

WOMAN TELLS OF RAPE TRY

Hope Creeley of Newport Beach testified that murder defendant Azul Mercante had once tried to accost her in the spa of the plush Surfside Club in Newport Beach.

The 24-year-old Creeley, widow of drowned Surfside co-owner Burton Creeley, said that she lived in fear of Mercante following his attack on her at a Fourth of July party this year.

Mrs. Creeley was called to the stand by prosecutor Jim Peters, who has claimed throughout the trial that Mercante is a "dangerous sexual outlaw."

Following Mrs. Creeley's testimony, another Surfside member, Tim Algernon, said that Mercante often made suggestive remarks about women at the club and often expressed a desire "to have relations" with several.

The damaging testimony was brought by Peters to show that Mercante entered Mrs. Shephard's home Sept. 9 with the "singular purpose of sexual assault."

He is asking for the death penalty.

Shephard broke into a fresh sweat as he finished the article. Standing up on nervous legs, he lit a cigarette and took the scrapbook with him to the window. In the bright afternoon light that shot through the blinds, he scanned ahead to the final article on the trial of Azul Mercante, killer of Colleen. There was a picture of Mercante being led from the courtroom, his face glaring at the photographer.

He was judged guilty by Francis Rubio, and sentenced to life imprisonment at Folsom State Prison, California.

Rhythms that by now seemed ancient found their way back from Shephard's memory.

Liars Burn and Little Liars
Burn First

And the long-delayed, but painfully obvious:

THIS BIBLE PROPERTY OF
FOLSOM STATE PRISON

Shephard brought the last rumpled Identikit sketch from his pocket and held it beside the hateful face in the photograph.

There was a difference. But with a pen from Helene's nightstand, he drew—with shaking hand—a beard onto Mercante's face in the newspaper, and the difference all but disappeared.

It was impossible: he knew that. But the harder he tried to listen to the voice of his own reason, the louder the roar inside him grew. He looked out at the rioting ocean, waiting for his ears to explode.

PART THREE

TWENTY-TWO

He was playing the dark notes now: he could feel them in his nerve-heavy legs, hear them in his voice as he bought a ticket at the AirCal counter.

A few minutes later, the 12:40 flight from Orange County to Sacramento groaned into the sky. Shephard leaned back and watched the buildings tilt away below, shrinking as the landing gear thumped into place.

What if Hannover knew he was looking for a dead man? Or Wade? Or Tina Trautwein, who believed in getting deeper than the headline? He waited with a cigarette in his mouth and a lighter in his sweaty hand, hoping the No Smoking light would hurry the hell up and go out.

When the jet leveled off, Shephard smoked and tried to take stock. He had two victims, three if he wanted to count Colleen—and he did. He had a motive. He had a suspect who'd been dead for half a decade. Shephard tried to imagine the lines he'd use at Folsom Prison, but they just didn't play. Johnny Cash's blues kept moaning into his mind instead. On the other hand, he thought, then listed the things that still seemed to make sense to him. Cal. The Jota. Ten stitches, holding nicely. Jane . . .

For the moment, a few other things would have to hold, too. He had left Helene's apartment, locked the door, and told Mink she'd killed herself. The Newport Beach police would be calling on him, soon.

At the Sacramento airport he rented a car, making Folsom just after three in the afternoon. The town was quaint and somewhat sorrowful. He looked out at the old houses, Victorian and a little self-conscious, he thought. The prison was away from the city, a steadfast brick building with ivy-covered walls and an appearance of absolute lifelessness. The desk guard, one of those minor officials who take pleasure in bearing bad news, offered a crisp litany. "Can't see the warden 'cause he's home, and can't see the assistant 'cause he's busy. Can't get into records without permission from one or the other. Sorry, detective."

Shephard dredged up the name from memory. "Assistant Warden TeWinkle is a friend. Call him for me, would you, buddy?"

"Told you he's busy. . . ."

"Don't know he's busy until you try, now do you? He's expecting me."

The guard poked the telephone buttons with martial address, waited, explained the situation. Then the hold button: "Never heard of you, Shephard. Maybe you ought to make an appointment and—"

"I got people back in my hometown dying by fire, mister. You heard of that? I'm a cop and I need some help, so tell TeWinkle this is the biggest emergency he's had all night."

The guard eyed him, sighing. This time his tone was a little more encouraging. He explained again, nodded, hung up. "Be right with you."

"Thanks, chum. You've done a fine thing, really."

Assistant Warden Dave TeWinkle was right with Shephard a half hour later. He was a thin, wiry man in his late fifties, Shephard guessed, with taut orange hair and the bright nose of a drinker. He led Shephard upstairs to his office, which was paneled in redwood and oppressively hot. "Mercante? Sure. Won't ever forget that sonofabitch. Killed in the riot of 1980, along with fifteen other inmates. Could have saved yourself a trip and used the phone, detective."

Shephard gathered what assurance he could muster. "What I want, Dave . . . what I need is to talk to someone who was there. At the riot. Someone who knew Mercante."

"Well, I was there. Me and a riot gun, holding down what was left of the east wing for twenty-four hours. Watched most of it burn." TeWinkle jerked his thumb toward a photograph framed on the wall. Behind the dense smoke in the picture's foreground, Shephard could see the forms of men scurrying through the cellblock surrounded by flames, like bodies lost in hell.

"What happened to Mercante?"

TeWinkle chortled, as if he were being pestered by a four-year-old. "He died. I wasn't *that* close. I didn't blast him with the twelve gauge, though I wouldn't have minded too much. What do you mean, what happened?"

"How did he die? Fire? Shot? How?"

TeWinkle leaned back, put his hands behind his head, and stared up at the ceiling. "Guess I don't remember exactly how it went down for old Azul."

"Can you get the account? The record? His file?"

"Get anything I goddamned want," TeWinkle said with a dry smile. "Stay put."

He was back in five minutes with a thin manila folder that bore a red sticker saying INACTIVE on it. He laid it on the desk in front of him, hunched over, and brought a pair of reading glasses from his pocket.

"Bad time," he said. "Late summer and *quiet*. That's how you know something's up in the joint. You come to work and the men are fighting and swearing and generally making a scene, you know things are okay. You come in and it's nothing going on, look out. I was in charge of guards back then. Supervisor. Spent a lot of time in the north tower, just watching." TeWinkle flipped a sheet and nodded.

"Started about this time of night," he said. "Fight in the mess hall got out of hand, and when the guard came to break it up they were ready for him. Half a dozen of them was the story. Beat the hell out of him and dragged him off to the east block and put him on the phone to the warden. They had a whole list of crap they wanted. Longer time in the yard, better *extermination*, I remember. The summer was a hot one and the place was full of fleas and roaches. Full of inmates, too. Much too crowded. Warden said he'd see what he could do if they'd let Connell go, but they killed him instead, then started setting fire to things. Mattresses, blankets, their own stuff mostly. Everybody runnin' wild. Couldn't hardly tell who was who, so much fire and smoke. Got into the rec room and set that on fire too.

"The prisoners held the blocks for four days. Guards shot three of them dead. Couple more died in the fire. One or two got killed by their own kind . . . here, that was Mercante. Says right here: 'Killed by unknown assailants during prison disturbance of August, 1980. A piece of sharpened bed frame was driven into his chest.' Someone shanked him. Couldn't have happened to a better guy. Open and shut, Shephard. That do ya?"

He handed the folder across the table. Shephard studied the profile and face shots, a fresh set taken every few years. In the last pictures, taken in May of the year Mercante died, he wore a full beard and mustache.

"Strange fellow, that Azul," TeWinkle said. "Little guy, but everybody scared of him. Even the gangs left him alone. Got sent up for murder, life, I think. Now I'm a skosh hazy on this—you can check it there if you want—but I think he killed a guy while he was inside. Long before I came here, late fifties maybe. A fight down in the showers, and when it was over, Mercante had busted the fella's head open on the tiles. So they tacked on another life sentence for that. Hell, he'd a been out a long time ago if he'd stayed low. Life is more like twenty if you do it straight up and keep clean."

Good memory, Shephard thought, reading a paragraph from the third sheet in Mercante's file. The man was jumped in the shower—three on one—and he lived to be sentenced for it. Azul's first five years had been hard time: three fights, two vacations in the cooler, moved to the trouble block, then back out with the regular population until he tried to use the bathroom. But after 1962, Shephard saw a change in the man's lifestyle.

"Understudy to the prison priest?"

"The worst of them always end up on God's side," Te-Winkle said as he fiddled with a pipe. "No wonder He's losing. Look at Manson out at Vacaville. Everybody's saved. Know why? Because it makes them feel good."

Shephard looked back at the file. Mercante, the acolyte, had outdistanced three prison priests in his twelve-year career. He witnessed daily to the prisoners, made some converts, upped the church attendance. He still had time for a job in the Folsom records room, $1.25 an hour, a trusty.

And he painted. The transcript mentioned a "successful" business he ran, charging inmates to have their portraits done. His work was featured twelve years running at the annual prison arts and crafts show. The guards commissioned him in 1972 to do a likeness of a retiring warden. He gave classes. And if his file was accurate, Azul Mercante changed. A 1953 entry described him as "deceitful, extremely violent, untrustworthy and not improving." Ten years later he was "patient, agreeable, and apparently without violent tendencies." By early 1973, his goodwill was no longer a hot topic among prison observers, and Mercante was "quite simply a model prisoner in all respects. It is regrettable that the inmate's past record prevents his consideration for parole."

"Detective?" Shephard looked up to find TeWinkle studying him from behind a thin cirrus of smoke. "Mind me asking just what the hell you're looking for?"

Shephard tossed the INACTIVE file onto the desk. "Someone who was there. When he died. Right in the middle of it."

"If I knew what you were—"

"If I knew, I'd ask, Dave. Someone inside at the riot. Someone who might have picked up the gossip afterwards. A man who's been inside a while. It's important. Can you get me inside, alone, with someone like that?"

"Shephard, you expect the damndest things. Yeah, I can get you into a visitor's room. If you want somebody who's been here and knows the place, I got that too. Ed Matusic, but we call him Shake. Writes all the time."

"Not the visitor's room. I need to see him on his own ground, where he's comfortable."

"It isn't comfortable anywhere in this place."

Shephard set his Python on TeWinkle's desk and stood up.

The sounds of West Block echoed around him as he stepped through the last set of sliding steel doors, flanked by two solemn guards. Music blurted from several of the cells, cacophonic and competitive. Two men screamed at each other—one dressed like a woman—from inside the cubicle to his left. From down the block, something raked against the bars in a clanging, methodical riff. Someone was singing and strumming a guitar, and a harmonica whined accompaniment from across the walkway. A Dylan song; Shephard recognized it. He could see faces coming into the dull light as he walked by, hands wrapping around bars. Somebody yelled, "Hey, sweet thing, come here to daddy." The guard on his right nodded to the stairs at the end of the hall. "Matusic, two hundred B, as in boy. Upstairs."

Shake got off his bed and came to the bars as they approached. Shephard studied his small eyes, set like jewels in the meaty face. He was a big man, but plump, and his expression hinted at a boy picked on for his softness. But when he smiled, Shephard saw the brutish guile of a man who'd learned how to get even. There was something damaged in it.

"Got a visitor, Shake. Mr. Shephard. Behave yourself, and show him this is a joint with class." The guard opened the door. "I'll be top of the stairs. Call when you're done."

Shephard stepped in, glanced at the open notebook on the bed, and the pen beside it. "A writer. Shake for Shakespeare?" The door slammed closed behind him. He'd forgotten to ask what Matusic was in for.

"And 'cause I shake when I move."

They shook hands. "Tom Shephard. What are you in for?"

"Mostly rape. You're a cop."

"Laguna Beach."

"Never heard of it."

"It's a long way."

"You can sit on the bed or the chair." Shephard took the chair, and Shake fluffed his pillow before sitting back on his bed. He balanced the notebook on his belly. "I don't want out. So if you're here to make a deal, forget that kind of stuff. I'm home. Everything in the world I got right here."

"Not a thing you want? Nothing?"

Matusic pondered the question, doodling in his notebook.

Shephard looked around the cell: two stacks of books in a corner, piled almost head-high; more books under the bed; a sink and toilet; one wall covered by a huge photograph of mountains with flowers in bloom; the other by large sheets of graph paper clotted with tiny, dark handwriting.

"Always use a little money," Shake said finally. "I collect it. What you want's the question, isn't it?"

Shephard studied the man's face for some avenue of appeal. "Where do you keep your stuff? Your writing?"

"Under the bed. This is my hundred and forty-third book, when I'm done with it. Collect them, too, like the money." He tapped the notebook with the pen, and something seemed to catch his eye. He wrote slowly, his face tensing with concentration. When he was finished, he looked back to Shephard, relaxed and grinning as if he'd been caught torturing a cat. Shephard felt the hairs bristling up his neck. He put a twenty on Shake's bed.

"I need to know some things about the riot in 'eighty, Shake. Nothing you tell me is going to come back on you, on anyone. It's a . . . personal thing for me."

Matusic's little eyes seemed to light up. He crumpled the bill toward him and grinned. "Bad riot. Four days of confusion and pain. Sixteen men and one guard died. Brought in the National Guard, finally." He leaned forward, catching the notebook as it slid away. "Fire everywhere and everything busted up. Guards thought we caused it, but it was the fleas caused it. That, and too many of us in the blocks." He spread out the twenty, pressing it against his knee.

"Do you remember it well?"

"I wrote nine books about it."

"I want to know what happened to Azul Mercante."

"He died. How about some more money?"

Shephard put another twenty on the bed and Shake pounced. It was time now: if Matusic had what he needed,

243

this is where it would be. "How? And don't tell me he got shanked, Matusic. I'm not here to buy shit."

Shake blushed, tried to straighten himself into composure, looked at Shephard with a worried grin. He's afraid, Shephard thought. Here's my way in. But don't turn your back on him, not for a second. Matusic lowered his voice, speaking confidentially: "The real story is he burned to death," he said. "That stuff about the shank was never true. This is what really happened. . . ."

Shephard stared at him as Shake told the story, about the mattresses piled up in the black man's cell and the way they caught fire with the paint thinner from the supply room, and the cell door slamming shut at the last minute with Azul inside and no one could get him out, so he burned up right there, I remember it, East Block number fifty-one Z.

"I heard he might have died from the guards, too," Shephard said quietly. "Shot him, Shake, is one way I heard it." He put down another twenty and Matusic collected it with a grin.

"That's possible, too," he said. "The way it happened was this."

Shephard stared at him again as he told the story about Mercante shot by a tower guard when he tried to make it from the rec room across the exercise yard with some more towels to burn. . . .

He studied Matusic's carnivorous smile, which grew bigger and more eager to please. The big man folded his new-found wealth, then unfolded the bills and straightened them against his leg. He laughed, unsurely.

When Shephard stood up, he watched Shake bring up his legs and wrap his hands around them, leaning his face onto his knees, still laughing quietly. Shephard looked outside to the guard, who was kibitzing with a prisoner near the stairway. The music was still loud. "You know what happened to Azul, don't you?" No change from Matusic, just little eyes laughing from atop his wide knees. The twenties were still in his hand. Go for broke, he thought. He brought the last of his money out, a twenty and a bunch of ones, but it looked good. He waved it.

Matusic's big head shook sideways. "I told you," he said quietly.

"You told me," Shephard whined back. Fast as he could move now: the money back into his pocket with one hand, ripping away the pillow with the other, then a grab at Matusic's throat, jamming his head into the corner of the mattress while he hopped on top and braced his knees on the big man's belly. Shake moaned, swatted up with his empty paw, and—Jesus Christ, Shephard thought—worked his money hand between the bed and the wall where he wouldn't lose his paycheck. Knees on the flabby arms now, and both hands secure around his neck. The longshot: "Mercante didn't die in that riot, Shake, we all know that. Your problem now is to tell me what happened before you choke to death. How you going to manage that, buddy?"

Matusic pushed out a strangled whine; his legs pounded the bed behind Shephard, and his good hand waved harmlessly from the outside of Shephard's knee. "I can't . . . I can't . . ."

"Can't breathe? That's a problem, Shake." He loosened his hands a little. "We were talking about Azul, remember? How it went down in 'eighty. You still there?" Cinching his hold again, hoping the guard wouldn't wander back.

"I can't tell you, I swore."

"Unswear, Shake. I'm either going to strangle you or take my money back, or both."

Incredibly, Shephard thought, Shake used what strength he had left to jam his money down farther toward the floor. Behind him, the sounds of a radio shrieked, and there was laughing too, excited and cruel. Showtime, Shephard thought. He let up a little. "Matusic, if you've got any brains in your head, listen up. You're going fast, another few minutes of this and you're history. Mercante. What happened? Tell now, you can keep your money and twenty more. That's a lot of money, Shake." The poor man really was gasping, he thought. He loosened his grip a little more. "You're not quite sure on that, are you? Shake? You there? Come clean, goddamnit, I'm getting tired of choking you."

One last try. He readjusted himself over Matusic's arms, then closed his grip with a slow, patient strength. He could hear the laughter from behind him, quiet enough not to draw the guards. Shake was gurgling something. ". . . I . . . rrr . . . rokay . . . rokay." Shephard let up. "I'll tell you . . . no more. . . ." Shake's chest was working deeply.

"You're on, Shake. Spill it and grow rich."

Then the big man's arm fell to the mattress, and his expression relaxed. Shephard got off and pulled him up, propping him against the cell wall. Face to face, Shake's lips trembling into a smile. Still, he kept the money, clutching it away from Shephard like a child.

"Mercante . . . just died. Like I told you."

"Shake, you disappoint me." Shephard wrenched the man's money hand from behind the bed and tore away the bills. He put them in his pocket and retreated to the far end of the cell. Then, a sound more agonized than any he'd managed to beat out of him, a high-pitched sorrowful keen that came from deep inside.

"Nooo . . . oooh nooo! I earned that. It's *miiine. . . .*"

"Death and taxes, Shake. I'm charging you this sixty plus the twenty more I was going to give you. For feeding me a bunch of shit and making me break a sweat. Deal's off."

Shake scooted up against the wall again, eyeing Shephard with a heartbroken pout. His chin trembled. "You can't do that."

"I just did."

"You broke the deal."

"Shut up, Matusic. Have a nice life." He leaned toward the cell door, looking for the guard.

"Wait! I can maybe tell you something."

"I just about strangled you. Now you want to talk."

"It's a matter of honor."

"Tell me about it. I'm all ears."

"The money?"

"Stays where it is until I hear what I need."

Shake buried his fleshy face in his hands. Shephard heard him sigh. "Okay, but when I tell, you pay. Right?"

"That was the deal ten minutes ago. Weren't you paying attention?"

"This is it. Come here. Come a little closer and I'll tell."

Shephard sat on the end of the bed. Shake scrunched up closer to the wall, hugging his legs to his chest. It was almost a whisper: "Azul didn't die in 'eighty. He just played a little cut and run."

"Cut and run?"

"Get somebody else's tags. Get their clothes and cell. *Be* them, if they're up before you. You know . . . out before you."

"Won't work unless they're twins, Shake. Am I going to have to keep your money?"

Shake leaned forward, licking his lips, boring into Shephard with his tiny eyes. "They practically *were* twins, except for a beard. Azul grew a beard, and when I saw him do that I knew what he was gonna try. Knew it. They were real alike. Enough to make it work. And Azul worked in Records, so I'll bet that helped. He could *change* shit. Azul even cut off his middle toe—right behind the first joint—because that's how—"

"What was his name?"

"Manny Soto . . . because Manny had a joint missing. Azul pulled it off during the riot. Caught Manny alone, then shanked him, dragged him off to his own cell. Changed everything with him and left him there. I was the only one who ever knew. I . . . swore I'd never tell."

"And he helped your money collection to make sure."

"Five hundred dollars. It's still under the bed, with my books." Shephard stood up, his mind racing but his body heavy, as if in a dream. "I never thought he'd get away with it. After the riot was done, bunch of us got transferred out so they could rebuild what we wrecked. I think Azul went to Lompoc. I never saw him again. He just got lost. I thought they'd find out, send him back. After a year I quit even thinking about it. Azul gave me money lots of times."

"I'll bet he did."

"Wanna see it?"

Shephard went to the door and called the guard, yelling over the din of the music and singing. The prisoner below was still mangling the Dylan song, but the harmonica had wandered off to its own wild melody.

"Hey . . . what about our deal?"

Shephard tossed the sixty on the bed, then chased it with one more twenty. He had eight dollars left. "Shake, Azul bought a lot of honor for five hundred bucks. I almost strangled you and you wouldn't give. But I take away sixty dollars and you squeal. Why?"

Matusic gathered up his hard-earned pay, organizing the bills in a neat stack. "I told you. I collect it."

"But what the hell for, if it's sitting there under the bed?"

The damaged grin again, self-satisfied and cruel. "Don't you know anything about the world? Shit man, money is *freedom.*"

TeWinkle was in his office, halfway through dinner. "Ah, Shephard. Find anything?"

"Manny Soto. Remember him?"

TeWinkle rearranged his diced carrots, frowning into the

plate, then looked back up with a nod. "Vaguely. I think we relocated him after the riot. In for murder too, I think. You keep some nice company, Shephard."

"Lompoc?"

"Think so. Here. Try 'em yourself." He pushed his telephone toward Shephard, who dialed and was put on hold. Five minutes later, he was put through to the assistant warden. No need to check the files, said the assistant, Manny Soto was released two weeks ago.

Shephard hung up, retrieved his Python from the desk, and walked out.

TWENTY-THREE

As the last boarding call for Flight 321 droned through the Sacramento terminal, Shephard repeated the three names to Pavlik. Judge Francis Rubio, District Attorney Jim Peters, Wade Shephard.

A condemned trinity, he thought. "Carl, you've got to get them *out* of wherever they are, and into someplace else. *Anyplace.* Just get them out. You got that?"

Pavlik's voice came back thin and unsure over the long-distance wires. "Tom, would you mind telling me—"

"I can't, Carl, buddy. My plane's leaving without me, and this is one I don't want to miss. Trust, Carl. Call me at my father's in an hour and a half." He gave the number. "And Carl, try Wade last. I just called the church and he's gone home. Should be there in half an hour." He hung up, hustling toward the gate with a sweat-drenched boarding pass in his hand.

The landing at Orange County was vicious and abrupt, the jet buffeted by winds that still howled in from the desert. Even the LaVerda seemed tentative as he sped down 405, for the first time in his recent life keeping an eye out for cops.

Wade's car wasn't on the street, nor was it in the garage. Shephard wheeled in his motorcycle and closed the door. He let himself in with a key he hadn't used for a decade and a growing sense of dread.

The house smelled of dried eucalyptus, and of Sunday bacon and eggs. He realized he had been expecting smoke.

"Pop?"

The living room was empty, the kitchen as spotless as ever, the den door closed. He listened, then pushed it open. The evening sunlight slanted through the blinds, ribbing the wall in light and shadow. He passed down the hallway with a faintly growing optimism, went through the main bedroom to the bath. "Pop?" When he pulled back the shower door, he saw only the glistening tub and a bar of soap that had slid off its tray and now covered the drain. Shephard picked it up and set it back in place. Wade's secretary had said he'd left, he thought. Almost two hours ago, for home. Dinner? Date? A party?

He heard a car pulling into the driveway, and went to the window. His .357 clunked against the frame as he moved aside the curtain and watched his father step from the car, then lean back in and take out two big bags of groceries. Shephard could not remember being so happy to see him in all his life. He met him at the door and took a bag, Wade studying him intently. "You look like a young cop with something on his mind," Wade said.

While his father put away the groceries, Shephard told

him the story. Wade's face tightened, and he feigned concentration on the chore at hand. The toothpaste went into the refrigerator. Shephard outlined his evidence: the threats to witnesses Tim and Hope, the cobalt and cadmium traces used in paints, the near match between the Identikit and the old Surfside photograph of Mercante, Ed Matusic's tale of violence and cunning at the Folsom riot, and "Manny Soto's" release two weeks ago from Lompoc. Wade leaned against the counter, the color draining from his face. "Mercante . . . simply *can't* be alive. He died, five years ago."

"The cons call it cut and run, pop. Azul raised it to an art form." Shephard filled a glass of water from the tap and handed it to Wade. "It's Mercante. He may as well have signed his name. You said it yourself once. Money, a woman, silence, or revenge. He wants revenge. He wants you. By the way, pop, Helene Lang is dead. She killed herself this morning."

He watched his father close his eyes, try to stand straight and reconstitute himself. Wade labored into the dining room and slumped into a chair. Shephard followed.

"She may have been a crazy old woman," he said, "who thought Joe was in love with her, that Joe killed Burton. But she believed it right to the end." When Wade looked up he seemed smaller, as if what part of him had slumped into the chair had continued into the fabric and vanished. Shephard wondered if he would ever get it back.

"I suppose she did," Wade said, in hardly more than a whisper.

When the phone rang, Shephard answered it. Pavlik's voice came through, rushed and excited: "Tom, I did your homework. Jim Peters doesn't have anything to worry about today. He died a few years back in an auto wreck. But the Honorable Francis Rubio is alive, *somewhere.* I got in touch with his son, Francis Junior, but he won't give us the old man's address. Did you find Wade?"

Shephard looked into the dining room. "He's here."

"What next?"

"Give me Rubio Junior's number. Maybe I can . . . make an impression."

Wade eyed Shephard quietly while he hung up from Pavlik and then dialed. On the fourth ring a woman answered hastily. "One moment," she snapped.

A very long moment later, Shephard found himself talking to Frank Rubio, Jr., who spoke in a clipped and irritated voice. "He doesn't live with us any more," he explained. "I'm handling medical and estate matters now. I suppose that's what you're calling about." Mr. and Mrs. Rubio are in the middle of a nasty one, Shephard thought.

"Not exactly. Can you tell me where he lives?"

After another long silence, Francis Rubio, Jr., said that his father was now in a very fine house in Santa Ana, but had all but lost his mental faculties. His Newport Beach home was in escrow, his finances in order, and visits by old friends, new friends, and financial sharps of any kind would be useless. Was this clear?

"Clear as day, Frank," Shephard answered. "How about a visit by an old enemy?"

"For what purpose?" Rubio demanded, losing patience.

"To kill him," he answered flatly. He waited for the click of the receiver. "Rubio, are you alone right now?"

"No."

"Can you get that way?"

The phone hit something hard. Shephard heard their voices in the background, then Frank Rubio was back. "Okay. Now just what the fuck is going on? Who are you?"

Shephard explained. He told Frank Rubio that his father had heard a case thirty years ago, that he had sent the defendant to prison, and the man had been let out. He explained that two of the witnesses had been murdered, and

Francis Rubio stood a good chance of being next. Rubio listened without comment, then grunted.

"Sounds pretty farfetched to me," he said. Years of experience had taught Shephard that the best antidote for stupidity was silence. He waited and Rubio grunted again, but with less conviction. "You're not kidding?"

"I'm not kidding, Frank, buddy. And this isn't my idea of a fun Sunday. Give me your father's address. How much longer do I have to sit here and beg you to help me save his life?"

Another long pause, then: "Maybe you're not who you say you are. How do I know you're not the one who's after him?"

"Francis, I'm a detective. My badge number is two-seven-one-eight, my partner is Carl Pavlik, and you can call him at the station right now to check me out. I'm demanding your help. And I'm telling you, the more time you waste, the sorrier you might be."

"It's called . . . Ross Manor. He's . . . in a nursing home, a very good one, though. Ross Street in Santa Ana, it's in the book. The director is Claire Bailey. I—"

"Don't even think of going out there. Stay put and wait for my call."

When Shephard heard the woman's voice again, he realized Rubio was speaking under pressure. "Maybe we could bring him back here," he said quietly.

"You might have to." Through the line, Shephard heard a door slam.

"I can do that," Rubio said finally. In the background, the woman's voice barked impatiently. "I can at least goddamned do that much."

Wade had disappeared down the hall. When he came back a few minutes later, with his white suit hanging on him and his eyes remote in thought, he gave Shephard the least convincing smile he'd seen in thirty years. Shephard had never seen him so dispirited, as if something inside him had slowed. Even his voice was brittle. They agreed— though Wade argued until his arguments made no sense— that he would leave town. "And what do you plan to do, Tommy?"

"I don't know yet. I've got to get to Francis Rubio. Get him out of Santa Ana for a while. Take a vacation, pop. Let your assistant deliver the sermon next week. Your ratings will soar when you get back."

His father smiled feebly, his eyes still gazing inward, lost on some solitary vision. He brought a .38 snubnose from his coat pocket, and a box of ammunition. "Don't look at me like I'm a helpless old man," he said finally. "I can still take care of myself. I think I'll go down to Mexico for a few days. See the hospital site. I'll leave you a note, here on the table, when I leave." He stood up, hugged his son, and walked down the hallway toward his bedroom.

"Dad, your toothpaste is in the refrigerator."

The LaVerda carried him out Laguna Canyon Road, onto Interstate 5, and through Irvine, Tustin, into Santa Ana. The wind continued unabated, casting him from one lane to the next without warning, stinging his face with sand. At Irvine Boulevard he angled to the off ramp, caught the green light, and headed downtown. A tumbleweed, strangely out of context in the city, rolled across the street in front of him and ran up against a chain-link fence. The elm trees that lined Ross Street tossed in the wind while two children on skateboards held out their coats to harness a free ride through the darkness.

Ross Manor was a converted Victorian-style home with a sprawling green lawn studded with empty white chairs. As Shephard pulled his motorcycle to the curb, he noted that two old men were sitting on the wide porch, facing each

254

other, rocking slowly in the porch light. They eyed him silently as he came toward them.

Inside, he faced a large, hotel-style desk, behind which an elderly woman sat knitting. Not far in front of her was a television set with the volume turned up. She looked at him through thick glasses, put down her needles and yarn, and stood up. Her badge said Claire Bailey.

"Miss Bailey, I'm Tom Shephard. I'd like to see Francis Rubio."

The woman turned down the volume on the TV, and when the music dissipated, Ross Manor lapsed into silence.

"I'm the director," she said, pulling a sweater around her thin neck. "Francis Rubio?"

"Please."

She checked a ledger of some kind. "The former judge is with his attorney right now," she said with polite firmness. "He asked me to let them conduct some personal business undisturbed."

There was a giddy swirl in Shephard's stomach. Business at nine o'clock?

"Mr. Rubio asked you, or the attorney?" He smiled, praying it didn't look false, as he scanned the ledger for a room number. Nothing but orange yarn and blue needles; Claire Bailey had set her knitting on the book.

"The attorney," she said. "His new attorney, in fact."

To hell with the Santa Ana police, Shephard thought. He brought out his badge. "Claire, I'm a policeman and I must see Francis immediately. Please, it's extremely important." When she hesitated, he lifted his coat away and exposed the Python. Her eyes widened and she stepped back.

"Two-oh-six."

Shephard looked to his right, then to his left: two stairways leading up in Victorian symmetry.

"It's in the middle of floor two," she said hurriedly. "Take either one. The room is right in the middle of the hallway."

Shephard chose the right. His footsteps echoed in the silence of Ross Manor, the click of shoes on wood. Halfway up, he heard a door close. Then footsteps away from his direction, deliberate, unhurried. They found the stairs and began down.

A faded green runner split the hallway in half. The narrow passage was lit by a lamp fastened to the ceiling midway, emitting a dull yellow glow that seemed to come more from the polished wood of the hallway than the bulb. There was a smell of disinfectant and old bedding. Odd numbers on his left and even on his right. Somewhere, a TV droned. Outside 206, he tried the knob and found it locked. Downstairs, a door slammed.

Then a muffled thrashing from inside the room, followed by muted groans, as if someone were screaming from under water.

Shephard pushed off from the wall behind him, aiming his shoulder at the door. He smashed against the old wood, a solid, bone-jarring collision that sent a wide throb of pain through his back and stopped him as decisively as if he had hit cement. The door shuddered and held. He charged again, this time with his other side, and again the thick wood punished him. Inside he could hear a high-pitched popping noise, then a hiss followed by splattering. The muffled groans had turned to thick, choked yelps. Against the wall again, Shephard pushed off and hurled himself again. He hit, rebounded in a shudder of pain, and watched the door swing open slowly before him.

Smoke and water pelted him from inside. Flames ate upward from the bed, growing from the white blanket toward the ceiling. A sprinkler showered the room, the water hissing violently as it streamed down on the fiery bed. He picked up a chair and threw it through the window. Under the flaming cover Shephard saw movement, a stifled struggling that sent sparks popping to the floor. The yelping sounded desperate, abandoned. With one quick movement that sent a puff of heat into his face, Shephard grabbed the end of the bedspread and flung it into the middle of the floor. The covers below, body-shaped, shook and trembled. He gathered them up and caught a glimpse of the man bundled underneath as he threw them down with the bedspread and trampled the heap. The sprinkler began to do its work. The sparks popped up, the water showered down with a fierce hissing. Shephard stuck his foot into the cooling stream.

When the fire on the floor seemed dead, he moved to the bed and looked down on the man whose quivering legs and arms were tied snugly to the railings with the strings built into his pajamas. The white feet continued to thud against the mattress. His arms were tied in place, but his hands clutched at the side of the bed, the knuckles purple with blood. And above the wide strips of tape that mummified the lower half of his face, two terrified eyes stared upward. Droplets of water splattered onto his head. Shephard moved his hands over the body, and his voice sounded high and foreign as he told the man that he was all right, buddy, chum, you're going to be all right, Mr. Rubio, you're going to be all right. Under his hands, Rubio's withered body was miraculously cool.

Heads appeared in the doorway. Shephard stripped open the pajamas and looked down with almost tearful relief at the unburned chest and stomach of Francis Rubio.

Murmuring from the doorway was a small crowd of old people—one man adjusting his hearing aid, a woman in curlers, the horrified face of Claire Bailey as she struggled to get in. Water pelted down from the sprinkler. Through it all, Rubio's eyes never strayed from Shephard.

Claire Bailey stood beside him. She had already called the fire department and the police, she said. In the quiet that followed, the sprinkler overhead shut off and Claire Bailey started weeping. She helped Shephard peel the tape from Rubio's face. When they lifted the first wide white strip from his mouth, the man's heels began pounding the bed again, his hands opened and closed around nothing, and he bellowed into the silence of Ross Manor.

Shephard eased his way through the people outside the door, looking them in the eyes and telling them that everything was okay now, just a little trouble with Mr. Rubio's new lawyer. One man said that attorneys were always a pain. He broke into a run when he reached the hall, and headed for the stairs. As he clambered down the stairway, two sounds echoed in his ears, even through the din of Rubio's wailing. One was the sound of footsteps going down the stairs when he had first climbed them, the other was the slamming door he had heard as he stood outside room 206. He reached the lobby, panting. On the porch, both of the men had risen from their rockers to stare at the overstuffed chair that had landed, as if dropped from heaven, on the lawn. Shephard ran to the LaVerda and was about to jump onto the seat—the key already in his hand—when he saw the spark plug cables, neatly severed, lying across the leather. He cursed and looked up Ross Street, where less than a block away a convertible red Cadillac and its gray-haired driver lurched around a corner and out of sight.

TWENTY-FOUR

The cops were waiting for him when he finally came home that night, as he knew they would be. Benson from Newport Beach and Hudson from Santa Ana. They stared at him appraisingly as Little Theodore delivered him on the back of his Harley-Davidson.

"Little trouble in Newport I'd like to talk to you about," Benson said with a crooked smile. He was short, with a combative face, and looked younger than Shephard.

Hudson was bulky and unshaven, and apparently not a talker. "Ditto in Santa Ana," he said, as if it were an effort. "At Ross Manor."

They came upstairs, surveyed his stripped apartment, and asked their questions. He modified the truth for Benson, saying only that he had waited for Helene Lang to meet him, then gone upstairs to find the door open, and let himself in.

It was news to Benson that her name wasn't Dorothy Edmond. He made a note of this, then sat stroking Cal. "If the door was open when you found her, how come it was locked when we got there?" he asked.

"Just thinking of you," Shephard said. "Didn't want anybody tampering with your scene."

Benson seemed to ponder this for a moment. "The next time you want to help me, stay the hell out of Newport, okay?"

"Ditto in Santa Ana," Hudson managed again.

After an hour of questions, Benson and Hudson closed

their notebooks as if on cue, took a last look around the inhospitable apartment, and left.

Later that night, as he studied the face of Azul Mercante in the pale light of his living room, Shephard could feel something foreign inside himself, a barely recognizable emotion, like an unwatered seed only now beginning to grow. He considered Mercante's haughty smile, the superiority in his eyes, the way he had forced himself into Shephard's own home and tried to drag his mother down. Images flickered through his mind. Looking at the sketch, Shephard saw in the man everything he had learned to despise: arrogance, violence, recklessness, and a belief—most difficult of all for Shephard to understand—that everything is legitimized by one's own passion. He recognized the crude emotion growing inside him. It was rage.

And he realized, as he listened to the sound of someone coming up his stairway, that Azul Mercante had yet to understand the full rage of revenge. That rage must have been written on his face when he opened the door and beheld the windswept beauty of the young woman in front of him.

"Hi, Tom," she said finally. "You look like hell." Jane handed him the Identikit he'd given her. "You said this was an excuse to see me again. Well, now it's mine to see you. I've never seen this guy before."

He stepped aside to let her in. "This is it."

"Your apartment . . . well . . ." She looked around at the bleak living room. Shephard watched her, wondering at the perfect match between the blue of her eyes and the blue of her blouse. Really, he thought, is she any of my business? Then she brought her lips to his mouth, and they stood there so long, wrapped silently together, that Cal finally came in from the patio to investigate. "He's cute," Jane said.

"If you think Cal's cute, you need a drink. If I had some

wine I'd offer you a glass, if I had a glass. It'll have to be vodka. Rocks or neat?"

"Rocks. It's a blazer tonight again."

"So you're thawing out? No more fires on August nights?"

"Guess so."

They sat on the floor, Cal working his way between them in sly jealousy. He seemed taken with the guest and panted up close to her face; a charmer in all respects, Shephard thought. Cal had never been shy with the ladies.

"You were right about animals being easy to love," she said. "And safe. Dad and Becky, you and Cal, Buster and I." She smiled and stroked Cal's head. The dog wiggled appreciatively, then snuck in a sloppy kiss.

"You asked for it," Shephard said. "Get away, Cal. She's not yours." But Cal had teamed up, and he turned to Shephard with a look of immunity.

"Sorry about the other night. I didn't mean to come off like the ice bitch. Make me another drink, would you? Then I'll try to explain myself."

She lay back and talked to the ceiling, Shephard beside her. Her first love, she said, had been in high school, and she still thought of the boy, who was now somewhere up north and married. He had proposed to her the night they graduated and she had refused out of principle. And it was the right thing to do, she said, because the boy had found a girl to marry not long after, and Jane had fallen in love with an older man her second year out of school. She was working as a waitress in New Orleans, had gone there on a whim, with a friend. Charlie. It was easy to fall for his dark good looks and his quiet attentiveness. "Besides, he wouldn't come around all the time," she said. "You know how it is when you can't always have what you want. So I loved him all the more."

But Charlie was a philanderer—the more she suspected it, the more she wanted him—and he finally left her in a bitter Southern winter, with nothing but syphilis as a good-bye. "I was young, dumb," she said, tilting the vodka to her lips. "But I wised up a little that winter."

She came back to California. She was twenty-one, broke, and didn't have an idea of what to do with herself. Shephard tried to picture her, stepping off the bus with her bags, a California beauty returned to the motherland. Charlie blew it, he thought. If he ever ran across him he would tell him so, and perhaps break his nose.

"I was pretty low," Jane was saying, "but as soon as I met Raymond, that all changed. He was a year younger than I was, a pretty, pretty boy. Strong face, a good heart, full of art. He wanted to be a painter. Met him here in town, at the Festival. We got an apartment and moved in together, got engaged, planned everything for the wedding. Two days before the big one, Ray just disappeared. He left a little note saying he couldn't do it, had to be free to find himself, or something. I really loved him. I still see him around, but he gave up the art and starting dealing cocaine. Makes a lot of money, too. Don't bust him, Shephard. He's an alright guy. I guess."

"Can I break his nose?"

She slapped him gently on the arm, then turned to face him. "After that, I just said fuck it, Tom. I traveled Europe and South America, a bit of the East. I did what I wanted, when I wanted. I took some men, mostly the ones who were most sincere about me, and spit 'em back up fast as I could. It was a way to get free, you know, a way not to fall. I kept it up for a couple of years after I got back. That's how I learned about that cold something inside of me—that thing I can use if I need to—and I made an art form out of it. Then I just quit. I'd proved whatever the point was and I wasn't very happy. I realized the one thing I'd always loved, even at the worst times, were the beasts. Like him." Jane rubbed Cal's belly. "So I enrolled at UCI in biology, and I'm going on to veterinary when I get out. To tell you the truth, I haven't really felt much of anything for a long time. Then along comes this lanky detective who won't take the hard line for an answer. You spoiled the whole program, Tom." She ran her fingers through his hair, gently across the stitches.

"Well, you're a couple of years ahead of me in the pain and heartache school. Though I've learned a few lessons, I guess." Shephard tipped back his vodka, mostly water by now.

"Tell me about them."

"No. Some other time. Enough for tonight."

"All that make you think I'm not exactly the woman you had at Diver's Cove?"

"No, Jane. It just makes me want to take you in the bedroom and love you for a long slow time."

"Would you do that now? Please?"

Two hours later they were still there, Jane resting peacefully with her dark hair spread against a pillow, Shephard staring at the clock. Their lovemaking had been desperate, almost frightening to him, and mixed with the haunting face of Azul Mercante, which invaded the room each time he closed his eyes. It had left him overloaded with possibilities, premonitions. The alternating current of love and hatred was a voltage he could scarcely stand.

"Time won't stop just because you stare at a clock, Tom."

Shephard ran his hand over her forehead, through her hair. "Sorry."

"You want to tell me now, just what's going on?"

He lay back and started at the beginning, the summer of bad luck at the Surfside. Burton and Hope, Joe and Helene, Tim and Margie, Wade and Colleen. Azul Mercante. Jane leaned against the wall, drawing the sheet over herself, listening silently through the rest of his story: the Bibles, the cobalt and cadmium, Mercante's transfer from Folsom and release from Lompoc. When Shephard finished, Jane was looking at the clock too. "So Rubio is hidden, and Wade? Where's your father?"

"On Isla Arenillas by now. Joe sent him down on his jet."

She turned to Shephard and kissed him, then settled her head on his chest. "You know, Tom, I've got one more question to add to all this. All those bills that dad ran up when mom had the cancer? The forty thousand? He never paid them. There's not a single canceled check to the hospital for all those years. And he kept canceled checks too, *all* of them."

"Maybe the insurance covered it."

"He didn't have any. He'd always lecture me on getting good insurance, because of how much that treatment cost him."

Shephard added this riddle to the bagful that already seemed to be weighing down his mind. Take a number, he thought, stand in line. "What year was it she first started treatment?"

"Nineteen fifty-one."

Of course, he thought. When else?

Just before two in the morning, the phone rang. Jane flinched at the sound. Shephard pulled his robe from the bathroom door and lit a cigarette on his way to the living room. The voice that greeted him was shaky, the music in the background was new wave.

"Tom Shephard?"

He recognized the voice, but couldn't place the agitated, nasal tone. "Speaking, chum."

"This is Ricky Hyams. At Valentine's, you know?"

"Rick, buddy. Sounds like a rockin' scene down there."

"Tom, uh, I think there's . . ." The phone was lowered. Shephard heard two men talking quickly, some decision being reached. Then Hyams was back. "Tom, I think there's something here you should see. In regard to, uh, what we talked about last week."

"What is it, Ricky? And why should I see it when I've got a lovely woman in my bed?" Shephard heard the muffled movements of Jane in his bedroom, then the closing of his bathroom door.

"I can't talk. But come here, I, uh, think you should come here right away if I were you." It struck Shephard that Hyams was drunk, high, or both. "I'll meet you outside the front door, okay?"

The wind had dissipated, leaving the city clean. A sparse trail of taillights glittered ahead of him down Coast Highway like the red scales on a winding snake. The oncoming headlights bore into his eyes with a new intensity.

The gay corner of town bustled with people, men arm-in-arm filling the crosswalk at Crest Street, and the liquor store seemingly crammed with bodies. A white convertible slowed in front of him as the driver considered a young hitchhiker. Shephard swerved around it onto the narrow Crest Street cul-de-sac and parked the Mustang along a red curb.

The door to Valentine's was hidden by a crowd of men waiting to get in. They sprawled around the entrance, some dancing to the music that was loud even outside the bar. Ricky Hyams broke away from the jam and waited at the bottom of the steps. Behind him was a large man, dressed in full leather regalia, who nodded officiously at Shephard and parted the bodies as they made their way to the door.

Inside, the Valentine's lobby was a cramped stampede of men, bunched, talking, laughing, drinking—an animated cast. Hyams nodded and chatted briefly with his constituency, guiding Shephard by the arm until they broke through the knotted bodies and into a short hallway marked by a Do Not Enter sign. The music was so loud Shephard could feel it in his bones. It receded to a series of muffled thuds when Hyams closed the door to his office after them. He had looked at Shephard once, and said nothing. When he sat down and lit a cigarette, Shephard noted the way it trembled in his hand. Ricky Hyams, Shephard thought, looked dead in the eyes.

"He was here," he said finally. "The man in the papers. I think it was him." He looked up at Shephard as if he expected to be hit. "It wasn't until, uh, just a few hours ago that I realized it might be him. Then, again, Tommy, it might not be, so if it isn't don't get down on me too hard about tonight, but better than not calling at all, isn't it?" He looked down at the blotter on his desk. "Oh hell." The bottle of gin that he took out of a drawer was a pint, and still half-full. "Been at this bottle all night," he said, holding it in front of his face. "I don't drink very often."

"When did you see him?"

Hyams gulped, but not much gin seemed to disappear. "First time last week. Monday, I think it was. Off and on since then. But he's gone now. Left late tonight with a suitcase, and took a taxi. I know because I can see the courtyard from my apartment."

"He had a room here?"

"Checked in Monday afternoon. Older guy with gray hair and beard, and blue eyes that you don't feel good looking at." Hyams attacked the bottle again, slurping. He lit another cigarette even though the first one was half alive. "Shit. Dammit to hell. Tom, you're not the first one interested in this guy. Monday night, a man showed up at the desk and asked to see me alone. He said he was interested in getting a key to the apartment that John Dixon had just rented. Dixon is your man, Tom." Hyams scanned the room, as if looking for something he had lost. "That isn't such an unusual request around here. Our clients tend to become familiar with each other rather quickly, and sometimes, uh, well, a room is a room, right?"

"So you gave him a key?"

"He insisted on leaving me a hundred for my graciousness, as he put it. And he said that due to some rather tender circumstances, he'd appreciate it if I forgot his face." Hyams drew sharply on his cigarette, then flicked his fingernails against the bottle. "I didn't think much of it until this envelope arrived on Wednesday."

From the bottom drawer of his desk, Ricky produced a plain white envelope with his name typewritten across it. He handed it to Shephard with a woeful look on his face.

"When I opened it, I knew that something wasn't right."

Shephard lifted the flap and drew out five one-thousand-dollar bills. They were so new they stuck together.

"How do you know it came from . . . ?"

"Russell Dulak, that's what his name is. Tom, around here you get used to a certain kind of man. I thought at first that Dulak might have been, uh, finding himself sexually. Coming out, as they say. But the hundred was strange, and the thousands, well, I just knew they were from him. No doubt. And the way he started coming and going around Dixon's place, well, it wasn't a personal kind of thing. I thought drugs, and I don't like big drugs, but I wasn't sure. Dulak came late at night, parked on the red where you did —I, uh, saw you from my apartment. And he only came when Dixon wasn't there. He knew because he'd call and ask me. That's how I knew the money was from him, too."

"What kind of car?"

"Dark Porsche Carerra. Beautiful car."

"What does Dulak look like?"

Hyams sighed and drank again from the gin. Shephard wondered what else was making his eyes gape. "Big guy. Dark hair and brown eyes. Always wore real nice clothes, I noticed."

Bruce Harmon, Shephard thought, always right on the

scene. Waving money at Hyams like he'd waved it at Jimmy and Dot Hylkama. So he *had* found Hodges–Steinhelper–Dixon–Mercante first, and not even bothered to call. Somehow, Shephard wasn't surprised.

"Tom," Hyams continued, staring down at the blotter again. "I think I did something wrong. So I called you. I was scared. When Dulak brought the suitcase and Dixon left in the taxi, I figured they'd be out of my place for a while. It's a good place here. You might not understand it, but there's a lot of good things here for a lot of people. I don't want it, uh, fucked up."

"What kind of car did Dixon drive?"

"Red caddy convertible. Nice one."

Shephard studied the man in front of him, and saw something sincere in the haggard young face. "You knew it was the man in the Identikit sketch I showed you Saturday, didn't you?"

Hyams downed the bottle in one gulp. "Dulak said I could keep the money, and my life, by saying and doing nothing. Russ. Shit, I knew it was wrong."

"And Dixon left here with the suitcase Dulak brought?"

"I'm sure it was the same one."

"Let's see his room, Ricky."

Hyams rose, swayed, steadied himself against Shephard's shoulder, then led him back down the hallway and through Valentine's dense lobby.

The apartments were clustered around a small courtyard behind the club. In the center stood a planter filled with banana trees, their fronds lacerated by the recent wind. Hyams took him to the second story, up a cement staircase that was swaying by the time they reached the top. The railing was littered with beer cans. The doors of several dilapidated apartments were open and couples kissed, laughed, spilled from the rooms. At the last door on the left, Hyams stopped and fumbled for the key. Mercante knew

268

the out-of-the-way places, Shephard thought. He had hidden himself in town like only a man who had once lived there could.

The reek of chemicals hit him as he stepped inside and turned on the light switch beside the door.

The shock that rocked his body as he looked at the huge painting in the middle of the room rattled Shephard clear to his fingertips. Smiling at him from the canvas, revealed in all her golden youth and beauty, a beauty that hurt him to look at, was his mother, Colleen.

"Dixon's a painter," Hyams offered. "I could see him through the window, working on her. Pretty, isn't she?"

Shephard's heart was beating in his ears. "Close the door, Ricky, would you?" he heard himself ask. "And don't touch anything, please."

He stepped away from the canvas and surveyed the rest of the small room. It was chaotic: tubes of paint—Winsor & Newtons, he noticed—lay strewn on the dirty carpet; dishes were littered on the floor and couch; magazines and newspapers had been discarded in one corner, and now the pile reached nearly a foot high. Other paintings hung on the shabby walls, discordantly, as if thrown there without regard to balance or order. A violent seascape, a still-life that emitted a jittery anxiety, and a painting that arrested Shephard's attention immediately. A self-portrait.

"Pretty, uh, riveting stuff, isn't it?"

Shephard studied the sallow face in the portrait. Mercante had chopped his own face into green and yellow bevels from which his eyes arose narrowed and grim, like those of a viper about to strike. He might act like a god, Shephard thought, but he sees himself as a serpent.

In the kitchen, tossed beneath the cheapish table, Shephard found a pair of cowboy boots, the right one cloven at the heel. Sitting between the salt and pepper shakers on the table was a roll—barely used by the looks of it—of white surgical tape. Beside it was a Bible, open to Revelation.

The page had been kept by a brightly colored ticket envelope for AeroMexico, which contained no ticket. The date, scrawled by hand on the cover, was *August 31*. So, he's traveling by air now, Shephard thought. The gate number was 42, the flight number 217, and whoever made the reservation had preferred—he read the words with a mirthless laugh—non-smoking. Shephard's insides twisted.

"Is there a phone in this rathole?"

Hyams pointed to the couch. Shephard dug out the phone from under a dirty pillow and dialed Los Angeles.

The AeroMexico counter at International was still open, but the ticketing agent mournfully told Shephard that Flight 217—L.A. to Cozumel—left at 10:15. He asked what time the the next flight departed.

"That will be nine-fifty this morning," she said. "Arriving Cozumel at seven P.M. May I reserve you a seat?"

Shephard took the reservation, hung up, and tried to find an earlier flight. Six phone calls later he had come up with nothing.

Then he thought of Marty Odette, who owed him one. Shephard dialed again. A song by the Rolling Stones echoed from the background of the Sportsplace when Odette answered the phone.

"Marty, buddy, this is Tom Shephard. I'm coming by in ten minutes and I need your help. Close the bar if you have to, you're flying to Isla Arenillas."

TWENTY-FIVE

What I like about the Lear is the velocity," Marty yelled as the jet careened down the dark runway. The scream of the engines rose to a soprano whine, the main wheels broke loose, and Shephard was pushed into his seat as the nose lifted into the air and the runway lights rapidly fell away below him. "Louder'n hell, but that's the price you pay for speed."

The Learjet angled upward and banked south toward Mexico. When Odette had climbed to thirty thousand feet, he left the jet in Shephard's control and disappeared into the passenger cabin. Shephard grasped the yoke and held course by doing nothing. A moment later Odette returned with two heavy Scotch and sodas, light on the soda. He worked his way back into the tiny seat, strapped the headphones on, and reclaimed the controls from Shephard.

"This ain't exactly legal, but that gun under your coat ain't either, Shephard. We'll ditch it under the seat when we go through Customs in Veracruz. They probably won't even look. The Mexicans don't care much what we bring down, as long as we got some dollars with us." Marty sipped his drink and settled into the seat. Shephard gazed out the window at the dull glow of San Diego to the west, the blackness of the California desert in front of them. "Well, now that we're comfortable, what the hell are we gonna do on Isla Arenillas? It means Island of Fine Sand, you know. And the airport there won't accommodate this baby."

"You're going to drop me in Cozumel, spend the afternoon, turn around, and come home. I'm going on to Isla Arenillas for a date with an old . . . acquaintance." Odette studied Shephard with his gambler's deadpan. "That's the version you give back home, if anybody asks. It's all I can tell you now, Marty."

Odette turned his attention to the instrument panel. "Do what you got to, Shephard. Being a betting man, I'll give you even odds down there. Yucatan isn't California. You run into the law and you might not ever get out. You run into something that isn't the law, and, well, there's plenty of jungle to fertilize with gringos."

Shephard sipped the Scotch and listened to the hypnotic crackle of voices on the radio. He sat back, running all the possibilities through his mind, coming up with nothing. How, he thought. How did Mercante find out Wade had left for Isla Arenillas? Was it Harmon? And if it was Harmon, how had he found out, and so quickly? An hour later he dozed off, his head resting on his jacket, his dream visions returning incessantly to the golden-haired woman in the portrait.

He woke up later with the back of his shirt drenched in sweat and the sick premonition that Mercante had lured him out of town on purpose.

Two Customs officials at Veracruz examined their passports and papers, one finally nodding while the other lowered the official stamp. The morning was overcast and humid, smelling of stagnant ocean. The first official stood, cast a disinterested glance at the Lear, then told them to have a good stay in Mexico. Odette had told them they were divers. Shephard reset his watch to match the wall clock noting that his palms were damp.

Ten minutes later they were high above the turquoise

water of the Bay of Campeche, climbing to cruising altitude for the two-hour journey to Cozumel.

"Ought to do some fishing if you have the time," Odette offered. "Boats run about twenty bucks an hour down here. White marlin, bluefin, sailfish, wahoo. Some of the best in the world."

Shephard lit a cigarette and put on his sunglasses, feeling the delirious swirl of exhaustion in his brain. "I'll think about that, Marty."

Odette gazed out the window, rubbing his tired eyes. "One last offer, Shephard. I'll stay in Cozumel while you do what you do, then bring you back out. I could use a day or two of that fishing myself. What do you say?"

Shephard thought a long moment before answering, his mind filling with visions of arrest, extradition, the foreign bureaucracy led by humorless Mexican federales. "Do that for me, Marty. That would be great."

"I'll book at La Ceiba if they've got room. If not, try the Cozumel-Caribe."

"I'll call you tonight. Thanks, Marty."

"It's not exactly police business, is it?"

"Oh, mostly."

He left Odette at the Cozumel airport and found an information booth, where he learned that charter flights to Isla Arenillas left from a number of small airstrips around the city, but not from the main terminal. The woman at the booth suggested the Hotel Presidente, which handled the flight bookings. Even inside the airport it was humid, sticky-hot.

"Taxi?" he asked, seeing none.

"No taxi from airport—the law," she said. "The bus goes downtown every fifteen minutes. Catch it right out there by the sign, señor."

Shephard waited in the vaguely air-conditioned airport, a tiny and still-unfinished cluster of buildings that seemed no more than a temporary intrusion on the jungle. The bus—a Volkswagen van already loaded with passengers—picked him up half an hour later and began its cumbersome trip to downtown Cozumel. It was unbearably hot, even with all the windows down and a large fan whirring from its mount over the rearview mirror. A picture of the Virgin Mary dangled from the roof. The passengers were all Americans, drained of energy by the long flight from the mainland, waving hands or newspapers in front of their faces to break the wet heat.

"I can see why the prices drop thirty percent in summer," a Bermuda-shorted man joked. All he got from his wife was a disgruntled "Yeah." "Where you staying?" he asked Shephard. Behind his sunglasses, the man looked like a shark.

"The island. Arenillas."

The man noted that Shephard was traveling alone. "Hear it's nice," he said with a minor grin.

The Presidente was the third stop. Shephard got off, tipped the driver, and refused help with his suitcase, which he had packed hastily and poorly in the five minutes he'd spent at home before picking up Odette. He thought of the tenderness in Jane's voice as she said good-bye. He suddenly wondered if he'd see her again.

The one-way ticket on the seaplane to Isla Arenillas cost thirteen dollars. Back outside, in the sweltering heat, he flagged a cab. An hour later—it was nearly one o'clock—the rickety seaplane groaned off a dirt airstrip on the outskirts of the city, overloaded with gleeful tourists. Most of them had brought their diving gear. Some wore only swimsuits, sandals, and T-shirts. A pretty young woman dug into her purse, applied lipstick, and smiled at Shephard. Her boyfriend had his face to the window, enumerating the sights from above. An hour later Shephard saw the island in the distance, a tiny strip of jungle green outlined in talc-white sand. The water surrounding it was a pale and unrippled blue, *azul* in Spanish, he thought, like the eyes of his enemy. The plane bumped down on a small runway.

The smell of Isla Arenillas was one that Shephard had never experienced before: a muggy, humid-sweet mixture of ocean and vegetation, sea and jungle. The airstrip had been cut from the dense foliage, which crept nearly to the edge of the runway and looked as if it could reclaim the thin landing area in a weekend.

He climbed off the plane, lugging his suitcase behind. Above him, cirrus clouds flattened high in the sky and a flock of seagulls stirred and cackled. A stand of banana trees, short and green, was clustered at the far end of the strip. Shephard followed the tourists toward a path leading into the jungle, turning briefly to see the pilot, beer in hand, trudging toward a dilapidated cantina on the end of the strip. The pathway was soon engulfed in green. Shephard moved his suitcase from one sweaty hand to another and listened to the musical riot of the jungle birds hidden around him. He stopped to light a cigarette and watched a pair of bright monarch butterflies winging silently against the undergrowth. The tobacco—a Mexican brand he'd bought in Veracruz—tasted black and dank, like the humid air. As he picked up his suitcase, a dark iguana lumbered across the path ahead of him, unhurried.

The pathway widened, left the jungle, and opened onto a neat dirt road that swung to the right. Ahead of him, he could see that both sides were spotted with hotels and restaurants, with many of the guests drinking outside under palapas. Beyond the hotels, the ocean sparkled blue and lazy. Walking past the tables of a restaurant called Tortuga, Shephard added the aroma of boiling shrimp to the smells that, like the heat, seemed intensified to the point of unreality. It occurred to him that of all the people on Isla Arenillas, he was the only one still wearing a coat, lugging a suitcase, or moving faster than one had to. And, he was sure, the only one carrying a .357 magnum in his suitcase. Two girls sped past him on motor scooters, each somehow balancing a bottle of beer on the handlebars. "Hey, gringo," one yelled back at him, "lose your load."

Wade had not specified a hotel. His note said only that he would check in under the name Frank Seely, if Shephard needed to reach him. What a surprise this will be, he thought, praying that Mercante hadn't surprised him first. The AeroMexico flight had arrived at six o'clock, just under five hours ago. Surely, he reasoned, it would take Mercante all of that to locate Wade, make his plans, and wait for night to carry them out. Longer maybe. Without knowing that Frank Seely was the man he was looking for, Mercante would have to loiter around the town in hopes of spotting him. The unnerving thought that Mercante could be sitting in one of the outdoor restaurants, watching him as he walked into the hotel, haunted Shephard as he pushed into the mercifully air-conditioned lobby of the Rocamar.

No Señor Seely, they told him. And no Señor Mercante, very sorry. The desk clerk offered him a cancelation, but Shephard declined. He bought a can of Tecate beer from the cantina and a Panama hat from the gift shop before heading back out into the sweltering afternoon. Outside he took off his coat and draped it over his arm, feeling for a moment as though he had arrived in paradise.

He worked his way down one side of the main avenue, enquiring at the hotels after Señores Seely and Mercante. When he had exhausted the possibilities and found himself facing a pen fenced off from the ocean and filled with huge sea turtles, he crossed the street and worked the other side.

At the Mesón del Marquez, Shephard found that Frank Seely had checked in the night before.

The porter had snatched his suitcase away and was heading toward the hallway before Shephard could protest. He fished some change from his pocket as he followed the man down the hall to room 26, which was ground floor, facing the main street. The porter set down the suitcase and smiled, not counting the coins that he slid into a pocket in his shirt. A moment later, looking haggard and scared, Wade opened the door, smiled, and stood back as worry overcame the smile.

"Tommy, what are you doing here? Are you okay?" Shephard saw that his father had been lying on the bed, reading the Bible. The look of control, compassion, still hadn't returned to his face.

"He knows you're here, pops. He flew down last night, from L.A. You've got bad security leaks."

Shephard called room service for a bottle of Scotch and ice, which was brought ten minutes later by the same eager man who had carried his bag. He pushed the cart into the room with some ceremony, arranged the ice tub on the desk beside the window, and presented Shephard with a bottle and a bill. When the door closed behind him, Shephard made sure it was locked, poured himself a stiff drink, and told his father about the near death of Francis Rubio and the grim room at Valentine's. Wade sat on the bed, listening intently, looking out the window with newfound anxiety.

"So?" he said finally. "What do you propose to do?"

"You're going out the way I came in," Shephard said.

"No I'm not, son. That's something I can't consider. He's crazy. You'll need all the help you can get."

Shephard drank from the Scotch, then put his face in front of the air conditioner. "This is the way I see it. He's looking for you, one man alone in a hotel room. This is a little town. Word gets around who's where, what they're doing. If he senses anything wrong, he'll never show himself. Point two, pop: you get mixed up in this now, it's going to be real hard on you. Even if everything goes like I hope it goes, there's going to be an arrest, extradition, publicity. Look real bad for you stateside, but bad down here, too. Who's going to want your hospital here if you're mixed up with some killer?" He stood at the window and looked out at the street, saw a fishing boat easing into dock in the shimmering distance.

Wade hadn't moved. "You might need me, Tommy. Another body can be a help."

"Another body is what Azul wants," Shephard said quietly. "This is what I've learned to do, pop. You taught me some of it yourself. You had a chance at him thirty years ago. This one is mine."

Wade rose from the bed and slowly paced the floor, his head down. "You're remembering your mother," he said.

"Aren't you?"

"It's too late for hatred, son."

"It's too late for a sermon." Shephard sighed. "I'm sorry." He picked up the telephone and called La Ceiba.

"You're playing the dark notes, after all."

A moment later, Shephard was put through to Marty, who was disappointed that his fishing trip would have to be canceled.

"Pop. You're going back to Cozumel on the seaplane. You're going to wear my clothes and sunglasses, and carry my bag. Here, wear this hat, too. If Mercante hasn't seen either of us yet, it might help."

Half an hour later, they stood facing each other in the small room, Shephard buried in his father's white linen suit, Wade squeezed into his son's clothes. Shephard helped his father pack the rest of his clothes into his own suitcase. With the sunglasses in place, the resemblance was close. He looked at Wade. When you go, I'll be here. I'll be the Reverend Wade Shephard.

He called the desk for a taxi back to the airstrip.

TWENTY-SIX

He checked out of the del Marquez at four that afternoon, lugging his father's suitcase into the stifling heat of the island. The street was crowded with tourists and vendors. One withered old man approached Shephard with a collection of dried, shellacked sand sharks bobbing from a stick. Shephard bought a very small one, which looked like a goblin dancing on its tail. It satisfied his need for some local talisman. Inside his left coat pocket he felt the sea lion tooth given him by Jane, then slid the dried shark in to give it company. The Indians considered the teeth good luck, he remembered, issuing his own brief prayer that that luck would be with him in the next few hours. He had never thought of himself as superstitious, but the heat, the musical mystery of the language being spoken, and the heavy smells of this tropical Eden all condensed around him as a reminder that he was wholly out of his own context.

His first move was to arrange himself more visibly, and in a place where Mercante would have no trouble trying to kill him.

He strolled past the hotels and shops of the main street, wondering if Mercante had perhaps already seen him and was right now viewing him from some upstairs balcony, beer in hand, planning the logistics of murder. The thought unsettled him still more: he had never pursued a man of such brazen and unfathomable cruelty. He thought again of the cut spark plug cable lying on the seat of his motorcycle, an eloquent reminder that he had arrived late, anticipated poorly, and had been spared by only seconds the ordeal of having to stare into the lifeless face of the Fire Killer's third victim. Shephard stopped suddenly and looked behind him, half expecting to see Mercante trudging a block behind, closing in. But the sidewalk was filled only with tourists.

He registered at the Serenidad, which overlooked the beach on the north side of town. He signed in clearly as the Reverend Wade Shephard and requested an upstairs room. The bellboy was a cheerful man with the high cheekbones and subtly upturned eyes of the native Indians. His name was Cantil.

"Cantil, isn't that a snake?" Shephard asked as they headed for his room.

"Yes. Only a name for me. From when I was small."

"Were you like a snake?"

Cantil set down the bag and opened the door to room 58. It opened with a stale, mildewed puff. "Very quiet," he said.

"Why Cantil, I don't know."

Shephard gave the man a dollar, asking for a bucket of ice and two extra pillows. "For my back, chum," he said. "Gets sore in this heat."

He unpacked the suitcase carefully, hanging up the extra trousers and shirts, which were heavily wrinkled from the hasty switch with his father. The Colt Python .357, wrapped in a bath towel with two extra cylinders, he slipped under the bed. He noted the layout of the room: the door opened to a small hallway, with a large closet on the right. To the left of the closet, a doorway opened to a bathing area, and behind that a toilet. Five steps from the doorway the main room began, a neat square with a single queen-sized bed to the left, a dresser opposite, and a small table and chairs placed in front of the window that overlooked the street. He drew back the curtains and looked down. The foot traffic below was minimal, with most of the shops and hotels a hundred yards toward the center of the town. To his right, he could see a stand of banana trees whose trunks vanished into the dense green of the jungle. Beyond the trees the water, the sand, the mainland.

"Señor Shephard?" Cantil's voice outside the door. Shephard opened it and he came in.

"Call me Wade," he said. "I like that better."

The bellboy put the ice on the dresser and offered Shephard the two extra pillows. "For your back," he said.

Shephard stood close to him now, and spoke slowly. "I'm very interested," he said as he found another dollar, "in any visitors that I may have. If you can let me know of anyone asking about my room number here, or of anyone looking for Reverend Wade Shephard, I would appreciate it very much. If you are asked, say only that I am an *older* man. I would need to know, by phone, immediately."

Cantil understood perfectly. "I'll call you fast, Señor Wade, if anyone comes here for you. The snake sees all things in his hotel." He smiled, thanked Shephard again for the tip, and quietly disappeared, leaving the pillows on the bed.

Shephard sat in front of the air conditioner and smoked. Positioned in the far corner of the room, he could see down the street, which by seven was still filled with pedestrians and an occasional motor scooter. He studied again the Identikit sketch of Azul Mercante, placing it on the table in front of him, imagining what he was doing, where he was staying, what plans he had made for Wade, the object of his revenge. When the evening came, announced only by a slow darkening to the east, he ordered dinner from room service. The steak picado arrived an hour later, just as the sun was streaking the sky in orange, dripping its color into the water. He ate silently and drank a light Scotch.

Jane answered on the first ring. "Are you okay, Tommy? Is Wade okay? Did you find Azul?"

He let her breathless rush play itself out. "I'm fine. Wade's heading back to the States. No Azul, though, not yet. I miss you, Jane."

"I miss you too, but don't expect me to admit it." She paused, then spoke more quietly: "Tommy, you know the cardboard file cabinets where dad kept all his financial stuff? Well, they're gone. I left them in his living room, and went back to clean them out for good, but they're not there. And your friend who drives the dark blue Porsche was outside your place when I fed Cal this morning. I'm a little scared."

Shephard felt the adrenaline coursing through his veins like fuel. He closed his eyes and tried to quiet his breathing. "Jane, listen to me. I'm going to send a man over to stay with you. He's big and he's scary, but you can trust him. Stay home until he comes—it should be an hour at the most. He'll know what to do." Though his mind was reeling, Shephard tried to bring some assurance to his voice. If Harmon hurts her, he thought, I'll kill him.

"I love you," he said.

"I love you," she said. Both at the same time.

He called Little Theodore and made arrangements, then dialed Louise's Malibu number.

"Lou? This is Tom."

"Where are you? I can hardly hear you."

"Far away. Look, I just wanted to tell you that . . . well, everything between us is okay, at my end. I've been sitting here thinking, and thought you should know that. If we don't get to see each other again, I at least want you to understand there's no hard feelings, Lou."

"I really don't think we *should* see each other. It's just too hard for you . . . for both of us."

Shephard grinned: same old Louise, he thought.

"Tom, are you drunk again?"

"I'll call you sometime. 'Night, Lou."

Just after nine, Shephard placed his dishes outside the door, which he left unlocked. He arranged the extra pillows lengthwise, molded the thin covers into legs, formed a dark shirt into a head. With the bedspread pulled up and the lights out he could see the man asleep there—the Reverend Wade Shephard, perhaps—conked out after a hot day.

Shephard brought the Python from under the bed and clicked the loaded cylinder into place, then put the second cylinder in his pocket. He unstrung two yards of dental floss from its container and tied one end to the pull chain of the light over the table. To the other end he tied a pencil, which he set on the floor beside him. The light flicked on as he pulled, then off again. He backed into the farthest corner of the room, his shoulders resting against the cool wall, the Python in one hand and the pencil in the other, and waited.

With his eyes closed in the darkness, his mind flickered with fatigued visions of the last week, and when Jane's image came he tried to hold it still to admire her beauty. He saw her bending back in ecstasy in the water of Diver's Cove; he saw her warm and silent in the bed beside him while he stared at the alarm clock; he saw her the first day he'd met her standing in the waders. Intermittently, another face began to appear beside Jane's, but it never materialized fully, remaining only half-formed, eclipsed by the raw energy that was Jane Algernon. It was only then that Shephard realized the fundamental change that had taken place inside him, that his heart was no longer a mourner for the woman who had left him, but a celebrant of the one he had found. For a moment the future—whatever it was and wherever it would be—seemed to overflow with possibilities of tenderness and love. He wondered if it was only the end of loneliness, an interruption of it. Among the images of Jane was the last he had seen of her, lying in his bed kissing him with gentle possessiveness, saying she would be with him. Then telling him again something that he had not heard in many years, words that seemed to have fallen from his own experience like extinct and useless birds: I love you.

If I die tonight in Mexico, it will be with you, he thought.

Just as he had done as a young boy, he released a flock of telepathic birds in the direction of California, trusting them to find her and sing the love that he would never be able to phrase himself.

Stiff and sore, his stomach queasy with fear and love, he stood, stretched, paced the room. It was nearly eleven. He slid open the window over the now-empty street and inhaled the clean night aroma of the ocean. With the air conditioner turned off, the only sounds were of an occasional scooter on the street and the muffled voices in other rooms.

Just before three in the morning, Shephard strapped on his shoulder holster and slid the Python into its place. He removed the extra pillows from the bed and untied the string from the pull chain. Locking the door behind him, he headed downstairs to the Serenidad lobby. The deskman was reading a magazine.

"Messages for Wade Shaphard?"

"No, señor," he said, checking the box for room 58. "No messages for you."

"How many hotels are there on Isla Arenillas?"

The desk man, whose badge said Aguilar, shrugged as if the question were too demanding for such a late hour. "Many."

"Exactly how many?" Shephard brought out a five-dollar bill and placed it on the desk. Aguilar grinned.

"I will tell you." He opened a drawer and removed a bright orange pamphlet, which he gave to Shephard. It was a listing of island hotels, complete with addresses and phone numbers. He counted twelve.

"Is this up to date?" Shephard asked. "Current?"

"Oh, it is the most up to date," Aguilar said with a nod. "Only place not listed is Hotel Cora, which is no open any more. Closed two years ago but they are soon to build it again. All others you will find on this." He reached out and pinched the pamphlet between his thumb and forefinger, shaking it quickly.

"Where is Cantil?"

The deskman looked disappointed. "Across the water. None of us live on the island."

Shephard turned for the door.

"Señor, *con permiso*, but the night life on Isla Arenillas is . . . minimal."

"Just some fresh air," he said.

Among hotel night clerks there is a universal reluctance to expend energy past midnight. Shephard encountered one sleepy deskman after another, all of whom eyed him as a nuisance rather than a potential customer, none of whom had any guests registered as Hodges, Steinhelper, Dixon, or Mercante. He made each clerk double-check the last name, using up whatever patience they had at that hour of the morning. In the lobby of the impressive Presidente Caribe, he was met as he left by a stout, steely-eyed security guard who took him aside for a terse interview. Shephard produced his passport and room key, explaining mournfully that he had had a terrible fight with his fiancée but loved her very much. Untouched, the guard watched him through the glass as he headed back down the curving entryway.

By four-thirty, he had gone through every hotel in the pamphlet except the La Palapa. The lobby of the hotel was engulfed in banana trees and illuminated only by soft neon light, which flickered onto the young face beneath it.

"*Buenos días,*" Shephard said, exhausting his Spanish. The young man nodded and put down the magazine. Shephard ran through his litany of names once again, and once again he was answered only by the slowly shaking head of the clerk. He explained that he was looking for his father, an older man with bright blue eyes who was a wealthy eccentric given to changing names and hotels on a moment's notice. He had arrived sometime yesterday—probably early morning—but had neglected to give him the name of his hotel. And now, desperate that the old man had become lost or worse, he had taken to the island on foot and failed to find his father at any of the dozen hotels. Shephard offered the man a cigarette, which he accepted with a smile.

"Very problem," he said. "Isla Arenillas not very big. Oh, five miles and two miles, but the jungle is very dark at night. Your father walk far?"

"He might. But I think he would want some place dry to sleep. I don't think he would sleep . . . under the stars."

The desk clerk examined the cigarette and nodded with concern. "Possible that if he is a little, you say, loco?"

"Yes, a little loco maybe."

"Possible if he walked to other side of island to Hotel Cora and got lost on his way back. Hotel Cora closed two years, but it is soon to be built again," he noted proudly. "Possible he is lost in the jungle. Hotel is very dark at night."

"There is nothing on the other side except the Cora?" Shephard asked.

"Only where the new hospital will be. Jungle is gone there now. New hospital will be Seesters of Mercy. Built by loco man of God with many pesos. Dollars really. He is American, Reverend Chephard."

Shephard considered Mercante's penchant for sliding in and out of derelict hotels and apartments, his talent for picking lairs away from—but somehow in the very midst of —where someone would look for him. It wasn't beyond possibility that he would hide in the Cora, and its closeness to the Sisters of Mercy made all the more sense. In fact, the more he thought about it, the more it fit into Mercante's twisted logic. And if Mercante was there, perhaps he would be sleeping, an easy mark for a morning visitor.

"How do I get to the Cora? I want to go there."

"Oh, señor. You must wait until light. Long walk, three miles now. Very dark and the path is full of iguanas and many *cucarachas*." The clerk held up two forefingers about three inches apart. Some cockroaches, Shephard thought.

"I can't wait. The poor man could be wandering that path right now, very terrified. *Comprende?*"

The clerk sighed and rose from his stool, tapping across the lobby in his hard shoes. Outside, he led Shephard past the first row of rooms, the porch lights of which swirled with moths and outsized winged beetles. Translucent lizards clung to the walls, darting intermittently. He stopped at the end of the cement sidewalk, as if going any further would offer him a personal risk. The clearing to which he pointed seemed large and passable enough.

"Here the path is wide, but farther away it will be small," the man said gravely. "About a half of mile from here, it will go to the right and to the left, and you go to the right. At the end you will be on the beach again, and the Cora is left, on a hill over the water. I don't think she has her lights because it is very expensive here. If your father is on the pathway, you will hear him because the jungle is quiet except for the monkeys and some pigs but they will run away. If you find a wild pig and babies, you should run first. They can be very, very *muy peligroso*. *Comprende*, señor?"

"Oh, yes. Thank you. I have a lucky sea lion's tooth." Shephard produced the tooth, which shone dully in the lights of the porches.

The footing was soft and moist. Shephard felt his heels sinking as he moved into the clearing and past the first cluster of banana trees. He stopped in the darkness for a last look at the light of the hotel, then located the moon, which was a full quarter now and clear in the eastern sky. He could see the pathway winding ahead, a shade darker than the trees that crouched at its borders. Another thirty yards, around a gentle right-hand bend that brought him under a bower of some sort—the smell was of honeysuckle—he stopped again and realized that even in so short a distance the jungle had consumed him fully. It seemed to hump around him in rounded forms that looked ready to uncoil. A dark shape cut across the pathway ahead of him, dragging a reptilian tail into the vegetation. He moved to the other side and continued, ducking low again under the banana leaves, using the moist trunks for balance where the trees threatened to choke off the path. Holy Christ, he thought, his mind filling with visions of fat tarantulas dropping like rain from the trees.

He lit a cigarette and began scuffing his shoes, slapping the leaves that reached out from the foliage. Halfway to the other side of the island—what he guessed was halfway, at least—he stopped dead in front of a huge iguana poised athwart the pathway in front of him. While Shephard choked his fear back down, he waited for the beast to move, but it didn't so much as twitch.

He bluffed forward a step, muttering a curse. Another step toward it—he was now within charging distance, Shephard guessed—the animal proved to be nothing more than a branch. He kicked it to be sure, picked it up, and brushed the damp earth from one end. Continuing on his way, he smacked the plants and trees around him like a city dweller whose lantern had blown out in the woods. Five minutes later the pathway forked and he bore right, quickening his pace.

The trail narrowed. He used his stick to part the fronds and began to hum a song that kept changing into other songs. At a small clearing he stopped and tried to find the moon again, but the tangled jungle over him offered only darkness. He noticed that the sounds—the piping of night birds, the occasional chatter of monkeys—always diminished around him, resuming only when he had moved on. He filled this portable silence with the whacking of his branch and a muttering threat to the jungle as it encroached onto his slim passageway.

A fat shape with tiny legs shot across the path ahead of him, followed by three more of the same, but smaller. *Muy peligroso,* he thought, very dangerous, the wild pigs. In the silence he heard them cracking through the jungle floor, a shuffle, a snort, then nothing.

Just as the jungle had choked the path into nothingness, he broke through a wall of fragrant foliage and saw the silver water of the Caribbean sparkling ahead. He threw the branch toward it with a silent blessing and watched it thud onto the powder-white sand. And just as the desk clerk had said, the dark shape of the Hotel Cora stood profiled against the sky on a hill overlooking the sea, a quarter mile to the west. It was completely dark, recognizable only by its angular symmetry against the blue-black sky.

Shephard followed the perimeter of the jungle, which zigzagged along a series of peaceful coves. The sand was soft underfoot, and the air was tinged with the clean and reassuring smell of ocean.

The outline of the Hotel Cora grew larger as he rounded a small lagoon. Behind him he could hear the busy chatter of the jungle, and in front the ocean against the shore. He stopped for a moment to look behind him and studied the series of tiny footprints that trailed off into the darkness from which he had come. The far side of the lagoon ended in an outcropping of dark rocks, which in the pale moonlight he saw was alive with iguanas, loafing in and out of each other's shadows. No wonder they eat them, he thought, big as pheasants.

He cautiously rounded the rocks, looking up when he

reached a dilapidated boardwalk that had once served as an entrance to the Cora. The hotel stood above him, large and decrepit, the sagging posture of the unused. Against the main wall, which was now covered by foliage nearly to the center, the words *Hotel Cora* were written in graceful wrought-iron letters. One of the wooden double doors was all but torn away, left dangling by a disfigured hinge. An iguana pulled itself across the porch, then dragged its dark weight up the decaying flanks of the colonnade. Shephard could hear its claws finding their way through the rotted wood. He studied the three floors of darkened windows, only a few still with glass. Two years, he thought, may as well be two centuries in the jungle. The glass of an upper-story window, the one farthest from the entrance and nearest to the water, seemed for an instant to move.

Shephard backed away from the boardwalk and stepped down onto the sand. He kept near the front of the building, squinting at the window, now with a copper glow behind it, now with an orange flicker.

Candlelight.

And a moment later the silhouette of a man at the window, looking down at the sea.

TWENTY-SEVEN

He watched the orange spot of a cigarette rise, brighten, trace downward again. A moment later, the man moved away.

Shephard worked his way back to the hotel porch, whose

boards sagged pliantly underfoot. The iguana twisted around the colonnade as he passed it, keeping to the deepest shadows. He ducked through the broken door of the lobby and stepped inside, waiting for his eyes to adjust to the greater darkness of the once-splendid Hotel Cora. The lobby smelled of rotted wood and mildew. Out of the blackness, shapes began to solidify: the desk was to his right; two columns rose ahead of him; behind them a wide set of stairs swept upward from the lobby floor to the upper stories. Its balustrade gaped with holes, and some of the pillars still lay scattered on the floor where age, or vandals, had dumped them.

As Shephard's eyes strained in the darkness he saw that the shapes were blurred and rounded, and a moment later he realized that everything in the lobby, from the walls to the strangely lumpy desk to the drooping chandelier above him, was covered with a carpet of jungle moss. He crouched and ran his fingers along the floor: the moist springiness of sphagnum gave way to cool tile. A rat squeaked, scampering across the moss in front of him.

He padded his way to the stairs and tentatively tried the first step. It was stout and resilient. Good, he thought, concrete or stone. He rose a step at a time, careful to test each plank before putting down his weight. High as the chandelier now, he stopped and looked down over the moss-draped lobby below him. Above the entryway door, a broken window gave him a view of the Caribbean, which lay flat and unperturbed to the east. The moon hovered low over the horizon, like a last beacon for travelers at the end of the world.

The stairway widened, easing onto the second floor. He stopped at the head of the stairs, unsure of how to go around the gaping hole in front of him. Below, he could see the door through which he had come twisted obscenely out and hanging by the stubborn hinge. Finally, he stepped across, his foot hitting the solid plank of the next step. Pushing off the mossy handrail, he heaved himself over the hole and onto the stairway, teetering momentarily when his full weight hit the other side. His shirt and jacket were soaked through, and his own smell was as strong as the smell of decay around him. The holster scraped against his wet ribcage, leather on soggy cloth.

As he took the last steps upward, his hand on the balustrade for balance, Shephard felt his stomach beginning to weaken as the anger that had brought him this far began to disappear. He stopped, listened to the shallow quickness of his breathing, heard his heart thumping in his ears. The darkness worried him. He considered settling onto the stairway to sleep until daylight, and finishing what he had come to do in the clean light of morning. Would Mercante come peacefully? Did he have the gun? Was he alone? Shephard conjured visions of his mother, her golden hair shifting as she played tennis, her smile as she held her son in her arms on the Surfside beach. Then he saw Hope Creeley again, and Algernon's head blighted by the sharp rock as he lay by the stables, and Jane's grieving face as she spoke of him in his living room the day after. He thought of his father on the witness stand, his long jumps from the pier at night.

Everything, Shephard thought, had its seeds in the man he had come to find. He stepped from the stairway onto the third floor and carefully began making his way to the outside balcony that would take him to the room at the far end.

With his back to the building, Shephard moved onto the balcony and stepped past the window of the first room. Lizards scattered over the railing as he moved, quicker and more agitated with the nearness of morning. Far to the east, he could see the first mellowing of the black, a fading of stars, the moon giving up its crisp outline.

Two rooms beyond, the window at the end still glowed. He opened his left palm against the wall for support and brought the Python from its holster with his right. Revolver in hand, he could feel the old terror creeping back into him —Pico Boulevard in the rain, Morris Mumford on the wet grass—and he wondered if when the time came, he would be able to make the gun obey his trembling fingers. *Too-Long Tom, Too-Long Tom.* With his back flattened against the building, Shephard edged to the last window, waited, then looked in.

The man sitting at a table, his face turned downward to a book, was Azul Mercante. Two candles threw a burnished orange light onto his old and wrinkled face. He turned a page of the book—Shephard saw it was a Bible—yawned, then looked at his wristwatch.

Keeping close to the wall, Shephard crept back to the balcony entrance and turned into the hallway, breathing rapidly.

With the rooms to his right, he stepped carefully across the moss-heavy floor, past the first three doors, over a small crevice to the last. The hallway was narrow; he gauged that two yards' running start was all he would have. He heard the blood rushing in his head. What if the door were as stout as Rubio's? Directly in front of it now, he moved his back to the wall opposite. Christ, he thought, won't the pounding stop so I can think; and he shoved off the wall, charged across the hallway, lowered his shoulder into the soft door, and crashed through. Splinters showered his head as the wood shattered. Light. But no movement. Only the glow of candlelight and the calm and hateful stare of Azul Mercante.

Shephard had the man's face just over the front sight of his pistol. He was surprised how familiar it looked, how well he knew the haughty eyes, the superior smirk, the wide forehead and dangling gray hair.

"I'm on target, asshole. Don't even blink."

Mercante was standing, his hands flat on the table in

front of him. He was thin, and shorter than Shephard had imagined. His shirt looked new. From the stare in the man's eyes, Shephard seemed to have made no impression whatsoever; they considered, then dismissed him. The full madness of the man didn't hit Shephard until Mercante finally spoke.

"You are disturbing the work of the Lord," he said. "But, please, sit down."

"I'm a cop. You're under arrest for the murders of Tim Algernon and Hope Creeley. And the attempted murder of Francis Rubio." Shephard's voice sounded shrill to him. He tried to lower it when he spoke again. "You're coming back to the States with me. You're going on trial again."

Mercante sat down, carefully sliding his chair back under him. He poured a glass of wine from a bottle on the table and held it out. Shephard stepped forward and slapped it away, resting the barrel of his revolver against Mercante's head as he worked his hand over the old man's body. The derringer was in a shirt pocket. Shephard eased it up and out, keeping Mercante in the sight of his Python as he backed away.

"You're Tom Shephard," he said. "I used to hold you in my arms when you were just this big." Mercante smiled and stretched his hands. "I consider it one of the great ironies of my life that you have come to take me back."

"It'll be one of the big pleasures of mine, bud. You're the only man I've ever hated."

Mercante shook his head and motioned again for him to sit. Shephard lowered the gun to Mercante's chest, his arm growing tired.

"That gun must be getting heavy. Sit down across from me, Tommy. What can an old man do to you now? We shouldn't be walking around this old hotel in the dark. When it's light again, I'll go with you, agreed? Besides, since you're going to take me back, there are a few things I want you to know about me." Mercante brought a fresh wineglass

294

from a table tray. He poured, and Shephard noted that Mercante's hand was steadier than his own. With his foot, he pulled back the chair and eased himself down into it. Mercante held up the bottle and Shephard shook his head. "So, you want me to go back to prison? Do you know what a living hell that can be?"

"If you want to talk, hell, let's talk Hope Creeley's eyelids."

Mercante rolled his eyes and drank again. "The woman was a liar and a cheat. Her punishment was terrible but brief. And Tim, too. Such a cowardly man, always. In his living room that night he tried to pay me money to let him live. Can you imagine?"

"I saw where you put it. Why didn't you just take it?" Shephard's hand was quivering now. Did Mercante notice? He lowered the gun butt to the table, its barrel still pointed at Mercante's chest.

"That would have been wrong. And unnecessary. The Lord has provided me with all I need for my revenge. I've never done anything in my life for money. It is a filthy and corrupting commodity. I don't need it. I am protected by Him. I've walked through your town, unseen. I've driven the car He sent to me. I've left my voice on Hope's answering machine. You see . . . I've simply been above your rules."

"You changed a few, too, didn't you? While you were working in the Folsom Records section?"

Mercante smiled proudly. "Eighteen months to turn Manny Soto's official records into mine, and mine into his. A miracle."

Through the window behind Mercante, Shephard could see the first gray of morning. "And the airline ticket? Don't tell me the Lord sent that to you personally, chum."

"Oh, literally He didn't. He used the form of a man, a man I don't even know, to aid me. He provides for me. I do not question, I only accept gratefully." He glanced down at the open book in front of him. "It says to do so in many places."

"Well, He just provided you with me. I don't think you'll be too grateful when you're making your last walk to the gas chamber."

Mercante studied Shephard with his bright blue eyes. "That will never happen. You must be thirty-two years old now. You weighed six pounds and four ounces when you were born. Colleen was very proud of you." Shephard felt a stony hatred at the mention of her name. "In fact, your birth kept Colleen and me from marrying. She was reluctant to leave your father because of you. I understood. Here, look at this." Mercante unclipped a chain from around his neck and swung it gently across the table to Shephard, who gathered it up with his left hand. The pendant was a deep blue stone framed in gold. "The rock is lapis, which Colleen said reminded her of my eyes. The inscription on the back, of course, is hers."

Shephard set the pistol on the table beside him, watching Mercante as he brought the pendant close. Mercante folded his hands. The inscription said: *So much for so many, so little for us. Love, C.* Shephard threw it back.

"And here, look at these. All from Colleen. I've kept them with me since the day I received them. Older than you are, Tommy." Mercante slowly unfolded his hands and sorted out an envelope from the papers stacked beside the Bible. He slid one down the table.

It was a letter in a woman's handwriting. The paper was yellowed and limp with age; the blue ink had turned to purple. Shephard read the salutation: "My Dearest Lovely Azul." He again felt the blood rushing to his ears; his eyes stung with the pressure.

"This is shit," he said. "You made it all up, *amigo.* Bought the necklace yourself and wrote the letters to yourself. You tried to rape her and you killed her when she

296

wouldn't submit. You're crazy, cheap, and stupid. Didn't work on Rubio. It won't work on me."

Mercante shrugged, holding out his hand. Shephard stuffed the letter back into the envelope and threw it across the table.

"You have your father's temper," Mercante said finally. "I could have used those letters in court, but that would have been a desecration of everything we were together. Besides, the Honorable Rubio was corrupt and ignorant and little could have changed that. You saved him?"

"I saved him."

"He really is a very inconsequential man. I pity his uselessness as I pity your father's. I searched for him all day yesterday, and the Lord kept him from me. I came here to be alone. It's good that you don't believe me about your mother. In the absence of truth, it is healthy to nurture illusions."

Shephard saw that the sky outside had reached a pale blue. The water was nearly the same color and the sand was beginning to regain its white, powdery softness. But inside, he felt a darkness descending, as if the night had left the sky and settled into him.

"The *truth* is you killed a woman. My mother. The *illusion* is that she loved you. You can take that with you to your deathbed," Shephard said.

Mercante studied him for a long moment, and the look on his face was one of pity. "We loved each other very much," he said, slowly brushing away the love letters to uncover a .45 caliber pistol. It lay on the table, inches from the old man's fingers. "Now, everything is fair again, as it should be." Mercante lowered his hand to the table.

The roaring in Shephard's ears as he looked at Mercante's pistol mounted to a whine that made the man's next words almost impossible to hear.

" . . . not going back with you . . . suppose I'll need to

go and find Wade . . . can't do it with you around, Tommy. . . ."

The roar inside was so loud now that Shephard felt tears coming to his eyes. Then it stopped abruptly, leaving only a tight and brittle silence.

Mercante's hand flashed forward behind the candle flame. Shephard reached for the Python as he pushed off from the chair. He watched his own fingers straining for his gun—how long can it take to get there, he wondered—and he could see Mercante moving too, then the Colt was in his hand and jolting his arm twice while orange flames shot across the table. Three cracks shattered the silence, one of them bringing a zip of heat to his ribs. He hit the floor on his stomach, the pistol held out before him. Two things reached his senses at once: the acrid sting of gunpowder in the air, and the bottoms of Mercante's feet dangling over the seat of his fallen chair.

It was a long time—an absurdly long time, he remembered later—that he lay there, keeping those unmoving feet in the sights of his gun.

He remembered, too, as he lay in the soft moss of the floor, his fingers finding the little hole in his side, and his thumb finding the larger one behind it. Between them, he realized, was what little fat he had collected in thirty-two years, and perhaps all of the luck.

And, he remembered finally standing up to the early colors of morning, the rich ocean blue in the background, the room encased in green moss, and the man lying back in the toppled chair, motionless except for the purple on his shirt and the first breeze of the day in his gray hair.

TWENTY-EIGHT

For the next three days Shephard remained on the Yucatan, explaining and reexplaining his presence on Mexican soil, his pursuit of the American Azul Mercante, the attempted arrest that had ended in gunfire and death. A Cozumel detective named Ruben Cortez received Shephard, exhausted and bleeding, on Monday morning, and drank hot coffee in his sweltering office while Shephard recounted the night's events. When Cortez had made copious notes and finished his fourth cup of coffee, he entrusted Shephard to the care of two uniformed deputies, who drove him to the small infirmary that passed as the city's hospital.

When his turn finally came, Shephard was stretched out on a cool white table, where he was X-rayed, bathed, and after an inexplicable wait of an hour, stitched shut. By then, the city's mayor had arrived to regard Shephard with a curious but unmoved expression. He was particularly interested in how the gringo had entered his country with a gun but no fresh pursuit papers from his department, as was the usual procedure. As Shephard lay on the table and explained the casual methods of the Veracruz federales, his mind constantly wandered north to Jane, her lovely face, her words, "I love you." When he finally sat up and felt the tight pinch of the new stitches in his side, he realized that over the last couple of days, few waking moments had not included thoughts of her.

The mayor was satisfied that the federales had done a

poor job at Customs, willing as are all minor officials to blame their superiors in government. He turned over the matter to the governor's assistant.

The assistant, a dapper man named Jaime Vogel, arrived an hour later, read Cortez's report, then dropped the papers to the desk with irritation. Shephard looked into his half-Aryan face: high cheekbones and pale eyes, framed by jet black hair that was oiled perfectly into place. Vogel smelled of after-shave.

"No papers of pursuit," he began. "No license to carry a firearm in Mexico. And you turn Isla Arenillas into the O.K. Corral. Mr. Shephard, this is quite irregular. Perhaps your Justice Department should know of this."

Shephard was allowed to call Hannover, who thought at first that it was all a joke. But as the story came out over the static-cluttered lines, Hannover became attentive and businesslike, congratulating Shephard on a job "splendidly handled and executed." He hung up in order to contact the U.S. Justice Department "with our end of the story." Shephard was freed on his own recognizance for one hour, which he used to walk to the Presidente, charge another night's lodging to his sadly overdrawn credit card, and to call Jane. There was no answer.

Justice Department officer Paul Rodriguez arrived late that afternoon. He locked horns with Vogel on official matters—mostly in Spanish—and Vogel seemed to be taking some pride in his stubbornness. When an agreement was reached, Rodriguez, speaking in English, asked Vogel how his sisters were and sent regards to Vogel from someone in the States.

Around eight they crowded into a tiny room behind the jail, where a white-clad assistant uncovered the body of Azul Mercante. Lack of refrigeration had made itself apparent. Rodriguez and Vogel haggled over photographs and dental records, which appeared from the former's fat briefcase

Vogel finally signed the release papers with a flourish, then shook hands all around and excused himself into the streets of Cozumel.

Shephard was back at the hotel just after nine, taking the elevator to his second-floor room. From his window he could see the water surging onto the rough rocks below. He smoked a cigarette on the balcony, where the billowy blue smoke hung in the humid air. The radio in his room played only Dixieland jazz, which he turned off before calling Jane.

She finally answered. She had been outside with Cal, whom with the help of Little Theodore she had relocated to her house on Laguna Canyon Road. "At this point, Cal and Buster are getting to know each other," she said.

"When can I get to know you?"

"Please make it soon. Tom, are you all right?"

He told her only that everything had been taken care of, and he would explain later. Then they talked for nearly an hour, about trivial things mostly, with Shephard unwilling to speak of the last days, and Jane respectful of his distance. It was a lovers' talk, he thought later: enthused, aimless, and with a pleasure that would carry over into his dreams.

"Has Harmon been back?" he asked.

"I don't think so. And Theodore hasn't slept a minute."

Shephard spent the next day on the beach, drinking Tecate beer with limes, dozing, watching the iguanas basking on the rugged rocks. That night he dined alone in the hotel, which he judged to be very good but overpriced. He called Jane twice and talked too long. As his adrenaline slowly subsided, he began to feel a deep exhaustion setting in, one that a night's sleep would not cure. It was a draining of spirit, a hollowing, a need that he wasn't sure how to fill. He called his father and was happy that he had returned safely, but Wade's voice somehow depressed him. He talked to Louise again, and ran out of things to say.

Late the next morning he flew out on reservations made

by Hannover at the department's expense. Coach, but a window seat just the same.

Jane was waiting for him at the terminal, and Little Theodore was with her, grinning through his tangled jungle of beard, sipping a Bloody Mary that seemed miniaturized by his hand. "Aw, ain't that cute," he growled as Shephard and Jane kissed. "You stayed down in Mexico one day longer, I was gonna ask this princess to marry me."

Theodore drove them back to Laguna in a big Cadillac that listed heavily to port when he got behind the wheel. "This runt gives you any trouble, just call Theodore," he told Jane as she got out at Shephard's apartment. "Good work, Shephard. I'm glad to hear you shot that sonofabitch."

Late that night Shephard was lying flat on his back in his apartment, recounting to Jane his trek through the jungle, the moss-encrusted ruins of the Hotel Cora, and the ghostly presence of Azul Mercante. He didn't mention Mercante's story about an affair with Colleen; the words seemed unfit to repeat, unnecessary.

"Well, I guess it's all over now," Jane said. "But that hole in your side is awful. And I'd still like to know why Harmon wanted those files of my father's—if it was Harmon who stole them."

Sal came upstairs with a halibut he'd caught at Moss Street that evening, a joint clenched between his teeth. "Good to have you back, bro," he said. "This halibut is the *kind*. Filet it and fry it with a little lemon and butter. The next time you go to Mexico, try an' get a little fishing in, will ya?" He left a few minutes later with a wink at Shephard and a lewd glance at Jane, who had stretched out on the floor for a nap.

At nine the phone rang and Shephard immediately recognized the voice.

"Tom Shephard, Marla Collins here, from Bruce Harmon's office. Hey, I read in the papers what happened in Mexico, and I thought it might not matter much, but I want to tell you who Bruce has been working for. The rotter fired me yesterday, so I guess I'm getting even. Still interested?"

"Sure. Shoot."

"He's had one client, and one client only, for the last week and a half. Called off all the others for this one, farmed them out to the other dicks. You might have heard of him, a real dandy from Newport Beach. Owns the Surfside Club. Joe Datilla."

"Oh sure," he said dreamily. "We're old friends."

"Really?"

"Just an expression. Thanks, Marla, you're a sweetheart."

When Shephard hung up, his mind was so confused it didn't want to work.

"What's wrong, Tom?" Jane asked, propping herself up on her elbows. Her skirt hiked up onto her thighs and Shephard felt a distant tug in his guts.

"Everything."

When Datilla strolled onto the Surfside tennis courts the next morning to play against himself, Shephard was waiting on the bench beside the fence. A cool fog had come over the coast during the night, and Datilla looked surprised when he set down his bucket of balls.

"Hello, Tommy." His grin was wide. "Congratulations, young man. You've got a whole city sleeping easier now." He offered his hand; Shephard kept his inside the windbreaker.

"You're in trouble, Joe. You hired Bruce Harmon to find Mercante, and when he did you funneled him cash, a car, and an airline ticket to Mexico to kill my father. Know about all that, don't you?"

Datilla touched his toes with a grunt, then began a series of knee-dips. "Might need a lawyer here, Tom, if you want to continue along those lines. Joking, aren't you?"

Shephard watched Joe's silver hair fall over his tanned forehead as he dipped. The fog made his face damp. "No joke, Joe. One of the things that Helene left me before she checked out was something from your safe. Plates to the Cadillac Mercante was driving, so we wouldn't spot them. I ran them past Sacramento, twice, and they're yours. A terrified man who works at Valentine's told me about Harmon's easy money and little favors. You gave Mink the day off so Harmon could borrow the car without a fuss. A few hours after your jet took my father to Mexico, Harmon delivered a ticket and a suitcase to Mercante. The only people who knew he was going to Isla Arenillas were you and the pilot, and of course Harmon, who's been handling your account exclusively for a week and a half. So go ahead, Joe. Get your lawyers out here if you want to. Personally, I'd be a tad embarrassed at what they'd have to hear."

Shephard stood up and faced Datilla, who had stopped the knee-bends and was now midway through a jumping-jack routine. Shephard lit a cigarette and looked out through the fog. When Datilla spoke again, his voice had an edge.

"Do you know what you're getting into, Shephard?"

"What am I getting into, Joe?"

"Let me tell you something as a friend, Tommy." He continued his jumping jacks and still hadn't lost his breath. "Azul Mercante is dead. He killed Tim and Hope and almost got Frank Rubio. He killed your mother. The guy's a badass, and he got what he deserved. But it's over. You're a bit of a hero, and your father's church gets a hundred grand out of me for that fucking hospital. If you can clear it with Hannover, I'll just sign the rest of the reward money over to you. Hell, I'll do it anyway. Be happy to. Anything beyond that is going to hurt us all. And I mean you, too, Tom, in a bad way." Datilla went from jumping jacks to running in place. "Some things you just have to leave alone."

Shephard considered Datilla's words: he could remember speaking ones just like them to Dr. Zahara, hardly a week ago. Something about deserving to have secrets, like everybody else. The dark notes, he thought. Playing them with a vengeance now, the whole orchestra. He knew that there was no turning back from what he was about to do.

"Nice proposition. But unless you tell me a little more, I'm going to arrest you for conspiracy. Right here in your little club."

"I don't want that."

"Then spill. The cuffs are in my pocket," he lied.

"Stubborn little prick, aren't you? Stubborn like your old man, same righteous cant. It makes me sick. Okay, Shephard, listen up and take your notes carefully." Datilla was breathing quickly now. A thin stream of sweat broke over his face. "I helped Mercante get to Hope Creeley. And I helped him try for your old man, too. Why? Let's just say they both knew things I'd rather they didn't. And Mercante was an easy and convenient way to get that taken care of."

"How did you know he was out of prison?"

"I saw him hitchhiking, of all the damned things. Right down Coast Highway toward Laguna. Couldn't believe my eyes, so I turned around and passed him again. Third time clinched it, Tom. Azul Mercante. Alive and well in his old town. It took Bruce two days to find him, but he still beat you."

Shephard struggled to piece together Helene Lang's account of the death of Burton Creeley. Her story seemed to have been told a century ago; only the heavy smell of her lilac perfume came into his mind.

"You wanted Hope Creeley dead because she knew you had her husband drowned."

"Wrong, detective. The bitch never even suspected it."

"Then why?"

"Same reason I wasn't too sad to read about Tim Algernon."

"Just what was it they knew, Joe?"

Datilla's legs stopped pumping. He put his hands on his hips, breathing deeply, still looking straight at Shephard. "I nudged Hope in a certain direction once, with some pressure, some cash, and a steady stream of phenobarbitol. Tim? He needed some money because his wife was sick, and I gave it to him—a lot of it. What they did for me in return was use a little . . . imagination. I paid for some imagination to protect a good friend of mine. And I simply didn't want any of that story to get public, Tom. That's what I mean by covering bets."

"What kind of imagination are you talking about?" Shephard felt his mind struggling to calibrate what he was hearing against what he thought was true.

"It's called perjury, Tom." Datilla picked up his racquet and slashed it through the air in front of Shephard's face. "One last chance to leave, detective. Take it while you can."

"If I leave now, it's with you, Joe. All the way to the station."

Datilla slammed the racquet to the ground. "All right boy, you've made yourself a deal. I bought them off to try to help your father. Just like I kicked in another twenty thousand dollars. Those were 1951 dollars." Shephard remembered the check that Helene had given him, Datilla to Wade, 1951. "That money made sure that a lab technician would find gunpowder on Mercante's skin, when in reality there wasn't any. Tim took the stand and said Azul made passes at his wife. Imagination. Hope told the court he tried to rape her, and God knows Mercante did make a pass at her one night. But in her state of mind she didn't know how to take it, so I told her it was an open and shut case of attempted rape. Tim and Hope were insurance against Mercante, even though we already had his ass framed to the wall. You stupid prick, Mercante didn't shoot Colleen. *Wade* did."

For a moment Shephard felt as if his insides were scrambling to get out.

"That's right, Shephard. Wade barged in on Colleen and Mercante, going at it in the living room. They were having quite a torrid little thing, you know. So Wade, drunk as usual back then, draws his gun and fires, and she jumps in the way. Mercante stands there like a dope while Wade falls on his wife—he couldn't believe he'd missed, the dumb shit —then he picks up Wade's gun. For a minute he held it to your dad's head—Wade told me this—then he lost his nerve and ran for it. Too bad. Azul's prints were on the gun, and a little money was all it took to make the lab tech report berium and antimony from the wax test."

Like a man deep in the woods just realizing he is lost, Shephard felt panic. He stumbled ahead with the most obvious question of all. "So what you say is true. So it's not. Why did you want him dead? What's he got on you?"

Datilla paced the courtside. He stopped a few yards away, looking through the fog toward the Surfside A Dock. "Wade *earned* that money," he said finally. Shephard could scarcely hear the words. But when Datilla turned back to him they came loud, bitter, and clear: "He did me a favor once, a business favor. He gave Burton Creeley a chilly ride from the waters of Laguna to the Newport Channel. He was a cop then. It was easy. Used a 1950 Chevy to do it."

Shephard watched Datilla return to his racket, sweat dripping from his face, and heard the wicked swish of the graphite cutting the air again. The sound was somehow far away. "That's what he's got on me. Burton and me. So I wanted rid of him, too. I hate his hypocrisy; I hate his righteous generosity. I hate any man who'd shoot a woman like Colleen, accident or not. But more important, like I told you, I don't take chances. I cover my bets. I didn't want Wade to get confessional about things. He's got that in him. To spill it all in the name of God. To purify himself, or some vague notion like that. Go ahead, Tommy Shephard, take me downtown if you want. But you'll be taking Wade, too, because when I start talking I won't quit until his name is so foul he'd be laughed off any pulpit on earth.

"You see this? See all this?" Datilla held out his racquet, sweeping it across the Surfside, its apartments and restaurants, lounges and docks, across the bay in the distance, smothered in fog. "I built it all, covering the bets, and I'll cover them until I die. Mercante *did* it all. I just gave him a little help. Listen, you came through it clean. So did Wade, and so can I. Think of the thousands of sick little souls he can save with his new hospital. Look to the future and get your ass out of the past. *You're* betting the hundred now to get fifty. And I promise you one thing, Shephard" —Datilla stepped forward and pressed the end of the racquet into Shephard's chest—"If I go down, Wade goes down, too. It's as simple as that."

He stooped for his bucket and took it to the far end of the court. Lost in the fog, his voice seemed to come from nowhere, Shephard thought, or maybe from everywhere.

"I'll be right here, Tom. Don't worry. Think about a hundred grand of my money in your pocket, and the same for those folks south of the border. Everybody's happy now, and getting happier. I'm a little more secure. Join the club, Tom. Everybody profits. The hawks always eat the sparrows—Wade told me that." Shephard heard the muffled pop of a tennis ball through the fog. Then Datilla's voice again, strangely distant: "Pretty funny, isn't it? You still there, Tom? Wade puts the wrong guy in jail to save his own ass, and when he gets out, you shoot him. Hell, with a little luck, Azul could have *been* your father."

TWENTY-NINE

S hephard spent the next hours wandering his city, a lanky figure with a stiff walk, scarcely aware of the life that bustled around him. He stopped for a beer at Marty Odette's Sportsplace, a cup of coffee at the Hotel Laguna, and an ice cream, which he gazed at momentarily, then gave to a boy on a skateboard.

He walked until his legs were weary and his mind wanted to give up. By afternoon the thoughts that were wrenching him had blurred and all but lost meaning, but Shephard still felt no closer to a just decision. When he looked behind him he saw a sky swirling with the ghosts of the past; when he looked forward he saw where they would surely land. To take down Datilla would bring those ghosts to rest on his father, on himself, even on Jane. And what good would there be in it, besides the downfall of Datilla, a man who had once saved his father from shame, then tried to take his life, and now was offering to pick up the tab for everybody's damages?

Shephard's hatred was gone, spent with his bullets in the Hotel Cora. His sense of forgiveness was bankrupt, his sense of betrayal complete. When he looked inside himself he saw no signs, heard no counsel, received no guidance from his own unparticipating heart.

Dr. Zahara changed an appointment to accommodate him. She studied him quietly from the depths of her big chair. They smoked. Shephard was aware of her green eyes prying into him.

"There's something I should do," he said finally. "Something that the law says should be done. Must be done. But if I do it, I'm not sure it will make any difference, and some people I love very much are going to get hurt. One of those —a woman I'm in love with—is innocent. The other is my father."

A long silence followed. Dr. Zahara lifted the telephone and asked her receptionist to reschedule the next appointment also. When she was finished, she brushed back her black hair, then settled still farther into the shadows of her chair. "I'd like you to explain."

When he had finished, Shephard could hear the traffic outside, thickening toward rush hour. Throughout his story, he had noticed that Zahara made no notes. She tapped her pen on the desk and turned her green eyes on him. "So, to get Joe, you must sacrifice the career and public standing of your father. How would the arrest affect Jane? I'm not sure you explained that, Tom."

"Tim Algernon perjured himself for money. To pay for his wife's cancer treatment. Jane and Tim weren't very close at the end of his life. She seems to have made a peace with him that I don't want to shatter. He's all the family she . . . had."

"I can appreciate that. Would such a detail be likely to arise from the arrest of Joe Datilla? Tim's perjury?"

Shephard thought it over, trying the angles. "It's possible. Joe will play dirty."

"Then we're back to those secrets you wanted to keep,

aren't we? This time to protect a woman you love, rather than yourself."

"I guess we are."

The silence that followed was a long one.

"There's a voice in there somewhere," she said, "trying to be heard. Let it come to you. Go somewhere quiet if you can. I'll tell you just one thing. When you consider all the people you may hurt through your actions, don't forget to include yourself. You're responsible for *you* as much as for your father, even Jane. Don't sacrifice yourself. It might be easy, but it would be wrong."

"I'll try to find that quiet place."

"When you first came here, it was for post-shooting trauma. Strange, Tom, but that's one thing we haven't talked about. Have you . . . come to terms with Morris Mumford? With Mercante?"

Shephard considered her words. "I left them both in Mexico," he said finally. "At the Hotel Cora."

In the end, as always, it was instinct that took him forward.

Late that evening he found his father in the garden, tending the roses that had been ravaged by the last wind. Shephard came quietly through the living room and into the kitchen, watching through the glass patio door as Wade touched a yellow rose and tried to catch the petals that drifted off and floated to his feet. Wade turned and smiled as Shephard slid back the door. The Reverend Wade Shephard, he thought, all smiles.

"Tommy, I thought you'd sleep a week." He peeled off his garden gloves and hugged his son, then pushed away and glanced at his side. "How is it?"

"Just a little stiff. Fine."

Shephard sat down at the patio table in the shade of a large umbrella. The sunset was accumulating high in the west, a wispy, cirrus-streaked tableau that promised reds and blacks. Wade brought lemonade and two glasses.

"To God's own sunset," he toasted. "And your good work. Salute."

"Salute."

They exchanged not-very-happy smiles. From across the table, Wade seemed to read his thoughts, or at least some of them. He sighed and folded his hands.

"I know how you feel, son. When I was just a little older than you, I shot a man. He would have pulled his trigger first if I'd let him, but even then I felt like my heart had broken when it was over. You'll get over it. You will."

Shephard tested the waters: "Some things you don't ever get over, do you?"

His father sipped from his glass and looked out over the Pacific. Testing his own, Shephard thought. The burden of three decades showed on Wade's face, in the creases around his eyes, the droop of his mouth, in the hollow, inward expression.

"Some things, no."

"I think you tried, though. Miracle bricks, you called them. Those regrets that build up inside and grow into something good." Wade smiled shyly. He loves it when someone remembers his sermons.

"Ah, you remembered," he said. "We all have our miracle bricks. Azul Mercante is now yours."

For a brief moment Shephard felt the roar returning to his ears, the same one that surrounded him before he'd pulled the trigger at the Hotel Cora, the one that whined through his brain only to vanish and leave him with that awful moment of silence. He listened now to the same nothingness. Maybe this is it, he thought, Dr. Zahara's quiet place. As if from far away, he heard himself speaking.

"I know he didn't kill her. I know that she and Mercante were lovers." Shephard forced himself to look at something other than his father, choosing a red rose at random. He heard Wade's glass lift from the table, a gulp, the sound of glass on wood. When Wade spoke again his voice was grainy and soft, as if it belonged to a much older man.

"You're the only person on earth I'm ashamed to have know that." After a long pause he spoke again. "Do you understand what I mean?" Shephard's silence answered for itself. "I mean that I know I have sinned. And I don't mean against God, but against another man. Every day of my life I've thought about confessing that, about telling everyone the truth. Sometimes when I'm home alone at night. Sometimes Sunday mornings on the pulpit. But I couldn't do it, Tom. I couldn't let you see that happen." His voice was soft and distant, as if coming from under the earth.

"Well, it happened, pop." Shephard looked at his father's quivering face, then to the glistening Pacific beyond.

"I knew about them for quite some time," Wade began. "A month maybe. I couldn't confront her with it. It's . . . one of my flaws not to be able to confront people with things. I hoped it would end. I tried to improve myself. But when it just kept going and going, I gave up and drank instead." Shephard watched his father study the glass in his hand, recollecting perhaps the days when it was filled with bourbon and not lemonade.

"I remember one day I asked a friend on patrol to go by the house and see if his car was there. She was leaving then, so he followed her to a hotel where they met. And the next day I had her followed, too, and this time they went to his studio and they made love on the patio outside under the trees. I don't know what all my friend saw, but that was all he told me. Then, I decided it was enough and I couldn't go on any more. I was going to tell her I loved her. Tell her she could go with him if she wanted. I wanted her to be happy, truly. I think only a young man can love so much.

"So I drank a lot that morning when I was on patrol

because the liquor made it all seem unreal and almost tolerable, and I drove here, to this house, and I came up the walkway. I remember it was a hot day and clear and I could smell the eucalyptus and the bourbon mixed together. Something inside me just gave out. I remember thinking it would feel good to have it over with, so we could go our separate ways and maybe be happy again with other people. So I walked through the door and there they were, right in there, in my living room. Up under her dress and I saw the underwear at her ankles and her eyes closed and his arm down there and him kissing her neck. She was groaning, I can remember that too."

Wade's eyes were pools and his face sagged as if it was being pulled by invisible strings. He was staring out at the water.

"We were friends, you know, Mercante and I. Tennis partners at the Surfside. We drank and made jokes. He was a fine painter, an energetic, funny little man. Your mother admired him very much. She started painting herself, you know.

"But when I saw them against the wall in the living room, I felt so outside them, so violated and betrayed. So foolish. And the look on his face when he saw me wasn't humiliation or fear, but triumph. He looked at me like I was a fool to let this happen and a dunce to be there to witness it. So . . . so I pulled my gun and shot him." Wade's face succumbed; it shattered. "But she was there instead . . . Good Christ; she was there instead."

In the long silence that followed, Shephard searched for something to say. Dr. Zahara's words came back again. Sometimes when we lose ourselves, we find ourselves, too. When Wade turned to look at him, his face was glazed, his eyes wide, as if in amazement.

"And I lay there on top of her for a long time. I heard Mercante pick up the gun and I felt him holding it to the

314

back of my head. I hoped he would do it. Then he dropped it and ran out the door. Colleen was . . . not breathing any more. And I breathed into her for a long time but nothing happened. So I stood up and went to the phone to call the watch commander. To tell the watch commander that I had just shot my wife but it was an accident. And I dialed and got him and I said, John, John, my wife's been killed. Colleen is dead. And he said, good God how did it happen, and I said she was shot. Her lover shot her. Azul Mercante shot her and I watched him do it. And it was then, Tommy, that I knew what it meant to sin, to kill someone you love and make someone else pay for it. It was so easy. So easy to back out. Joe loaned me a little money for a favor and that was that. Later, a few days later I think it was, Joe called on me to return the favor and I took a dead man in my car to Newport Beach. It just got deeper and deeper."

Shephard looked at his father again, the picture of a man holding himself together by sheer willpower. Everything about him seemed ready to dissolve.

"Every day I thought about changing it. Setting Mercante free. Telling. Confessing. And years later, when I was finished wishing I could die, I thought the next best thing was to help someone else live better. And I prayed and prayed and God asked me to act on his behalf. I felt that He asked me. I wanted it. I wanted to do something I could feel good about, finally. When I heard Azul died in prison, all I could do was double my prayers for him." His father looked up, and Shephard held his gaze. "That's why I understand forgiveness," he said. "Because the hardest thing I ever did was to try to forgive myself. And when I had done as much of that as I could, I started trying to make up for it all. I think everything decent I've ever done since that day was for Colleen. I think maybe . . . she was my God." Wade's voice trailed off to nothing, a whisper against the background surge of the sea.

"It was Datilla who hired Harmon, pop. They gave Mercante a car and money. He sent him to Mexico to find you. He wanted you dead."

It was apparent from the vacant, infant-like expression on his father's face that Wade didn't understand.

"Joe told me he was afraid you might make that confession someday. He was afraid he'd finally have to pay for Burton Creeley. He helped Mercante get Hope."

"Joe did?"

"He did. It's conspiracy, pop. Conspiracy to commit murder. Do you understand what that means?"

In his confusion, the reverend was a cop for a moment. "More than one person planning, arranging, or intending to bring about the—"

"Not that, pop. Do you understand what it means to you? If I take Joe for conspiracy?"

Wade leaned forward, as if the news to come should be told in secret. Later, Shephard remembered thinking that it was at this instant his father finally broke. Wade slowly shook his head. The evening breeze stirred his father's hair, much as the breeze on Isla Arenillas had stirred Mercante's.

"It means that if Joe goes for conspiracy, he's going to take you with him. Everything you just told me. Colleen, Burton in your car. Everything." Shephard heard his own voice trembling, and he fought to control the heaving of his heart. And then, in a moment of clarity that all of his previous thoughts had failed to bring· to him, Shephard knew what he should do.

No, he thought. Never. I can't do that to him.

Wade stood up and put his gloves back on. Behind him, the sun had nearly touched the horizon, and the island of Catalina lay balanced like a gray body on the rim of the ocean. The water danced in crimson. It will be better this way, Shephard thought, as his father moved toward the rose bushes. It has to end somewhere, why not here, while something remains.

"What are you going to do?" Wade asked. He had picked up a pair of pruning shears and was nudging them into a thick bush near the center. "Come here, son. Come here." There was a new tone to his voice, a tone that Shephard hadn't heard in years. Ten, he wondered? Twenty? "Tommy. Get the other gloves. In the garage, far wall." As Shephard walked off to the garage, he recognized the difference. It fit with the walls of the house, the flowers, the same carpet and wallpaper he had always known, the smell of his father's breakfasts cooking on Sunday mornings. It wasn't Wade the lawman; it wasn't Wade the man of God.

He got the gloves off the wall and returned to the rose hedge. Wade's head was angled down at a bush that he seemed to be inspecting in some minute detail.

I can let him be, Shephard thought. After all this, I can let him be.

But the feeling inside him was not relief, only surrender, and it was the first time he could remember ever giving up on something he truly cared about. The thought of Datilla going free brought a sick lump to his throat.

"Put the gloves on, Tom, and go through these bushes after the dead branches. The wind was pretty hard on them this time. All in all, roses are pretty hardy flowers, but sixty miles per hour off the desert is just too much. The little branches didn't make it. The big ones are okay."

Sure, Shephard thought. I know that voice.

Then Wade had turned away and was working silently, pruning the limbs, tossing the outcasts into a neat pile on the lawn. Shephard looked out and watched the last sliver of sun dunk behind the island. Wade turned and stared at him.

"What are you going to do, Tommy?"

Shephard could not answer the question. He fiddled idly with a branch.

"I ran a little experiment on these roses years ago," Wade said as he clipped. "When I planted them. The ones to your left I just stuck in the ground that was here when your mother and I bought the house. Then I went to the nursery and found out the proper way to plant roses. Got mulch, vitamins, a book about it, the whole shot. The ones over there I planted with all the knowledge of just how to do it. Well, when they grew up and started giving us flowers, guess what? The ones on the left grew better. The flowers weren't any bigger and there weren't any more of them, but they were shaped better. They were tighter, brighter, more be-lievable." He stood back and made a show of studying the roses on the two sides. "So much for the mulch, I said. And from then on I just stuck them in the ground without the additives and let them go. Careful to keep the pests away, of course."

He shot his son a smile, one that Shephard hadn't seen in years, one that went with the voice. Not the cop, not the reverend, but just the man, and the father. Uncluttered, unforced. Believable.

"Tommy, if you don't take Joe, I'll be deeply ashamed of what I raised. You wouldn't for a minute entertain that idea, would you? Because when you've done that, I can take myself and plant me in some real soil. I think it's time for that. It's not too late for me to quit living the lie, but it's much too early for you to start. You have my blessing."

After a brief time in which Shephard decided to let a half-dead branch stay on the bush, he felt his heart settle and a new balance spreading inside. He thought of Jane. At the cove again, tonight.

"Thank you," he said.

They worked after dark amidst silence and small talk, and when the roses were in order, Shephard went home.

THIRTY

The moon appeared an hour later, low on the horizon, dangling strings of light over the water at Diver's Cove. Shephard and Jane crossed the sand barefoot and worked their way north past the tidepools, which shone up at them like mirrors. As they walked toward the cave, the waves that lapped at Shephard's feet seemed to nibble away at everything that had happened to him in the last few days, just as they had done the first time he walked the shore with Jane. A week ago, he wondered, or a century? The memories seemed to be inching out of him: the three shots cracking through the early morning in the Hotel Cora; Datilla's bitter confession; Wade's enfeebled, then rejuvenating voice. Even before they found the cave and stripped naked in the glow of the flashlight, he could feel relief and forgetfulness pouring in.

The stitches in his side brought him sharply back to reality.

"Ouch," Jane said, running her fingers over them for the hundredth time. "Sure you want to do this?"

"This is where I got to know you, chum. I'll never get tired of that."

This time they undressed each other, eagerly. She came close and put her arms gently around him.

"How are you?" she asked.

"Let's talk later," he said, wondering about Tim. Would t do any good to tell her?

319

They waded together through the rocks, and when they were knee-deep in the rolling waves, they dove under. The first wave thumped him as he went under it, stinging his side. He came up and saw Jane pulling through the water ahead of him. Another wave, another thump, but he was closer to her now and each time he brought up his head for air he could hear her laughing.

Silver shoulders, silver arms ahead in the moonlight. When he came up even with her, she was still laughing, but it didn't seem to be the right time to ask why. Later, he thought.

And the farther out they swam, the less things back on shore seemed to matter: absurdly, what was ahead of them was suddenly more important than what was behind, although he knew that it was just the Indicator rocks, the Inside Indicator coming up not far ahead and somewhere behind it the Outside Indicator where Jane said all real lovers go. They passed the first rock side by side and neither of them stopped to pay it any attention.

Good God, he thought, she laughs so well it's like music, or even better; must be hard when you swim.

It was all he could do to keep up, right then left, a sting in his side with each stroke. Saltwater must be good for gunshot, he thought, or maybe that was just an old wives' tale. No need to tell her about Tim, at least not tonight. Then they were even again and he kept up, right then left, right then left, heading for the Outside Indicator.

EPILOGUE

Joe Datilla and Bruce Harmon were arrested for conspiracy to commit murder. Harmon turned state's witness, and Datilla skipped his considerable bail but was arrested again in the border town of Calexico. He was found guilty and sentenced to thirty years in prison for his part in the death of Hope Creeley and the assault on Francis Rubio.

Before Datilla's trial began, Wade Shephard publicly confessed the truth about the death of his wife, Colleen. Tom tried to watch this confession on television, but he could not. The district attorney chose not to reopen the case. The Reverend Shephard turned over leadership of the Church of New Life to his young and earnest assistant. Taking his personal savings with him to Isla Arenillas, he opened a small infirmary, effective and growing daily, but considerably more humble than the hospital he had envisioned.

Jane Algernon returned for her last year of school, looking to a career in veterinary medicine. She released Buster to the ocean when she had diagnosed and cured the infection that beached him in the first place. Cal stood at the rocks, barking.

Tom Shephard quit the department and opened his own office on Coast Highway, near Diver's Cove. He is engaged to Jane, and a wedding is planned for next spring on Isla Arenillas.

Business is good. To the people who keep track of such things, he is known as a competent and reasonably priced private detective.